The
Staycation

Cressy grew up in South-East London surrounded by books and with a cat named after Lawrence of Arabia. She studied English at the University of East Anglia and now lives in Norwich with her husband David. *The Staycation* is her eleventh novel and her books have sold over half a million copies worldwide. When she isn't writing, Cressy spends her spare time reading, returning to London, or exploring the beautiful Norfolk coastline.

If you'd like to find out more about Cressy, visit her on her social media channels. She'd love to hear from you!

f /CressidaMcLaughlinAuthor
𝕏 @CressMcLaughlin
◉ @cressmclaughlin

Also by Cressida McLaughlin

Cressida McLaughlin

The Staycation

HarperCollins*Publishers*

HarperCollins*Publishers*
1 London Bridge Street
London SE1 9GF

www.harpercollins.co.uk

HarperCollins*Publishers*
1st Floor, Watermarque Building, Ringsend Road
Dublin 4, Ireland

Published by HarperCollins*Publishers* 2022
1

A catalogue record for this book
is available from the British Library

ISBN: 978-0-00-851894-3

This novel is entirely a work of fiction.
The names, characters and incidents portrayed in it are
the work of the author's imagination. Any resemblance to
actual persons, living or dead, events or localities is
entirely coincidental.

Typeset in Birka by Palimpsest Book Production Ltd, Falkirk, Stirlingshire

Printed and Bound in the UK using 100% Renewable
Electricity at CPI Group (UK) Ltd

MIX
Paper from
responsible sources
FSC® C007454

This book is produced from independently certified FSC™ paper
to ensure responsible forest management.

For more information visit:
www.harpercollins.co.uk/green

To Kirsty Greenwood, for being the best

Chapter
One

Thursday

Hester Monday stood at the end of the hotel corridor, on carpet thick enough to lose her heels in, and looked from the door on her left, to the door on her right. It would be helpful, she thought, if she knew which one she was supposed to knock on. Was Jake Oakenfield behind the door labelled Avalon, or the one named Merryweather?

Hester's job was all about opening doors. Doors to hotels like this one all over the world, where the attention to detail was astounding, but not as astounding as the price people paid for it: doors to log cabins on African game reserves that were more well-equipped than most people's homes; doors to penthouse apartments with views over Central Park and 100-foot yachts and islands that were exclusively yours for the duration of your stay. Islands might not have physical doors, but the ones she dealt in certainly weren't open to everyone. She was a high-class travel agent. Luxury destination facilitator. Keyholder to the escape of your dreams, if you have enough pots of money to spare.

And now, here she was, standing outside suites that cost several thousand pounds for a single night's stay. The most she had ever spent on a holiday was four hundred pounds. It had been an all-inclusive trip to Spain with her friends Amber and Glen, and she hadn't even made it to Departures. Four hundred pounds to stand, shaking, in Stansted airport while strangers looked on with obvious wariness, and her friends hid their pity behind concern. Hester pushed the unwelcome memory aside. This was not the time to spiral down that very unwelcome episode in her recent history.

Now, Hester had a fifty-fifty choice. The suite names were delicately embossed, picked out in antique gold on pristine white doors, inviting her finger to trace the curves of each letter. She had a vague idea that Avalon and Merryweather were both varieties of plum, but that wasn't going to help her right this moment.

Of course, she wouldn't have this quandary if she'd been paying attention to the receptionist of the exclusive London hotel where she'd ended up on this sweltering September day, the short walk across Hungerford Bridge enough to create a sheen of sweat that plastered her skirt to the backs of her thighs. If she had listened to the black-haired man who had spoken to her with silky patience, who had checked his notes and discovered that she was, in fact, expected.

Hester had listened to his descriptions as far as the floor she needed to be on, the corridor, the suites at the very end. And then her mind had gone elsewhere, distracted by the old woman wearing a buttercup-yellow trouser suit, standing in the middle of the marbled foyer as if she owned it.

Otherwise, she would have known if it was Avalon or Merryweather where she was supposed to be: the door her newest client lay behind.

She raised her hand, about to knock on Merryweather, when she heard the door behind her open. Reception must have told him she was coming. She spun a hundred and eighty degrees, her warmest smile on her face.

The man stopped in his doorway and looked at her. He was a few inches taller than her and fairly wide, gravity settling in his stomach to pull it lower than the waistband of his trousers. His suit was an uninspiring grey, his shirt not quite white, his tie navy and slightly shiny. His features seemed lost inside his fleshy face, making his expression hard to read.

Hester couldn't help the disappointment that thudded into her like a heavy shoe. She enjoyed building a rapport with her clients, especially the ones she went to visit, seeing them on their turf – even if that turf was a hotel, rather than a home – rather than in the office of Paradise Awaits. She thought that it would be hard to build a rapport with this man.

'Who are you?' he asked. 'Are you here to see me?'

'Jake Oakenfield?' She glanced down at her iPad, checking she'd got the surname right. He didn't look like a Jake.

'You're called Jake?' He sounded sceptical, as well he might.

'No, I'm Hester. Hester Monday. Are *you* Jake?' She held out a hand, but this interaction already felt off-kilter. It wasn't one of her most successful openings.

'I am not,' he said. 'You're clearly in the wrong place.'

'Oh.' She smiled. 'OK. Phew. Sorry about that, then.'

He glared at her for a second longer, then stepped into the corridor, shut the door behind him and strode away. Happy that Sagging Man wasn't her client, Hester smoothed down her blouse, straightened her skirt, and turned back to Merryweather. And then she realized something: the man hadn't looked like the recent victim of a car accident.

Jake Oakenfield, Carrie had said to her before she left, perching on the edge of the white metal desk so her skirt rode indecently up her thighs to reveal acres of fishnet stocking. *Over here from New York on business, got hit by a car saving an old lady near Trafalgar Square the day he landed. His sister, Beth, wants to cheer him up so she's asked us to book him a trip to Thailand. He loves travelling apparently, and needs something positive to focus on while he's recovering.*

God, Hester had replied, wiping croissant crumbs off her keyboard and focusing on her boss. It wasn't often that drama swept through the doors of Paradise Awaits. She had got used to the super-rich and their taste in holidays, and nothing much about their demands shocked her any more. This was a new sort of intrigue. *Is he OK?* she had asked. *How badly was he hurt?*

Cassie had shrugged. Nothing fazed her: not weather disasters or plane strikes or clients demanding Tiffany's open after hours just for them. *A few broken ribs*, she'd said. *Bruises. He was lucky, according to Beth. But his spirit's been dented, because he likes spending as little time in London as possible, and now he's stuck for the next week. The doctors have told him he can't fly home immediately, and he can't go living it up in town, because he's in a lot of pain and he's supposed to be resting.*

Why doesn't he like being in London? Hester had asked, curious.

Because he grew up here, Cassie had replied, as if that was explanation enough.

Baffled, Hester had waited for her boss to email the details over, before gathering up her things. Jake Oakenfield was already more interesting than most of the people she dealt with, and she hadn't even met him yet.

She'd spent the walk from their office near Waterloo station to the hotel wondering about the gaps in his story. What kind of business had coaxed him all the way from New York to London? What had happened to make him dislike it here? Where did he live in New York, and what did he fill his time with? And, the part she was most curious about, how had the accident unravelled? Who was this old woman that he'd saved, and what had made him realize she was in danger, and react the way he did? Had he rolled across the car's bonnet, or been sent flying? What had happened to the driver of the car: had their spirit also been dented, or just their number plate?

These thoughts had kept her occupied throughout her humid walk, passing the beggars and buskers taking advantage of the good weather to ply their trades on the wide, tourist-filled walkway of the bridge, the white supports rising above her like the ribbons of a maypole. Portrait painters and pan-pipe players, bracelet weavers and one young boy performing a magic trick with a coin, over and over, even when nobody stopped to watch him. The Thames glittered, for once a pale blue instead of murky green. No dark depths to it, only light and shimmer, reflecting the sun back so that Hester couldn't help but be buoyed by it. *How could anyone hate London?* she had thought.

And then she had arrived at the imposing hotel and – as she often did in her job – felt like a fraud, because she would never get used to setting foot inside these places. Thoughts of her new client and the task at hand had gone out of her head as she used up all her energy on not turning and running: on planting her feet, one after the other, on the polished floor surrounding the curved reception desk.

And now, here she was. She'd picked the right door – it wasn't her fault that the man behind the wrong one had interrupted her – so she gave herself a mental pat on the back. She was calm and in control, and she knew she could plan the perfect Thailand vacation for this man. She would have him salivating over luxury treehouses on Phuket Island, the soft creak of a hammock outside swaying in the breeze; imagining the aromatic flavours of the spicy chicken coconut soup, Tom Kha Gai; picturing sipping Thai pearl cocktails in iridescent bowl glasses. His current woes would fade into the background at the promise of a fort-night of endless white sand and water that was both cerulean and crystal clear, all the way down to the soft seabed.

She knocked on the door of the Merryweather suite, and waited. Further along the corridor, a soundless member of staff slipped out of a door, a stack of fresh, fluffy towels under her arm. Hester wondered what it would be like to do a job where you had to be invisible. Was her job like that? She had been trained to put the destination centre stage, but she had always hoped, always believed, that the way she presented it made a difference to the outcome.

She heard no voices, no footsteps approaching on the other side of the door. For a few, idle moments she wondered whether Jake Oakenfield was even inside. Or perhaps he was in the bath, soothing his aching body, or asleep under the influence of heavy painkillers. Cassie had said it was all arranged: that Beth, Jake's sister, had called ahead and Hester was expected.

She raised her hand to knock again, but her closed fist met air as the door swung inward. She let it fall to her side as she took in the man standing in front of her.

Dark brown hair in untidy curls that were restricted to the top of his head, blue eyes a shade darker than the Thames that day but seemed to glitter just as much, full lips that made her think of plums all over again. He was about five inches taller than her, around six foot, and the thick white towelling robe he was wearing softened the edges of the All Man air he gave off. He had purple smudges under his eyes, dark stubble that looked a couple of days old and hollowed out his cheeks, and a greenish bruise skirting one side of his face, from his jawbone to his temple. One arm loosely clutched his torso, and the other, now the door was open, rested against the frame.

Hester took a calming breath. So *this* was Jake Oakenfield.

Chapter Two

Thursday

'Hello,' he said. The word, in his deep English accent, brimmed with exhaustion. Only his eyes shimmered with life as he looked her up and down.

'I'm Hester,' she said. 'Hester Monday. I believe you're expecting me? From Paradise Awaits?' Her surprise made her squeaky. She hated anyone who gave their sentences an upward inflection, as if they were always waiting for a 'no' even when they weren't asking a question. Today, she hated herself.

Was it that Sagging Man made Jake Oakenfield seem more attractive, despite his recent altercation with a swift-moving lump of metal, the way a toffee cappuccino from the coffee shop near her office tasted like nectar after a morning of grainy instant with on-the-edge milk? Or was he actually, objectively, this beautiful? Lord knows how anyone coped when he was looking his best.

'Paradise Awaits,' he repeated slowly, as if weighing the two words up against each other. His long fingers curled over the doorframe, and Hester's awareness deepened.

She was aware of the sweat cooling between her breasts, and how her shoulder-length, dark blonde hair must look like unwoven hessian after her humid walk, and that the mascara she used to frame her large, hazel eyes might have made a run for it down her cheeks. But mostly she was aware of how Cassie's luxury travel agency was exceptional in every way except for its name, which made it sound like a high-end escort business. This was what Jake Oakenfield was thinking: that the hotel had sent him a woman to soothe his aches away with pleasure, taking everything slowly and gently, making him forget all the bad sensations and focus on the good.

But Hester would never pass for a high-end escort, even if she wanted to. She lacked the gall needed to pull it off. Still, imagining taking her time with Jake Oakenfield was— God, entirely not appropriate. She'd been in his presence for a minute, tops. Sagging Man had really done a number on her.

She rushed to get the truth out. 'Beth has asked me to build you a perfect Thailand experience. So you have something good to focus on, for when you're recovered.'

The gleam in his eyes dulled, and irritation flickered across his face. 'You'd better come in.'

He turned and walked back into the room, his progress slow and stilted. Hester hovered just inside the door, watching him, and thought that, even though his movements were guided by his recent injuries, he did look like a man whose spirit was broken. She couldn't fail to notice that her announcement about booking him a holiday hadn't made him any happier.

'Take a seat,' he said, as he did the same. Only for him it looked like a mammoth task, the way he turned and lowered himself, putting his arm out so that he could control the pace of his descent onto the plush, cream sofa: a sofa that looked wide enough and comfy enough to sleep on, let alone sit.

The rest of the living space was the same, and she could see, from glimpses through doors, that it was just one room in the luxurious suite. The colour palette was expensively subtle, the furnishings and woodwork displaying every shade of cream, biscuit and beige. The carpet was a tone away from rose gold, and the sparse ornaments – a vase with a bulbous base like a pear; a silver candelabra; a couple of abstract statuettes that looked like people caught in a volcanic blast, their features melted off – added elegant, shimmering highlights.

It was a neutral room, but it erred on the feminine side. Or maybe that was the flowers? Hester counted six bouquets standing on tables around the suite: pink chrysanthemums and yellow gardenias; purple freesias; and one bunch of vibrant orange roses, their heavy heads bowing under their own weight. It was a space that Hester thought she would be able to fit her entire flat into, and probably her neighbour Vanessa's, too.

'They're get-well flowers,' Jake said mildly, and she realized she was still standing, iPad in hand, her curiosity overruling her professionalism. 'Not my taste, exactly, but people have been kind.' He gestured to the sofa opposite his, and as Hester went to sit down he lifted his feet onto the strategically placed pouffe in front of him. She noticed he'd made himself a little squirrelly nest, everything within

11

reaching distance. TV remote, iPad, a bowl of nuts, a copy of the *New York Times*. There was a jug and a glass of water on the gleaming coffee table, next to a blister strip of pills. Hester felt a moment of kinship with this stranger, because she would have done exactly the same thing: nesting was one of her best skills.

'I was sorry to hear about your accident,' she said, as she sat and smoothed out her skirt. The backs of her thighs had dried, and the air con was making short work of the other patches of sweat that had bloomed during her walk.

'Why?' he asked. 'Presumably you knew about it at exactly the same time you heard I existed.'

'Why wouldn't I be sorry?' She frowned. 'Even though I didn't know about you beforehand, I'm not going to rejoice in a stranger being hit by a car.' A memory, of her dad leaning over a body on the floor, slid into her head, and she forced it away.

Jake pursed his lips, blew air out quietly between them. 'Sorry. It's been a rough couple of days.' He gestured to his robe-clad form, and Hester took it as an invitation for her eyes to sweep up and down him again. 'This is Beth's doing, you said?'

She nodded. 'She contacted Cassie, at Paradise Awaits, and—' His lips lifted in amusement, and Hester, to her mortification, felt hers do the same. She cleared her throat. 'Apparently she wanted you to have something good on the horizon, to look forward to when you're fully recovered.'

'What I'm most looking forward to is getting home. I don't need a trip to Thailand.'

'Is home New York? You don't have an accent.' She had

12

expected it; conjured it up while she was unravelling his brief story on her way over here.

'I moved there when I was twenty-two. It's definitely home.'

He said it with conviction, and Hester resisted the urge to ask more. New York was at the very top of her travelling bucket list. Inconvenient, considering its distance from London, but that was part of what made it so desirable.

'And you don't want me to book you a trip to Thailand?' she said instead. 'Cassie assured me the cost would be covered by your sister. Her treat.'

Jake gave a humourless laugh, but then his face twisted and he leaned forward, clutching his ribs. Hester jumped off the sofa, discarding her iPad as she came round the table towards him. Panic made her limbs tingle, but she crouched next to him and reached her hand out, wary of touching this stranger, but hating how his pain was so obvious.

'What can I do?'

'Nothing,' he gritted out. 'This happens. It'll pass.'

'OK.' She sat back on her haunches, waiting. She filled up the glass from the jug on the table, then took the jug and went in search of a tap, her gaze tracking back to where Jake was bent double. He turned his head to look at her, and gestured vaguely behind her. Hester saw a glimpse of palatial bedroom, the sheets twisted as if something much more fun than a night of agony had happened beneath them, and then, keeping her eyes straight ahead, walked through it to the en suite, filling the jug in the deep sink.

There was a toothbrush, and a carelessly squeezed tube of toothpaste on the marble surround, along with a heavy-looking glass bottle of aftershave called Ocean Haze. Hester paused for a second, then picked it up and took the lid off.

She sniffed it, and shuddered at the complex, delicious scent. She imagined Jake Oakenfield in a sharp suit, sprayed in this combination of cedar, lemon and sea salt, and decided it should be illegal for something so enticing to exist. Would he be clean-shaven or still slightly fuzzy? Would she start by kissing his cheek, or reaching out to take his hand?

'What are you doing back there?' he called, and she could tell, as she almost dropped the aftershave bottle, that it was an effort for him to raise his voice.

She hurried back through the bedroom, holding the jug like a trophy. 'Replenishing.'

He narrowed his eyes. His face was two shades paler than it had been before.

'Is this whole holiday thing a cover?' he asked. 'What are you really here for? Are you a spy? Did my mother send you?'

'What? No. I promise you I am from P— the travel agency. Are you OK?'

She put the jug down next to the glass, saw a few drops of water on the table where he must have spilled it taking a sip, then sat back in her place.

Jake watched her for a few seconds, his expression unreadable. 'No,' he said finally. 'Nothing about this is OK.'

'Because you're in pain, and you want to go home,' Hester confirmed. 'And you don't want a holiday.'

'Got it in one, Hester Monday.' He gave her name a little too much focus, over-enunciating it. 'My sister means well, but she always interferes. I am uncomfortable in my own skin, and in these surroundings. All I want to do is go home and recover in my apartment, and I can't even do that.' He rubbed his forehead.

'They're not the *worst* surroundings to get better in,' Hester said carefully.

His smile was small and bitter, and didn't make full use of those beautiful lips. Hester did not tell him this. 'Rosalie's gratitude on full show.'

'Rosalie?' Without her conscious permission, Hester's bum settled further into the sofa cushions. She wasn't going to get a successful outcome or any commission out of this trip across the river, which made it all the more imperative that she got what she could in life-experience terms. Cassie wouldn't be happy, but Hester's soul would, and long ago she had made a promise to herself to feed her soul in any way she could. She was limited by her circumstances, so she had to make the most of what *was* on offer to her. This luxurious suite, and Jake Oakenfield, were the most compelling things the universe had delivered to her in a long time.

'Rosalie Dewey,' Jake explained. 'She's eternally grateful that I pushed her out of the way of the car, so she booked me into this suite to recover. I promise you, I don't make a habit of staying in these sorts of places.'

'You make it sound like a crack den,' Hester said, laughing. 'It's pretty swanky.'

'Is *pretty swanky* a travel agent term?' He raised an eyebrow.

Hester felt the blush in the roots of her hair.

'I'm kidding,' he said. 'And you're right, it is better than a crack den, or at least the last few I've been to. But I don't feel comfortable here.'

'You can't really be comfortable anywhere if your ribs are broken,' Hester said, caught off guard by his sudden humour, albeit drier than a Martini. At least she hoped it was humour, and he wasn't hiding a drug-riddled lifestyle in plain sight. But then, no. Not with those cheeks, that glossy hair. She'd seen the before and after pictures of meth addicts on the *Daily Mail* website.

'Thank you, Captain Obvious.'

This time, Hester just stared.

Jake sighed. 'Sorry. That was uncalled for.'

'Why aren't you comfortable here? Other than your ribs.'

'Because I don't want Rosalie feeling like she has to pay for this place for my recuperation. I was already booked into a hotel – one at a tenth of the price – and that would have done me fine.'

'Surely it's because she's grateful for what you did? Anyone would be. You saved her life.'

'I probably stopped her getting a bruised leg, if that. It wasn't Superman stuff.'

'But *you* got more than a bruised leg.'

'I tripped as I ran, and got the full force of the car's bumper. It was stupid.'

'It was brave.'

'Are you going to give me a sticker?'

'I left my roll of *brave little soldier* stickers at home today. Didn't you get one from the doctor?'

'No, I got the kibosh put on my trip home.'

'Bad doctor,' Hester said soothingly.

This time when Jake's lips curved upwards, the smile ignited his eyes. 'Anyway,' he said. 'I don't want to be here, I don't want all the flowers, and I definitely don't want a trip to Thailand. The first two I'm stuck with for the time being, the last I can do something about. I'm sorry, Hester Monday, to have wasted your time, but I don't want what you're offering.'

16

Chapter
Three

Thursday

Hester put her iPad in her leather rucksack. 'No problem, Mr Oakenfield. I hope you recover quickly, and can get back to New York sooner rather than later.'

His eyes followed her up as she stood, as she dithered. *Goodbye, Jake Oakenfield,* she thought, her inner voice overly dramatic. She walked to his side of the coffee table and held out her hand.

'It was good to meet you,' she said.

A beat, and then he reached up and wrapped his hand around hers. Hester pressed her lips together as her palm sizzled at the contact. Was her skin as warm as his? Was his skin that warm all over? Were his ribs purple beneath that robe? Was his bum a perfect Merryweather plum? Her brain had forgotten that she was meant to let go, but thankfully his seemed to have, too. She met his gaze, and the shock of the connection jolted through her. His blue eyes blazed, a Bunsen burner flame in a long-ago Chemistry class. She much preferred this kind of chemistry.

'You know,' he said, 'I've completely forgotten my manners. Would you like a drink before you go?' Hester wondered if she was imagining the slight rasp in his voice. He let go of her hand and Hester pressed it to her chest, pushing against her breastbone.

He was prolonging their meeting. Should she accept?

'I mean, it's obviously hot out there,' he added.

'Why "obviously"? Your suite is air-conditioned.'

'Weather app,' he said, holding his phone up.

'Oh. I—'

'And your hair,' he went on. 'It's curled around your temples.' He made spirals in the air with a finger. 'Beth's does the same, in the heat.'

'Yes. Well. It *is* hot.'

'So, a drink, then? I can order up any kind of cordial you can think of. One of the perks of my plush prison.'

'Lime cordial,' she said. 'Or – no. Do you think they have pink lemonade?'

'I would put money on it.' Jake picked up the cordless phone that was in easy reach on the table and pressed a button. 'Hi, yes Marty, it's me. Could I have a couple of pink lemonades, and some of those rice crackers? Can you put it on my tab, not the room's?' He paused. 'No, I know she said that, but I really would feel better if— yes. Thank you.' He hung up.

Hester was still standing within hand-shaking distance, and Jake gave her a sheepish smile. 'I don't want to take liberties with Rosalie. She may be paying for the room, but she doesn't have to foot the bill for everything else.'

'If you never wanted to take her offer, why didn't you just go back to your own hotel?'

'Because she arranged everything while I was in hospital, and I was on some pretty impressive painkillers. I wasn't in a position to do my own thing, when it came to it.'

'And Beth didn't help?' Hester asked. 'If she's so concerned about you that she wants to buy you a holiday, why didn't she make sure you ended up where you wanted to?'

'Beth's generosity is very much on her own terms,' he said. 'She is the most kind-hearted person I know, if she's doing what she thinks is right for you. Your own opinion tends not to come into it.'

'And she thought it was right that you accepted Rosalie's offer?'

'She's got me exactly where she wants me. Coddled, drugged-up, placid, and not on the other side of London from her. Look, you don't have to stand there, looming over me. I don't need so much close scrutiny.'

'Oh! Sorry, I—' Hester hurried back to the opposite sofa, sat down too quickly and was caught in a hug by the cushions. God, this place was luxurious. She would be fully prepared to put aside her moral stance for a night in a suite like this. *What sort of morals?* her brain whispered, and her eyes tracked back to the man sitting across from her. *What if you could have both? Think how much that would do for your soul.* 'You're not usually placid?' She imagined he could be very much in control if he wanted to be. She shuddered.

'Are you cold now? I can turn the air con down.' He pushed his palms into the sofa as if about to get up, and Hester held out a hand.

'No, I'm fine. *Fine.*' Shit.

19

She was saved from her embarrassment by a knock on the door. She got up and hurried over to it, finding a tall, willowy woman with ice-white hair on the other side. In front of her was a trolley, and on it were two tall glasses and a silver dome covering a platter. Hester had to chew her cheek to hold in her laughter.

'Mr Oakenfield's room service,' the woman said, and as Hester thanked her and wheeled the trolley into the suite, the woman craned her neck, trying to peer around the open door.

Yeah, I don't blame you, Hester thought as she smiled at the woman and slowly, politely, she hoped, closed the door. It was not a good sign that she already felt proprietorial about a man she wouldn't see again after this glass of pink lemonade.

'Your room service, Mr Oakenfield,' she repeated, giving a small curtsy as she pushed the trolly over to where he sat.

'Thank you,' he said drily. 'Please, help yourself.'

The two tall, straight glasses were filled with lemonade in a deep, raspberry red; ice clustered at the bottom; a strawberry sliced almost in half and balanced on the rim; a sprig of fresh mint partially drowned in each glass. Hester lifted the cloche with a flourish to find two Chinese-patterned bowls of rice crackers, glossy and enticing, and a small, cracked-porcelain dish containing four rose-shaped chocolates.

'Oh my God,' she breathed. 'This is unreal.' She took a glass and a bowl off the platter and placed them reverentially in front of Jake. Then she took the others back to her seat across the wide glass table. The chocolates she left where they were. Somehow, it was all too much for her brain to process.

'Unreal?' Jake echoed. 'For someone who works at a place called Paradise Awaits, you seem pretty surprised by what goes for paradise these days.'

Hester stared at her bowl of crackers. She felt fully unpeeled by his comment; his perceptiveness. She sipped her drink, trying not to let her sheer bliss at the pink lemonade's fruity flavour show on her face. This wasn't something she could find in a supermarket, not even Waitrose. She wondered if Jake would introduce her to Rosalie Dewey. Then she could follow her around and avert another disaster, and then perhaps *she* could end up somewhere like this.

'Sorry,' she said, when she saw Jake was waiting for an answer, his glass hovering inches from his lips. 'I hadn't realized how hot I'd got, walking across the river. The sun is baking.'

Jake nodded slowly. She could tell he didn't believe a word of it. Still, what did it matter? She wouldn't see him again after this.

Hester glugged her drink, holding the glass with two hands like a chipmunk. Then she put it down and picked up a perfect rice cracker. She was about to put it in her mouth when she saw that he was still watching her, his eyes narrowed. His chest moved up and down evenly, his breathing steady or, perhaps, slightly laboured. Another flash of panic gripped her, but when he spoke his voice was calm, no hint of his earlier discomfort.

'Why do you do what you do?'

'You mean my job?'

He nodded. 'Surely you have experience of what you're selling? You can't wax lyrical about the benefits of a new BMW if you haven't taken it for a test drive.'

21

'We're well-trained,' Hester said quickly. 'We've got contacts in all our destinations. Built relationships with hoteliers and resort managers. Of course, we're passionate about travel, about giving our clients the best possible experience. Every hotel, every tour, every option is fully explored before we consider adding it to our portfolio. Nothing is too much trouble.'

'Great spiel.'

'Thank you.' She chose to ignore his sarcasm. She was good at her job: nobody could tell her she wasn't. Personal knowledge of the destinations was desirable but not essential. And what did it matter if she'd never taken advantage of the generous discount she got? She'd been able to pass it on to her friends.

She wished she could show Jake how capable she was: how she could have him picturing his arrival at his five-star hotel the moment the sun set in a burst of colour on the beach; the pure white sheets and urns of lotus flowers; the clean scent of the sea and whispered breeze tickling the blinds; the feel of the sand between his toes. She would have him aching for it, and booking that holiday at his sister's expense, in a heartbeat.

Hester thought of her desk at Paradise Awaits. Currently, it was more like *Paperwork Awaits*.

This was the best part, sitting with the client, slotting flights and hotels and experiences together like a big Lego palace of possibility, their excitement palpable. She felt a sudden longing to come back to this unbelievable room and this plum of a man, with his injuries and his stubble and his dry, cracked humour nestled amongst layers of cynicism.

'I'd better be getting back.' She stood and put her bowl of crackers next to his. 'It was good to meet you, Mr Oakenfield.'

He ran a hand through his hair, his fingers briefly straightening the curls. 'You too, Hester Monday. Sorry, again, that you weren't what I was looking for.' He seemed so weary, Hester wished she *could* be what he wanted; that she could spend time with him and make him laugh, help him forget his troubles and see that there was something to be said for having a luxurious holiday in your near future to aim for. But maybe he was a doer, suddenly thrust into a world of being helpless and relying on other people, and the thought of lying on a sun lounger and being waited on was his idea of hell.

'No problem.' She shrugged. 'There's always someone waiting for me to brighten up their day.'

She wondered whether to shake hands again, but that might result in another delay, and she was too full of nervous energy to let the sofa swallow her again. She needed to get away from Jake before she found another reason to linger. The longer she stayed, the harder it would be to leave.

'Bye then,' she said.

'Goodbye, Hester.' Somehow the use of her first name alone, dropping the formalities at the last minute, was the saddest thing of all. So much potential, wasted.

She walked to the door and turned. He was in the same place, his head leaning against the back of the sofa, his eyes closed and a hint of a smile on his lips. It was the first time she'd seen him anything like relaxed, and it took all her willpower to stop staring and close the door behind her.

She looked up at the gold, embossed Merryweather nameplate, stroked it gently, and then strode back down the corridor, her heels sinking into the soft carpet as she went.

Chapter
Four

Thursday

Hester escaped the cloying confines of the hotel, almost galloping down the wide front steps and back into the sunshine. She felt disheartened, all the questions buzzing in her thoughts on her way to the meeting still there, but with nowhere, now, to land.

She had got *some* answers. Jake had pushed the old lady out of the way and sacrificed himself, being hit by the bumper of the oncoming car. She tried to play the accident through in her head, wondering what frame of mind you'd have to be in to rush into danger without any thought for yourself – or perhaps it was his hesitation that had led to his injuries being that much worse. The broken ribs, the bruise on his face somehow dashing; a mark of bravery, enhancing his features instead of marring them.

But there was no point in thinking about him any more. He didn't want the holiday. She hoped Cassie wouldn't be too disappointed. She tried to push away the unease settling in her gut; her boss had specifically chosen her, and the last thing she wanted to do was let her down.

The sun was even hotter now, the glittering Thames in contrast to the still, stilted air that felt as if all the oxygen had been sucked out of the city. Hester slipped her sunglasses onto her nose, not minding the sweat so much when she was on her way to see friends instead of a client.

She was meeting Glen and Amber outside the Festival Hall, on the wide concrete terrace that, in the summer months, boasted overpriced outdoor bars and a fountain set into the floor, its multiple water jets launching into the air in a seemingly haphazard fashion, catching tourists unaware as they strolled over the innocuous-looking rubber square, soaking them in seconds.

The three of them could spend hours watching it – their favourite spectator sport, accompanied by bottles of wine – arguing about whether the jets were on a random timer, or if there was someone in the bowels of the cavernous hall watching the flow of people, young and old, hurrying and lingering, on CCTV and choosing when to strike. Hester had decided that would be her ideal job, and certainly less fraught with danger than extolling the virtues of places she'd never been to.

She pictured Jake's look of amused disbelief when she'd reacted to the trolley of treats, and cringed. Of course, Amber noticed her doing it. Her friend had commandeered a table, and was looking up from her phone while simultaneously typing on it, her fingers flying across the screen.

Amber was a marketing manager at a large software company, deeply driven, deeply together, kind but with a no-nonsense approach to all aspects of her – and her friends' – lives. Hester didn't want to think about the number of headphone sets and external iPhone speakers in her flat, all bought because her friend had convinced her she needed them.

'What's up?' Amber asked, standing while still typing. 'You've got that *look*.' She hugged her while still holding her phone, and held out a glass of red wine with her free hand.

'What look?' Hester asked, accepting the embrace and the drink.

'The look of doom. You've had a bad day.'

'I've had a good day actually,' Hester said, sliding onto the stool opposite her friend. There was a shriek from behind her, and she turned to see a couple dressed for the theatre standing, soaked and stunned, on the low rubber square. Amber and Hester winced in unison.

'Why was it good?' Amber asked. 'Come on, traffic lights.'

'I am too tired for traffic lights.'

'Don't think too hard; go on instinct. Green for what went well, red for what could have gone better, amber,' she paused to gesture to herself, 'for a moment when you felt undeniably hot and invincible.'

'Kill me now,' Hester muttered, even though her friend's strategy could be useful, if a little egocentric. It had certainly helped her at times when she was feeling lost, and incapable of finding anything positive in a situation.

'Start with green.' Amber folded her arms and pinned Hester with her large brown eyes, her shiny black hair swept artfully over one shoulder.

'OK,' Hester said. 'Green. I met a client at the Duval hotel, where I drank pink lemonade with a real strawberry on the side, and I didn't even have to find the guy a holiday.'

'Oooh, the Duval. Fancy. Why didn't you have to book the holiday? Did the fire alarm go off?'

'I'd been arranged as a surprise by his sister, and he didn't want me after all.'

'That's utterly implausible,' said a gruff voice, as a hand landed on Hester's shoulder and stubble brushed her cheek. 'Nobody who saw you wouldn't want you.' Glen swung onto the remaining stool, pulled his satchel over his head and poured himself a glass of wine in one elegant swoop. 'Who was this dickhead?'

Hester hadn't thought of Jake Oakenfield as a dickhead. She gave a tiny shake of her head and her friends picked up on it. They had spent so much time together, their reading of each other was attuned enough that they might as well be nonidentical triplets.

Glen managed a trendy bar in Hoxton, was laid back where Amber was clinically efficient, but was also supremely confident because – he'd told them years ago – being a pure ginger meant he'd absorbed as many insults as he could and no longer got offended by anything. Hester thought his pale red fuzz – almost the same length on his jaw as on his head – and green eyes were attractive, and whenever she visited him at work he had women gazing at him as if he was a rare breed of highly desirable poodle. But he only had eyes for his girlfriend, Elise, who never made it to their Thursday drinks because she was training to be a midwife and Thursday was her busiest day.

'The dickhead,' Hester said, answering Glen's question, 'was not a dickhead at all. He just didn't want a holiday.

And that's my red,' she added, going back to Amber's traffic lights. 'I wish I'd been able to convince him to book one. My conversion rate is pretty good.'

'But if he's already staying at the Duval then he probably doesn't need one.' Amber frowned in a *duh* way, and Hester sighed. She should have sidestepped Amber's questions about her day, but it always seemed so innocuous. Just three little things about your day, Hester. Where's the harm in that? *For someone who works at a place called Paradise Awaits, you seem pretty surprised by what goes for paradise these days.* She shifted uncomfortably on her stool.

'He's staying at the Duval because the woman whose life he saved booked him into a suite to recuperate, and he was on too many drugs to protest.' If she was going to have to tell the story, she wouldn't do it half-heartedly. She watched, pleased, as Amber and Glen turned towards her, lips parted, wine forgotten. Even when a group of teenagers made an ungodly racket after one of them pushed another into the path of the water jets, Hester retained her friends' attention.

She may not have the life experience of other travel agents, but spinning stories, she could do. She folded her arms on the table and told her friends everything.

'So he basically outed you because you got squeaky about a fancy drink?' Glen raised a pale eyebrow. 'Have you never been to my bar?'

'It came with a *cloche*,' Hester said. 'Didn't you hear that bit?'

'So several years working as a travel agent,' Glen said, 'a job that you are singularly unqualified to do because you haven't actually been anywhere, haven't set foot in a country other than the UK since you were eleven, and—'

'You don't *have* to go anywhere to be a travel agent,' she protested. 'And I never intended to make a career of it. It was one admin job, at one travel agency, because it was round the corner from my flat and then . . . when I got the chance to sell holidays, it turned out I was good at it. Paradise Awaits was the next logical step.' She sighed. 'I know that it's a different ball game, that Cassie is expecting me to represent her company at resorts, to test these places out. But maybe it will help me finally get over this thing. Sooner or later she's going to force me to go somewhere.' And yet, if Hester kept finding excuses for the invites Cassie sent her way, she would be forever treading water.

'Whatever happens,' Glen said, 'you can't be fazed by a metal dish over a bowl of crackers, or more people will get suspicious.'

'We've spent enough time over the years debating Hester's confounding career choices.' Amber slapped her palm down on the table. 'We need to focus on the fact that you liked him; this Jake guy. You got that dreamy look in your eyes. The one you last had about Pierre.'

'Ugh,' Hester and Glen said together. Pierre the French chef, who, after charming Hester's socks off, had turned out to care about only two things: food and himself. The food part was good for a while, but she soon got bored of being less interesting than a gooey Camembert.

'In the early days, obviously,' Amber clarified. 'But you *did* like him, didn't you? Jake the almost-client.'

'He's roadkill,' Glen objected. 'He'd *literally* been scraped off the pavement a few days before.'

Hester narrowed her eyes at him, and he grinned. She hated the word "literally" being misused – it was a lazy way to add drama to a story – so Glen baited her with it at every opportunity.

'Dark, moody, and slightly damaged.' Amber shuddered theatrically. 'Sounds delicious.'

'Is that your new marketing slogan, Ambs?' Glen asked. 'Not sure you're going to sell many units with it.'

They glared at each other across the table, and Hester took the opportunity to go and replenish their drinks. The waiter had a tea towel slung over his shoulder, designer stubble and an eyebrow piercing. His movements were liquid; efficiency without any real effort. He smiled at her with his blue eyes, and Hester pictured other, slightly darker eyes in a bruised face, glinting at her over a glass coffee table as big as her bedroom.

Why hadn't she glossed over the meeting, found three different things to tell Amber about her day? She'd sat next to a woman with really great hair on the train coming in: all the colours of the rainbow and a fuck-off glare for anyone who dared to smirk. She'd got a Pret salad with a particularly good chicken to leaves ratio at lunch. Her red would have been that she hadn't bought a muffin to go with it, a decision she regretted. She wasn't sure what her amber would have been, but that was always the hardest one.

Anyway, it was too late. She'd gone over the afternoon in detail, not needing to admit how attractive she had found Jake, because her friends had picked up on it anyway. She'd brought it to the surface like lost treasure recovered from the deep. She would never see him again, but she had allowed him to stay, gleaming in the silt of her thoughts, instead of falling, forgotten, to the bottom.

When she got back to her friends they were still bickering,

the topic of conversation long since moved on from the Duval and its occupant, and they barely noticed when she placed the bottle of rosé between them, which showed just how seriously they were taking their argument. Amber was red wine all the way, Glen thought it was better to pay more for a good bottle of white, and they both agreed that rosé was the worst of both worlds and Hester's taste buds must be dead. Hester would defend her beloved rosé – not as tart as most whites, not as dehydrating as a lot of reds – until the cows came home. Tonight, she didn't have to.

She settled back as much as the stool would allow, and let her attention drift between Amber and Glen, the activity surrounding the fountain, and the day cruisers and clippers passing on the wide river, while the sun sank lower behind the Houses of Parliament, turning the magnificent building that housed so much rot into a stark silhouette.

A few more hours of this, and Jake Oakenfield would be gone from her thoughts for good. As she poured the peach-hued liquid into their glasses and tuned into her friends' discussion, she almost let herself believe it.

Chapter
Five

Thursday

Hester got on the train at Waterloo East in a slightly hazy wine fug that meant she didn't notice anything except other happy people, smiling back at her as if they were sharing some deep secret instead of simply trading alcohol fumes across the carriage.

Less in control of her thoughts, they kept tripping back to the hotel. The feel of the carpet through the thin soles of her shoes; Jake leaning on the doorframe, his blue gaze latching onto hers; her brazen few minutes snooping in the bathroom; that strange ache of wanting to belong – to be there as more than just a favour from his sister that he had no intention of cashing in. She rolled her eyes and a woman sitting opposite her, wearing a navy suit with a sparkling, strawberry brooch on the lapel, gave her an indulgent smile.

'Don't worry about it,' she said.

'Worry about what?' Hester asked, keeping her voice low. The carriage was full of post-work and pub-people, the slightly scruffier set before the theatregoers emerged from their evening performances and filled the trains with glamour and the shared frisson of having had their minds and emotions stretched by art.

'Whatever it is you're berating yourself for,' the woman said. 'Let it go. It's done. Move forward.' She turned to the window with a satisfied smile, as if she'd imparted a piece of wisdom that would change Hester's life.

Hester was grateful, but she also wanted to point out that it wasn't as easy as that. Everyone had some element of their past nipping at their heels. Whether it was good, bad or indifferent, you couldn't just pretend you were born fresh every morning, a grown adult, and nothing had shaped you into the person you were. Still, she wasn't up for a slightly drunken philosophical argument with a stranger on a train, so she followed the woman's example and stared out of the window, the figures inside the carriage imprinted gauzily on the pockets of night-time London they passed.

She got off at Kidbrooke and took her place among the shoal of commuters slipping out of the station, then walked the short distance to her flat, her footsteps echoing in the dark. The block had been sleek and pristine in the nineties, the ad had told her when she'd gone to the viewing, but now it was decidedly less so. Still, her flat was cosy and convenient, with its minuscule entranceway and living room-slash-kitchen, boxy bedroom and a bathroom she couldn't turn around in with her arms fully outstretched. Her personal space in the world was enough for her, she told herself for the millionth time. What more did she need?

She passed the light on the first-floor landing that flickered and buzzed like an angry wasp was trapped inside it, and the graffiti scrawled in pink paint asserting that *Rose loves Dick,* and she wondered, as she always did, whether Dick was a person or an appendage. She was putting her key in the lock when she heard the door behind her open. She turned, her smile genuine as her neighbour, Vanessa, appeared in the doorway.

'Darling Hester,' she said in her melodic voice, spreading her arms wide and shuffling forwards. Her dress had a bold pattern of pink and indigo swirls, the hem dragging on the floor. 'What news are you bringing me today?'

Hester leaned against her own door and put her handbag on the floor.

This was their almost-daily ritual. Vanessa never complained about the pain in her legs and lower back, the result of a fall she'd had several years ago, before Hester knew her. She was mostly restricted to the second-floor flat which she'd made a colourful home – so much cosier than Hester's own attempts – fit to bursting with reminders of Barbados. Like so many people seemed to be, she was fascinated by Hester's job, imagining glamorous colleagues and endless trips abroad, private jets and five-star resorts, and Hester, not wanting to put any more limits on Nessa's restricted life, had tried to live up to her expectations whenever they passed on the stairs.

Now Vanessa listened out for her return every evening, wanting updates. It was obvious that she knew Hester embellished her stories, but they had a silent understanding that formed part of their friendship.

'Well, Nessa,' Hester started, 'what would you say if I told you I spent this afternoon in one of London's most exclusive hotels, being wined and dined' – on lemonade and rice crackers – 'surrounded by delicious scents' – she would never forget the smell of Jake's Ocean Haze aftershave – 'and hearing someone tell me about a dramatic, life-or-death rescue that put them in hospital?'

Vanessa narrowed her eyes and folded her arms across her bosom. 'I'd say it sounds a little too exciting to be true.'

Hester gasped. 'But Nessa—'

'Why would you be hearing about rescues, when your job is booking these fancy trips?'

'I was in the hotel meeting a client,' Hester explained. 'The rescue was—' She stopped. She didn't want to go through it again. It was one unusual day that had made her life seem more interesting for a few hours, but now it was over. 'It doesn't matter.'

'Why not, darling?' Her friend's suspicion was replaced by concern. 'What's the problem? Where did this tale come from? All your friends and family OK?'

Hester nodded. 'Everyone's fine. I just . . . missed out on an opportunity, that's all.'

'That Cassie keeping back the good stuff?' Vanessa clicked her tongue against her teeth. 'She doesn't know what she's got in you.'

'No, Cassie's been great. She always is.' Hester didn't want to tell Vanessa how many chances to trial new, exotic hotels or overseas tours she'd passed up, always finding excuses she was sure her boss didn't believe but had given up challenging her on.

'So what's this, then?' Vanessa shuffled forward and poked

36

a finger into Hester's cheek, her turned-down mouth. 'Why are you so sad?'

'Not sad,' Hester said. 'A bit drunk. A bit hot. When is this weather going to break?'

'You need the sea,' Vanessa replied. 'A good sea breeze makes the worst heat feel like paradise. Why do all these people choose to live away from the ocean? It makes no sense.'

'Will you be by the sea when you go back to Barbados?' Hester asked. 'You and Lyron?' Lyron was Nessa's grown-up son.

'Lyron won't come back with me. He's got a home here now, a good job. Lyron will be in London, sweltering and suffocating. I will be by the water. You should get out there, too. When was the last time you had a trip that wasn't work?'

'I went to Devon last summer with Mum and Dad,' Hester said. 'The sea there is beautiful.'

'But you need the heat, Hester. Heat and blue sea; sand and soul. You have to be overwhelmed by your surroundings. Devon won't hit you in the face with its beauty. Get one of your fancy brochures, bring it here and I'll tell you exactly the place. Now sleep, darling. Smooth out those worry lines. No more thoughts of death – it's not healthy.' She tapped Hester firmly on the head, the underside of her rings connecting with Hester's scalp, then turned and went back inside her flat.

Hester opened her front door, dumped her bag on the carpet and kicked her shoes off. She switched the fairy lights on, and her living room was transformed. The cracks in the plaster, the red wine stain on the rug and the photographs on her flimsy bookcase – they all faded to nothing against the white, glowing lights.

With them on and the rest of the room in shadow, Hester could be anywhere. Somewhere far away, with the sea breeze Nessa had talked about and tables under a vine-entwined veranda, the breathtaking landscape hidden by darkness, the lights a reminder that this was a magical place. The unreality of holiday created by spending £34.99 at Lisa Angel. Everyone underestimated the power of fairy lights except her.

But she didn't tell anyone, not Nessa or Amber or Glen, and certainly not Cassie, Seb or Danielle at Paradise Awaits, that you could create a romantic otherworld without going anywhere near an aeroplane: that you could conjure up the atmosphere of a holiday by filling your senses with the sounds, smells and tastes of your dream destination without actually being there. She didn't tell them because she was a travel agent and if she was too convincing she'd talk herself out of a job, but also because nobody needed a get-out like she did. None of them had a problem that prevented them from travelling, so there was no need to find an alternative.

Hester poured herself a glass of water, managing to splash it all over her thin blouse as she did, then gave in and switched the main light on, the fairy lights diminished in the stronger, yellowish glow. Her eyes latched onto the photo on her bookshelf, next to her Gene Kelly signature edition box set. Guilt and regret made her stomach ache, and she wondered if she would ever be able to look at the still of that happy, Italian memory without thinking about what had come afterwards.

One flight to Edinburgh, when she was twelve years old, and she still felt the impact of it. Her parents hadn't given up their holidays abroad. They went to Spain and Greece, occasionally America, and they always invited her; her mum's tone cautious, her dad's boisterous, verging on belligerent, as if positivity could erase what had happened and the way it had changed his daughter. The Devon holidays were a compromise, and as much as Hester enjoyed going away with her family, she felt ashamed, too. As if her phobia made her weak; as if she should have got over it long before now, and her parents were pandering to her.

Hester looked at the photo of the three of them standing at the end of the jetty on Amalfi's charmingly cluttered seafront. Her head was tucked into her dad's armpit, her blonde hair a frizzy, out-of-shape halo, her mum on the other side. Her dad's grin was wide and white, her mum's gentler, and eleven-year-old Hester gazed up at them, wanting to see if they were as overwhelmed by their first twilight view of the Italian town as she was; the way the houses and hotels ran in jumbled, coloured rows up the cliff, lights twinkling and the sea a purplish-grey behind them.

Hester had been full of the sights and sounds, the strange language being spoken around her, the sea that seemed so different from the Kent beaches she was used to. She knew, then, that she wanted to travel, to soak in as many places as she could. She had been determined, at that young age, that whatever else her life was, it would be one bursting with new locations: Hester would be a Jetsetter.

But, just a year later, the option was taken from her. That was how she chose to see it − as something that had happened *to* her − but perhaps that was part of the problem. Nobody else was stopping her. Nobody had put all those plans in her head and then decided that, no matter how hard she tried, she wouldn't be able to make it through airport security, let alone on an aeroplane.

Sighing, she unzipped the side pocket of her handbag and took out the piece of malachite she always carried with her, wrapping her hand around the impossibly smooth, green crystal. It felt cold, glasslike, against her warm skin. She closed her eyes. *The guardian stone for travellers,* she remembered Betty telling her, holding it out to her over the back of the seat, her green eyes wide with excitement. *I carry it everywhere. You should get yourself one, if you're going to be like me. It's a talisman.*

Hester had wanted, more than anything – in that obsessive, all-consuming way things came to her when she was twelve – to be like Betty. But the irony was that if it hadn't been for Betty, for meeting her on that fateful flight, Hester wouldn't be in this position. She might be taking her own malachite talisman on endless international trips, instead of carrying the one she'd stolen onto the train every day, hoping that, eventually, it would help her go further.

She went to bed, the hot weather finally breaking as a distant rumble of thunder, heard through the open window; the golden fairy lights strung around her headboard making her dream of an Italian veranda, a Neapolitan pizza shimmering with olive oil, the glint of a glass aftershave bottle on a marble bathroom countertop.

Chapter
Six

Friday

This week it was Hester's turn to collect the doughnuts, Paradise Awaits' traditional Friday routine, which fitted in well with her Thursday nights with Amber and Glen, as the sugar was a surefire way to ease her hangover. The day was crisp and sweet after the thunderstorm in the night, the roads left damp rather than puddled, the slight rasp of tyres on the wet tarmac a sound that, as she stood outside Tom's Bakery, she realized she loved.

She selected the doughnuts she needed: chocolate sprinkles for Danielle, classic jam for Seb, lemon-iced ring for Cassie and maple glazed for her. She walked the short distance from the bakery to the Paradise Awaits office, which was down one of the cobbled side streets close to Waterloo. It looked exclusive, with its arched glass panel above the door and large, captionless photos of idyllic destinations in the windows. Hester thought it seemed somehow covert, as if the travel agency was a cover for international mercenaries.

The Paradise Awaits logo was black and gold, the font slightly italicized, and it oozed the luxury Cassie wanted to portray in every aspect of their business. Danielle saw Hester through the window and hurried to the door, opening it to admit her. Hester knew that this wasn't out of kindness. For Danielle, Hester was a means to a doughnut rather than a person with a heart and soul, ambitions and beliefs.

'Thanks, Danielle,' she said anyway, putting the box on the nearest desk and waggling her fingers where the cardboard had cut into her skin. The office was brick-walled, with simple white furniture and more oversized prints of tropical seascapes looking down on the Mac-adorned desks. It had a New York loft vibe without the views over Central Park.

'No worries,' Danielle said, smoothing down her long chestnut hair. She had started working for Paradise Awaits at the beginning of the year and was unwaveringly ambitious, her dark eyes gleaming with interest at the sight of every new travel brochure or mention of an island hideaway. Hester sometimes imagined her as a crab, scuttling along behind her, desperate to get onto Hester's back and then, with a few quick snaps of her claws, snipping off Hester's legs so she could overtake her and hurry, sideways, into a perfect sunset horizon.

'Have a good evening?' Danielle asked, peering at Hester closely.

'Great thanks,' Hester said perkily. She would not let Danielle see any signs of alcohol-induced weakness.

'Lovely people!' Cassie swooped out of her office and raised her hands to the sky. 'St Lucia is calling us. A new resort close to Fond Doux, rivalling the plantation. I want to add it to our books and I need a full assessment. Hester.' She spun round.

Hester was waggling her mouse to wake up her computer. 'Yes?'

'Fancy being our St Lucia scout? A few days to check it's up to scratch, personal guest of the owner?' Cassie was wearing a long scarlet dress that emphasized her slender frame, her dyed black hair hanging loose over her shoulders, her blue eyes catlike.

Hester felt herself simultaneously shrivel and go cold, like some freeze-dried food in one of those expensive diet programmes. Seb looked up from his desk, flashy silver-framed glasses on his nose. Danielle froze, chocolate sprinkled doughnut in hand.

'When is it?' Hester hoped she sounded casual.

'Three weeks' time,' Cassie said. 'Could be a big player for us if it's as good as they're promising, but it's a new company so I need to check the teething problems are being ironed out. You'd be great, Hester.'

'Three weeks? I'm – umm. It's my mum's birthday. We've got a spa weekend planned.' The birthday part wasn't a lie, and her mum might well be having some kind of spa treatment in the Madrid hotel Dad had booked for them, but Hester wouldn't be with them, even though, as always, she'd been invited.

'Really?' Cassie raised a perfectly sculpted eyebrow.

Hester didn't need to look at Seb to know he was staring at her with incredulity, or that Danielle had started salivating at the prospect of another discarded opportunity.

'Really. Thanks though, Cassie. For asking me. I've got a

bit of a backlog anyway.' She picked up some white ring binders from the edge of her desk, the Paradise Awaits logo flashing under the spotlights set into the low ceiling. 'Probably best if you or Seb go.'

'OK.' Cassie nodded, unflappable as always. 'Seb?'

'Sure.' He said it easily, but Hester knew he was vibrating with excitement. People wanted to be travel agents so that they could travel, immersing themselves in a world of eternal vacations, securing hefty discounts to far-flung places when they weren't working. Paradise Awaits provided all those opportunities, and one day, *one day,* Hester would be able to enjoy them all, too.

'In my office in ten minutes, then,' Cassie said, 'and I'll give you the details.' She turned and, as she passed Hester's desk to get her lemon doughnut, tapped the ring binders. 'Next time, Hester. Don't keep turning me down. I don't want to see your potential wasted because you won't go the extra mile.'

'Literally,' Seb called over, chuckling.

Both Cassie and Hester ignored him.

'Course not,' Hester said, feeling her cheeks flush pink.

Once Cassie was back in her office, Hester turned to her computer and avoided the disbelieving stares of her colleagues. She didn't have to explain herself to anyone, and she could still do a great job without having actually been to the resorts, whatever Danielle or Seb thought. She remembered Jake's words: *You can't wax lyrical about the benefits of a new BMW if you haven't taken it for a test drive.* But she could. She was making a career out of it.

* * *

The time went slowly, as it often did on a Friday. The doughnut kept her energy up for a while but then it came crashing down again, her hangover pulsing behind just one eye, which was more annoying than both.

She immersed herself in her work, planning a Scandinavian adventure for a couple celebrating their tenth wedding anniversary. Mr and Mrs Oliver wanted all the standard things: a night in an ice hotel, a trip to see the Northern Lights, a husky sled-ride. Hester couldn't blame them their clichés – those were traditional Scandinavian experiences because they were incredible. Who could imagine sleeping in a building made of ice, and not freezing to death? It would be like being inside a diamond. And as for the Northern Lights: well, anyone who said they didn't want to see the real-life version of the iPhone Background was kidding themselves.

Hester flicked through the Aurora Borealis catalogue, browsing the different tour options, mesmerized by the pictures, and wondered which one would suit Mr and Mrs Oliver. They had married fairly young, were still only in their mid-thirties, so she thought a mixture of comfort and adventure would suit. Igloos and campfires, fully surrendering to the landscape while togged up in the warmest gear. It was the only way to do it.

'Each room has its own spa suite,' she heard Seb say to Danielle. 'And the hotelier will throw in premium economy flights if we book today.'

'Sounds extreme,' Danielle said, leaning so far over Seb's desk that Hester was worried she'd lose her balance and fall into him. Danielle said everything was extreme, good or bad. Hester always wanted to say, 'Extremely *what?* Hideous, delightful, disastrous?' But she didn't, because she didn't like drawing attention to herself after she'd turned down a trip. They already thought she was weird.

'Spa suite includes . . .' Seb flicked loudly through the folder Cassie had given him, his shoulders back, his voice raised so she couldn't fail to hear. 'Jacuzzi bath, sauna, steam room, and outdoor shower next to your own pathway down to the private beach.'

'Fuck,' Danielle breathed, the word conveying awe and envy. 'That is . . .' She shook her head, and Hester resisted the urge to finish her sentence. *Extreme?*

Seb was being *extreme*ly annoying. Not because she cared about giving up the St Lucia trip, not in any real sense because it was an impossibility, but because he was strutting about like a peacock. But if she told him she wasn't bothered he wouldn't believe her and think it was sour grapes.

'Golly, Hester,' Danielle said, turning to her. 'You've missed out on a real—'

'Hester,' Cassie said smoothly, appearing at her desk as if she wasn't even aware of Danielle's presence, though of course she was because she saw everything with those feline eyes. 'What's your schedule looking like for this afternoon?'

'Not too bad,' Hester said cautiously. 'I've almost finished the Olivers' itinerary. I've got the Bastians' Route 66 road-trip to confirm – just a couple of the hotels to finalize, and then it's some research for a couple who want a ten-week New Zealand tour, but I've got a few days to do that.'

'Do you think you'll be done with the Olivers and Bastians by two?'

Hester glanced at the corner of her computer, where the clock blinked away the time. How was it not even lunchtime? 'Definitely.'

'Good, because you have to go back to the Duval.'

It took her a moment for Cassie's words to sink in. And then they sunk all the way to the pit of her stomach, and didn't settle at all well. 'Oh?' She tried for breezy.

What had happened? Had Jake Oakenfield found something offensive in the way she'd behaved? Was it the bathroom snoop, or had accepting the drink from him been some kind of test that she'd failed? Or was it Sagging Man? Had he seen the relief on her face when he'd told her he wasn't the man she was looking for? She couldn't remember being particularly subtle about it. Or maybe she'd openly sneered at the receptionist? To be honest, in a place like that she could have offended someone merely by standing the wrong way, so perhaps it wasn't a massive surprise that—

'Yes, Mr Oakenfield has changed his mind. He's had a chance to sleep on Beth's kind offer, and he's decided he does want us to arrange a holiday for him after all. Are you happy to be back there for two-thirty? Beth's so relieved: she was at her wit's end with him.'

'You know Beth?' Hester asked, giving herself time to process this turn of events. She *would* see him again: those blue eyes and that distracting bruise, and his low voice lightly mocking her. She hadn't minded at all: it had been teasing, really, rather than mocking. It had drawn her to him, like a moth to an open candle flame, the burning somehow worth the brightness it let out.

'We do yoga together,' Cassie explained. 'She says Jake is more trouble than all her kids put together, and he's supposed to be an adult. Still, she can't help but mother him.'

'How many children does Beth have?'

'I think four, at the moment.'

Hester's surprise must have been obvious because Cassie laughed gently. 'She's a foster mum. She keeps more balls in the air than anyone else I know. Jake is a particularly slippery one, so it would be good to get this right, Hester. It's not as glamorous as St Lucia, but when it comes to client relationships you're the best I've got, so I know you'll do a good job.'

'Sure. Of course. No problem,' she said to Cassie's retreating back.

Her hangover pounded behind one eye and her heart raced. She was going to see Jake Oakenfield again. This afternoon.

Chapter
Seven

Friday

Hester stood at the bottom of the Duval's wide steps and stared up at the Palladian entrance, the thick pillars stretching up towards a pale blue sky.

After checking she had all the latest Thailand offers loaded up on her iPad, racing out of the office and across the bridge, then almost colliding with a Lycra-clad man on a bicycle when she reached the bottom of the stairs, she had come to a standstill. It was as if she'd run out of impetus, now that she had arrived and the reality of the situation was finally sinking in.

Traffic lights, she thought, a sense of calm descending as she went through Amber's ritual. Green was the fact that Jake had changed his mind, that she would see him again and book him an unforgettable holiday. She would cheer him up and, in the process, please Cassie too, by helping her friend Beth's brother out. Red was how she'd screeched like an angry banshee to the retreating back of Bicycle Man. It wasn't like her at all: she'd been scared by the near-miss, perhaps with Jake's situation at the forefront of her mind. Still, the less said about it the better. Amber? That had to be right now. She had to be hot and invincible *right now.*

'Are you all right, madam?'

Hester started. She hadn't noticed the doorman standing a few feet away. His expression was kind but assessing, the gold band around his top hat glinting in the light.

'I'm fine, thank you,' she said. 'I have a meeting with one of your guests, and I'm just . . .'

'Psyching yourself up?' His smile was warm, but there was a hint of amusement in his dark eyes.

'Something like that.'

'Well, good luck.' He pulled open the heavy glass door.

Hester walked through it, keeping her head high and her chin out, and wishing she'd brought some heels in her bag. She wasn't one of those people who felt underdressed if she didn't have heels – far from it – but a couple of extra inches gave her a poise she usually lacked, forced her to push her shoulders back instead of slumping forwards. And the gilded foyer of the Duval was not a place for slumping.

It was spacious and elegant, and everyone moved without any sense of hurry, as if time inside the doors had been put on the slow-speed setting. The archway into the lounge was so big she felt like a Sylvanian Family member playing at being human. Through it she could see a grand piano, its dark surface polished like glass, and a huge orb of a chandelier, the crystal nuggets that made up its whole twinkling like the world's most expensive glitter ball.

It was breathtaking.

It was awe-inspiring.

It was terrifying.

She was relieved to see that the man with dark hair from the day before wasn't behind the reception desk, and she stepped forward, about to announce herself, when a hand lightly squeezed her arm.

Hester spun round, nearly dropping her handbag. She had almost expected to see Jake, escaped from his decadent prison to come and meet her, but the two women in front of her weren't familiar.

One was her age or a few years older, dark hair kept back from her forehead by a leopard-print headband, denim dungarees making her blue eyes shine. She had delicate features and a wide, easy smile and, despite the animal print and denim, she looked elegant; relaxed; as if she belonged in places like this.

The woman beside her was, when Hester looked closely, actually a girl. Perhaps fifteen or sixteen, with a mane of curly hair around her face which, while undoubtedly beautiful, was expressing sheer boredom. Her spindly arms were folded across her chest, her T-shirt stopping a good couple of inches above the waistband of her skinny jeans to reveal a smooth, brown stomach.

'Are you Hester?' the woman asked.

'Yes, I . . . sorry. I don't think we've met?'

'No, we haven't.' The woman grinned. 'I'm Beth Law, Jake's sister. And this is Tamsin.'

'Hey.' Tamsin waved in a way that managed to convey sarcasm.

Beth's face was a mask of serene patience, and Hester

remembered what Cassie had said about her being a foster mum.

'Hi Tamsin,' Hester said. 'Good to meet you, Beth. Is everything OK with Jake? Cassie told me he'd changed his mind about the holiday.' Now she knew the connection, she could see the similarities between Beth and Jake. The thick, dark hair, the expressive blue eyes. Beth was a couple of inches taller than Hester, and slender, but there was a strength to her, too. Hester imagined she could appear both fragile and unbreakable, depending on what was required. The family had good genes, that was for sure.

'Shall we go and get a cup of tea?' Beth suggested. 'I won't keep you long, and Jake won't mind if you're a few minutes late.'

'No problem,' Hester said, snapping into professional mode as Beth led the way into the lounge. Beth was, after all, her client. 'I was pleased to hear that your brother had changed his mind,' she added. 'Having a holiday to look forward to is almost as enjoyable as the holiday itself.'

'Yes.' Beth glanced back at Hester with a smile. 'And Jake needs something positive, especially now.'

The lounge was a perfect balance of elegance and comfort, the furnishings in shades of gold and cream, accents of sky-blue subtle enough not to be glaring, but adding a pop of colour that made it seem more modern. There was a low hum of conversation as couples and friends had afternoon tea or late lunch, and Hester spotted a mother and daughter – their features so similar as to be obvious – clinking champagne glasses. She thought of her fib about her mum's spa weekend, and unease twisted inside her.

Beth picked a table close to the grand piano, the lid

currently closed, the room free of music. Hester sat opposite her and Tamsin took the last chair, not bothering to pull it up to the table, her gaze drifting aimlessly around her as if to confirm, without speaking, that she wasn't a part of the conversation.

'Tea, coffee?' Beth asked, glancing at the menu.

'Tea would be great,' Hester said. She didn't need any more coffee firing her nervous energy.

The waiter was with them in seconds, almost gliding across the floor, and Hester wondered what it would be like to live your life like this: everything you wanted on immediate, easy demand. Would it set you up for disappointment the moment you stepped into the real world?

'So, Hester,' Beth said, turning her full attention on her. 'Cassie says you're her best agent. She picked you specifically for Jake, and I'm glad.'

Hester was taken aback at the compliment. 'Thank you. I'm planning to book him the holiday of a lifetime.'

Beth gave her a smile that, Hester decided, was sympathetic. 'I'm sure you'll do just that. But I thought it was only fair to warn you that, while it was his decision to invite you back here, things have become slightly more complicated since then.'

'Complicated?' Hester raised her eyebrows.

The waiter reappeared with their teas and a glass of lemonade for Tamsin, who stared unforgivingly at the straw in it, and Hester had to stop herself from smiling.

'Jake had a visit from the doctor this morning,' Beth explained, 'and he's told him he can't fly yet; possibly not for another fortnight. Something to do with his broken ribs: he wants to keep an eye on them, make sure Jake stays free from infection. He should be doing breathing exercises, keeping his lungs clear, but all of that is painful and Jake's a hopeless patient.' She shrugged.

Hester looked for traces of concern on her face, but Beth seemed perfectly calm. Maybe being a foster mum meant this was nothing in the scheme of things, or maybe she had learnt to hide her emotions for the sake of the children she looked after.

'So he won't be able to go home as soon as he'd like,' Hester said, remembering that Jake had told her all he really wanted was to leave London and get back to New York. 'And he's not particularly pleased?'

'Not pleased at all,' Beth confirmed.

'And you wanted to warn me?'

'I thought it was only fair. I love my brother: he has a big heart and he's very generous, but he can also be single-minded when he's got something to aim for, and right now that thing is frustratingly out of reach.'

'Does he still want me to visit him this afternoon?' Hester hoped she was coming across as matter-of-fact. Since Cassie had given her the news, Hester's concentration had been shot, everything focused on returning here. How would she cope if she didn't, after all, get to see him again? She *should* be fine. He was just a client: a total stranger, really.

Beth nodded. 'I offered to cancel it, but he said he may as well see you again, now that he's going to be stuck here for the next two weeks.'

'Rosalie's letting him stay in the suite?' Hester couldn't keep the surprise from her voice. That would be equivalent to a generous deposit on a house.

Beth looked equally surprised. 'He told you about Rosalie?'

'He was explaining that he wouldn't usually stay in such an expensive hotel,' Hester said. 'I think he's a bit embarrassed.'

'He's embarrassed about the whole thing.' Beth sipped her tea, and Tamsin sucked the end of her drink noisily through the straw. Beth put a hand on her forearm and gave her a look that was both steel and cotton wool, and the girl put the glass down and shifted in her seat.

'The rescue?' Hester prompted. Now Beth had sought her out, she couldn't resist gathering information on Jake.

'The rescue, the fact that it was Rosalie he saved – because she won't let him forget about it – and that he's incapacitated. He's always valued his independence, and this feels cloying for him. The attention, the praise, the mollycoddling.' Beth grinned. 'I do feel sorry for him – though I wouldn't ever tell him that – but it's nice to have him here. I don't get to spend a lot of time with my little brother, and now he can't escape. I would have had him at home, but we're full up, and the comfort he's getting here is significantly greater than the camp bed I could offer him. But,' she added, her smile fading, 'I can handle his moods, and I don't want you to be offended if he's not particularly charming. The moment he's rude, just tell him you're not doing it and leave.'

'Got it,' Hester said. 'Don't take any rubbish from him.'

'Exactly,' Beth replied. 'Cassie and I are good friends, I love Paradise Awaits, and I would hate to be responsible for you having a horrible time when you're doing this, partly, for me.'

Hester sipped her tea. It was smoky and delicious, with deep layers of flavour that laughed in the face of the organic teabags Danielle insisted on having in the office. 'I don't often deal with disgruntled clients,' she admitted.

'Booking a holiday is usually a positive experience, but I am fully prepared to stand up to your brother. Thank you for the warning.'

'Good,' Beth said. 'And although I'm not one for having spies,' – Hester thought she heard Tamsin mutter 'yeah right' – 'if you want to call me, any time, just to give me an update, then I wouldn't be against it.' She slid a pearly white business card across the table, the font slanted and delicate.

'Of course,' Hester replied, hoping that didn't commit her to actually doing it. She put the business card in her purse, thinking that this was the strangest meeting she had ever had in this job. Her clients could be eccentric, but she'd never been intercepted before, given warnings and been asked for covert follow-ups. *It's a holiday,* she felt like saying. *Not an international anti-terrorist operation.*

But Beth made it impossible for her to be annoyed. She was friendly and warm and complimentary, and Hester didn't get the sense that she was putting on a front. She was genuinely concerned about her brother's welfare and, it seemed, Hester's too.

'I'm going to find the toilet,' Tamsin said. She stood and flounced off, and Beth watched her go.

'You'd have thought I'd asked her to spend three hours in a rat-infested dungeon, instead of visiting my brother in one of London's most exclusive hotels, the way she's behaving.'

'Perhaps she had other plans this afternoon?' Hester suggested, though it was a long time since she'd considered the inner workings of a teenage mind. Were they even the same species now as she'd been back then?

'Nope,' Beth said. 'When I told her I was going to visit Jake she volunteered to come. The moment we said goodbye to him, her oversized attitude returned. She's generally a good kid, though. She's come a long way. Maybe she just ran out of patience?' Beth shrugged and then smiled at Hester, her blue eyes bright.

Hester thought of the man she was about to see, and her nerve endings fizzed to life. Beth might be astute and intuitive, but Hester suspected that when it came to how attractive her brother was, and how appealing he might appear to hormonal teenage girls, she had a wilful blind spot.

Chapter
Eight

Friday

'Hester. Monday.' There was a definite pause between the words. He didn't look, or sound, pleased to see her. The dressing gown was gone, replaced by a pair of loose jogging bottoms and a bottle-green T-shirt, and the bruise on his face seemed darker. He was still gorgeous, but the weariness of the day before had been replaced with anger. His blue eyes shone with it. Hester thought that all her anticipation, building up since yesterday – because she hadn't stopped thinking about him even when she believed she wouldn't see him again – had been for this moment. He wasn't a disappointment, and Hester was so ready to not take any shit from him.

'Jake Oakenfield,' she said brightly. 'Here I am, back again.' Her pulse was pounding in her throat, an uncomfortable sensation that made it hard to swallow.

'Yes, you are.' His arm was above him, his hand pressed

into the doorframe like yesterday, but this time his stance was more aggressive: a blockade.

'Am I coming in, or are we going to go through it all out here? The man opposite might have something to say about that.'

Jake's eyes narrowed. 'What do you know about him?'

'I met him yesterday, before I saw you. It turned out that neither of us were called Jake, so we couldn't help each other.'

'That's a shame.'

'He didn't want a holiday either, or at least I didn't get around to asking him. Anyway.' She exhaled, trying to settle her nerves. 'None of that is relevant. It turns out you *do* want a holiday after all, so here I am.'

Jake dropped his hand and walked slowly back into the room. Hester went straight to the sofa opposite – as if she already had her own spot in this plush suite – but Jake sat and gestured to the cushion beside him.

'If I'm going to see the screen, you'll need to be next to me, not over there.'

'Which is possibly in a different postcode,' Hester mumbled, nodding.

She walked around the table and sat next to him, keeping a polite distance between them. His posture was upright, his arm wrapped loosely around his torso, and Hester thought that, regardless of the discussion with Beth about his frustration at not being able to go home, he must still be in constant pain.

'You know,' she said gently, 'if a doctor tells you that you shouldn't fly, then there must be a good reason for it. You should listen to them.'

Jake's gaze settled on her, not unkind, but still assessing. 'Beth told you?'

Hester nodded, surprised that he didn't seem annoyed by this revelation.

'She said she was going to warn you about me.' His lips nudged up at one corner, his smile wry. 'I never thought of myself as someone who needed warnings attached to them, but then I never imagined I'd end up here, either.'

Hester ran her finger along the velvety softness of a caramel-coloured scatter cushion, felt the money embedded in its thick weave. 'Flying when you're unwell or injured is never a good idea,' she said. 'It's risky: you don't know what might happen.' Her thoughts tripped back to that flight, all those years ago, when one minute everything had been fine, and then . . .

'You learnt about this as part of your training?' Jake asked.

'Yeah,' Hester said, which wasn't true, but was an easy, obvious lie. 'I am sorry, though. I know you want to get home.'

Jake rubbed his cheek, and Hester heard the rasp of stubble against his palm. 'Thanks. It wasn't the best start to the day.'

'At least I can help cheer you up!' She forced brightness into her tone, gave him her most winning, professional smile as she took her iPad out of her bag. 'I've had a look at the latest Thailand exclusives, and I've got a couple of wonderful options, depending on what type of holiday you're after: whether you want a pure beach vacation, or prefer something a bit more adventurous. Our partners, Thalios, have got these—'

'Where would you go?' Jake asked, cutting her off. 'If you could pick anywhere for a holiday of a lifetime, somewhere to go to celebrate not being dead – which is what I assume Beth thinks this is for – where would you choose?'

Hester looked up. Jake was leaning forwards slightly, one knee bent on the sofa cushion. He looked warmer, softer, than she'd seen him up until now, and she felt a glimmer of silent vindication that just *talking* about holidays could do this to him. She considered his question, her list almost endless since she spent her days absorbed in details of the world's most exclusive places, but had never actually been to any of them.

'Me?' she asked, stalling for time.

'You.'

She sat back, briefly shutting her eyes, conjuring up her most relived, travel-related fantasies. 'And I can only pick one place?' She opened her eyes. Jake was watching her, and she noticed that he had a smattering of freckles across his nose. *Unfair,* she thought.

'Just one,' he said, his voice low and quiet. 'I want to know where you'd go, if you were in my position.'

She nodded, swallowed, examined her knee for several moments before looking back up. 'I would go to Canada. British Columbia,' she admitted, exhaling. 'Somewhere secluded and surrounded by nature, far away from the bright lights of the city. In the Skeena Valley, maybe: there are some beautiful lodges hidden away in that area. I would arrive just after dusk had fallen, after a journey that was comfortable but felt very long—'

'I suppose you can't ever describe the flight as tortuous, even though everyone knows it will be, in case it puts your clients off,' he said.

Hester laughed, the sound coming out slightly strangled. 'True. But still,' she went on, holding his gaze, 'despite the extreme comfort of the journey, it would be long, and the jet lag never helps. So I'd be weary, but I'd arrive, in a sleek black car, at my log cabin. The exterior would be floodlit, welcoming against the inky sky and surrounding forest, the smell of cedar embracing me when I pushed open the door. The furniture would be deceptively simple, the comfort that comes with understated luxury. It would be all the little details that let me know, without question, that this was special.' She picked up the scatter cushion that was lying, like a barrier, on the sofa between them.

'There would be blankets, softer than this.' She ran her palm over the sumptuous fabric, then presented it to Jake like a trophy, and he did the same. She noticed his fingers were long, his nails short, as he caressed it, and she cleared her throat. 'The fire would have been lit, warming the cabin before I arrived, its gentle crackle mirrored by the flickering candles on the mantel above. It would smell of wood, clean air and fresh pine, and lamplight would soften all the dark corners, making cosy nooks out of them.

'In the kitchen, a platter of local meats and charcuterie; fresh, crusty bread with pillowy insides; salted butter and cheeses, would be waiting, along with a bottle of champagne chilling in an ice bucket. Underfloor heating would warm the tiles, relaxing the soles of my feet in my warm, Canada-appropriate socks, and a long, low bench in front of a window would promise a view, in the morning, of mountains and endless sky, more shades of green than I'd ever seen, but when I arrive would show silky blue and the endless stars of an unpolluted night.'

'Would you go and stand on the doorstep?' Jake said softly. 'Once you had settled in?'

Hester nodded. 'It would have a wraparound veranda; a swinging chair that creaked ever so slightly, that I'd go and sit on once I'd popped the champagne and poured myself a glass, tasted the soft, creamy cheese on a torn piece of bread.' She licked her lips as she imagined it. She could see Jake was captivated by the picture she was weaving around them both: perhaps almost as captivated as she was.

'There's a tour I've always wanted to go on,' she continued, 'ever since I heard about it. You start in a helicopter, flying over valleys and fjords, the rugged, breathtaking landscape, then transfer to a boat, to watch grizzly bears in the wild of the Khutzeymateen Provincial Park. There are bald eagles, too, and killer whales sometimes—'

Jake shook his head, but his eyes were bright with interest.

'What?' she asked. 'You don't like wildlife?'

'I do, but you've skipped ahead.'

'What do you mean?' She moved further back on the sofa. She was so close to slipping off her shoes, feeling the thick carpet between her toes, drawing her legs up under her and giving herself fully up to this space, to Jake and to her imagined dream holiday.

He smiled at her: the first proper smile she'd seen from him. Even on low wattage, it shone brightly. 'I mean that you didn't tell me about the upstairs of the cabin. The bedroom, the bathroom.'

'Oh!' Hester's cheeks heated, and she glanced at her iPad, buying herself a bit of time. When she looked up again, she noticed that the neck of Jake's T-shirt was slightly stretched, and she could see the shadowy ridge of his collarbone. It looked strong: lickable. She swallowed. The weather had broken, but she felt like all the pressure was building up inside her, instead. 'The upstairs of the cabin is palatial. The bed, facing a floor-to-ceiling window, is emperor-sized—'

'Is that bigger than a super king?' Jake asked.

'It's the biggest size,' she explained. 'It's piled high with cushions—'

'Why is everyone so obsessed with pointless cushions?'

'—and has a sofa at the end of it,' she went on, ignoring him. 'And when I sink into the mattress, it feels like sleeping on silk clouds.' She knew her voice had taken on a dream-like quality. 'The roof above the bedroom is slightly angled, with a huge skylight that shows off the starry sky, and that wakes me with the sun, so I can get up and stand at the window, with a cup of coffee brewed fresh in the bedroom espresso machine, and gaze out at the panorama of mountains and glassy lakes, vultures flying overhead, so overwhelming that, in that moment, I can't ever imagine being back in my flat.' She met his gaze, saw that his lips were slightly parted, his blue eyes locked onto her. 'Even where you live,' she went on, 'your house – home – would be a distant memory.'

'My apartment,' he murmured.

'Exactly,' she whispered. 'Even a New York apartment couldn't live up to it. The bathroom would have a jacuzzi tub, a window that slides fully open next to it, so you can have fresh air surrounding you while you soak. The lights would be subtle, relaxing, fading from one colour to the next – no disco bathtubs in this cabin, where it's all about bringing the outside, inside.'

'No *disco bathtubs*?' Jake let his smile break through, showing white teeth, one canine cutely crooked. Fuck him, honestly; all his flaws made him more perfect. 'What if I wanted a disco tub on my Canadian Rockies holiday?'

Hester sat up straighter. 'You might well do, but you asked me what *I* wanted. And I want piles of cushions and a relaxing jacuzzi bath surrounded by cool, mountain air. I want to hike for miles, until my legs ache and my heel is threatening a blister, and see animals I've never seen outside of a David Attenborough documentary. Then I want to come back to my indulgent, decadent hideaway and soak my aches away in steamy bubbles with another glass of crisp, chilled champagne.'

She waited for Jake's cynical reply, but he was rubbing his lower lip with a finger, his expression slightly dazed, as if that last description had put him under her spell. She'd done it to herself, as well. God, she wanted that holiday so badly.

'I would like that, too,' he said eventually. 'Much more than Thailand.'

She exhaled. 'Great. So. That's what we're going for?' She set her shoulders back, trying for professional again as she tapped her iPad, angling it slightly so she could open it with Face Recognition. 'We can absolutely book you this holiday instead. I've got all the details of the lodge, the tour. There's the Skeena train, which travels through the mountains to Prince Rupert—' She faltered when he touched her arm, the press of his fingers warm through the thin cotton of her shirt.

'Why would you go on your own?' he asked.

'Sorry?' She frowned.

'Your dream holiday – which you have completely sold to me, by the way – you described it all as if you were there on your own. You said *I,* and there was no clinking of champagne glasses with anyone else. Is that because you go away for work so often?'

Hester froze. She hadn't realized she'd been speaking like that. Usually she conjured up the ideal holiday for her clients, put *them* in the spotlight, but Jake had specifically asked about her. And in her fantasy, she *was* on her own. Was that because she felt so alone with her phobia: the only person in her immediate circle who couldn't travel abroad so that, when she finally did manage it, she would be solo there, too? But Jake had given her another, easy out.

'Yes,' she said. 'Work trips aren't quite the same: you're there to check things out, not share indulgences with your nearest and dearest.'

Jake laughed. It was deep and low and, after a couple of seconds, turned into a cough. He sat back against the sofa, not doubling over this time, his face creasing with a mixture of laughter and pain.

'Are you OK?' Hester asked.

Jake nodded, pressing a fist to his mouth as he coughed and breathed and winced and then, after a while, settled to stillness. His cheeks had blushed red, and his eyes were bright, but his amusement hadn't gone.

'Are you sure you're all right?' Hester asked. And then, 'What was so funny?'

'You said work trips weren't the same as dream holidays, but if that Rockies experience you just created for me was one you went on for Paradise Awaits, then I'd like to change careers.' He shook his head. 'No wonder Beth said you were the best they have; I forgot where I was for a few minutes.'

Now it was Hester's turn to smile. 'I'm glad. You know, I can make all that a reality for you. I just need to look up the details: I had all the Thailand holidays prepared.'

'Hang on a moment, Hester Monday.' He rubbed his flattened palm over his chest, and she wondered if he was conscious of doing it, or if it was a tick he'd picked up since the accident.

'Why do you have to say both my names like that?'

He looked surprised. 'I don't know. I guess I like the way they sound together.'

'Well, *Jake Oakenfield*,' she said, emboldened by her successful sales pitch, 'what are we hanging on for? I can't stay here all afternoon.' She would *love* to stay all afternoon, weaving escape fantasies in this sumptuous suite that made it easy, with a man she could picture by her side on any one of them.

'Of course not,' he said, sobering. 'Friday-night plans?'

He'd asked it casually. A bit *too* casually, Hester thought, then chided herself for the idea. 'Just meeting some friends in the pub.' It wasn't entirely true, but she didn't want Jake to think she was going home alone to her flat on a Friday night. She wasn't sure why not.

'Oh, right. Sure.'

'What about you?'

Jake gestured around the room. 'I have my pick of films to watch. I might take my sorry ass downstairs to the restaurant, do a few laps of the stairwells. I'm supposed to rest, but also keep up with breathing exercises, stay fairly mobile so my lungs stay clear and I don't stiffen up. But the pain means I don't exactly feel like wandering miles from the hotel. The whole thing is like purgatory, to be honest.'

'Your doctor probably knows what they're doing,' she said quietly. 'They just want you to get better.'

'Yeah, well.' Jake ran a hand over his face, and Hester felt the mood sink between them like a deflating balloon at the end of a child's birthday party.

She touched his hand quickly, felt the prickle of contact, of skin on skin, even though it was only for a second. 'Let's sort out this trip to Canada.' She turned back to her iPad, her fingers feeling hot and fat as she pulled up the right screen.

'No,' Jake said, and this time his hand was back on her arm, squeezing gently.

'No?' She folded her iPad cover over so it would stand on the glass table. She wouldn't look at him or where his hand rested. She barely understood what he was saying.

'I've been thinking, and I don't want a trip to Canada, or Thailand. Not a real one, anyway. Not right now.'

Now it did sink in. 'Excuse me?' She looked up, a kernel of annoyance solidifying inside her. 'You dismissed me yesterday, and then you called me back, and I've come all the way over here again, had tea with your sister so she could warn me about you – which honestly felt pretty weird, by the way – and now you're telling me, again, that you've wasted my time?' The anger built with her words. Beth had warned her not to take any shit from him, and she had to stand up for herself.

'I don't want you to book me a holiday,' he said, calm in the face of her fury, 'but I hope I haven't wasted your time. Will you at least stay and hear me out?'

'Why?' she asked, her shoulders dropping slightly.

'I have a different proposition for you, Hester Monday. Just let me tell you what it is.'

Chapter
Nine

Friday

'I have just been to the Canadian Rockies, to a five-star log cabin with world-class views,' Jake said.

Hester blinked. 'I know. And I can take you there, but we need to—'

'The way you described it,' he went on, 'it was as if I was really there, even though it was only you, and your words, and this cushion as a prop.' He held it in front of her, mirroring her gesture of a few minutes ago.

'That's what we do,' she said, shrugging. 'We sell holidays. It helps if you make them sound good.' She laughed, but it sounded weak in this huge suite, and in the face of Jake's conviction about something she didn't understand.

He nodded. 'But couldn't you just recreate them, instead? For me? For the next couple of weeks?' His cheeks tinged pink, and her anger was dampened by his vulnerability.

'I'm sorry,' she said. 'I don't really understand what you're suggesting.'

'That you could come back here and repeat what you just did, but on a bigger scale. Take me to different places, locations that you've been to and love, from this room. You must have so many stories, and Marty could help with the setup; giving the suite the feel of wherever we were going, bring us some authentic food, maybe. It's what you do with clients, when you're making those destinations irresistible to them, just levelled up.' He waggled the cushion.

Hester stood up and folded her arms, then walked around the square made by the two huge sofas facing each other over the glass coffee table. 'This is ridiculous.' She laughed.

'Why?' He sounded completely calm, reasonable. Determined.

'You want me to come back, while you're staying here, and take you on holiday without either of us leaving the suite?'

'Exactly. You've summarized it perfectly. Why is that ridiculous?'

She shook her head. 'You want me to pick the destinations?' she asked. 'Do everything I can to whisk you away to far-flung places: the sights, sounds and smells, the food and drink, while we both stay right here?'

'You would have all the hotel's resources at your disposal,' Jake said. 'Marty would help.'

Hester stopped in the middle of the room. She felt confused, torn in half by her desire to really listen to what he was asking, and also run away.

'I don't know why you're finding this so hard to grasp,' Jake went on. 'Armchair travel is all the rage these days, isn't it? Lower carbon emissions from less flying; every country bleeding into one another; cultures and traditions mixing. I'm all for it, and I just thought—' he stopped, sighed, and Hester saw his fragility in that one, small action. 'I thought it would be a good way to keep occupied. Something that would help me take my mind off all this.' He gestured at the room, but also at himself. His poor ribs. His instant sympathy card.

'It's not what I do,' Hester protested weakly, but then she thought of the fairy lights in her living room, and all that they symbolized. 'I book real holidays. I contact hotels and tour operators, and I build magical experiences for people. But with the expectation that they actually *go* to those places, not just hear about them.'

'I have faith that you can do this, and I will pay for your time and expertise.'

'Why?'

'Because you're providing me with a service, and I appreciate that it's a bit out of the ordinary.'

'No, I mean why do you have faith that I can do this?' She perched on the edge of the sofa, as far away from him as she could get. The sun had sunk lower and was burning in through the window, hot on her face as if she was under a spotlight.

'Because it's your job,' Jake said smoothly. 'And because of the last half an hour. I forgot about feeling trapped, about how much my ribs ache, how bloody itchy my stitches are. I was there, in that cabin – even though you'd supposedly gone on your own – wondering if we'd hear coyotes while we were looking at the stars.'

'You've got stitches?' She looked at him properly for the

first time in a few minutes, her curiosity outweighing her growing panic.

'The edge of the bumper,' he explained, and lifted one side of his T-shirt to reveal taut, toned skin and then, where his stomach met the bottom of his ribcage, there was an angry red line with minute, expert stitches crossing it. Around it, and spreading up under the T-shirt, the bruising was almost black.

'Holy crap,' Hester whispered, leaning forward. 'That looks so painful.'

Jake nodded. 'I wasn't trying to get you to feel sorry for me,' he said quietly, some of his certainty gone. 'But I will, if it'll help you say yes.'

'What about your other visitors? All the people who've sent you flowers? Can't they keep you entertained?'

Jake sighed. 'Beth and Tamsin, and Beth's husband Duncan, have been here, but Beth is constantly on my case about something. Tamsin swings between being sullen or showing me her latest TikToks' – he rolled his eyes – 'and Duncan is good fun, but they're so busy at home. They've got three other kids besides Tamsin at the moment, and Alfie's only two, so . . .' He shook his head. 'I think Rosalie would spend every evening with me if she could, but she just wants to make it up to me, and I keep telling her she already has a hundred times over, even though she didn't need to, and that conversation is so circular I'm bored of it.'

'You don't have any friends left in London?' Hester felt sorry for him then, and it must have shown because he gave her a look that said, *Don't you dare.*

'My best mate growing up, Dan, lives in Sheffield now.

There's Richard, who I know from the London office, and he'd be round in a shot if I told him where I was, but there's no way.' He shook his head, a smile playing on his lips.

'Why no way?' Hester asked.

Jake reached forward and picked up his glass of water. Hester could almost hear him suppressing the groan. 'Because every time I see Rich I get so drunk I can't remember anything, and if I invited him here he'd have emptied the mini bar in three seconds flat, and I'd end up with a hefty room bill and a lost night that would make me feel even worse than I do now.'

'Ah,' Hester said. 'One of those friends.'

'You have those friends?'

'Doesn't everyone? Though, to be fair, they don't force us to drink, do they?'

'No, but it's somehow inevitable. They lower our defences, make it seem irresistible.' He paused. 'I'm trying to imagine what you're like when you're drunk.'

Hester shrugged. 'Generally quite happy and silly, until I reach the dreaded tipping point into doom and gloom and lost loves and lost opportunities.' She laughed, thinking he'd join in. Wasn't that everyone's drunk pattern?

Instead, Jake looked at her as if he wanted to peel her open. 'Please do this, Hester. Keep me company in the evenings. Take me on a tour of your favourite places: all the places you've fallen in love with around the world, and could talk about for hours.'

And there it was. The reason that panic was filling her stomach instead of the Duval's superior tea. *All the places you've fallen in love with around the world.* Would he mind if they were limited to the Jurassic Coast, a quaint village in the Cotswolds, Italy and Edinburgh? Ugh, Edinburgh. No, she would never include that city, as beautiful as it was.

He was expecting exotic, exclusive. Like the Maldives, or Cassie's new resort in St Lucia. India perhaps, a boat-hopping tour of the Greek Islands. How would she feel if she told him that his home city was more exciting than anywhere she'd been: that it was on her bucket list of places to visit, but instead she'd resigned herself to watching Gene Kelly, Frank Sinatra and Ann Miller dancing through a stage-set version until she knew all the words off by heart?

'Can I use your bathroom?' She stood up.

'Sure,' Jake said, and she knew he was watching her as she went straight through his bedroom, into the marble bathroom as big as her flat, and locked the door.

She closed the toilet lid and sat on it, rested her knees on her elbows and her head in her hands. The bathroom smelled of lilies – there was a large vase on the shelf next to the sink that she thought must have been provided by the hotel, unless Jake had received flowers from someone he really hated and banished them here – and the Ocean Haze aftershave she'd sniffed the day before.

It felt like an impossible choice.

One, refuse to do it and walk away. It wasn't her job, she didn't know how to go about planning an armchair holiday, other than sourcing some authentic food, getting a slide-show of images up on the TV in the sitting area, researching local music, a few facts and maybe scattering some sand on the hotel's thick carpet. Would that really satisfy Jake?

But she supposed, if he was in pain, bored, frustrated at being unable to go home and all his friends were in New York, then it might be enough. He'd said the hotel would be able to help, and Hester was sure nothing would be too much trouble here – except perhaps the sand. If she said no her life would be easier. She could return to her job and the ball of panic working its way from her gut to her lungs would subside. Everything would go back to normal.

And she wouldn't see him again.

Or, she could accept. It would be utterly foolhardy. She would have to invent holiday experiences she'd never had. Research every place down to the last, tiny detail. Every evening, every occasion, there would be multiple opportunities for her to slip up, leaving Jake nonplussed and dissatisfied with the service he was paying her for.

But she was good at research: she knew some places better, she was sure, than some people who had been on holiday there. The offices and online files of Paradise Awaits were not short of destination details. She would have one of London's most exclusive hotels entirely at her disposal – when would she get an opportunity like this again? And Beth was Cassie's friend. If she could do this, unusual as it was, it would make Cassie happy and distract her from Hester's tendency to turn down trips abroad.

If she did a good job then it might even become a branch of the business: holidays in your own home. All the sights, sounds and sensations of a perfect holiday without the drama, travel hours or expense. OK, it could never live up to the real thing, but for people who couldn't travel, like Jake, or others with an injury or disability, a fear or *phobia* that limited their dreams, wasn't it an option? Couldn't it be a lifeline for some desperate, wannabe-travellers? The lump in her throat thickened. *Could this work?*

'You OK in there, Hester?' Jake called. She stood and

flushed the toilet, hurried to the sink and turned the tap on so quickly that her cream shirt and the poor lilies got a drenching.

'I'm fine,' she called, turning the tap off again, watching as her shirt turned translucent. 'Give me two secs.'

She gazed into the mirror that ran the length of the wall, expecting to see herself looking like a rabbit in the headlights, but somehow not that surprised when her reflection stared back at her, her face set with determination, eyes bright with excitement.

Of course, if she took Jake up on his offer it would mean spending more time with him. Whole evenings together, just the two of them, pretending they were on holiday. His every wish would be her command. The thrill of anticipation worked its way through her, from the top of her head to her toes.

She walked to the door and unlocked it, took a deep breath and stood up straight. She lifted her chin and pulled open the door, then strode through the bedroom.

Jake was sitting on the arm of the sofa, facing the door. His blue eyes were filled with concern and, if Hester wasn't mistaken, hope.

'What do you think?' he asked. She waited a second, expecting him to end his sentence with her full name, enunciating the words in his soft, low voice. But he didn't. She noticed that he was gripping the sofa with both hands, his faux relaxed posture unable to entirely hide how much he was waiting for her answer.

It gave Hester power, and clarity. It made her, in that split second, confident. She leaned on the doorframe, met his gaze, and smiled.

Chapter Ten

Friday

'We need more wine!' Amber banged the table hard enough to make it seem like the solid wood was shaking, except Hester thought it was probably because it was windy on the terrace and the empty crisp packets littering the surface weren't held down by anything.

'It's not table service,' Glen said, laughing lazily. 'You have to go to the bar.'

'I wasn't *demanding*.' Amber glared at him. 'I was stating it as a fact. Of life. Our life, right now.' She gestured at the three of them, her arm sweeping round and almost hitting Hester in the face.

God, they were drunk. It was Friday night, so it wasn't *that* unusual, although it was quite rare that the three of them could make it on a Friday as well as their regular Thursday. But Elise was out with her fellow trainee midwives for a birthday meal, and Amber had cancelled whatever else she had been planning on doing, and had refused to tell them what it was in case Hester felt bad.

Hester already felt bad. She'd messaged them both in a state of panic, once she'd left the Duval and after she'd called Cassie to explain what she'd done, part of her praying that her boss would call her out for being an idiot to accept such an off-the-wall request from a client they barely knew. It was as if the hotel was some kind of otherworld, hypno-tizing her with its glitter-ball chandelier and its suites of unending luxury, so that her thoughts twisted and anything seemed possible.

And it had felt possible when she was standing there, watching Jake, seeing his face light up in a smile so wide and glorious it was like a reward. One that, she already knew after two meetings, she wanted to keep earning.

Strangely, it had been Cassie's enthusiasm for the plan that had brought her bumping back down to earth as she made her way across Hungerford Bridge, a day cruiser gliding underneath, packed to the rails with tourists. Hester had waved down automatically at the children waving up, had taken a photo for a family who wanted a picture with the Houses of Parliament in the background, and then wondered if she'd actually pressed the button.

Cassie had been overjoyed, telling her to take all the time she needed, saying she would assign her current bookings to Danielle – which Danielle would *hate* – and leaving her free to get these staycations planned.

'You'll get extra commission,' Cassie had said. 'A higher rate than usual, because it's taking up your evenings as well as the working day. And it's what? Two weeks at the most? Easiest money you've ever made.'

'Has he been in touch already, then?' Hester had asked, staring longingly at the fountain outside the Festival Hall, desperate to call her friends. She thought that Jake must have agreed to pay a substantial amount for his ridiculous hotel vacations.

'He has.' Her boss had sounded smug. 'It seems Mr Oakenfield is very keen for these armchair holidays to go ahead. And in his position, who can blame him? The poor guy.' The smugness was replaced by indulgence, and Hester imagined Jake calling Cassie to make their arrangement formal, charming her with that deep, steady voice, a powerful tool even without the eyes and lips and hair to back it up. *Poor wounded soldier*, she imagined Cassie saying, and felt a shard of white-hot envy.

'So it's all settled then,' Hester had said, leaning against the wall next to the bust of Nelson Mandela. 'I'm really doing this.'

'Yes,' Cassie had replied. 'You really are. Well done, Hester. Trust you to think outside the box for this one.'

Glen and Amber had seen through the casual words of her WhatsApp to the panic within, and now they were sitting at a table outside the Founder's Arms, further up the river from their usual haunt, two bottles of wine and one round of dubious-looking yellow shots down. She should be at home, right now, getting everything ready for tomorrow night. Except she hadn't known where to take him, was completely at a loss as to where to plan her first night in with Jake, and had hoped her friends would be able to help her.

Staycation, she corrected herself. *Night in* sounded like a date. It was work, she reminded herself. Work, work, work.

'Yes, I find it as surprising as you do,' Glen said, putting a fresh bottle of white wine on the table. 'What?' he added, when she stared at him. 'You said that out loud. *Work work work.* Your job, which you wrote an application for and interviewed for, on purpose, is centred around foreign travel. Cruises sometimes, sure, but even those often involve flights to the right port. Why didn't you get a job with a UK booking agent if escapism is so important to you? Country house hotels, spa retreats on the Cornish coast and caravan parks.'

'You escape *from* caravan parks, not to them,' Amber said, sloppily topping up their glasses, not caring that Hester had some rosé left in the bottom of hers. 'And Hester's been there a year and it's all going swimmingly. Sort of. Cassie will get bored of asking you to go on scouting trips eventually. Or she won't, and she'll fire you.'

'Let's not dissect *all* my life choices here,' Hester said, because when asked why she'd stuck with this particular career path after that first admin job, she was hard-pressed to come up with a solid answer. Because she wanted to face her fears? The only problem was, she wasn't even starting to turn towards them. 'Let's focus on tomorrow. On the fact that I have to entertain Jake Oakenfield with a staycation of elaborate and exotic proportions, and it can't be one of the places I've been to, because I don't think he wants me to recreate my trip to the Christmas market in Stow-on-the-Wold.'

'But you know your stuff,' Amber said. 'You can do this in your sleep.'

'He wants the places that *I* love.' She pressed a hand to her collarbone. 'I can give him the spiel about the best

82

destinations to go to right now, but then he'll ask which bit I liked most or what happened when I went there and who did I go with, and I won't have any answers.'

'So just tell him,' Glen said.

Hester shook her head.

'Why not?' Amber asked.

Because she had the sense that he wouldn't be interested anymore. She remembered the light going out of his eyes when she'd told him why she was there yesterday afternoon. He didn't want the script. He wanted something personal: something entertaining, to keep his mind off the pain in his chest and the fact that he was stuck in London. And if he wasn't interested anymore, she would lose her commission along with Cassie's respect, as well as any chance she might have to gain some from Seb and Danielle.

'Because I can't,' she said, shrugging. 'It's not what we agreed.'

'So fake it,' Amber said. 'All women have experience of that.'

'Why not take him to Amalfi?' Glen cut in, not prepared to be excluded as the only man at the table. 'You went there and you loved it, even if you were only eleven.'

Hester nodded, but she'd already thought of that. 'It's like my one trump card,' she said. 'The one place I can legitimately take him to, and if I go there first, then I'll be even more stressed because I will have used it up and be stuck for all the other nights. And I can't *just* take him to Italy. Pretend I'm doing different regions each time and hope he doesn't notice. I need somewhere else to take him first.'

'That is a weird sort of logic,' Amber said, resting her cheek in her hand, her elbow sliding sideways on the table. 'But I get it, I guess.'

They needed to end this sorry night soon if Hester was to have any chance of being compos mentis for her stay-cation tomorrow night. A staycation that currently had no more of a destination than the Merryweather suite at the Duval hotel. It had started out almost victorious, as Hester had explained, albeit with a slight undercurrent of panic, that she had bagged a new client and Cassie was paying her extra commission for a project that would take two weeks. And then, as she let the panic out and her friends realized the seriousness of the predicament, their evening – and their drinking – had become slightly hysterical.

'And you can't exactly take him to Stansted airport,' Glen said. Amber glared at him and made frantic 'stop' move-ments with her hands as if, because she wasn't looking at Hester, Hester wouldn't be able to see her doing it.

'No.' Hester shook her head. 'No, definitely not. Tell him we're going to Spain, it'll be the best holiday he's ever had and to think how great he'll feel once he finally gets there, years of worry behind him. Bring him a limp bacon sand-wich and a glass of warm Prosecco, give him a giant Toblerone and a bottle of cheap perfume from duty free, then have a panic attack right in front of him.'

'Doesn't sound that great,' Amber said quietly.

'It wasn't great,' Glen added, and Hester could see he felt guilty for mentioning it.

'So we need another plan,' Hester said brightly, taking a sip of wine that, quality or not, burned like acid all the way down her throat.

'Australia,' Glen said into the subsequent quiet. A group of guys at the table behind them whooped loudly, as if it was the right answer.

'I've never been to Australia,' Hester said.

'I know, but our holiday was only last year, just before El started her university course. You've seen all the photos more than once, heard all the stories. I'll send you the pictures, email you my best anecdotes tomorrow. Not tonight.' He laughed and rubbed his forehead, his hair sticking up in a Tintin quiff. 'But that, along with your brochures from work, the help of his grand hotel, that should be enough.'

Hester chewed her lip. She did know a lot about Glen's trip up the east coast, and she'd booked enough luxury holidays there for other people. Could she pass off his memories as her own?

'That might work,' she murmured.

'You'd have to get on it,' Amber said. 'Be fully prepared. Stop drinking now and get a kebab on the way home to soak up all the wine. Get up early, coffee and egg on toast, get cracking. If Cassie's got your back on this one you can't let her down. Not if this client means a lot to her.'

'No,' Hester said. 'You're right. Glen, are you sure you've got time to do that?' He played football on Saturday mornings, then – because he'd been able to meet them tonight – he would be going straight to the bar and working through from lunch until close. 'It seems like a lot.'

Glen put his arm around her shoulders, bringing her towards him in a half hug, half headlock. 'For you, Hester, anything.'

'Then we can do Japan for one of the others,' Amber said. 'Especially if you've got a couple of days to swot up. I can load you up with facts and memories, photos of cherry blossom. You'll be a pro.'

'God, guys.' Hester reached her hand across the table to Amber, and squeezed Glen's arm. 'You're the best. What can I do to repay you?' Warmth spread through her, somehow neutralizing the acidity of the wine. She knew it didn't really work like that: if friendship was an antidote for alcohol poisoning she wouldn't have suffered a hangover in her life.

Glen shrugged. 'As long as you keep being petrified of flying and let us book our holidays with your discount, you never need owe us another thing.'

Hester grinned, and sighed, and asked Amber how she was getting on with her new flatmate, a woman who had recently converted to veganism, which was bringing Amber's decidedly carnivorous and fairly haphazard cooking style under scrutiny.

By the time Hester said a hazy, overblown goodbye and made her way to the station, she was all laughed out and feeling very grateful for her friends, and things were suddenly looking more hopeful. Of course, that could have been entirely down to the wine, but she didn't think so. It was Amber and Glen, and the readiness with which they'd come to her rescue.

Vanessa didn't come to greet her when she got home: it was too late for her tonight. The lamp flickered in the stairwell as she fumbled with her key, having to try three times before she got it in the lock. It was as she was heading to the kitchen for a pint of water, her jacket half off, that her phone buzzed in her bag.

She thought it was Glen, sending through some photos to get a head start on the morning, but the name in bold at the top of the WhatsApp notification made her freeze.

For a second, her drunk brain struggled to make sense of what she was seeing, and then she remembered exchanging numbers with Jake, him saying it would be easier if they needed to get in touch, that she might not want to look at her work emails on the weekend. At the time she'd been high on the power of the job she'd bagged, and the thought of spending all that time with him.

Hope your night was good. Looking forward to tomorrow. Jake

Hester couldn't help smiling as she plopped herself down in her tatty blue canvas armchair. There wasn't really enough space for it opposite the more sociable sofa in her living room, but it was the comfiest piece of furniture she owned. She tapped out a reply.

I had fun! Avoided the tipping point, just. Hope you've enjoyed your stair laps. First destination's a ripper. Hester

The clue was probably obvious. Subtlety didn't survive a few drinks.

Wish I could see you drunk was his almost instant reply. Laps exhausting, but good for me. Can't wait for tomorrow arvo, Hester Monday. J.

Hester grinned. He was no fool, and she was drunk. Then her smile slipped and her stomach churned as she realized it was really happening: that she was going to have to bring Australia to him tomorrow afternoon. She took her piece of malachite out of her bag and looked at the familiar green swirls, like a deep lagoon in a faraway place.

'What have I got myself into?' she said into the quiet. But there was nobody there to give her a reassuring reply.

Chapter
Eleven

Saturday

The first thing that was strikingly obvious about the piano room at the Duval was that it had no piano in it. It was tucked away down a seemingly endless trail of soundless corridors, black-and-white photos of the hotel through the ages widely spaced on the white walls. As Hester walked past they played a silent slideshow out of the corner of her eye.

The piano room had wine-red Chesterfield sofas and indigo walls and carpet, only getting away with the sombre colour scheme because of the tall windows that let in the early morning light. It smelt faintly of woodsmoke, and Hester could picture it in the evenings, lamp- and firelight making shadows of the corners and turning faces to flickering masks. She could easily imagine Jake in here: there was something strong and mellow about both of them. But she couldn't be distracted by thoughts of Jake right now. She had less than a day to get ready.

'Lights sorted, menu no problem, beach sounds good. There's a pulldown screen in the suite if you can get hold of the aerial tour of the Whitsundays, and that other thing you're planning, which would work better than the TV.'

'Excellent,' Hester said, looking up from her iPad, her Australia folders spread across the wooden table, her first coffee long since drained.

Marty replaced her empty cup with a full one.

'Thank you.' She smiled gratefully, marvelling again at how lucky she was to have Jake's favourite hotel employee at her disposal. 'For everything.'

Marty shrugged and grinned. 'It's my job.'

He was tall and wirily thin, dressed in a dark suit, white shirt and thick black tie. His salt-and-pepper hair was shaggy, the only part of him that was less than immaculate, and it gave him a rakish, mysterious air. Or maybe she had superimposed the mysterious part on him because Jake had told her that he would help with whatever she needed, and since asking for him at reception early that morning, he had done exactly that without batting a single eyelid.

'It's not really your job though, is it?' Hester said. 'All this extra stuff, to help me?'

'My job is looking after our guests, and Jake is a guest.'

'He says you've taken care of him really well.'

'I take my role seriously,' he said with a smile.

Hester chewed the end of her pen, feeling the plastic give beneath her teeth. 'Did you know him before this?'

'No.' Marty ran a hand through his hair. 'I know Rosalie, though.'

'Ah. So she's asked you to pay him a bit more attention?'

'She mentioned she was booking the suite and why,'

Marty admitted. 'We always take extra care if our guests have any health concerns, make sure there's a doctor on standby, that sort of thing. And Jake's obviously struggling with his situation.'

Hester nodded. 'He's frustrated about where he's ended up. No offence to the hotel – I would *not* be sad to have an enforced stay here.'

'Is that why you're helping him, then?' Marty gave her a wicked grin.

'It's *my* job,' she echoed back at him. 'Even if this is a more unusual project than most of them. I wonder why he hates London? I know New York is supposed to be incredible, but London's not horrible.' Hester, it seemed, could not resist gossiping about Jake Oakenfield. It didn't matter who it was: her boss, his sister, a hotel employee. She wouldn't be surprised to find herself telling the pan-pipe player on Hungerford Bridge about him after a couple more days.

Marty shrugged. 'He's not said as much to me. All I know is he's embarrassed about being here, that he's paying for everything other than the suite itself – the food, any extras – himself. He's changed his tune slightly, though. From one in a minor key to something a lot more cheerful.'

Hester laughed. 'What do you mean?'

'All this.' Marty gestured towards her, and everything laid out on her table. 'He's perked up a lot since you and he agreed on these hotel holidays, or whatever they are. He was whistling last night, laughing with Rosalie on the phone while I was in the room.'

Hester kept her smile small, her tone light. 'His luxury prison's expanding, which is what he wanted.'

91

Marty grinned. 'Luxury prison, eh? Wonder if the top boss wants to add that quote to the website.'

'Possibly not,' Hester said. 'But in a way it's good that Jake's grumpy about being here.' When Marty gave her a curious look, she explained: 'He doesn't seem too traumatized by his accident. Having flashbacks, panic attacks, that sort of thing.'

'Not everyone does, I suppose.'

'No.' It came out as a sigh, and Hester wondered, for what must have been at least the ten-thousandth time, if there was something genuinely wrong with her. She had only *seen* something horrible, and it had coloured her life in a way that was still holding her back, sixteen years later. Jake had been hit by a car a few days ago, and his dominant thought was that his injuries were inconvenient because they were keeping him here. 'Australia,' she said, when she realized Marty was watching her a bit too closely. 'Best get back to it.'

'Of course.' He grabbed the hem of his jacket and tugged once, sharply, to smooth it out. 'What more do you need?'

Hester looked at everything spread around her. 'I'm not sure yet.'

'I'll come back in half an hour. Those your snaps?' He pointed at the slideshow scrolling across her iPad screen.

She swallowed. Glen had sent through his photos and some stories just as he'd said he would, adding the caveat that he was so hungover he wasn't sure whether the anecdotes were detailed enough. But Hester was grateful. She had to convince Jake that the memories were her own, not somebody else's, and Glen had provided enough information for her to give it her best shot.

'It looks great,' Marty said.

'It was a great time,' Hester murmured.

The concierge strolled out, one hand in his pocket, leaving her alone with her thoughts and her plans, and her worries that she wouldn't be able to pull it all together into something believable.

She looked out of the window, a patch of blue sky and bulbous white clouds visible above the rooftops opposite, the sun flashing in and out of view. What would it be like, she wondered, to be hit by a car? Even though Jake had run towards it, did he, at any point in the few seconds after he'd decided he was going to save Rosalie, imagine he would actually be struck? Was he knocked unconscious, waking up disorientated in a strange hospital bed? The bruise on his face suggested he might have been. And then to be herded here, without being given a choice. It was no wonder he was frustrated.

Which made it even more important that she gave him the best possible experience. She forced herself to focus, sipping her coffee as she went through Glen's stories and photos over and over again, looking up the places he talked about, filling in any gaps he'd left about the locations and tours he'd been on.

It was like swotting for an exam when she hadn't studied the subject. *Or*, she told herself, trying to stay positive, it was a more in-depth version of what she always did. Making clients feel as if they could taste the salt on the air, smell the barbecue or the Greek coffee or the rose garden. Engage the senses, and she was halfway there.

Her phone buzzed, and she saw that it was Cherry from Bonza Experiences across town.

'Hi Cherry,' Hester said.

'Hester! Got that aerial you asked for. Where do I need to send it?'

'File-drop it over to the usual address, and I'll do the rest from here.'

'You sure you want the full thing, not the teaser?' Cherry had an Australian twang which made her sound constantly upbeat. 'If they get the whole tour they're less likely to book one as part of their trip.'

'Oh, don't worry about that,' Hester said. 'But actually, Cherry, could I ask you for a couple of other things? They wouldn't take too long, I don't think, and they would really help me out.'

By mid-afternoon Hester's mind was swarming with Australian facts, experiences and traditions, all of them running through her head in an antipodean accent. She was exhausted, wired, on the edge of her sanity. But she also felt, for the first time in a while, like she had put her heart and soul into her job. It was the equivalent of running a 10k around the park instead of taking a light stroll. She was tired, but she had also accomplished something.

The light had drifted across the piano room while she sat in the same position, her bum losing sensation. Marty had come in frequently, checking on her progress, taking her requests away and fulfilling them. He'd made it seem easy, though she didn't know how much work was going on behind the scenes. Wasn't that always the way in these places?

She hoped she would achieve a similar swanlike state tonight. Everything serene on the surface, her frantic paddling hidden from sight. Her eyes were sore, she had an ache between her shoulder blades and she had almost convinced herself her name was Elise, the amount of times she'd read through Glen's tales of his holiday with his girlfriend.

But, she thought, as she heard footsteps approaching, it would all be worth it if it made Jake happy: if it lifted his spirits and took his mind off the things he couldn't change. And if Jake was happy, then Beth would be happy, and Cassie would be happy, and Hester would get a temporary reprieve from being forced into a work trip she couldn't accept.

'Excuse me, is this room booked?' She looked up to see a thick-set man in a suit standing in the doorway.

'I don't think so,' Hester said. 'I was told I could use it today, but I'm done.' She gathered up her folders and iPad and put them in her bag, moving her dress to the top, so that it didn't get squashed. She had time to change and freshen up before Marty sent Jake on a few laps around the hotel, and he and Hester got the room ready.

Showtime, she thought, her insides alive with butterflies as she smiled at the businessman and slipped out of the room. She just hoped that, on this occasion, it was the varied eggfly butterfly, common in five states in Australia, that had chosen to take up root.

Chapter
Twelve

Saturday

There was a knock on the door and Hester pressed play on the Bang & Olufsen stereo, didgeridoo music filling the suite. It felt strange to be answering the door to him, instead of the other way around.

She pulled it open and said, 'Welcome to Australia.'

She had expected Jake to gaze around him, mesmerized by all the work she and Marty had put in while he'd been trudging up and down the stairs. The room, they had agreed, looked spectacular. But Jake's gaze was fixed firmly on her.

'Hey,' he said scratchily. 'That is . . .' He shook his head.

'Come in.' She smiled at him as she arced her arm, encompassing the entire suite, and stepped purposefully back, letting the sand crunch under her feet. The sound jolted Jake out of his daze, and he looked down for the first time.

'What the hell?'

'Your very own private beach,' Hester said proudly.

She had mentioned sand to Marty as a joke, and he'd told her they could have a small sandpit in the room for the evening. Hester hadn't believed him. Marty had said that compared to some of the things they sometimes had to clear up in rooms rented by billionaires, it would be a doddle. Hester had been stuck between wanting to know what those things were, and running screaming into the Thames.

Now Jake looked up at her, his lips lifting. The didgeridoo music was a low beat in the background, and he finally started to take notice of his surroundings. White lights twinkled enticingly around the room, several upright lamps emitting a soft glow, but on the largest, blank wall where, later, Hester would project Cherry's aerial tour of the Whitsunday Islands, was the image of the Sydney Opera House's impressive sails.

Hester had got hold of a recording of that summer's spectacular light show: The Lighting of the Sails, which saw the usually white, shell-like constructions transformed into huge canvases, this time showing high-definition images of famous Australian locations, from apricot sunsets at Uluru to the Great Barrier Reef, Darwin's lush green forests and the buzzing metropolis and elegant riverside of Brisbane. She could imagine what it would be like to stand beneath the opera house and see these giant images – she knew this was a pale imitation – but from the way Jake's gaze snagged onto the recording and held, she could tell that it was still captivating.

Marty had found a couple of potted eucalyptus trees at a florist, and they'd placed them either side of the bedroom door. They produced a fragrant, almost minty scent, which added to the exotic effect Hester was trying to create. They had laid out cutlery on the small oval dining table, along with a tall candle flickering in a jar, a trolley to the side with their first course waiting under cloches. The food was impressive, and while Hester had been trying for elegant with the trees and light show display, she hadn't been able to resist adding a few kitsch elements, too.

The temporary beach was one of them, and she had placed cuddly crocodiles, kangaroos and koalas strategically around the room, one of the smaller koalas balanced precariously in one of the eucalyptus trees. There was a life-sized cassowary in the far corner, that Marty had apparently borrowed from an Australian-themed restaurant near Piccadilly Circus.

'A paddling pool?' Jake asked, once he'd taken everything in. He sounded stern, but his eyes were bright with interest.

'It's your hilltop Australian swimming pool. Feel free to take a dip any time you like.' She didn't tell him that it was an inflatable dog bathing pool, from a dog groomer's nearby – fully disinfected for tonight's purposes.

'Love the wildlife.' He walked over to a large stuffed crocodile with an idiotic grin on its face, picked it up and held it against his chest. He was wearing jeans and a grey T-shirt, scuffed black trainers, and Hester thought he looked tired, a sheen of sweat on his forehead.

'That one's a salty,' she said. 'Be careful, they're the most dangerous. It could crush your pelvis with one strategically placed chomp.'

'I'd better not get too close, then.' He put the crocodile down and gave it a gentle stroke that made Hester bite her lip. She thought the scorn in his voice was a defence mechanism, to hide the fact that he was enchanted by what she and Marty had done. He turned to look at her, leaning against the writing desk. 'Great outfit.'

Hester went to tuck her hair behind her ear, then remembered it was up in a high ponytail. She was in a short, red dress and gold flip-flops, dangly gold earrings that occasionally grazed her jaw, trying to strike the right balance between Sydney glamour and the beach lifestyle Australia was so famous for. This was supposed to be a luxury staycation, but she had wanted some of Australia's unique character in there, as well. 'Thank you,' she said. 'I got some board shorts for you, too. They're, uhm, on your bed.'

'Sure.'

He disappeared into the bedroom and Hester took a deep breath. He was pleased, she was sure. Perhaps slightly wary, too, but who could blame him? She'd filled his hotel suite with sand and the world's smallest paddling pool. She busied herself switching off the didgeridoo music and prepping the next track, and didn't hear him return.

He cleared his throat and she spun round. He'd put on the navy shorts she'd got for him, and the black flip-flops – *thongs*, she corrected herself, if she wanted to be properly Australian – showing lean legs. He'd kept the grey T-shirt on.

'This is . . .' His gaze returned to the wall, the images on the opera house's sails shifting to a myriad of soft, rainbow colours, the display they'd gone for while New Year's Eve fireworks had exploded from the harbour bridge. Hester had no real fireworks, except for a couple of indoor sparklers she was going to bring out with dessert. 'This is exactly what I expected from you, Hester Monday.'

100

'There's more to show you, yet.'

'I can't wait.' He perched on the arm of the sofa and picked up a large shell from the coffee table.

Hester pressed play on the sound system, and Cherry's bright voice filled the suite.

'Welcome to Australia, Jake Oakenfield. Chill out as we take you on a tour of the East Coast of our beautiful country, enjoying perfect beaches and the Great Barrier Reef, shipwrecks and vibrant cities, rafting and paragliding, and some of the best food in the world. We aim to make your stay as beaut as possible, so sit back, relax and throw another shrimp on the barbie.'

Jake laughed.

'Speaking of food.' Hester crossed to the trolley. 'Are you ready for your aperitif?' She lifted the cloche, revealing a delicate dish of scallops in their shells, surrounded by a pale cream and whisky sauce, and decorated with edible flowers and thin slices of white radish.

'This doesn't look like an Australian barbecue,' he said, coming to stand next to her.

'The chef has recreated the à la carte menu from Bennelong,' she said. 'The restaurant in the opera house. If you'd rather something else—'

'No way,' he said, bending over to inhale the dish's aroma. 'This smells wonderful.'

'We have Wagyu beef for the main course, and Bennelong's famous chocolate crackle to finish.'

'Chocolate crackle?'

'I don't want to spoil the surprise,' she said, smiling. 'But the flavours are supposed to be unlike anything else. To drink we've got . . .'

'Beer?' Jake tried.

Hester shook her head. 'I couldn't ignore all those Australian vineyards. This one is a 2005 Arras rosé from Tasmania. Sparkling, of course, as we're on holiday.'

'Of course.'

Hester took the remote and pressed the button again, and this time the intro to a vintage Kylie Minogue song filtered into the room. She hoped she'd got the vibe right: the most decadent food on the table, the light show making the suite shift with different colours, like they were relaxing inside a stained-glass window, alongside the cuddly toys and paddling pool.

She gestured for Jake to sit, then said, 'Now, don't forget, you have to leave it at least an hour after our meal before you can go in the pool. You don't want to get cramp.'

Jake's eyes gleamed with amusement. 'You're in charge, Hester. I wouldn't dream of doing anything you haven't scheduled. Food from Bennelong? The light show? You've pulled out all the stops.' He watched as she poured two glasses of the sparkling wine into crystal flutes, and handed him one.

'I thought that's what you wanted?' She sat opposite him and raised her glass. 'Cheers.'

'Cheers.' They clinked. 'I just . . . I guess my imagination is lacking.'

Hester shrugged. 'That's what you're paying me for.'

He nodded and they ate the scallops, Hester closing her eyes in delight at the bite of their perfectly caramelized outsides, the gentle squish of the inner flesh, the way the smoky sauce and crunchy radishes brought the whole thing together. Marty had told her the chef had been more than happy to recreate the menu of the exclusive Sydney restaurant, and even though she had no clue how this compared to the real thing, it was one of the most delicious dishes she'd eaten.

'This has set my taste buds alight,' Jake said, holding up a sliver of radish on his fork. 'You'll have me booking a holiday to Sydney at this rate.'

'That was always a risk,' Hester said, laughing gently. 'Augmented reality is never as good as the real thing.'

'But it's what I need right now.'

Hester called Marty, requesting the main course, and it arrived minutes later. The Wagyu fillet was plump, the chips golden, and she marvelled out how something as simple as beef could be elevated to such a level. Jake was quiet, focusing on his food, and Hester watched him for a moment, his dark curls falling over his forehead.

'Why didn't you want a real holiday for when you're better?' she asked eventually. She wanted to know what made Jake tick, and hoped these evenings would allow her to find out.

'Because I do enough travelling for my job, so spending all those hours on a plane wasn't the right carrot for Beth to dangle in front of me. But she doesn't know that.'

'Why doesn't she know that?' Hester laughed. 'Why haven't you set her straight?'

He shrugged, his gaze on his plate. 'I'm a coffee buyer, which is a mix of visiting coffee plantations, managing relationships and the supply chain, keeping on top of logistics and quality issues. So I do travel a lot, but it's hardly ever relaxing. I see the airport, my hotel, the plantations. I spend a lot of time trying to balance costs, and I never get to the beaches or tourist sights: I don't have the time. Beth thinks I love my job because I get to see the world, but really I enjoy it because finding a new product, building relationships with the owners, seeing it go from green coffee to cafes and restaurants, is satisfying.'

'So it's demanding and challenging, but the payoff is worth it,' she said. '*And* it means your life revolves around coffee.'

Jake smiled. 'Yup.'

'It sounds like a dream job, apart from the maths. Why not tell Beth all that? You just explained it to me in two minutes.'

'Because Beth has this idealized idea of my life: living in New York, travelling around the world, discovering new coffee varieties in exotic locations. She thinks I'm happy, and I wouldn't want to dissuade her of that.'

'Which makes it sound like you're not happy,' Hester said softly.

His mouth twisted in a wry smile. 'It's never that simple, though, is it? I am, for the most part. In my New York apartment, in my work. She's busy enough with her own life, as you can imagine. She doesn't need to take on my problems too, which she would if I let her. But we're both adults. We're siblings, but we lead very different lives.'

'Which is why you resent her help? Her encouragement of Rosalie booking you into this hotel?'

He exhaled. 'I don't resent it: I'm not ungrateful. I suppose I'm not used to living to someone else's plan, and none of this is the way I'd play it.'

Hester topped up their glasses, watching the bubbles ignite and skitter up to the surface. 'So if you'd still had the accident, but it had been a different old lady that you'd saved – one without Rosalie's means or generosity – and the paramedics hadn't discovered your emergency contact in your phone and Beth hadn't found out, but thought you were still attending your conference or whatever it was, then how would you have managed it? The discharge from hospital, the delayed return to New York? How would you have looked after yourself?'

'I'd have managed,' Jake said tightly. 'It's not like I'm on total bed rest, I'm just limited by what I can do. Everything is painful and tiring right now, but it's not impossible. Except, apparently, flying, which is sod's law.'

'You don't look like you could wheel a suitcase at the moment, let alone do anything else.'

She saw something flash in his eyes, could sense he was tamping down his anger. 'I would have been fine, Hester. Anyway, we're not here for that. We're here for this.' He gestured around the room. 'I want to hear all about Australia. I want you to tell me what it was like for you.'

Chapter Thirteen

Saturday

She had known it was coming, of course. The sick, unsettled feeling she'd had all day was a portent of it, and nothing to do with the stupid yellow shot Glen had bought them all in the pub the night before. Hester was used to embellishing in her job, but now it was time to outright lie. To the one client she didn't want to, but who she would have already lost if she hadn't agreed to it.

They ate the chocolate crackle dessert – the rich taste of dark chocolate mixing with the sharpness of sea salt, a dose of nostalgia in its crunchy, chewy texture, the elegance of a whisper of gold leaf on the top – sitting on the sofa. Hester played the tour of Airlie Beach and the Whitsunday Islands, the commentary from Bonza Experiences pointing out the wildlife: the shoals of yellow snappers they zoomed in on; the tiger shark that made her shudder just looking at it; then Whitehaven Beach with its curve of gleaming white sand. A slice of pure, holiday perfection.

'Did you go here?' Jake asked, leaning over to top up her rosé. 'I've always thought it looks fake.'

Hester laughed awkwardly, and swallowed a large mouthful of wine before replying. *Here goes.* 'It's not fake, and it is even more beautiful in real life than this gives it credit for.'

'How did you get out there? Helicopter?'

'Inflatable boat. It was a day tour. We got the boat just after dawn, and cut through the blue water out to the island. You could sit on the side – it was almost like one of those inflatable bananas – and have your feet in the water, as long as you held on. At one point, dolphins swam alongside us. And then,' she swallowed, hoping she was doing Glen's story justice, praying it sounded natural, rather than robotic, 'all that over-the-top view, of the swirls of colour?'

Jake nodded. 'Like bubblegum and vanilla ice cream.' With the suite lights dimmed, the white LED bulbs were mirrored in his eyes as he looked at her.

Hester laughed. 'Exactly like that. Well, we hadn't seen it on our approach: the boat stops in a different bay. Our guides led us on a walk through the forest. They told us we didn't need shoes, and like the hapless tourists we were, we believed them. It was so painful, all these leaves and twigs and God knows what else digging into the soles of our feet; there was so much grumbling and complaining on that walk.'

'Not from you, though.' He said it as a statement, not a question, and she wanted to tell him that, if she had really gone there, then of *course* she wouldn't have moaned. She would have embraced every second, every sensation.

'No,' she said. 'I was too busy looking out for deadly spiders.' She laughed. 'Anyway, we kept walking and sweating, moaning or rolling our eyes at the moaners, but then we emerged onto this wooden viewing platform, right at the top of the forest canopy, and—' she paused, widening her eyes theatrically.

Jake's lips parted, his attention fully on her. 'Bubblegum and vanilla ice cream,' he murmured.

'Dotted with boats that looked like ants – chocolate chips, maybe – from where we were. It was beautiful.'

He glanced at the screen. 'Even more beautiful than that?'

'Even more beautiful,' she said, because she was sure it was true. 'There was a gentle wind, a freshness in the air that cleared out your lungs. We were right at the top of the forest, looking down on this . . . paradise. It was unreal.'

Jake shook his head, exhaled slowly.

'We haven't been in our swimming pool,' Hester said, desperate to get away from the lies. 'It's been an hour now.'

'Not since dessert,' Jake corrected. 'What was your worst experience? Were there any parts you hated?'

She closed her eyes. She could feel her mouth drying out despite the fruity, zingy wine. Her heart pounded, and she shuddered.

Jake's hand on her bare arm jolted her back to the moment. 'Are you cold?' he asked. 'I could make the air con match Australia, too? Wearing that dress – it's meant for real sunshine, surely.' His smile was lopsided, embarrassed, and Hester wondered how recent his last relationship was: if he was as rusty at flirting as she was. Or maybe he was in a relationship, and there was a woman waiting for him in New York, calling him daily and texting him photos of what he was coming home to. Would it be disingenuous of him to invite her to do this if he wasn't single? She had never considered it: the attraction was hers, and entirely unprofessional, and should have no bearing on what she was doing here.

'Hester?' he prompted. 'Are you all right?'

'I'm not cold,' she said. 'I'm fine. Just thinking . . .'

There was a knock on the door, and she tried to hide her relief. She smiled, getting up and hurrying over to open it.

'What's this?' Jake asked. 'Not more food, surely.'

'A piece of real Australia,' she said, opening the door to reveal Marty and a short, dark-haired man wearing a green shirt and jeans, with a large, open bag strapped over one shoulder. 'Hi. Andy, is it? Come in. Thanks, Marty.'

The concierge grinned, gave Jake a quick wave and left them to it.

'Hi Jake,' Andy said. 'I'm Andy Simmons, here with my friend Jackman. Named after Hugh Jackman, of course, one of Australia's greatest exports.'

'Hi Andy. Who's Jackman?' Jake gave Hester a bemused glance and sat forward on the sofa, his wince there and gone in a flash.

Andy approached Jake slowly, and Hester stood back against the wall and watched as a pair of ears, and then a snout, lifted up over the opening of the bag.

Jake sat up, his eyes wide as he coughed out a laugh. 'It's a . . . Jackman's a—'

'A joey,' Hester finished, as the miniature kangaroo lifted his head fully out of the opening, Andy supporting its weight, cradling the bag with both arms.

'Do you want to hold him?'

Jake was shaking his head, but he grinned and said, 'OK.'

'You'll have to put the bag over you,' Andy said, as he walked round the table, and gently lifted the wide strap over his head, then lowered it over Jake's. He settled Jackman on Jake's lap, and Jake brought his arms around the bag, his movements tentative, concentration creasing his brow.

'How old is he?' Jake asked softly.

'Four months, now. His mum died just after he was born, so we've been hand-rearing him. This is the best way to replicate the experience he'd get in a pouch, and it's pretty full on, to be honest, but my team loves him. As you can see, he's hard to resist.'

'He's so placid,' Hester said, sitting gently next to Jake, reaching out to touch the soft fur of Jackman's nose.

Andy nodded. 'He's actually very gentle. He's curious, mostly: always wants to know what's going on, where his surrogate mum is. But on the whole he doesn't cause too much fuss. We've got a couple of possums, and they're a nightmare, but cute with it, so they get away with a lot.'

'Would I find one of these in Sydney?' Jake asked.

'Not in the centre,' Andy said. 'But in the bushland surrounding the city, sure.'

Jake nodded, looking at Jackman's face, his arms cradling the bag while the joey peered out at his unusual surroundings. He asked Andy more questions, while Hester sat back and watched, thinking that this was a rather ridiculous, but also fairly amazing thing she and Marty had achieved. It reminded her of the zoo visits she'd had at primary school, meeting a chinchilla and a tarantula in the dusty assembly hall, but she didn't think a visit from a baby kangaroo was something that would be routinely available to just anyone. Eventually Andy took Jackman back, carefully put the makeshift pouch back over his shoulders, and wished them a good evening.

Jake and Hester washed their hands, then settled on the sofa again. Hester poured the remaining wine into their glasses.

'I can't believe you brought a real kangaroo to the suite,' Jake said, laughing. 'I can't wait to tell Rosalie: show her what her generosity has led to.'

Hester grinned. 'You wanted the souped-up Australia experience. And you're right, Marty can get hold of just about anything. Though I don't think this would have been possible if they weren't hand-rearing Jackman. I don't think I could have got someone to bring a wombat here.'

'Did you see kangaroos in the wild when you were there? Koalas? No poisonous spiders or snakes, I hope.' He frowned. 'I'm not a fan of snakes.'

'No,' Hester said lightly. 'No deadly animals encountered at all.' *Obviously,* she thought, because meeting Jackman was the closest she'd ever got to Australian wildlife. She'd never even seen an adder, let alone a brown snake or black mamba slithering through the grass. 'But there is something I'll never forget,' she added, before she could talk herself out of it. 'Though it's not particularly positive. I had a panic attack.'

Jake's gaze sharpened. 'In Australia? What happened?'

Hester looked at the hem of her dress, resting just above her knee. She could see a few fine hairs where she'd missed a patch of skin with the razor. 'It was – I was booked in to do a bungee jump. I was brave, full of bravado. I thought

I could do it, even though just thinking about it made my palms sticky.'

'A *bungee jump*? You're braver than me,' Jake said, shaking his head. 'I wouldn't go near anything like that.'

'It's almost a rite of passage on some of those backpacking trips,' she replied. 'And I got all the way there; I held onto my smidgen of confidence right until the last minute, could hear the whoops and calls of the people ahead of me, the terror and exhilaration, the line getting shorter and shorter as I reached the edge of the bridge. It was over this deep valley, you could hear the river rushing, far below. The sky was so blue, it was a beautiful day, but I got near the front and then . . .' She wiped her hands down her dress.

'Then?' Jake swallowed, his Adam's apple bobbing.

'Then my vision went blurry and I couldn't take in any air: it was as if the path to my lungs was blocked, and my breaths couldn't go past my throat. My legs felt like pipe cleaners and I—' She shook her head. 'I couldn't do it. My friends took my arms, they walked me away from the line, and I remember . . .' She looked up at him, smiling, because this was real. The situation wasn't as she was telling it, but the emotions, the relief, were all hers. 'I remember lying on the grass, feeling the prickle of its blades against my ears and the backs of my calves, the firmness of the ground beneath me, gazing up at a blue sky with white, streamer-like clouds sliding overhead, and being so grateful that I was OK. Ashamed that I hadn't made it, especially when I'd been so determined, but mostly grateful.'

'You got closer than I ever would,' Jake said. 'I think you were courageous to even attempt it.'

Hester accepted his compliment, felt warmed by it, because

113

what did it matter that the bungee jump had actually been a flight to Spain; the queue of people waiting by the bridge the other passengers queuing up to go through airport security; the grass she'd lain on and sky she'd looked up at, in her parents' garden – after she'd said goodbye to Glen and Amber and made it back from the airport – instead of in Australia? She knew what terror felt like; what it was to be so certain, so hopeful, and then not quite make it over the hurdle.

Hester laughed. 'I felt grateful to be alive right then, even if it was a rope I'd been facing, rather than a deadly snake.'

'I'll toast to that.' Jake held up his glass and Hester nudged hers against it. They smiled at each other, and then Jake leaned back against the deep sofa cushions, an arm around his ribs. Hester felt the room deflate slightly, as if they'd both run out of steam.

'You're hurting?' she asked.

'Just stiffening up, that's all. Your time in Australia – most of it, anyway – sounds like bliss. I want to go to that restaurant in Sydney Opera House, and see the sails all lit up.' He laughed. 'I wonder if the Duval chef would do us a different selection from the Bennelong à la carte menu another night?'

'Another night is another country.' Hester stood up. 'You need to get moving if you're stiffening up: aren't those your doctor's orders? And what, honestly, is the point of having an *actual* swimming pool, if we don't make use of it? I can't miss the last train home.'

'Understood,' Jake said.

Hester held out her hand, her breath catching when he took it. His hand was warm, his grip firm. She gently pulled him up and he staggered forward, putting his other hand on her shoulder to steady himself. Now there was no reason to turn the air con down. The strap of her dress was thin, and she could feel the heat of his skin go through her. She needed the dial turned all the way to arctic to combat the fire racing through her.

'OK?' she asked lightly.

'Fine.'

'Come on, then.' She lifted her glass and waited while he did the same, then led him over to the tiny swimming pool. She stepped inside, the water reaching just over her ankles, the temperature ticklishly cool, and Jake joined her. They faced each other, the twinkling lights draped along the wall putting silver highlights in his hair.

He laughed softly. 'Not much room for diving or splashing. Or even lounging.'

The pool was so small they had to stand close together, and Hester was very conscious of her dress, and its low-cut neckline.

'I didn't think this through,' she murmured.

'You thought everything through,' he said, his gaze taking in every inch of her face. 'Tonight has been better than I imagined. Can I keep Stanley?'

'Who's Stanley?'

'The saltwater crocodile.'

Hester grinned. 'You can keep Stanley, but not the cassowary. He has to go back to Australia. Where all these things came from, I might add.'

'Even the sand?'

'Whitehaven Beach's finest.'

The smile flickered on Jake's face. 'I know what we can do in here.'

'What?'

'We can dance.'

'Dance?'

'That's something people do on holiday, isn't it? Room,' he said loudly, 'play "Waltzing Matilda".'

'*Got it,*' said a smooth, electronic voice. '*Now playing "Waltzing Matilda" by The Seekers.*'

The opening bars started, and Jake held out his hand.

'How did I not know there was voice activation in here?' Hester whispered, taking his hand as they started to sway in time to the music.

'I only discovered it because I told the room it was fucking lame after I tripped over the rug and jarred my ribs. She told me she wasn't going to respond to language like that and I almost had a heart attack.'

Hester laughed, and it felt like the most natural thing when Jake took her drink and put it on the mantelpiece alongside his, then drew her closer, his hand on her hip, the press of his fingers tantalizing. She rested her head on his shoulder, her cheek brushing against the soft cotton of his T-shirt. She put her hands gently on his waist, keeping her touch soft, unsure how far down the pain went. He felt toned, and she was so tempted to slip her palms up, under the hem of his T-shirt, to have the chance to touch more of his skin, but she didn't.

She could feel him whispering the lyrics against her neck, the water around her feet warming to room temperature. It was a slow, sultry dance under shimmering lights, in a tiny paddling pool surrounded by sand and cuddly crocodiles. It was a fantasy; as unreal as the stories she'd been spinning him all evening. And now they were here, dancing close together, and she felt—

'I should go,' she said. She pulled herself out of his arms and stepped out of the pool, her foot skidding on the protective undercoating beneath the sand so that she nearly fell into the sofa. 'Shit.'

'Are you OK?' Jake stepped out after her, handing her one of the towels that was draped over the back of a nearby chair.

'I didn't realize how late it was. I really need to get going. I'm just going to get changed.' she pointed at the bathroom door. 'This dress doesn't really feel public transport appropriate.'

'Sure,' Jake said.

'Won't be a sec.' She hurried into the bathroom, shut the door and pressed her forehead against the cool glass of the mirror. This time when she looked at her reflection, her excitement had been replaced by fear. Regardless of the shallow water in that doggy bathing pool, Hester knew she was completely out of her depth, in more ways than one.

Chapter
Fourteen

Sunday

'Happy Sunday, Hester,' Vanessa said as she stepped out onto the landing. 'Off to see your mum and dad?'

'That's right,' Hester replied. 'What about you?'

'Lyron will be over soon, with a lamb to roast and some plantain.'

'Sounds delicious,' Hester said. 'We're having beef, I think.'

Her parents lived in Blackheath, which wasn't far from her: she could walk it in twenty-five minutes. Even so, it was like being in a different city. Blackheath was more like a village, in fact, with its hilly high street strewn with independent cafes and restaurants; the flat beauty of the heath, the church and the pond nestled in one corner, where she had sailed toy boats as a child; the grand mansions surrounding it. The sky there was empty and huge, so unlike the rest of London.

'You were in late last night,' Vanessa added, her tone curious.

Hester paused. She didn't have the heart for any more make-believe right now. 'I was with a client,' she said. 'I just made the last train.'

'Good night?' Vanessa folded her arms. Her dress was orange with blue flowers, vibrant against her dark skin. Her eyes were pinned on Hester.

'It was fine. Fun.' She swallowed. 'We both had a good time, I think.'

She had come home and climbed into bed, Betty's piece of malachite on her bedside table, gleaming under the glow from her lamp while she fretted about what she'd said to Jake. She had reminded herself that he was just a client, that she would entertain him until he got better and went home to New York, and then she never had to see him again. He would never know about her lies. It wasn't all that serious, was it? She needed to get some perspective, zoom out and see the bigger picture.

'You look tired,' Vanessa said.

'I didn't sleep well. I can have a snooze at Mum and Dad's, especially after a roast.'

'Knock on my door when you're back. Lyron might still be here, and he'd love to see you.'

'I'll do that, thank you. See you later, Nessa.'

The September day had started out grey, but as Hester walked patches of blue split the clouds, tentative rays of sun settled on cars and paving stones, and the fresh air and exercise lifted her spirits. Jake hadn't seemed to notice her discomfort at the end of the evening, and they'd agreed that the next destination would be on Monday night. He didn't want her working all Sunday, and she needed time to prepare. Hester had sent a text to Amber that morning, asking for a download of all her Japanese experiences from her trip at the beginning of the year.

'Darling,' her mum said as she opened the door to the deceptively spacious house. 'Just in time for tea. The roasts's in, and your dad's working on the gravy.' She made it sound like he was giving it mouth-to-mouth.

'Hi, Mum.' Hester followed her into the airy living room, the walls a sunshine yellow, the wooden furniture all painted white, the chunky sofas covered in woven throws in blues, pinks and purples. Each room was painted a different colour, and all were accented in white, straddling the border between tasteful and garish. The design complemented her parents' different personalities: Dad, who was eternally sunny, outgoing and competent, and her mum, who was more thoughtful, calmer, everything she said or did carefully considered beforehand. Hester imagined she fell somewhere between the two of them, though when it came to her dad's attitude for getting things done, breezing through every challenge as if it didn't trouble him in the slightest, she felt distinctly lacking.

'Sit there, darling,' her mum said now. 'The light'll be round in a few moments and it's the warmest patch. I'll get you a tea.'

Hester wanted to point out that she wasn't a cat, that she didn't need a square of sunshine to bask in, but she did as she was told, putting her handbag on the floor and taking out the box of Ferrero Rocher and bottle of red wine she'd bought as gifts. She felt nervous, which she never did in this house. The weight of her evening with Jake, and all it had asked of her, sat heavily on her shoulders like a too-thick cardigan.

'There you go.' Her mum came back with a mug of tea, and Hester clutched it gratefully, taking a sip even though it was still scalding.

'Thanks. How are you, Mum? How's it all going?'

'Oh, you know. Not too bad.' She waved a hand, her smile gentle, as always. Their features were similar: the same delicate, slightly snub nose, high cheekbones and large, hazel eyes. But where her mum's hair was a dusty brown, now sprinkled with a few grey highlights, Hester had inherited her dad's thick, blond locks, wearing them just longer than shoulder-length, unable to stop the strands frizzing in humid weather.

'Is the surgery busy?' Her mum was office manager at the local doctor's surgery, a job she played down as "just admin", but which Hester knew was a juggling act of managing staff and dealing with disgruntled, unwell customers. She was one of those people, Hester had come to realize, that wanted her imprint on the world to be small: to slip through it almost unnoticed. Her dad easily took up the space she refused to fill. He was always cheerful, his stance relaxed, his smile almost permanent. He sold insurance, but had somehow made his occupation the least noteworthy thing about him. He packed his time outside work with other pursuits: tinkering with engines, playing badminton some evenings and golf at the weekends, even convincing his wife to go salsa dancing with him, an occurrence that had made Hester almost fall over in shock.

'Gravy's gravied,' he said, rubbing his hands as he walked into the lounge. 'Hester, my sweet.' She stood up as he came over and hugged her, and she returned it with her free arm, holding her tea away from his purple jumper, before putting it down. 'How's my favourite daughter? Keeping out of mischief at that holiday agency?'

'Sort of,' she said, her smile mirroring his. 'It's all a bit full-on at the moment.'

'Oh?' her mum asked, and Hester heard the hope in her voice.

'I've been planning a lot of stuff. In London, actually.'

Her dad laughed. 'Jet set holidays to London? That sounds intriguing.'

'I'll tell you about it over lunch,' Hester said, handing the wine to her mum and chocolates to her dad, hoping to distract them long enough to get her thoughts in order.

When the roast was ready, they sat around the table in the lime-green dining room, and Chess, her parent's black-and-white cat, took his place on the fourth chair. He sat with his nose in the air, with his one black ear and one white ear, watching the proceedings as if, at any moment, he would be given a full plate of roast dinner as was his right. Hester loved Chess, but Chess didn't love her back, and she didn't try to stroke him for fear of getting scratched.

The food was delicious as always, and despite her Australian feast the night before – her dad's roast beef not quite as melt-in-the-mouth as the Duval's Wagyu – Hester tucked in eagerly, to the point where her mum gave her a curious look.

'What's this new thing you've got on at work?' she asked. 'It sounds a bit different to your usual.'

As with everything work-related, her mum approached with caution. Her parents had been on the flight that had traumatized Hester: they had witnessed the tragedy alongside her. But whether it was down to Hester's impressionable, twelve-year-old brain, or because she'd struck up a short-lived friendship with Betty, the impact on her had been much harder.

Hester was lucky that her parents were so supportive, but their gentle coaxing, her dad's often-repeated suggestion that she should try again – get back on the horse, as it were – sometimes made her feel like a failure. Of course, she felt that way most days, because she had intentionally stepped into a world that embraced long-distance travel. But when her parents walked on eggshells, Hester felt the crunch right to her bones.

'I've got a client who's stuck in London and has asked me to plan some virtual holidays for him,' she said. 'Sort of themed nights in his hotel, set in different destinations.'

Her mum and dad looked at her as if she'd told them she'd been booking trips to Mars.

'We went to Australia last night,' she continued. 'The food and music, the beach.'

'In this man's hotel room?' her mum said.

'That's right. It went well, I think.'

'You've never been to Australia.'

'No, Mum.' Hester sighed. 'But I've never been anywhere, really, have I? It doesn't stop me being able to advise people on their luxury cruise or six-week American road trip. I'm good at research.'

'Sounds like a great night,' her dad said affably. 'Though I can't quite get my head around how you did it.' He laughed. 'Was it your idea to take him to the other side of the world, or was that wishful thinking on your part?' His eyes shone with humour and something else: something that looked like sympathy.

'He wanted luxury, exotic.' She shrugged. 'And Glen went

to Australia last year with Elise, so he gave me a few pointers. When I think of Oz, I think of fun, and that felt right for the first destination. It wasn't too heavy. I'm just testing the waters at the moment.'

'Where are you taking him next?' her mum asked.

'Japan. Amber went earlier this year, so she's sending me some photos and . . . other bits and pieces.'

The silence was thoughtful, and Hester had the impression that her mum and dad couldn't quite grasp what she was doing. She wanted to tell them they weren't the only ones. She sipped her wine and looked at them over the rim of her glass. She glanced at Chess and he turned his head away, not prepared to dignify her with his attention.

'What about Amalfi?' her mum said eventually.

'You loved Amalfi,' her dad added. 'Couldn't get enough of it, at the time. You had all these plans . . .' His voice tailed off.

'I know,' Hester said quietly. 'I am planning on taking him there, but I think I . . . I want to save it. It's the one place I can talk about honestly. It feels like it should be the grand finale, somehow.'

'Why don't we look at the photos after lunch?' her dad said. 'Remind yourself of everything.'

'It might give you a bit more confidence,' her mum added, 'if you do the next . . . holiday in a place you've been to. More confidence for your future evenings.'

Her dad nodded. 'I'm guessing this client is important to you – or to Cassie, at least – if you're prepared to do something so unusual for him? If you want to take him somewhere you're passionate about, then Italy seems like the perfect choice.'

Her mum smiled, her hands clasped in front of her. 'If your memories have faded, then Charles and I can fill in the gaps.'

'We'd like to help you, sweet.'

Hester nodded, swallowing a piece of potato that had lodged in her throat. Her dad's tone was serious, and she knew he was talking about more than just Jake's next staycation. Perhaps they thought this project was Cassie's way of helping her. Cassie didn't know about Hester's phobia, but she must have guessed, by now, that there was something stopping her from accepting the scouting trips she was offering.

'Come on then, darling,' her mum said, when all their plates were clear. 'Tell us about this client of yours and why he's so important. We'll take your nutty chocolates into the other room.'

'Jake Oakenfield,' Hester said, feeling a spark of excitement at having a reason to say his name. 'He's recovering from an accident. He stopped this old woman from being hit by a car, and ended up getting hurt himself.'

'Goodness,' her mum said as they went through to the sunny living room and she pulled a navy, leatherbound photo album from a bookshelf. 'The poor man. No wonder he's looking for a way to escape.'

'And Amalfi *is* pretty luxurious,' Hester agreed, sitting next to her mum while her dad went to put the kettle on. She had never said it out loud, but knew her parents must have realized that it was a totemic destination for her: the last place she'd been when everything still felt possible, before that fateful trip to Edinburgh. They had spent time on the beach, visited the quaint restaurants, climbed up to the huge crematorium that looked down on Amalfi bay, and she had thought this was the first of many – endless – holidays. Now it shone, dreamlike, in her mind. She was eleven when she went, an age when cares were for other people, and all she had to do was enjoy herself. Would she have treasured it more if she'd known what was to come?

'I don't know why your father felt he needed to take a photo of the departure lounge,' her mum said, turning to the first page of the album.

'Because we were on holiday!' her dad called, laughing, from the kitchen. 'Wait for me! I'll be two secs.'

While he made the tea, Hester stared at an eleven-year-old version of herself, standing next to her mum, below the backlit yellow sign that read "Naples". Both their smiles were wide, expectant, but she felt a familiar tightening in her throat, an unwelcome pulse at her temples, and this was just a *photo* of the airport. She ran her hands down her jeans, clutched her knees tightly and took deep, subtle breaths. And then her mum flipped the page, and the airport was replaced with Amalfi. Her panic faded, and she swallowed, reminded again of how beautiful it was: how special that holiday had been.

Her parents sat either side of her as they went through the photographs: the ferry ride they'd taken to Capri, then the sumptuous gardens at the top of the island with views over to the mainland; the pillars and cobbled streets of Pompeii, so thronged with tourists it was hard to really feel how ancient it was; a patchwork Bay of Naples laid out below cottonwool clouds from the top of Mount Vesuvius. All those memories, the unreality of being somewhere so different to home, that she had taken for granted.

Her mum turned the page, let out a breathy, 'Oh,' and Hester was shaken out of her daydream.

'Should we . . .' Her dad went to close the album, but Hester put her hand in it, stopping him.

'I don't remember this one,' she said.

'I have a few photos from that Edinburgh weekend, but—'

'You took a photo of me and Betty?' Hester whispered. 'I never realized. Or I – I forgot.'

'You might have blocked it out,' her dad said gently. 'After what happened.'

Hester nodded absent-mindedly. The photo was taken from a high angle, because Hester was sitting in a window seat on the small plane – a bus with wings, really – and Betty had been in the row in front. Her mum had angled the camera so she could fit them both in, the back of Betty's seat between them as Hester grinned, her hair much longer than it was now, the frizz round her temples much less controlled.

Betty's flame-red hair was cropped short, and Hester realized she had never forgotten how green her eyes were: had, in fact, thought she'd been exaggerating their shade in her memories, until this picture confirmed it as the truth. They were alive with possibility, ready to drink in every new experience. She looked at her now, this person she thought had been consigned to her hazy memories forever, and wondered if she'd had an inkling. Had she felt ill or weak when they were chatting, when she'd been telling Hester to follow her dreams everywhere, because what was the point of being born onto this miraculous planet with all its diversity, if you didn't try to reach every corner of it?

Her mum closed the album, shutting it on that snap-shot, wiping out Hester and Betty's carefree smiles. 'Do you want to take the album and scan in some Amalfi photos for your Italy night?' Her mum's voice was brusque, almost businesslike.

'Sure,' Hester said quietly. 'That would be great. Thanks, Mum.'

Her dad squeezed her knee and held the Ferrero Rocher box out to her, and she took one without meeting his gaze, because she didn't want to see the pity in it.

'Take this client to Amalfi,' he said. 'It'll be a surefire triumph. You can worry about where to go next when he's too full of authentic Neapolitan pizza to move.'

It was dark when Hester said goodbye, the navy photo album stowed safely in her handbag. Chess was lying on the sofa, the sunlight he'd sought out long since fallen behind the roof of the house opposite.

She felt buoyed up, determined, but still slightly shaken by the unexpected photograph. Betty had become almost a figment in her thoughts and dreams, represented by the piece of malachite she'd left behind, and which Hester had grabbed hold of. Now, she was vivid again: almost as vivid as she'd been in the short time – less than an hour, in fact – that Hester had known her. Had she followed the travel agent route *for* Betty? To live up to the expectations of the woman who was so filled with wanderlust, but whose own journey had been cut short? If she had, then she was doing an awful job of it. Hester hadn't been able to follow her dreams very far at all.

'Bye, puss,' she said, boldly reaching out a hand towards the cat. Chess swiped out a paw before Hester had time to react, and left a long, angry scratch down the inside of her arm.

129

Chapter
Fifteen

Monday

She woke on Monday morning with anticipation fluttering in her chest. After the afternoon with her parents she felt stronger, happier, ready to face a day of research at the Duval and then an evening with Jake, *not* lying to him while she transported him to one of the most beautiful countries in the world. It was a country that oozed love and romance; the food and architecture, music and dancing and landscapes. It thrummed through the heart of Italy, as if it was infused in the country's sunlight. But her night with Jake had to be entirely platonic: he was a client, and she had to be professional. OK, so maybe she didn't feel *quite* so ready to face this particular challenge, but it was a brand-new week, and Hester Monday was determined to make *this* Monday a great one.

'We have a problem,' Marty said as he greeted her in the piano room, a mug of coffee held out in a placatory gesture.

'Oh no! What is it?'

'I think he's guessed where you're taking him.'

Hester took the mug from Marty and put it on the table. She could hear someone playing the grand piano in the lounge, a cheery tune that wasn't quite 'The Entertainer' but had that same, learning-the-techniques feel about it. 'How come?' she asked. 'Has he been pestering you, too?'

Marty leaned against a chair. 'Yup. Started when I took him dinner last night. What did I have planned; what were my tasks for today; why couldn't I give him just one tiny clue? He played the invalid card too, the little shit.'

'He messaged me as well, asking for hints. I've been ignoring him.' It had been so hard, her fingers itching to tap out a reply. 'Why do you think he's guessed?'

'Because when I went to check if he needed anything just now, he was whistling "That's Amore". I think he got it out of Felicity or Dana, who have been helping me get some of the items you texted over last night. Frankly, as professional as they are, I wouldn't be entirely surprised if one – or both – of them gave in. Jake's got rough-around-the-edges charm even before you add in his injury. He'd have every female staff member looking after him if we gave them the chance.'

'If he's already guessed it's Italy,' Hester said, pushing down a pulse of jealousy at the thought of Jake flirting with Flick or Dana, 'then we're really going to have to up our game to make it even remotely surprising.'

Again, they sent Jake off to do his stairway walkabout while they got the suite ready. They wheeled in a trolley on which were hefty ceramic pots bursting with pink and

132

red bougainvillea, and Marty arranged a decorative wooden arch, complete with real vine tangled around it, in front of the bedroom door. There was a polystyrene fountain doing a very good impression of stone that Hester had noticed in a boutique window on her walk to the hotel, and Marty had phoned up to secure a loan of for the evening. She still marvelled at the lengths the Duval staff would go to, at short notice, to fulfil the wishes of their guests.

She looped delicate pink lights around the window seat that looked out over London rooftops, lit a lemon-scented candle on the dining table, then tested out the voice activation.

'Room,' she said. 'Play Pavarotti.'

'*Got it*,' said the electronic voice. 'Best of Pavarotti, *now playing.*'

The opening of 'Nessun Dorma' almost burst her eardrums, and she shouted, '*VOLUME DOWN! VOLUME DOWN! VOLUME DOWN!*' until it was a charming background noise instead of an assault. Marty, she saw, was trying hard not to laugh.

'Oh my God,' she said, exhaling. 'Has Jake been trying to deafen the other guests?'

The concierge shrugged. 'Who knows what he gets up to in the endless hours when he's waiting for you to arrive?' Now that everything was in place he left the room, giving Hester a last, lazy wave.

She wiped her palms down her jeans. She'd gone for a casual outfit this time: her favourite worn-soft jeans and a T-shirt in the colours of the Italian flag. Taking Jake to Amalfi felt more authentic than Australia, and this time the room was more elegant, less fun. She didn't want to be too over the top, because Italy was already seductive enough, and the jeans and T-shirt felt like the right balance. Now, all she had to do was set up the entertainment, and wait for Jake to arrive.

She had a slideshow of photographs on her iPad, which she could project onto the wall if anything went wrong with her other plans. Most of them were professional shots, but she had taken a few from her parents' album, even though their age meant they were film rather than digital and the quality – especially blown up onto the wall – would be pretty bad. But they were genuinely hers, and that seemed to matter more than anything. She dimmed the main lights so the strings of twinkly bulbs would shine out around the wooden arch and the window seat, and surveyed the room.

It was magical. Beautiful. Hugely fucking romantic. Hester closed her eyes and groaned, wondering if she had time to escape before Jake arrived, but there was a knock on the door and she knew the answer was no.

The look in his eyes was pure triumph. And then his expression softened, his lips parted, and Hester thought that not even the most unromantic of people could fail to be moved by the transformation his suite had undergone, and she didn't think Jake fell into that category anyway.

'You sure this is my room?' he asked, walking slowly around it, touching the petals of the flowers and then bending to sniff them. He was wearing dark jeans and a casual white shirt, proving that things that were naturally stunning needed no embellishment whatsoever. He was holding himself slightly straighter, and Hester realized the weariness she'd come to expect from him wasn't quite so evident.

'Of course it's not your room,' she said. 'It's Amalfi.'

He nodded, distracted, as he completed his circuit and came to stand in front of her. 'I got you something.'

'You got *me* something? Why?'

'Castagnole.' He held out his gift: a square box full of little crispy pastry balls, dusted with icing sugar. 'They're filled with coffee, seeing as that's my speciality, though I had no hand in making these.'

'You guessed,' she said. 'Marty thought you had.'

'I did my own research.' He sat on the sofa and she did the same, not hesitating to open the box of delicate patisserie and hold it out to him. 'The chef made them earlier,' he added. 'I haven't ventured outside yet.'

'Did your research involve guilt-tripping impressionable young women with your twinkly eyes and woe-is-me rib-clutching?' She leaned forward, mimicking the pose she'd seen him do so often.

'Hey,' he said, laughing. 'They do still hurt, you know.'

'I know that really. I'm just annoyed at being sprung. *Again*.'

'You gave away Australia with your drunk messaging. I didn't have to work at all to guess that one.'

'Fair. And – oh my God, these are incredible.' She mumbled it, her mouth full of superior Italian patisserie.

'Mmm.' He moaned in appreciation as he ate one. 'You shouldn't be annoyed,' he said when he'd finished. 'Once again you have knocked it out of the park. Fresh flowers, vines. Fairy lights. Again.' He narrowed his eyes.

'What?'

'Are fairy lights that universal?'

'You don't see them everywhere in New York?'

Jake shook his head. 'I haven't really been looking for them.'

'Then you're missing out. Fairy lights can transform a space completely. Soften it or lift it up. Life is full of simple, uncomplicated joys, and fairy lights are one of the best.'

'Which philosopher said that?'

'Esteemed philosopher Hester Monday.'

'She sounds wise. I'd better listen to her.'

Hester put the box of treats on the table and scooted further back on the sofa. Pavarotti sang about something heartfelt in the background. 'I think you should,' she said. She smiled at him, and his eyes shone back.

Their silence held while the operatic tenor reached the climax of his song, and all the hairs stood up on the back of Hester's neck. Even at a low volume, the emotion in his voice soared inside her, touching skin and blood and sinew. She was taken back to her own holiday all those years ago, the specific quality of the air, lights from boats reflecting on the water while she strolled through the cobbled streets with her parents, this song, or one very similar to it, drifting out of a window higher up the hill. The photos had brought it all back to her. And then there was the one she hadn't expected: the one of her and Betty smiling for the camera.

'Hester?' Jake said quietly, 'is something wrong?'

'Of course not!' She smiled at him. 'We shouldn't let the food get cold.'

'Pizza?' He followed her to the dining table. Hester didn't think she'd ever get used to the cloches, like huge silver boobs with delicacies hidden underneath.

'I may be obvious with my destinations,' she said, 'but I've tried hard with the detail. There's a takeaway seafood stall halfway up the main street of the town called Cuoppo D'Amalfi, that sells mouth-watering cones of calamari.

That's what we're having to start.' She lifted off the cover to reveal two paper cones full of seafood covered in crispy, golden batter. The smell that wafted out seemed to zing straight to her taste buds. She'd worked through lunch, she realized, and was fuelled almost entirely on coffee. She wondered if Jake was as hungry as she was.

He looked sideways at her, giving her one of his gentle smiles. 'Calamari is one of my favourite things. I could eat it for every meal, breakfast included.'

'Good.' Hester flushed with pleasure. 'And we've got Aperol Spritz to drink.' She went to pull out a chair and Jake squeezed her arm.

'This window seat,' he said, 'the one you've dressed with flowers and lights, looks particularly holiday-like. If the view outside was a beach or harbour instead of London rooftops, it would be a hundred per cent authentic. I think we should eat these here.'

'OK, then.' She waited while Jake sat sideways on the plush cream cushion nestled in the deep-set window recess and pulled his legs up, crossing them, his brows knitting together as he got comfortable. 'All right?' she asked.

He nodded, his jaw clenched. Clearly, he didn't want to draw attention to his injuries tonight.

'Hang on a moment,' she said. 'Our entertainment for the evening is about to begin.' She picked up a remote, bringing up a menu on the blank wall at the other end of the suite, where a couple of nights before the Sydney Light Show had played. 'I hope you'll forgive me the slight detour, but there aren't a lot of opera houses in Amalfi itself, and Accademia di Santa Cecilia have a live-screening of *La Traviata*. I thought we could bring the performance to us.'

Jake sounded surprised. 'Opera?'

'We don't have to watch it intently – unless you want to? I'll keep the volume low.' She pulled up the right image, of a darkened theatre stage, the soundtrack a low thrum of the orchestra tuning up; the shuffle of papers; a couple of people coughing. She turned the volume down a couple of notches, then dimmed the lighting so the stage was more prominent.

She joined Jake on the window seat, facing him and crossing her legs in front of her. The window was open, and the breeze that licked in could have been Italian because they were so far up, away from the London streets, with their petrol fumes, car horns and siren blares, and the sky was turning an inky, purplish blue.

They ate their calamari with wooden forks, while the overture to *La Traviata* began. Jake's gaze flicked over her shoulder, watching for a few moments, then returned to her.

'I realized that I should have started off by asking you where you've been,' Hester said. 'For all I know I could be taking you to countries and cities you visit every year.'

'It wouldn't matter. These are your interpretations of them: the visions of an imaginative, professional, well-travelled expert. That's what I wanted, and you know you're already exceeding my expectations. I can believe these came from Amalfi, they're so good.' He speared a calamari ring and held it up in front of him, so Hester could see one of his blue eyes through the hole in the middle.

'You've been to Italy?' she asked, ignoring his description of her.

'Rome and Florence, Bolzano a couple of times, but never the Amalfi coast. And I didn't go to the music academy, or

138

see any operas in Rome. I want to go to Sicily at some point. On a real visit, involving flights and passports.'

'Because *The Godfather* is your favourite film,' Hester said, rolling her eyes.

Jake laughed. '*Godfather II* actually, which is by far the best.'

'If you say so.'

'You've never seen it?'

Hester shook her head, waiting to finish her mouthful before she spoke. 'Sorry. I like the classics, and Gene Kelly particularly. *Singing in the Rain* never gets boring, no matter how many times I watch it.'

'Are you saying that the *Godfather* films aren't classics? Because if so, you're going to have to take it back immediately.'

Hester held her free hand up in submission. 'I haven't seen them. I will bow to your superior knowledge.'

He stared at her for a second. 'Acceptable,' he said eventually.

'Phew.' Hester grinned.

'But not that you haven't seen them,' he added, his eyes narrowing. 'I'm sure we could find it in the film library once this is over.' He gestured in the direction of the projection.

Hester laughed. 'I think this is almost three hours long; we can't fit in another mammoth performance afterwards.'

'Because of your last train.'

She nodded, and it looked like he was about to say something else, find some way of removing the restraint, and for a moment Hester thought of that train as a gleaming glass carriage that would, if she stayed with Jake and watched the film, turn into a pumpkin. But instead of speaking, Jake took a long, slow sip of his cocktail. His white shirt was open at the neck, and one of his dark curls had formed a perfect circle, right on the top of his head. It reminded Hester of a rubber duck on a pond at the fair, and she realized she had never wanted to hook something quite so much in her entire life.

'I approve of our Italy trip so far,' he said into the silence, lifting his empty cone.

Hester nodded, aware that the atmosphere had shifted, the air charged. 'After the Australian swimming pool I was tempted to turn your bathtub into a jacuzzi,' she told him. 'But I thought that would be taking things a step too far.'

His lips parted in surprise, and Hester realized she'd stepped too far by even mentioning it.

'The bath actually has jets,' he said, after a moment. 'I tried it when I first got here, because I thought it might be soothing.'

'It wasn't?'

Jake shook his head, his grimace explanation enough.

'I haven't got my costume anyway,' Hester hurried on, trying to ease the tension but knowing, even as she spoke, she was making it worse. 'I'd have to get into the bath with my clothes on, and that would be far too symbolic for our first European holiday together.'

Jake's features crumpled in confusion. 'What are you talking about?' he said with a laugh. 'It's *symbolic* to get into a bath with all your clothes on, as opposed to just unhinged?'

'Oh come on, you know,' she said. 'Those scenes in films or TV shows where one person is already in the bath and then someone joins them with all their clothes on, because they're delirious with happiness or love or—'

'That makes no sense.'

'Of course it does! Getting into a bath with all your clothes on is the ultimate expression of conviction; it shows you really *mean* it, whatever "it" is. There are no other forces that compel you to do it, unlike rushing into the sea to save someone. If someone's in trouble in a bathtub, you can reach in and pull them out. There is always, *always* a choice about getting into the bath without undressing, which is why it's so symbolic.'

'Getting into a bath with all your clothes on is the ultimate symbolic gesture,' he repeated slowly. 'You fundamentally believe that?'

'I do,' Hester said, nodding.

'You are a strange person, Hester Monday.'

She grinned, because he wasn't looking at her like she was strange: he seemed intrigued, as if he wanted to know more rather than run in the opposite direction.

'I want one of yours next,' she said, then took a sip of her cocktail. It was fizzy and fruity, and went down easily. 'One of your fundamental beliefs.'

He raised his eyebrows. 'I'm not as weird as you are, so don't think you're going to catch me out.'

'I'm not trying to. I just want to know what you *truly* believe in.'

'OK,' he said. 'I believe Sunday mornings should be exclusively about long, lazy breakfasts, preferably with eggs – always with coffee – and reading the newspaper. You should never feel guilty about doing fuck all on a Sunday morning.'

'Good belief,' she said. 'Is that what you did yesterday?'

He shook his head. 'I slept until gone midday.'

Hester laughed. 'Our paddle to "Waltzing Matilda" tired you out?'

Jake shrugged. 'I've been struggling to sleep, then making up for it when I finally drift off. Anyway, that's my main belief. Sundays are for worshipping your own space, giving yourself time to do nothing. What's another of yours?'

'I don't really know if I have—' She didn't get to finish her sentence because there was a knock on the door.

'Shit.' Jake sighed. 'I'd better see who it is.'

'Let me.' Hester jumped off the window seat and hurried to the door. She pulled it open, fully expecting to see Marty with one of the items they'd talked about but had so far failed to track down, but it was someone else entirely. Someone she had never met in her life, but could instantly put a name to.

Chapter Sixteen

Monday

'Is my darling boy there?' the woman asked.

For a moment, Hester thought she had got it wrong. She hadn't believed this neat, polished woman, with a room-appropriate plum-coloured coat and matching handbag, kind grey eyes in a rounded face, could be Jake's mum. Not least because, unless she'd given birth to him in her fifties, the ages didn't match.

'Hi Rosalie,' Jake said, coming to stand beside Hester and confirming what she'd thought at the beginning. 'I wasn't expecting you this evening.'

'I was passing on my way to my club, and thought I'd pop by and see how you were. I didn't realize you'd have company. I'm so sorry.'

'I'm Hester.' She held her hand out. 'Jake's hired me to take him on a few virtual vacations while he's here.'

'Oh yes, he did mention something.' Rosalie stepped

into the room. 'And look at this! Goodness! How marvellous. Italy is the most magical destination. *La Traviata*, too,' she added, pressing her hand to her chest as she turned to the performance playing out on the wall.

Hester grinned. 'That's exactly what I thought.' She caught Jake's eye, and saw amusement there, and also warmth. Jake liked Rosalie, despite his complaints about not knowing how to deal with her gratitude. 'Would you like a cocktail, Mrs Dewey? I have the ingredients.'

'Oh, dear, I wouldn't want to put you to any trouble.'

'It's no trouble,' Jake said. 'And what about the food. *Is* it pizza?'

Hester shook her head. 'No, but I can make sure we have enough.' She called down to Marty, who took her instructions with his usual ease, then went to the drinks trolley next to the dining table.

'Are these photos of Amalfi?' Rosalie called, and Hester looked up to see the older woman holding her iPad aloft.

'Yes,' she said. 'You can look through them if you like.' She didn't think they would get around to having them on the big screen, and a slideshow of photos felt like a copout compared to live opera performances and Sydney light shows.

She made a third Aperol Spritz, measuring the ingredients carefully, and topped hers and Jake's up. Rosalie had her hand on Jake's shoulder while he scrolled through the pictures on Hester's iPad. Whatever she was saying was making him laugh, and Hester wondered if there was anyone in the world who wasn't smitten with him.

'Here we go.' As she carried their drinks to the coffee table, there was a knock on the door. She went to answer it, admitting Marty who was at the helm of a fresh trolley, the smell emanating from under the silver domes all-consuming in its deliciousness.

'Marty!' Rosalie waved.

'Good to see you, Ros,' he said. 'I didn't realize this extra plate was for you: I thought Hester and Jake must be particularly hungry.'

'What is it?' Jake asked.

Marty looked at Hester, his lips twitching.

She took a deep breath. 'Linguine all'astice. Lobster spaghetti, in a shallot, tomato and white wine sauce. We got the recipe from one of Amalfi's exclusive seafood restaurants, so it's . . . special, I hope.'

'Wonderful!' Rosalie said. 'I'm extra glad I made a detour, now. I would have ended up having macaroni cheese with crispy bacon bits at the club. Wheel it over here, Marty. Hester, thank you so much for letting me stay.'

'Jake's in charge,' she said.

He laughed. 'No, I'm not. I'm a willing participant in this magical mystery tour, but you're pulling all the strings.' He was still looking at her iPad, swiping through the photos, and Hester felt a prickle of uncertainty at him seeing her holiday snaps: what if there was one that somehow revealed, unequivocally, that this was her last holiday abroad? Of course, that thought was ludicrous, but before she had time to feel at ease, he swiped to a picture she remembered scanning – because there was a part of her that wanted to hold onto it, to deepen the connection between her memories and the piece of green stone she looked at so often – but had been sure she hadn't added to this folder: her and Betty, their smiling faces on the flight to Edinburgh.

'Oh, who is this with you?' Rosalie asked, leaning over Jake, the lobster momentarily forgotten. 'I assumed the other woman, with darker hair, was your mother, because she looks so like you.'

Hester caught Jake's eye, and he looked back at her with open curiosity.

'It's Betty,' she scratched out. 'I met her on a plane on the way to Edinburgh. It was years ago, as you can see.'

'Is she a friend?' Rosalie glanced up briefly.

Still, Jake said nothing, but it was clear he was waiting for her answer. He had noticed her change in demeanour, she thought: the way she had frozen, caught out by her own, stupid mistake.

Hester turned away, grateful to be able to help Marty serve the steaming plates of lobster spaghetti, and hoped it would distract the older woman from her questioning. But even when they all had their dishes, when Hester had sunk onto the opposite sofa, Rosalie's eyebrow was still raised in question.

Marty made a swift, almost silent retreat, and the soprano of Violetta Valéry soared in the background.

'I'm sorry,' Hester said. 'That photo wasn't supposed to be in there.'

'Why not?' Rosalie asked.

Hester wrapped a strand of spaghetti around and around her fork. It smelled delicious, but she wondered if she'd manage even a single mouthful. 'She died,' she said quietly. 'I didn't . . . shall we eat? We don't want it to get cold!' Her attempt at perky was pathetic, and Rosalie's expression changed from curious to mortified.

'Oh dear,' she said, her dinner forgotten. 'Oh, my darling.'

'I'm sorry, Hester,' Jake added.

She shook her head. 'I didn't know her – not at all, really. It was just a shock . . .' She reached over and gently took the iPad, putting it next to her on the sofa, then turned up the volume of the opera, until it swelled into the sadness she'd left behind, filling up the space. Hester felt the band around her chest loosen. 'There.'

Nobody spoke, and even while they ate, it was clear that Rosalie was unsure what to say, and that Jake was watching Hester with the calm scrutiny she was coming to expect but which still unnerved her. Her words must have left them with more questions, but she didn't feel up to answering any right now.

'You know,' Rosalie said, when there was a lull in the singing, 'when Jake saved me, I was on my way home from the hospital.'

'Oh,' Hester said. 'I'm sorry.'

'You didn't tell me that,' Jake added.

Rosalie shrugged. 'It wasn't important at the time. But I'd just been given the all-clear from breast cancer, after two years of treatment. I was in a daze. I thought I'd had my run, you see. I'd almost come to accept it, and then to be told I was free of the disease, that I was getting more years – in my ninth decade – it felt unfair to everyone who isn't so lucky. And then, of course, because of this astounding news, I wasn't paying attention, and if it hadn't been for Jake . . .' She patted his knee.

Jake shook his head. 'You wouldn't have been seriously hurt, even if the car had hit you.'

'You can't possibly know that, my dear boy. You got a glancing blow to your chest, went down and hit your head

147

on the kerb. I was convinced you were dead, and I wasn't the only one that day who thought your light had gone out. The relief when your eyes flickered, well, I almost fainted myself.'

Hester swallowed, her gaze going straight to the bruise on Jake's face. He'd been luckier than he'd led her to believe. She might never have ended up here, because there would have been no Jake Oakenfield left, on this planet, to need entertaining. The realization made her feel chilled, despite the snugness of the suite.

'Rosalie.' She heard the protest in Jake's voice.

'All I'm saying,' the older woman continued, 'is that every day we're faced with reminders of our mortality, so we need to live each moment as if it's our last. Transform hotel suites into Italian verandas; drink strong cocktails; and, if we're over eighty and have survived breast cancer *and* almost been hit by a car, take advantage of the man we've held captive out of gratitude and crash his dates with beautiful women in order to eat lobster and listen to *La Traviata*.'

Hester laughed, feeling instantly better. Rosalie looked like butter wouldn't melt, but she was clearly a powerhouse. Hester hoped that, if she reached that age, she would have the confidence to be just like her.

Jake picked up his drink, positioning the glass to hide his grin.

'Come on then,' Rosalie said to him. 'What Italian did you learn to impress Hester?'

'Oh, I don't think—' Hester started, but Jake's cheeks went a startling shade of pink.

'You see.' Rosalie's eyes gleamed. 'I have the measure of him, Hester. All the stubbornness in the world can't disguise who he really is: how soft his centre is. I had a boyfriend,

148

only a couple of decades ago, who set out to learn Italian for an upcoming trip by watching films with the subtitles on. Sadly, the only Italian language films he could find were porn films.'

Hester spat Aperol Spritz all over the table.

'I did tell him that "My God you've got a big cock" wasn't likely to be a phrase you'd need in an Italian restaurant.'

'At least you'd hope not,' Jake added, drily. 'Though I guess it depends on the kind of establishment you were aiming for.'

It took Hester at least five minutes to recover, tears of laughter streaming down her face as surprise mingled with the tension she'd been feeling all evening, the unexpected appearance of the photograph bringing her emotions rushing to the surface. By the time she'd calmed down, Rosalie had her coat back on and Jake had poured Hester a glass of water and was perched on the arm of her sofa, the amusement gone from his eyes.

'I won't take up any more of your evening,' Rosalie said, leaning down to peck Hester on the cheek, then pulling Jake into a gentle embrace and planting a kiss on the top of his head. Hester's eyes were still watery, but she didn't miss the intent in the old woman's gesture. She didn't think Rosalie would let Jake out of her life even when he was an ocean away. 'Goodbye, my darlings. I hope I'll see you again, Hester. I'm glad you're keeping this boy entertained.'

'You've been doing most of the entertaining tonight,' Hester said. 'It was lovely to meet you, Rosalie.'

She waved and slipped through the door, and then it was just Hester and Jake and the opera, continuing without their attention in the background.

'I think the gelato's probably melted,' she said. 'Pistachio soup for pudding, sir?'

Jake smiled. 'We could dip the castagnole in it.'

'Oooh. Now you're talking!' She moved to get up, but Jake slid from the arm of the sofa to the seat, so he was next to her.

'Are you OK?'

'Fine. Why?'

'That photo of you and your friend, it seemed to knock you sideways.'

'Betty wasn't really a friend.' She shook her head, because that seemed disloyal. 'I knew her for such a short amount of time, and I hadn't meant to show it, here.'

'To a near stranger, in a hotel room, when you're working?'

'I wouldn't say you were a near stranger. Not any more.'

Jake nodded, then shifted on the seat so he was facing her. Hester did the same, her left leg dangling off the side of the sofa while her right was crossed in front of her. Jake rested his arm along the back, his fingers close to her ear.

'What happened to her?' he asked.

Hester waited for another swell of emotion to pass, her internal sea getting choppier, then smoothing out, and exhaled. 'She collapsed on the plane,' she said. 'Half an hour out of Edinburgh.'

Jake winced. He slid his finger gently into the hair above her ear. 'Shit, Hester.'

She swallowed, his touch making her scalp tingle. 'I was twelve in that photo, on the way to Edinburgh with my parents for the festival. The flight was a treat, because I'd loved Amalfi so much the year before, and decided I wanted to travel – to fly – everywhere.'

'It must have scared you, at that age. I think someone collapsing on a flight would scare anyone.'

She nodded, even though it was the understatement of the century. She couldn't tell him that it was the worst day of her life so far; that it meant she had been unable to get on a plane since. He believed, wholeheartedly, that she was always jet-setting from one place to another, had been all over the world, seeing the sights that were so absent from his own work trips, living in luxury to prepare her clients for the same.

She didn't want to lie anymore. 'I was young,' she explained. 'I didn't really understand what was happening, at the time. She was so vibrant while I was talking to her, like a giddy, happy, human whirlwind. And then . . .' She took a deep breath. 'Anyway.'

'I'm sorry,' Jake whispered, adding a second finger to the first, the movements against her temple rhythmic and soothing. 'I'm so sorry that happened to you.'

'It was a long time ago,' she said, which was true, but didn't remotely convey the impact it had had on her. Betty, who had turned to her on the flight, who had sought her out and made her feel special, realizing that she was a fellow adventure-seeker, only to fade in front of her, collapsing onto the man in the next seat. There had been panic from the other passengers, a flurry of urgent activity from the flight attendants that Hester couldn't follow while her parents tried to shield her from what was happening. The horror of everyone on board; the shouts and crying; the moment when an oxygen mask was produced signalling a terror that perhaps there was something wrong with the plane, rather than just one, solitary passenger.

Hester took a long, slow swig of her drink, then let herself lean into Jake's touch. It wasn't fair, she realized. She was keeping so much from him, and he was giving her unreserved kindness. Still, she couldn't seem to stop herself from accepting it. He made her feel more grounded: everything about him was calm and solid, and tempered her waves of emotion.

'Rosalie guessed you had learnt some Italian for this evening?' she said, desperate to move away from Betty, back to the holiday she was supposed to be taking Jake on.

His gentle smile turned to a grin, and he wiped a hand over his face. 'That bloody woman! How did she know that?'

'What did you learn? Come on, Jake, tell me. Look at the setting. We're *in* Amalfi. If there was ever a place to practice your Italian, that place is here, the time is now.'

'OK, but I only learnt one phrase, and I don't know if the pronunciation is any good. I only thought of it this afternoon, so—'

'Stop adding caveats,' Hester said, laughing.

'OK. OK, then. Here goes.' He looked up to the ceiling, where the golden lamp above them, a smaller, subtler version of the glitter-ball chandelier in the lounge, was letting out a muted light. Hester stared at his throat, his collarbone, the skin tanned against the crisp white of his shirt. He dropped his head, looked her in the eye and then spoke, his voice lower than usual, the opera singers' world-class performances unimportant compared to Jake's words.

'Hester Monday,' he started tentatively. '*Sei una donna bellissima e generosa. Ti*—' He swallowed. '*Ti ringrazio dal profondo del cuore, per la tua gentilezza e il tuo tempo. Stasera é perfetta.*'

'Oh my God,' she whispered. 'That sounded . . . that was beautiful.'

Jake's smile was verging on shy.

'What did it mean? I got a couple of words, but—'

'Nope.' He shook his head.

'Jake?'

'Tonight we're in Italy, so you'll have to settle for the Italian. Shall we have some pistachio soup with pastry balls? The lobster was delicious, but I have space for pudding.'

Hester tried again, but Jake held firm, and she wondered about it all the way home, typing the words she remembered into her notes app as soon as she left his suite, with his warm kiss branding her cheek and an agreement to be in touch tomorrow. It was futile. She had no idea how to spell the few words she thought she could remember, and anyway, she had been mesmerized by the beautiful language – the language of love – spoken in his soft, deep voice.

She got home and made herself a cup of night-time tea, the piece of malachite warm in her palm, her fragmented memories of the flight with Betty closer to the surface after seeing the photograph again, having to recount some of the details to Rosalie and Jake. She was cleaning her teeth when Jake's message came through, repeating the words he'd said to her earlier.

Hester Monday. Sei una donna bellissima e generosa. Ti ringrazio dal profondo del cuore, per la tua gentilezza e il tuo tempo. Stasera é perfetta. Jx

Sitting on the back of her armchair, Hester copied his words into Google Translate and hit the button. Her whole body flushed warm, and she was glad that he hadn't translated it for her then and there, because she knew her self-restraint would have deserted her, that she would have leaned forward and pressed her lips against his, never mind polite pecks on the cheek and damn professionalism all to hell.

Hester Monday. You are a beautiful, generous woman. I thank you from the bottom of my heart for your kindness and your time. Tonight is perfect. Jx

Chapter
Seventeen

Tuesday

A takeaway coffee cup and a vanilla custard Danish were plonked on Hester's desk. Her colleagues were never this generous – apart from on doughnut Friday – unless they wanted something. She looked up from the photos of cherry blossom in Ueno Park sent to her by Amber, and smiled at Danielle.

Danielle rested one bum cheek on her desk, fluttering eyelashes coated in enough mascara to weigh her down when swimming. Cassie was out at a board meeting for one of the charities she was trustee of, and Hester was sure Danielle wouldn't be over here if their boss was in her office.

'Hi Hester,' she said. 'Got you a little treat.' She circled a finger above the cake.

'That's really kind of you, Danielle. Thanks.' She gave what she hoped was an end-of-interaction smile.

'How's it going?'

'How's what going?'

'This . . . thing. With your new client. Cassie said you were working on something special. I've picked up some of your work: Seb too. Must be important.'

'It is,' Hester agreed. 'It's going well.' Apart from having to transform Jake's hotel room into Japan in only a few hours' time. Amber's photos were beautiful, it was clear she'd put time and effort into planning each shot, methodical as always, but unlike Glen's Australian anecdotes, the stories she'd passed over were like something out of the *Lonely Planet Guide to Japan*.

They lacked the personal touch of Glen's trip through the forest to see the swirling sands of the Whitsunday islands, which meant that she would really have to work on creating something human and Hester-like in the titbits Amber had given her. And she didn't want to be inventing things at all.

'What you up to today?' Danielle leaned over to peer at Hester's computer screen, almost planting her elbow in the custardy middle of the Danish.

'Working on something with a bit of Eastern promise,' Hester said.

'Ooh Japan. I *love* Japan. You've never been there, have you, Hester?' She raised her voice, and Hester heard a guffaw from Seb's desk.

'Which means I really need to focus on getting this right,' she said firmly. 'Thanks for your help, Danielle. If you have any questions about the work Cassie's given you on my behalf, please just ask.'

'Oh, really? There was one thing, actually.' She sauntered over to her side of the office, picked up a ring binder and brought it back across the room. This time she plopped herself into the chair facing Hester's desk and pulled it up close. 'Could you go through the Holloway family's Orient Express trip with me? I'm struggling to see which bits you've booked, and which are still to do.'

Hester gritted her teeth. She didn't believe Danielle was really struggling – she'd left the Holloways' account in perfect order – and didn't understand why she wanted to sabotage her: unless she resented having to pick up Hester's work, when Hester had been chosen for something out of the ordinary. But she *had* offered. She would give Danielle half an hour, and that would still allow her time to gather her files and research, then get over to the Duval for lunch-time to see how Marty had got on with the items she'd asked for.

Hester could still fit everything in and not disappoint Jake. *With your lies*, her conscience taunted her. Hester pushed the thought away and focused on Danielle who, for once, was the lesser of two evils.

An hour later, she was beginning to despair. Danielle was acting like she'd never heard of geography before, let alone knew how to book a holiday for someone. Hester was being played and pushed, and was holding onto her patience by a thread.

'And so this hotel, here . . .' Danielle squinted and typed with one finger on her keyboard, spelling out *Gritti Palace, Venice* incredibly slowly. Hester took a deep breath and pushed her chair back.

'I'm sorry, Danielle, I'm going to need to pick this up with you tomorrow. I have to get on.'

'Oh.' Danielle looked up at her, wounded. 'OK. It's just you said you'd help, and I—'

'I'm sure you'll be all right now. Get Seb to help you if you have any more issues this afternoon.' She went back to her desk, unlocked her computer and stared forlornly at the photographs of the temples in Kyoto. Her head was too empty of facts, and she was running out of time. She needed fresh air and better coffee.

She picked up her handbag, put it on her desk and automatically pulled out her phone. Her screen had a slew of notifications on it, the top one from Marty:

Will save Japan for tomorrow. Let me know when you want to catch up. M.

Frowning, Hester scrolled further down. Had Jake cancelled on her? There were three messages from him.

Change of plan for this evening. Can do your destination tomorrow. Jx

Hester, OK? Let me know you've got this. Jx

Meet me outside the hotel at 7 p.m. We're going for a walk! Jx

She pressed her phone to her lips for a kiss, then dropped her gaze when she noticed Seb staring at her. She had a stay of execution, and could brush up on her Japanese trip for the rest of the afternoon and in the morning. It wouldn't give her time to create some *real* memories, but

158

it would give her the confidence to make it authentic, and for her client that was what mattered.

She sent him a message:

That's not part of the plan! You're paying me to send you to exotic locations. x

He replied almost instantly.

No arguments, Hester. 7 p.m. outside the hotel. Jx

Relief squashed her caffeine craving and she returned to her work, ignoring Danielle's loud, fake protestations from the other side of the office. She would not be manipulated by the woman determined to take her job and see her fail.

The Thames was green-grey and fast moving when she walked across the bridge that evening. Jake's meet-up time had allowed her to stay at work later than usual, giving her a quiet hour once Seb and Danielle had left to finalize her plans for the following evening. Cassie had returned at three o'clock looking harassed, and shut herself in her office for the afternoon, so Hester was undisturbed. By the time she left she felt much more prepared, not to mention curious about what Jake had organized. Whatever it was, it wasn't part of their arrangement. She was supposed to be entertaining *him*.

London was busy with post-work people sliding into bars and restaurants, commuters heading for trains and buses, a mass of faces and colour and noise. Hester felt the giddy rush of anticipation as she joined the throng, tasting the brine of the river and exhaust fumes in the air, feeling the setting sun against her face. She knew that, as much as she would love to spend time lying on a sun lounger on a tropical island, staring at her painted toes and the picturesque tableau of the sea and sky beyond, she wouldn't ever tire of her home city.

A city that, for the next few days at least, also contained Jake Oakenfield.

In a place so busily chaotic, he was a calming pool of shimmering blue water that she was hopelessly drawn towards. There was something solid and steadfast about him, even though proximity to him made her heart race. He never seemed embarrassed about showing himself to her: even dressing-gown clad and in pain, he had let her in, had spoken to her frankly. *Honestly*. Hester picked up her pace, hurrying down the steps of Hungerford Bridge and onto the bustling Embankment, as if she could run away from the discomfort of that thought.

Was she blowing it out of proportion? If she admitted to Jake that she'd never been to Australia, that the last time she'd seen those Italian views had been that holiday, when she was eleven, would he brush it away as nothing? Would he see that she'd understood what he needed and brought it to him, and that was all that mattered?

She was torn, because if he wasn't bothered, then it meant that he saw her as nothing more than her job: a woman who could provide the entertainment he'd asked for. If he was upset that she'd lied, then she'd be gratified that he cared enough about her to mind, but she would never be able to take it back. What she *should* be doing was treating it like any other project: giving him all the promise of these places, just as she would with a family or couple who were travelling there, and not think anything more of it.

The sun hit the upper windows of buildings as she got nearer to the hotel, heavy clouds meeting overhead as if gathering for a clandestine meeting, squeezing the light into intense, golden rays. Away from the river, Hester could smell rain in the air, feel a hint of the autumn that was fast approaching, crisp and fresh and renewing after the sultry Indian summer.

Jake had taken control of tonight, and at least, Hester thought, as she hefted her handbag higher on her shoulder, she wouldn't have to lie. She would put the professional travel agent aside and be Hester Monday for the evening. She hoped Jake wasn't disappointed.

She turned the corner and faltered. He was standing at the bottom of the steps, waiting for her.

Chapter Eighteen

Tuesday

Jake looked like something out of a horny dream Hester had had when she was sixteen years old: dark jeans and white, scuffed trainers, a plain white T-shirt under a battered brown leather jacket. His brown curls were more dishevelled than usual, and he hadn't shaved, perhaps thinking that the stubble would distract from his yellowing bruise. The effect was overwhelming.

'Hey,' he said, raising a hand in greeting.

'You're outside!' Her eyes slid up and down him as she got closer, the view as addictive as a sunset over the Manhattan skyline.

'It's a lot,' he admitted. 'Fresh air and sunlight. I'd almost forgotten.'

'You need vitamin D.'

'I need a change of scene.' He leaned down and kissed her cheek, the brush of stubble making her skin tingle.

'Isn't that what I've been doing?'

Jake gave her his lopsided smile. 'Believe me, I would have lost my mind before now if it hadn't been for you, but tonight I thought we'd go somewhere I'm familiar with.'

Hester laughed. 'London?'

'New York.'

'You're kidnapping me and taking me home with you?' She wouldn't even mind.

'There's a restaurant in Soho. New York decor, New York food and cocktails.'

'You're homesick.'

'You already know that. Shall we?'

'Soho's about fifteen minutes away. Do you want to get a taxi?'

Jake started walking. 'I swear to God the other guests think I'm some kind of hotel pet, wandering along the corridors in my joggers. I'm surprised I haven't been told that I'm putting them off their caviar, but I suppose that's Marty's doing, making sure my weird behaviour is accepted. But I need to get back to doing normal things: walking properly, rather than shuffling.'

'Doesn't it hurt?'

'It does, but that doesn't mean I shouldn't be doing it. Come on, I promise this'll be worth it. How often do you go to New York?'

They stopped at a crossing, the traffic idling engines at the lights like restless horses, and Hester glanced at Jake, wondering if he felt any kind of nervousness around cars. If he did, it was likely to be a bigger problem than her phobia of flying. But he didn't seem tense, and she resisted the urge to squeeze his hand because, even if he *was* worried, he would hate her making a thing of it. Getting back to normal was his goal.

'I've never been to New York,' she admitted.

He looked at her, surprised. 'Seriously? It's not a hot destination for your clients?'

'It is, but I could never get to all the places I send people to, or I wouldn't have any time to book holidays for them. I would love to go, though. Which part do you live in?'

'The West Village,' Jake said. 'It's pretty great. It's got a lot of heart, some really interesting architecture. Good independent cafes and restaurants, ideal for those Sunday mornings I was talking about: reading the paper, drinking coffee and people-watching. I can't believe you've never been.'

'Get over it, Hot Shot.' She nudged his arm.

He laughed and coughed into his hand. 'OK.'

'What's with the get-up, anyway? This looks like it's a few decades old.' She pinched the sleeve of his jacket. The leather was impossibly soft.

'It is,' he admitted as they walked into Leicester Square, a funfair squashed into the tiny garden in the centre, a Ferris wheel and carousel a wash of gaudy lights and electronic music, the air filled with the sweet scent of candy floss. 'I was only meant to be here for three days, so I haven't got much stuff with me. Beth got some old clothes from Mum's house: T-shirts and jogging bottoms. I think she brought me the jacket as a joke: as a *look what you used to wear* offering. But I loved this jacket, and it seems that, as unfashionable as it is, I still love it.'

'You look great in it,' Hester said.

'Thanks. I will be auditioning for *Top Gun Three*, obviously.'

'You can't unless you have Aviators.'

'I've got some of those, too.'

'Oh God, don't put them on. I'll have to spend the evening standing around while people ask you for autographs, even though they don't know exactly *which* film star you are.'

'You think I look like a film star?'

She did, but she wasn't going to admit it. 'I think that no sensible person would be stupid enough to walk through Soho on a cloudy September evening wearing a battered leather jacket, white T-shirt and aviators, unless they really wanted to be noticed.'

'You're being pretty brutal tonight,' he said, stopping outside a glass-fronted restaurant and holding the door open. 'You're crushing my happy nostalgia, wiping away the Vaseline lens glow. I'm going to have to put the jacket back into storage.'

Hester grabbed his sleeve and pressed her nose into the soft, worn leather. 'Never put it into storage,' she whimpered. *'Never.'*

When she looked up, a woman in a uniform of white shirt and short black tie was staring at her from just inside the door.

Jake cleared his throat and Hester let go, stepping behind him as he walked into the restaurant. 'Smooth,' he whispered.

'Thanks,' she murmured.

'Reservation for Jake Oakenfield,' he said to the woman, and they were shown to a table at the back of the restaurant, Hester letting her gaze settle on every inch of their impressive surroundings.

The room was double-height, with bottles of every spirit imaginable nestled on shelves around a pillar in the centre of the 360-degree bar, creating a tower of multicoloured glass that was reflected in large mirrors on the walls. Hester wondered if anyone asked for a single malt from the top shelf just to be difficult, but thought that they probably had one of those wheelie ladders to deal with requests like that. Against the back wall and towards the ceiling, there was a huge, glittering photograph of the New York skyline at night, a thousand crystallized lights in silhouetted buildings drawing Hester's eye. It looked like a window, as if they really had been transported to one of the most famously vibrant cities in the world.

The bartop was dotted with lush green ferns in coloured pots, smaller versions in place of flower vases on every table. The floor was black-and-white checkerboard, the bar stools were cream, and the booths around the edges of the room had claret-red leather benches and granite-effect tabletops. It was to one of these that the woman led them, handing out menus as Hester slid into the curved booth and Jake followed.

They sat at right angles to each other; not quite opposite, not quite adjacent, both with a good view of the space, which Hester decided was magnificent. Why had she never been here before? It could be a special occasion destination for her, Amber and Glen, even if it was out of budget for their regular Thursday night catch-ups.

'This is New York, then?'

'It's a slice of it,' Jake said. 'I love this place.'

'I can see why.' She scanned the menu, overawed by the cocktail list. 'It has to be a Manhattan, doesn't it? For the full experience.'

'I'd say so.' Jake was giving her that amused, affectionate smile that Hester found so distracting.

'What is it?'

'You're so wide-eyed about this place, and at the hotel. It's refreshing. Despite your job, you're not jaded or cynical about anything: you don't seem tired of any of it. It's as if your mind is wiped clean when you sleep and everything is fresh and new in the morning.'

She shrugged, returning her gaze to the menu. 'I'm surprised by at least one thing every day. Aren't you? I mean, I've lived in London all my life and I never knew this place existed.'

'I suppose not everything meets our expectations,' Jake said.

Hester laughed. 'I meant in a *good* way. Happy surprised, not disappointed. If that's your attitude, then I feel sorry for you.'

'I guess these last few days I've had more of an idea what you're talking about.'

'Live opera performances and cuddly crocodiles?'

'He does have a name, you know. Stanley. Don't forget it, Hester.'

'How could I? The way you fell for that dude warmed the cockles of my heart.' She didn't admit that, after their Australian night and Jake's affection for the fluffy reptile, she'd asked Marty to save one of the crocodiles – the smallest one – for her. Stanley Mk 2 now lived in her cavernous handbag.

The waitress came to take their drinks order, and Jake asked for a Manhattan and a tonic water.

'You're not having one?' Hester asked. 'I'll start to feel like I'm being chaperoned.'

Jake laughed. 'I upped my painkillers to cope with the

walk, and I don't think mixing alcohol and codeine will make me a great dinner companion.'

'I don't know, it might have been highly entertaining. How *was* the walk?'

'OK,' Jake said. 'Not as tough as I thought it would be. I'm healing.'

'Of course you are. You're a young, healthy man recuperating in a luxury hotel. You'll be back on your feet – properly, I mean – and back on the plane home, in no time at all.'

She hoped her smile was easy-breezy, but he must have seen through it because the one he gave her in return was decidedly lacklustre.

The waitress returned with their drinks, and they ordered steaks with fries and peppercorn sauce, Hester's mouth watering at the thought.

'To New York,' she said, holding up her glass.

'New York,' he echoed.

Hester took a sip of the amber drink, and felt it burn all the way to her stomach. 'Wow.' She put it on the table. 'A cocktail to be sipped slowly. This is the strongest Manhattan I've ever tasted.'

'They don't pull their punches,' Jake said. 'With anything.'

Looking around the gorgeous space, Hester had to agree.

The steak was melt-in-the-mouth delicious, the sauce was fiery and creamy all at once, and the fries were crunchy and so salty they were almost encrusted. She could eat the whole meal every day of her life, and never get bored of it. She cleared her plate and saw that Jake still had a mound of fries left.

'Not hungry?' she asked.

'Go ahead.'

Hester did.

'Why did you bring me here?' she asked eventually, when she'd finished most of Jake's chips and was on to her second Manhattan. 'I'm supposed to be taking *you* on staycations. On our little hotel room holibobs.'

Jake winced. 'Do you have to use that word?'

'Holibobs,' Hester said reverentially. She slunk closer to him along the bench, letting herself drink in scruffy, Top Gun Jake, with his stubble and his bruise and those blue eyes, shining like sapphires in his pale face. 'Holi,' she whispered. '*Bobs*.'

'Shhhhh.' He leaned towards her, and she got a whiff of Ocean Haze aftershave.

'Do you want to go on your *holibobs* with me, Jake Oakenfield?' she murmured. 'Isn't that even better than a staycation? Let's get matching *holibobs* tattoos to remind us of this magical time.'

'Stop it.' His lips curved upwards.

'I do think it's a great name for them, though. Hester's Hotel Holibobs. Where shall we go on our next holibobs, Jake?'

He shook his head. 'Hester Monday.'

'Yes?'

'Be quiet, now.'

'Holibobs,' she whispered.

'OK then. You asked for it.'

He closed the gap between them and kissed her, his soft, full lips finding hers, the pressure enough for her to part them, to match him movement for movement, for her to feel it all the way down her chest, into her stomach, following the whisky's path, and then lower. He brought his hand to her jaw, and his thumb stroked her cheek, gently, rhythmically. Hester was vaguely aware that they were still in the restaurant, and very aware that she was on fire, that sensations that had been boarded up for a long time were breaking free, singing and dancing and clamouring for Jake. For more of him. All of him.

When he pulled back and dropped his hand, his eyes lit with the same flame that was scorching through her, she wanted to follow him, to touch him again.

He coughed, turning away from her, and when he met her gaze again, his cheeks were flushed.

'I don't like the word holibobs,' he said calmly. 'But I did like that.'

Hester wanted to laugh. She wanted to climb into his lap. 'What now, then?'

'Dessert?' he asked, and Hester wondered if he was referring to the sundaes on the menu, or something else.

Chapter
Nineteen

Tuesday

W hen they left the restaurant it was raining. Hester's jacket had a hood and she put it up, but she was concerned for Jake and his leather jacket. Not just because his jacket was soft and she loved it, but because Jake looked tired, with purplish smudges under his eyes. They'd talked easily over a shared piece of New York cheesecake – what else? – that had so much vanilla in it Hester had moaned out loud at one point, but the kiss had shimmered between them, a firefly of feeling and possibility.

'Should we get a taxi?' Hester asked, expecting Jake to protest.

'Sure,' he said, coughing into the collar of his jacket.

Car headlamps turned the wet roads into diamond pathways, and the smell of hot, damp tarmac was enticing and electric, like the static in the air after a storm.

Hester and Jake sat close in the back of the cab, but she

was careful not to slide into him when they went round corners in the late-night traffic, to spare his ribs and her growing desire. She insisted on paying, and they got out into the rain and hurried past the doorman, who smiled and let them into the hotel lobby.

Hester stopped just inside the door. 'I should go and get my train,' she said.

'Come up for a bit. We hardly talked about New York, and that was the whole point of tonight.'

'You—' she wanted to tell him he looked too tired, but he would hate that. 'What kind of hot chocolate do you get in New York?'

'The best kind,' he said, smiling. 'I'll order down for some.'

His suite looked strange without the trailing pink flowers or fairy lights, though Stanley lay along the back of one sofa, grinning at her. Hester shrugged out of her coat while Jake disappeared into the bedroom. She heard him cough, heard him swear, and went to the doorway. He had his arms raised awkwardly, a navy jumper half on, half off.

'Here, let me help.' She found the hem and pulled it down gently, and after a moment Jake's face reappeared, his curls a tangle, a sheen of sweat on his brow.

'Thank you,' he said. 'Are you warm enough? You can borrow a jumper if you like.'

Hester shook her head. She was wearing a thin red shirt, but the suite was cosy enough for her. 'You sure you want me to stay?'

He walked out of the bedroom and she followed, sitting beside him when he patted the cushion next to him.

'If you were making an itinerary for New York, where would you go?' he asked, ignoring her question.

174

'Uhm, West Village, obviously. Especially now I know you live there and love it: nothing beats a personal recommendation. I want to do the proper touristy things, the Empire State Building, Fifth Avenue, and I've heard so much about the High Line, I would love to go there.'

Jake nodded. 'The High Line lives up to the hype. Where else?'

'I want to do the Manhattan Island cruise and the sunset sail, and I want to eat at Katz' Delicatessen and wherever you like to eat most, especially after tonight's food. I want to—' She sighed, filled with a sudden longing for all the trips she'd planned and never taken, for Jake and his easy New York lifestyle, if that's what it was; if he was painting an honest picture of it. 'I want to do so much.'

He tucked a few strands of her hair behind her ear. 'I want to show you all those things,' he said. 'I'd take you everywhere.'

This time when he kissed her, it was slower, softer and even more arousing, as if he was bringing her to life one nerve ending at a time. She leaned into him, felt him grip her waist, only the thin fabric of her shirt between his fingers and her skin. She slid her hands into his hair, snagged a curl and twisted it around her finger, sucked on his bottom lip.

'Hester, fuck,' he whispered against her lips. 'I'm sorry, I shouldn't have—'

'What are you sorry for?' She laughed softly. 'This? This is what we should have had for dessert. I feel spoiled, getting both.'

He pressed his forehead against hers, his skin hot, and then kissed her again, pushing her back against the sofa cushions, sliding his hand under her shirt. She felt his chest on hers, felt him pull back and then settle, more gently, on top. He was solid and warm, and she loved the weight of him. She wished he hadn't put his jumper on because it meant there were more layers to take off. Still, her hands found their way to the hem of his jumper and pulled up just as she'd pulled down, and then there was a loud knock on the door, followed by, 'Room service,' and the sound of the latch turning.

'Shit,' Jake muttered. He braced his arm on the back of the sofa and got up. Hester heard the thud as Stanley rolled off and onto the floor, and hid her smile.

The door opened and Felicity came in, wheeling a trolley with two giant mugs of hot chocolate on it, a tower of cream and marshmallows adorning them.

'Here you go, Jake,' she said. Her eyes flitted from him to Hester and back again. Her smile was suddenly brighter, and a lot less authentic. 'Enjoy!'

'Thanks, Flick.' Jake followed her, waited for a few moments, and then, when Hester couldn't hear her soft footfalls any more, he flipped over the metal *Do Not Disturb* sign and shut the door. He leaned on it, closed his eyes briefly and then, ignoring the tray completely, came back to the sofa.

'Now,' he said, lowering himself down. 'Where were we?'

'I *think* you were telling me where you'd take me in New York,' Hester said.

'Oh yes,' Jake murmured, undoing the bottom button of her shirt. 'That's right. I didn't hear you mention Central Park. You'd want me to take you there, I assume?'

'I would,' Hester scratched out as his fingers touched

the sensitive skin of her stomach. She leaned back, watching a curl fall over his forehead as he made his way slowly up her body, undoing her buttons, exposing her purple, flowery bra.

He looked up at her. 'Nice,' he said. 'I approve.'

'So, Central Park,' Hester murmured as he kissed her jaw. 'It's worth going to?'

'Yeah, definitely.' He brushed his lips against her cheek, her jaw, the bow of her mouth, and then, just as she was about to kiss him back, he moved lower again, trailing a line of hot, tender kisses down her neck and to her collarbone.

'At the north edge, here, you've got the woods and Harlem Meer.' He planted a kiss at the edge of her bra strap. 'Then you stroll further down, along the trails, and you find the North Meadow. There are great views of Manhattan from here. You head further south, south . . .' He kept kissing her, his nose brushing her skin, his lips hot, and Hester closed her eyes and tried to stop a moan escaping. Jake was killing her one feathery kiss at a time, and she wasn't sure if she would make it to the other end of the park.

'What's south?' she asked.

'There is so much going on further down,' he explained. 'So much to explore. There's the reservoir, of course. Named after Jackie O. And on still autumn days you won't see a more beautiful sight. The water is a piece of glass, and the trees reflected in it are every shade of an American fall, framing the New York skyline. You can stay there for hours.' He pressed his lips to her belly button, kept them there for several agonizingly delicious moments, and then continued his descent.

'But there is so much more, still. You've got the Met, and this little pool called Turtle Pond. Though we're talking

177

American scale, so it's actually not that small.' He laughed softly into her skin, then coughed, clearing his throat, and Hester shuddered from the top of her head to her toes. This, she thought, was easily the best tour she'd ever been on. She waited, wondering what came south of Turtle Pond, her body thrumming with anticipation.

'What's next, Jake?' she asked. And then she realized she could no longer feel his breath, or his lips, against her. She opened her eyes.

He was kneeling on the cushion, one hand gripping the back of the sofa, his other arm clutching his chest. His head was dropped, but she could see that he was struggling for breath, his torso rising and falling unevenly.

'Jake?' She sat up and squeezed his shoulder. 'Jake, what is it?'

'Fine,' he managed. 'I'm fine.'

But he clearly wasn't. 'Jake.' She tipped his head up, her fingers under his chin. He was pale, apart from his cheeks which were flushed pink, and there was panic in his eyes. 'Cough, Jake. Can you cough?'

He drew in a breath, and she heard it rattle through his lungs, and then when he coughed it was like an explosion, shaking his whole body, going on and on, while he clutched the sofa with a white-knuckled hand. She could almost feel the pain that he was in.

'God,' she whispered. 'God oh God oh God.' She looked for her handbag, and saw it discarded on the opposite side of the room. She rushed over, grabbed her phone and took it back to the sofa.

Jake's coughs had subsided and he'd collapsed against the cushions. His gaze was slightly unfocused as he said,

'I'm fine. I need to finish your tour.' He smiled at her, but she shook her head. She didn't like how pink his cheeks were, or the sweat darkening his hairline.

'We're putting my tour on ice,' she said, pressing a number in her phone. 'Hi, Marty?' Jake made a noise of protest, but she knew she was doing the right thing. 'Are you working tonight? Oh, thank God. I'm worried about Jake.'

By the time Hester and Marty had convinced Jake to get into bed, Marty had called the hotel doctor just to be on the safe side, and the doctor had arrived and shut himself in the bedroom with his patient, Hester had convinced herself that Jake was mad with her. But she wasn't sorry: better he was mad and OK than passed out on his hotel room floor.

The doctor emerged and told them both that Jake was fine, that he was just exhausted and hadn't been doing the breathing exercises needed to keep his lungs clear, and that if he didn't start he was in danger of risking an infection – even pneumonia. Hester's relief that it wasn't anything more serious, even though it *could* have been, was like a ton weight being lifted off her own chest.

Marty said he'd show the doctor out, and said goodbye to her with a squeeze of her arm, and assurances that when he finished his shift, the other concierges would be fully briefed and know to treat any calls from this suite as a priority. Hester thanked him and shut the door, the quiet and calm profound after the flurry of panicked activity.

She padded on bare feet into Jake's bedroom, where the dim glow from the bedside lamps showed him propped up on a mound of pillows, his T-shirt back on after the doctor

179

had examined him. As Hester approached the bed, his eyes flickered open.

'What time is it?' he asked, his voice hoarse from coughing.

Hester glanced at her watch. 'Twelve thirty.'

'You've missed your train.'

'It doesn't matter,' she said.

'You're staying here?' His eyes were tracking her, and she was relieved that his colour had returned to normal, neither deathly pale or overly flushed.

She shrugged, held up the lilac throw she'd found in a drawer. 'The sofas are huge and comfortable.'

He shook his head, held his arm out.

'Jake—'

'I'm fine,' he said. 'Dr Hughes said so, didn't he? Just a reminder that I'm not back to normal yet. Besides, I'm not going to try anything. But you're stuck here because you were looking out for me, and I appreciate it.'

'You couldn't breathe, Jake.' She climbed onto the bed and crawled up it, towards his arm. 'I was hardly going to say '"see you later, got a train to catch," was I?'

'Shirt and trousers off. You can borrow one of my T-shirts, in the top drawer, then under the covers.'

'You're very demanding for someone who could barely speak an hour ago.'

Jake rolled his eyes and waited.

Hester pointed at the bathroom and then slipped inside. She took her time, washing her face and rubbing toothpaste against her teeth with a finger, her pulse refusing to settle even though she knew that, now, her place in Jake's bed wouldn't be under the same circumstances as she'd imagined it might be, earlier.

180

She tiptoed back into the bedroom, saw that he was still awake and went to the chest of drawers, taking out a grey T-shirt. She undid the buttons of her shirt and slipped it off her shoulders, sat on the bed and wriggled out of her trousers, then pulled on the T-shirt, aware of Jake watching her the whole time. She tugged back the bed covers on the empty side, slid in between layers of cool, pillowy cotton and nestled into the crook of Jake's shoulder, leaning her head gently against his chest.

His arm came around her, folding her into him. 'It's OK,' he murmured. 'I won't break.'

Hester closed her eyes and tried to slow her pounding heart. 'Night, Jake,' she said.

'Hester?' he whispered.

'Mmmm?'

He exhaled, and she felt his lips brush the top of her head. 'Your tour of Central Park.'

She smiled against his chest. 'It was a very tantalizing teaser.'

He groaned. 'I wasn't going for *teaser* when I started it.'

'I know, but we—' She brushed her lips against his chest, the soft fabric of his T-shirt. 'We can always try again, another day.'

'I'd up my game,' he said, his voice thick. 'Make it even better than I was planning to tonight.'

'Well then,' she said. 'How could I resist?'

He slid his hand down and wrapped it around her hip, squeezing gently, and Hester silently cursed his decision to leave the hotel tonight: to push himself to the point of exhaustion, despite their wonderful New York dinner.

'Goodnight, Hester Monday,' Jake said quietly. He kissed

her forehead, and she felt him shift against the cushions. It was a matter of minutes before his breathing settled, a slight rasp left over from his coughing fit, and his fingers loosened around her hip.

Hester moulded her body against his, and told herself that he was fine now: that the doctor wasn't worried, so she had no need to be, either. Still, it was a long time before she stopped listening to his breathing, and let sleep come for her, too.

Chapter
Twenty

Wednesday

She was woken by a stream of sunshine sliding through a crack in the curtain, picking her out like an actor under a spotlight. She rolled over, her brain registering that her bed felt particularly comfortable, before her memories filtered back and she remembered where she was, and what had happened the night before. A moment later, her body was tingling with awareness, and she turned her head and opened her eyes, finding a pair of blue eyes staring back at her.

'Jake,' she said. 'How are you feeling?'

'Good. Fine.' He smiled. 'I slept well for the first time in ages. Must be having you in my bed.'

'Or that you were completely worn out last night,' Hester said.

Jake made a noise of protest and leaned towards her.

The small part of Hester's brain that told her this was too good to be true was swiftly overruled, and she reached for him, twisting the fabric of his Top Gun white T-shirt as he kissed her, as he moved on top of her, sliding his hands up under her – *his* – T-shirt.

'Hester,' he whispered, between kisses. 'Stay here all day, with me.'

'Jake.' She arched into him, wanting to feel him everywhere, to match chest with chest, hip with hip, leg against leg. But she couldn't, not now. 'I have to go to work.'

'This could be a continuation of Italy,' he murmured, 'or New York. Anywhere you want it to be. I don't care. All holidays have beds. All the best ones should have great sex.'

'I know, but—' she gasped as his hand slid further up, his touch soft and teasing. 'But I need to go in to the office, to prepare for Japan.'

'I don't care about Japan,' he said. 'I care about you.'

It was like a bucket of iced water, drenching her. 'Jake!' She pushed down into the mattress and slid herself up the bed, out from under him. 'I need to go in. I'm spending so much time here, with Marty, getting things prepared. I need to show my face, at least.'

'Stay for a bit?' he pleaded. 'An hour?'

She shook her head. 'I'll come back this evening, I promise. But you need to rest after last night, and I really have to go to work. I can't just go AWOL because I . . .'

'Because you what?' Jake sat back on his haunches, his blue eyes fixed on hers, his lips looking so kissable as he smiled.

'Because I would rather stay here, in this bed, with you.'

'You admit it?'

'I'm not here under sufferance.'

He nodded. 'You want to be here as much as I want you here.'

She swallowed, forcing herself to keep her eyes on his face, and not let them fall lower, to see just how much he wanted her to stay. It would snap the last thread of her resolve.

'Can I use your shower?'

'Of course,' he said, and she scrambled off the bed, went into the bathroom and shut the door. She didn't have time to go home and change, so she would have to put up with Danielle and Seb's snide comments, because while they didn't notice much about her, they would certainly notice that she was in the same red shirt as the day before.

But that, honestly, was the least of her worries.

Jake had said he cared about her. But he couldn't really, could he? This time last week she hadn't even met him, and while they'd spent a lot of time together since then – intense time, too: basically several evenings of a holiday, of *staycations,* where senses and pleasure were heightened – what he was feeling, what *she* was feeling, couldn't be anything more than infatuation. It couldn't be real, because she'd lied to him from the beginning.

When she came out of the shower, Jake wasn't in the bedroom, and she dressed quickly, found her handbag and added what little make-up she had with her: mascara, powder and a bit of blusher.

Jake was sitting on the sofa, wearing the white towelling robe and flicking through a newspaper. The room smelled of coffee, and Hester saw a pot on the table with two mugs, and a plate of buttery-looking croissants. He looked up as she hovered in the doorway, and put his paper down.

'Will you eat something before you go?'

'Sure.' Her stomach rumbled, and she sat next to him, on the sofa where, the night before, he'd kissed his way down her stomach. He held out the croissants and she took one, began tearing it into pieces on her plate while he poured them both coffee.

'Milk?'

'A little, please. Thanks.' It was reassuring. He couldn't really care about her if he didn't even know how she took her coffee. It wasn't real: she hadn't lied to someone she had genuine feelings for. She had done her job, had met the brief she'd been given.

She accepted the mug from him, and they exchanged smiles.

'You are coming back tonight, aren't you?'

She thought of all the pictures and facts she'd collated, the stories she'd gleaned from Amber about her time in Japan, that she was preparing to adopt as her own for Jake Oakenfield's benefit. 'Of course,' she said.

'Because if what happened – what *almost* happened last night . . . If you're worried it shouldn't have—'

'I wanted you, Jake,' she cut in, not prepared for him to say anything more about feelings. 'I wasn't exactly protesting. I wouldn't have wanted to stop if it hadn't been for your . . .' She waved a hand in the direction of his chest.

He sighed. 'I am getting pretty bored of it now.'

Hester popped a bit of croissant in her mouth to give her time to think. 'It's just not what I was expecting, that's all. It's surprised me. Hasn't it surprised you?'

He nodded. 'But one of those good surprises, like you were talking about last night. I'm learning a lot from you, I like spending time with you, and I want to keep going.'

'So Japan, then.' She stood, leaving her breakfast and coffee unfinished. 'I'm already going to be late.'

Jake stood too, stepping towards her. 'I'll see you later.' He ran his thumb down the side of her face, leaned in to kiss the corner of her mouth. 'This can be whatever we want it to be, you know. If you have rules at work about fraternizing with clients, then I will stop being your client.'

'It's not – we don't. I have to go, Jake. I'll see you this evening.' She left him standing in the middle of the suite and slipped out of the door. It wasn't the walk of shame, she thought, as she hurried down the corridor towards the bank of lifts, but the walk of thudding realization.

Hester worried the events of the past sixteen hours over in her head on the walk across the river. Of course she fancied Jake: she had from the first moment she'd seen him. And she had known that he liked her, because it was part of the reason he'd invited her back, and obviously they had a connection. *Obviously*.

But he lived in New York. This was all temporary. They couldn't have genuine feelings for each other – not after such a short amount of time.

When she arrived at Paradise Awaits, Danielle, Seb and Cassie all greeted her, made no mention of – or gave her googly eyes about – her outfit, or the fact that she was half an hour late. It seemed they all had other things on their mind, and it was soon clear that it was destined to be one of those days where chatter was light, and everyone kept their heads down. Hester was so relieved, she got them all coffee from the cafe two doors down.

Then, when she looked at her Japan research, everything came back surprisingly easily, and instead of feeling panicked about later, she felt calm. It didn't matter that they had only known each other a few days: she wasn't going to lie to Jake any more. She would still dress his suite as Japan, she would still take him there, but she would tell him the truth about where she'd got the stories and photos. And then she would tell him she'd never been to Australia, and that the last time she went to Italy she was eleven. He might be furious with her or he might shrug and tell her it didn't matter, but whatever happened, she would be being honest with him.

And if he *was* OK with what she'd done – if he was prepared to forgive her – then she would take him back to that glorious big bed, and regardless of whether they were supposed to be in London or Japan or Timbuktu, she would kiss and touch him everywhere, and let him do the same to her.

'Hester?'

She looked up, sure her cheeks must be flushed, and saw Cassie smiling at her. 'Yup?'

'How's it going with Beth's brother?'

'Oh, good. Great, in fact. He's still a bit under the weather, but I think we're doing an excellent job of distracting him. It's Japan tonight.' She gestured to the brochures on her desk.

'Fabulous. Glad to hear it's all working out. I did wonder when he told me what he wanted, but it seems you're rising to the challenge. And it's showing you, I hope, that you have the ability to be flexible?'

'Of course,' Hester said. 'Though without the Duval's help, none of these nights would be nearly so impressive. It would take us weeks to source the kind of thing they can organize in a couple of hours.'

'I expect Jake was aware of that when he asked us to do

this,' Cassie replied. 'Beth says he's a realist, that he isn't the type to demand things for the sake of it. But that doesn't mean your input should be considered any less important. Without your vision, there would be nothing for the hotel to get hold of. You've created these occasions for him. Just *you*, Hester.'

She shifted in her chair, uncomfortable. 'What are you saying?' She glanced behind her, but Danielle was out to lunch and Seb was turned sideways, on the phone to someone while he clack-clack-clacked his biro against his desk.

'I'm saying that you shouldn't underestimate yourself. You're capable of more than you think you are, and the next time I get a hotel opening, I want you there. No excuses. Wherever it is, whatever else you're supposedly doing, it's yours, Hester. You're going.' Cassie gave her a triumphant smile, as if she'd just offered her the biggest prize of all, as if it really was as simple as that. Hester had no idea what expression she volleyed back, but if it was anything other than a panicked grimace she would have been surprised.

She was officially on a countdown. Her secret would be uncovered, and then her job at Paradise Awaits would be over.

Her project with Jake suddenly took on even more meaning, which was unfortunate when it was already so overloaded with emotion it was in danger of tipping over. Now it might also be her Paradise Awaits swansong: the last thing she achieved before she had to quit and find a career that she was much more suited to, without her fear of flying hovering like a devil at her shoulder, but also without the potential to get her over her phobia.

She had thought being a part of this team would mean

she would come to see flying as the norm, something to take in her stride. She had hoped that, after a year of working here, she would have got over it and taken numerous flights. But of course that hadn't happened. It had been easy to excuse herself, to hedge, and she hadn't even come close.

And now Cassie had finally run out of patience. She was giving her the opportunity that should have been the start of a new phase of her life, but Hester felt rooted to her chair, so filled with fear at the prospect of flying she felt physically sick. No, she had not eased herself into getting better. She had stuck her head in the sand and made it a hundred times worse.

She had to accept that she couldn't do it, that she would never be able to. She would organize a few more virtual holidays for Jake and then he would fly, out of reach, back to New York, and Hester would be left with no job, no idea what to do next, and no Jake Oakenfield.

Chapter
Twenty-One

Wednesday

'These cherry trees are beautiful,' Hester said in the lift, Marty half hidden behind the wide swathes of blossom, the two trees like oversized bonsais, perfectly shaped and in black marbled pots. They had just about managed to get them on the trolley, and Hester was sure her unexpected strength was due to the nervous energy firing through her veins like a ball in a pinball machine.

She was going to tell the truth. Jake would be OK with it, or he wouldn't. It was time, it seemed, for her to start being honest with everyone around her: to accept the consequences and see where it left her. It was ironic that it was her project for Jake that had encouraged Cassie to be more demanding, as if somehow, somewhere deep down, he already knew she'd been lying and was making her face up to it.

'The restaurant was very accommodating,' Marty said smoothly, which she thought meant that they had paid handsomely to borrow the trees. She would see later: he sent her his costings after every evening, and she added them to her spreadsheet. Some of the prices had made her eyes water – getting a visit from Jackman the joey especially – but Cassie had assured her she had carte blanche to do what she needed to. Hester had wondered whether that instruction had come directly from Jake, or if Paradise Awaits had simply charged him a premium for his strange request. That thought made her even more nervous, because she was potentially about to bring the whole thing crashing down.

'What are we going to do with Jake?' Marty asked now, as they reached the floor of his suite and the lift doors opened with a swoosh and a ping. 'Is he up to his usual circuit after last night?'

He wheeled the trolley out and Hester followed, staying close in case either of their trees decided to topple over. 'He should be. The doctor said he was struggling because he hasn't been doing his breathing exercises: that he's been letting the pain rule him when he should be working through it. How anyone's supposed to *not* let that sort of pain rule them, I don't know. The walk to Soho was prob- ably too much,' she added, wincing because he'd done that for her. 'But he still needs to keep moving.'

'Right then,' Marty said, knocking on the door. 'We'll tell him to sod off for a bit and do that while we sort out the room.'

'We should have got him out before now. It's going to ruin the surprise.' She gestured to the trees. She should have cared more, but Jake already knew about Japan, and this evening was about something else now, anyway. For her, at least.

'He's had a guest up with him,' Marty said.

'Oh?' Hester wondered if it was Rosalie or Beth. Maybe Tamsin had agreed to come too, so she could gaze adoringly at him.

'Some friend of his called Richard,' Marty said, and knocked on the door again, Hester's stomach swooping uncomfortably as he added, loudly, 'It's Marty and Hester, Jake.'

'Richard?' Hester whispered, a sense of foreboding making her shiver.

The door was yanked open and Jake stood there, in jeans and a tatty brown jumper that made him look rumpled and gorgeous.

'Marty! Hester!' He greeted them enthusiastically. 'Come in. Meet Rich.' He stumbled back into the room and Marty gave Hester a curious look before pushing the trolley inside.

'Actual fucking cherry trees?' said a voice. 'Seriously, man, this is fucking nuts.'

Hester stepped sideways so the trees weren't blocking her view. Her sense of foreboding turned swiftly to despair. There was a half-empty whisky bottle on the table next to two glasses, and a man with floppy blond hair sprawled on one sofa. He was wearing a blue-and-white striped shirt with a stiff white collar, his top button open, his tie half-undone. Hester *hated* those shirts.

'I know,' Jake said. 'I told you, there are no limits with this woman. This amazing woman.' He came towards her, held her face in his hands and kissed her. The tips of his fingers were cold and he smelt of whisky, dark and smoky. Hester backed away, glanced at Rich again and then, help-lessly, at Marty.

'I'll bet,' Rich leered. The grin he gave her made the back of her neck prickle in warning.

'Do you and your friend want to go down to the bar for half an hour?' Marty asked.

'No,' Hester said quickly. 'No need. We can work around you.' She smiled, hoping it looked genuine.

This was the friend Jake hadn't wanted to call because they always ended up getting drunk together. And Jake was definitely drunk, standing a few feet away from her, looking puppy-dog bemused that she'd rejected his kiss. Hester felt irrationally angry. The night before they'd had to call the doctor for him, and now he thought *this* was OK? If they went to the bar, God knows what state he'd be in when he came back.

'You sure?' Marty asked.

Hester nodded. 'We can work around them,' she repeated, and Marty, lifesaver that he was, took a single second to understand everything she was conveying with her eyes.

'Work around me all you like, darling,' Rich said. 'I'll just sit here and watch you.'

'That sounds like a good plan, Hester,' Marty said, ignoring Jake's friend. 'Shall I go and get the rest of the stuff, or do you want to do that while I stay here?'

'I'll be fine here,' she said.

'You're positive?' Marty's brows furrowed.

'Positive,' Hester said firmly.

'I'll order up some coffee.' Marty walked slowly, pointedly, to the door. 'I'll be ten minutes, max.'

Hester watched him go and then went briskly to the trolley, unravelling the strings of fairy lights, these ones pink to match the cherry blossoms. She stared at them, feeling for the first time a shock of embarrassment at her silly, childish attempts at being creative.

'Hester,' Jake said softly. 'Are you OK? Was work OK?'

'It was fine,' she said, not facing him.

She took a long, deep breath and went to the plug socket in the corner, the suite now so familiar that she knew exactly where to weave the lights – around lamp stands and on top of picture frames – where they would stay up and look pretty. *Pretty*. She'd never thought what she was doing was pathetic before, but now, with Rich's eyes on her – she could feel them, like a damp, cloying fog – she did.

'Are you sure?' Jake was slurring his words slightly, and she would have found it adorable if she wasn't so mad, so worried about him, so cross at his recklessness. He came up behind her and put his arms around her waist, and her body responded to the Jake it knew: the Jake who'd kissed her and made her laugh, who was thoughtful and astute, and who'd given her a tour of Central Park with his lips on her skin. She couldn't blame her body. Her mind was fighting her anger, too.

'Hester,' he murmured into her neck, and Rich gave a catcall from behind them.

'Whoop. Get a room, you two! Oh wait, you already have. Get in there, Jakey boy. She is a *stunner*.'

Hester pushed herself out of Jake's arms and spun round. 'How dare you speak about me like that while I'm standing here! Not even *to* me. I don't care if you're drunk, that is no excuse.'

Rich gawped, his ruddy face oozing surprise. Clearly he wasn't used to being stood up to.

Jake blinked and swayed, a rabbit in the headlights. He

reached out to her but Hester took a step back. 'I'm not doing this, Jake. Not now.'

'Hester, please. I had no idea Rich was coming, that he even knew I was here. I'm sorry, I—' His voice cracked, and he coughed, which fanned the flames of Hester's irritation. 'I'm sorry. Forgive me?'

Hester tried to respond, but found she couldn't. Those were the words she should have been saying to him tonight, but she couldn't do it now; not while he was drunk and Rich was here.

'Lovers' tiff, is it?' Rich called from the sofa.

'Shut up, Rich,' Jake said, without taking his eyes off her. 'Hester, I'm so sorry.'

'You shouldn't be doing this,' she said, unable to hold it in, even if it wasn't her place to tell him. 'You shouldn't be getting half-cut like this, not on the painkillers you're on, and not after what happened last night.'

Jake blinked. 'I thought you were cross because of tonight, because you're here with your cherry trees and your fairy lights. Again.' He grinned, but it was a sloppy grin, a caricature of his usual self, and Hester looked away. 'You're here and I'm a bit drunk. I thought that was why you were cross.'

'It is!' Hester shot back. 'Of course I'm angry about that. You knew I was coming, and you knew that—' She paused, breathed, not wanting to talk about that morning, about what she'd stopped between them in order to get to work, while Rich was listening. 'It's disrespectful. But I'm also angry because you seem unable to look after yourself. It's not my job to look after you – I am just providing a service, after all – but that's what I've ended up doing. Or maybe that's what you wanted the whole time? Someone to mother you.'

196

'That is *not* what you're here for,' Jake protested. He stumbled sideways, finding the back of the nearest sofa and leaning against it, his shoulders slumping. 'I know this shouldn't have happened, but it's just . . . it's so boring, being stuck here every day, waiting for you to turn up in the evenings. I was all ready to check out, to book my plane home and then, last night, that bloody doctor said—'

'You were going to check out and go home?' Hester cut in, his confession pushing everything else out of her thoughts. 'When?'

Jake must have heard the change in her tone, something about it lancing through his drunk brain, because he stood up straighter. 'Well, not immediately, but—'

'Tomorrow, you said,' Rich finished for him. 'One last night to have Hester here, and then you were fucking off out of London again, as bloody always. So you see, Hester love, this was *my* last chance, too. To get some quality time with old Jakey boy.'

'Tomorrow,' Hester repeated dully.

'I hadn't confirmed it,' Jake said, running a hand through his hair. 'I promise. I wasn't thinking—'

'No, clearly not,' she replied. 'Not about anyone other than yourself, anyway. But that's fair enough.' She swallowed the emotion burning up her throat. 'I'm just here to entertain you. No need to keep me informed about your plans. Use me until you no longer need me, then check out without looking back. I don't know why I'm surprised.'

'Hester, wait!' Jake stood up, but she slipped easily past him and opened the door, leaving behind the cherry trees and the fairy lights, feeling a swell of shock and anger, and a big, hearty dose of intense stupidity. Of course he hadn't

197

cared about her. He'd just wanted her in his bed, to *entertain* him before he went back to his precious New York life.

She headed for the stairs, not wanting to wait for the lift, banking on his drunkenness holding him back.

'Please don't do this,' he called down the corridor.

She didn't answer, didn't turn around. She hurried to the stairs, yanked open the door that slid back slowly on its expensive, weighted hinges, which only made her madder. Fuck Jake and his wanky friend and his deceit. He could go back to New York whenever he wanted, and she hoped he was in pain all the way through that long, arduous flight, and that his apartment was empty and cold and unloving when he got back.

Fuck you, Jake Oakenfield, she said to herself as she flew down the steps, only stopping when she'd reached the ground floor and was sure he wasn't following, and taking out her phone. She ignored his missed calls and was tapping out an apologetic text to Marty when she felt a hand on her shoulder.

She looked up quickly. 'Marty,' she said, her voice wavering with relief. 'I can't do tonight: I'm so sorry. Let me know what you've spent, and of course we'll still cover all the costs.'

'Are you OK?' he asked, his eyes sharp with concern.

'Yes.' She exhaled. 'No. Sort of. I'm going to go home, and then . . .'

'I'll get a car to take you over the river.'

'You don't need to do that.'

'I'd like to.'

She walked into the foyer, her gaze tracking back to the stairway door, the lifts, hoping she'd be out of here before

Jake appeared – if he was even coming after her. But he had Rich and his whisky, his flight home. He didn't need her anymore.

'Just out the front,' Marty said when he reappeared. He led her to a waiting black car, all sleek lines and gleaming door handles, that was idling at the bottom of the wide hotel steps.

'Thank you,' Hester said. 'And not just for this.'

Marty nodded. 'Jake's a good guy. I know he didn't give that impression tonight, but whatever's happened, I don't think he would ever intentionally do something to upset you.'

'It doesn't matter,' Hester said, forcing a smile. 'It was only ever going to be temporary. Maybe it's better that it ended like this.'

She thanked Marty again, said goodbye, then climbed into the back seat of the car, leaned forward and gave the driver her address. The man nodded, flashed her a warm smile, then pulled away from the kerb, into a London that was busy with post-work promise, the golden haze of a mesmerizing sunset falling below the buildings.

She made it to the end of the road, the car pausing at the junction, waiting to turn right onto the Embankment, before she decided that it was all wrong. She didn't want to be driven home by a chauffeur: she had never been a guest at the hotel.

'Excuse me,' she said. 'Thanks very much for the lift, but can you let me out here?'

The driver glanced in the mirror, then reversed slightly, bringing the car to a stop at the side of the road. He turned to face her. 'Are you sure?' he asked.

'I am. Thank you so much.' She stepped out into the cool evening, casting a glance back at the Duval's grand facade, which she could still, just about, see. She doubted she'd be back here again: not for a while, anyway.

By the time she was on her train home, her phone switched off and her attention firmly on the London sights slipping past her – so the other passengers couldn't see her red eyes – travelling out of the centre and towards the leafier south-east suburbs, all her anger had gone. She didn't want Jake to hurt on his flight home, or for his apartment to be unwelcoming. She wanted him to be happy. She just wished he'd been happy spending time with her, at least for a few more days.

Chapter
Twenty-Two

Wednesday

When Hester got back to her block of flats, the sun almost gone and the sky a deep turquoise, she was calmer. It might well have ended tonight, anyway. It was less than a week out of her life, and she need not let it upset or sadden her. She would ignore the fact that these last few days had taken a bigger proportion of her emotions than they were entitled to: that spending time with Jake had been exhilarating and fun, that she had started to crave his company, to think about him whenever they were apart.

She would have to put his blue eyes and his curls, the feel of his fingers and his lips – and his drunken, confused expression when she'd walked away – out of her mind. She would move on. Maybe she would even jump on the trip abroad that Cassie had promised her and fulfil all her potential, she thought, and then laughed as the stairwell light buzzed. No, of course she wouldn't.

'Hester.' Vanessa's door opened as she reached her landing.

'Nessa.' She turned round.

'My God, girl, what's up with you?'

'It's a long story,' Hester said.

'Good, I like those. Lyron's round for tea, and I've made extra. Get yourself sorted, wash your face, and be knocking on my door in fifteen minutes.'

'Oh Nessa, I don't think I can.'

'That's all the more reason why you should. Fifteen minutes, Hester, otherwise *I'll* come knocking.'

Hester nodded and went into her flat. She switched on all her fairy lights, dropped her clothes – yesterday's clothes – into the laundry basket and stepped into the shower, trying to wash away her regret, and the memory of Jake's expression when she'd left the suite. She hated that that was the last time she'd see him: that, after all the fun they'd had together, it had ended so badly.

She dried herself, wrapped her towel around her and wandered back into the living room. She switched her phone back on, waiting while it booted up and the screen filled with notifications, pinging and pinging into the quiet. She saw the messages, the missed calls, from Jake and Marty, and then Beth and Cassie. Her heart jolted. *Beth and Cassie?* Why on earth were they calling her?

She had a horrible thought: that Jake had followed her to the stairwell, had tripped or fallen in his drunken state, had done himself more damage. *No no no.*

She hurried to unlock her phone and then looked at the messages, scrolling through them quickly: Marty asking if she was OK, and why she'd cancelled the car; Jake pleading with her to answer; Cassie asking if she was all right, that she knew something had happened and she wanted to check on her; Beth apologizing for her idiot brother.

Hester looked at the times the messages had been sent, and saw to her relief that Jake had been texting her up until half an hour ago. The most recent message, sent twenty minutes ago from Marty, settled her pulse as she leaned against her armchair.

> That twat Rich is gone. Jake's drinking coffee, and if it's any consolation, he's mortified. I've never seen anyone so perfectly embody regret. Hope you're OK, love.

She replied.

> Thank you for letting me know. Glad Jake's OK. I'm fine. Will be in touch about settling up, and thanks again for all you've done. H xx

> That sounds like a goodbye, Miss Monday. I hope not.

Hester smiled, left her phone on the counter and got dressed, then went to spend the evening with her neighbour.

Vanessa's brown stew chicken was the perfect dish for Hester that evening, with its rich, creamy sauce, thick-cut vegetables and melt-in-the-mouth chicken, served with her non-alcoholic rum punch.

Her flat was a haven of colour and warmth, every surface covered in trinkets, rugs overlapping on the floor, crocheted blankets on the backs of chairs and photographs covering the walls – some landscapes, some close-ups of flowers, but most of them people: laughing children and families sitting round tables; costume-clad women lying on beaches with their hands up to shade their eyes from the sun. It was a hug of a flat. It said: this world, and everything in it, is for sharing with others.

'Sounds pretty terrible,' Lyron, Nessa's son, said, as he spooned stew into Hester's dish, and she'd come to the end of telling them about her evening, and all that had led up to it. 'Sounds like the guy is a douche.'

Hester shook her head, trying to laugh and brush it off. Lyron was a couple of years older than her, a family lawyer in the city, handsome, intelligent and funny, and committed to his girlfriend Allie, who worked as a freelance graphic designer.

'Jake isn't a douche,' Hester protested, gratefully accepting a full plate from him. 'At least, sober, not-influenced-by-Rich Jake isn't a douche. He was just drunk, and he's not had the easiest run of it, with the accident and being stuck in London, and maybe he needed to let off steam with someone he could talk rubbish with. Everyone needs that occasionally, don't they?'

'Of course they do,' Nessa said, bringing in a steaming bowl of rice from the kitchen. 'But he shouldn't have been talking rubbish to *you*. He should have respected you, Hester. Whether you were there as a professional or a friend. There were no circumstances where it was OK.'

'It was his friend who was the idiot,' Hester said, suddenly feeling guilty for talking about it. 'He didn't say anything offensive.'

'He should have apologized for this Rich bloke, then,' Lyron said. 'Told him to get out.'

'We all do stupid things when we're drunk,' Hester replied.

'Why are you defending him?' Lyron asked.

'Because he was more than just a client,' Nessa said. 'It's obvious, Lyron. Aren't you supposed to be able to read people in your job?'

'I can read people, Mum. I just—' He gave Hester a curious look. 'You liked Mr Douche, before he went all douchey? You only met him last week.'

'Attraction can be instant,' Hester said. 'And believe me, Jake is attractive. And it wasn't just the way he looked, either. After the first couple of times, when I planned those nights for him . . .' She shook her head. She didn't even have any photos of him, she realized, which was crap when they'd had three staycations together. How could she ever claim to be an expert on holidays? She'd taken a photo of him with Jackman the joey, so he could send it to Rosalie, but it had been on his phone, not hers. They should have had one selfie in front of the bougainvillea, at the very least.

'You were fallin' for him.' Nessa sat in her chair and sighed, then heaped a mound of rice next to Hester's stew. 'And then he was an idiot.'

'He lives in New York,' Hester said. 'If it was anything, it was an almost-holiday romance, and I've never had one of those before.'

'You've *never* had a holiday romance?' Nessa's eyes widened. 'Not with all those work trips you go on? Get away, girl.'

'Not exactly the most professional thing, is it, Mum?' Lyron suggested.

Hester wondered whether they would notice if she took her bowl of stew back to her own flat. Their good-natured bickering was usually fun to watch, to occasionally engage with, but tonight she wasn't in the mood.

'Those work trips are only ever for a few days,' she explained. 'So there's not a lot of opportunity.'

'But more chance with your staycation plans?'

'It was just me and Jake, night after night. Acting out these strange, virtual holidays, with the food and wine, the music and the views, flowers and fairy lights—'

'You and your fairy lights.' Vanessa gave her an indulgent smile.

'Always fairy lights,' Hester murmured, but her words were shining their own light on what had happened. 'I was forcing us into this weird, fake holiday state, so it's no wonder we ended up getting close, is it? I mean, he is completely gorgeous, but I don't know whether I really, properly liked him, because we barely know each other. And he said he cared for me, but I bet those feelings are as unreal as our nights together were. It's horrible now, because I feel like he disrespected me, getting drunk like that when I was coming over, but he's a grown man: he doesn't owe me anything. He can do whatever he wants. God, it's me who's been the idiot.' She rubbed her forehead and then, her speech over, she felt slightly lighter. She heaped a forkful of stew and rice into her mouth.

'Almost convincing,' Vanessa said.

'Almost,' Lyron agreed.

Hester chewed and swallowed, then glanced between the two of them. 'What?'

'You fell for him, my darling,' Vanessa said. 'It's all over your face, thick in your words. You're always good at the stories, always giving them to me with so much detail and

206

humour and romance, but this one is different. This one has a little more heart in it: more authenticity.' She spoke the word slowly, annunciating every syllable.

'You've got yourself a crush on a drunken douche,' Lyron added, his dark eyes sorrowful.

Hester couldn't do anything but laugh. 'He is *not* a drunken douche,' she said. 'Anyway, I'm not going to see him again, am I? We need to stop dissecting this and talk about something else. Nessa, your stew is incredible as always. Lyron, tell me about your latest case.'

He winced and shook his head. 'No can do. I can't give you any details, and even if I could, you wouldn't want to hear them.'

'Tell Hester about your puppy.'

'A puppy?' Hester sat up straighter. 'Oh yes, that is exactly what I need right now. Has he wee'd on your work shoes?'

'And my briefcase, and my suit jacket, and our bed, and my favourite chair.'

Hester laughed. 'Oh my God! What's his name? What kind of dog is he?'

'He's a cocker spaniel called Barkley, and he is driving me insane.'

'Why didn't you bring him round here? I would *love* to have a cuddle with a puppy right now.'

'He would have peed on you,' Vanessa warned. 'I've told Lyron he's not allowed here until he's toilet trained.'

'And I wanted a night away from his antics,' Lyron added. 'But, I give you this, you can't stay mad at him for long. He's got these big brown eyes, and he looks at you like he can't believe you're telling him off. I try to stay angry at him, Hester, I really do, but it's impossible. Once he's worked his way in here . . .' Lyron patted his chest. He was wearing a faded *Red Dwarf* T-shirt, had managed to change out of his work clothes before coming over, which was a rarity with his long office hours. '. . . which takes about two seconds flat, he's there for good.'

Hester fixed a smile on her face. She wasn't thinking about the puppy any more. Perhaps it hadn't been the right topic to take her mind off things, after all. 'I'd love to meet him,' she managed.

'One day,' Vanessa said, 'when he's learnt how to behave. Eat your food, Hester. I'm having none of that loss-of-appetite-heartbreak stuff. You need to keep your energy up, dust yourself off, move on.'

'I do,' she said. 'I will. Everything's good.' She pictured Jake, his blue eyes wide with surprise when she raised her voice. But he wasn't in her heart or her brain for good, was he? He was a client. She'd done what he'd asked and now it was over.

'Excellent.' Nessa pointed at her. 'So eat your stew and make sure you've got room for dessert.'

Hester ate. She cleared her plate, and then, when they were all finished, she took the used crockery into Nessa's kitchen, which looked so clean they could probably have eaten the stew directly off the counter, even though she must have spent most of the day in there making it.

'Do you want me to serve the pudding?' she called, but there was no answer from the living room. She put the bowls in the sink, squirted in washing up liquid and ran the water until it was hot, watching the foam bubble up. 'Nessa?' she tried again. 'Want me to serve the pudding when I've washed up?'

'Leave that, Hester,' Nessa called back, and there was something about her voice that made Hester turn off the tap and walk back into the living room, where she came to a sudden stop, her breath lodging in her throat.

Nessa and Lyron both turned to look at her, Lyron from his seat at the table, Nessa from next to the open door of her flat, where she was standing with her hand on the handle.

'Hester,' Jake said from the doorway, 'can I talk to you? Please. Give me a chance to explain.'

Chapter
Twenty-Three

Wednesday

She'd left her fairy lights on, and they taunted her as she walked back into her flat, but she didn't want to draw attention to them by switching them off. She went into the kitchen and ran the tap, filling two glasses with water. When she came back into the living room Jake was standing on the threshold, as if wary about coming in even though she'd said he could.

'How did you find me?' she asked, gesturing for him to come in and handing him one of the glasses. He was wearing his leather jacket over the scruffy brown jumper, and his eyes were bloodshot. He looked worse than he had last night, after the doctor had seen him.

'You know *Pretty Woman?*' He gave her a sheepish smile.

Hester sighed. 'The driver had my address.'

Jake nodded. 'Marty told me, once he was satisfied I was sober enough to see you. He said he didn't like the way it had ended between us. I tried Cassie, but she wouldn't give out your address – which is right, I know – even when I told her that I'd royally fucked up and needed to speak to you, and that you weren't answering your phone.'

Hester sat in her chair and pulled her legs up under her. She indicated the sofa opposite and Jake dropped onto it with a sigh.

'Did you come here by car?' she asked.

'Yes, with Adam, who drove you about ten metres before you bailed.' He drooped slightly, like a flower that needed watering. 'I am so, so sorry. About Rich, and what he said, which was unforgivable, and about my plans. I want you to know I hadn't booked a flight back tomorrow, not even before the doctor told me to hold off for another few days.'

'But you were going to?'

'I had been thinking about it, before you swept me off to Italy. But even after that first night, after Australia . . .' He shook his head. 'I wasn't quite so sure. But I must have said the wrong thing to Rich, made it seem like the flight was booked. I swear I didn't say anything about having one last night with you: I was drunk, but I would never have said that, because I had never thought it.' He leaned forward, his elbows on his knees. Hester saw him glance at the bookshelf, where she'd put her piece of malachite when she got in. It was glistening, lit from below by the white lights that snaked along the shelf.

'You don't seem drunk any more,' she said.

'Marty filled me up with coffee, and gave me a piece of his mind – not that he needed to. I'm so sorry I fucked tonight up.'

'Why are you friends with that guy?' Hester took a sip of water. 'He's a dickhead.'

Jake dropped his head. 'I know. When we were younger . . . he was fun to hang out with. Before today, I hadn't seen him for about four years. We don't keep in touch other than when I'm in London. But I guess . . . when I didn't show up at the conference, word got out about what had happened and Rich tracked me down. I meant to have one quick drink with him, but then . . .' He shrugged. 'It was an idiot move, and I am so sorry I hurt you.' He slid gingerly off the chair, onto the floor, and walked on his knees across the rug towards her. 'Hester, please. I'll do anything to make it up to you.'

She sighed. He looked miserable and genuinely contrite, and it would have been a long journey, even in the comfort of the luxurious car, stopping and starting in traffic for over an hour to get here, facing the possibility that she would refuse to see him and he would have to turn around and go straight back.

'You were a horrible idiot,' she said.

'I know. I know that. Anything, Hester.'

She bit her lip. 'Stop kneeling on the floor like that. And take off your coat.'

It was his turn to sigh. 'I can't be too long. Adam's waiting for me outside.'

But right now she had him in her flat, without any made-up stories or drunk dickheads or people bringing them room service. She didn't want to let him go, but if she had to, she would take these few precious minutes. She thought of Vanessa and Lyron, their knowing, smug faces when, despite all their talk about Jake being a douche, they had waved the two of them back to her flat, Nessa staring at Jake with undisguised curiosity. She wished she had her own *Do Not Disturb* sign to hang over the doorknob.

Jake got up off the floor and she moved to the sofa, so they were sitting next to each other. She sat sideways and cross-legged, so she was facing him. He twisted towards her.

'I forgive you,' she said. 'For Rich and for ruining Japan, and for the mix-up over the flights. I'm not your keeper: it's not up to me what you do. You are your own man, and you can get as drunk as you like and go home whenever you want to, but right now you're in my flat. You came all the way over here to apologize, and I would hate to waste this opportunity.'

'You would?' She could hear the hope in his voice.

She nodded. 'We don't have Japan, but obviously there are fairy lights.'

'Obviously,' he repeated, the side of his mouth kicking up. That one, tiny action transformed him. Solemn, weary Jake was gone, and Hester felt the impact of him all over again, awakening every one of her senses. 'No night would be complete without fairy lights.'

'And if you really want an authentic holiday experience,' Hester went on, 'we could go back over to see Vanessa and Lyron. I've just had the best bowl of Barbadian brown stew chicken. She always makes a mountain, and I don't think she hates you too much to let you have some.'

'Why would she hate me?' Jake asked, and then realization dawned. 'Ah. Of course. But I'm not hungry. Marty force-fed me chips to sober me up before he agreed to call the car.'

'OK, then.' She leaned towards him. 'But if you kiss me, I'll probably still taste of it.'

He didn't reply, but she heard his breath hitch in surprise. He didn't need to be told twice. He reached forward, cupped the back of her head and leaned in, bringing her to meet him in the middle, their noses brushing before his lips found hers. He tasted bitter with coffee, sweet with whisky, heady with relief and desire, and Hester matched his urgency, kissing him back, sliding onto his lap so she was straddling him. She moaned softly as he ran his hands up her sides, then down her legs, his fingertips grazing the backs of her thighs.

'Hester,' he said raggedly, between kisses, 'I can't stay.'

'You could send the car away,' she murmured. 'He'd have to go back over the river anyway, with or without you.'

'No, I—' He broke away, looking up at her. 'Not like this. Not now, when it feels . . .' He exhaled. 'I mean, it feels so good, but I came here to apologize. I didn't expect—'

'I should think not.' She tried to sound scolding. 'If you had assumed we were making up this way, I wouldn't have let you in.'

He pressed his forehead against hers. 'Let me plan something for the weekend.'

She sat back slightly, and he held onto her hips so she wouldn't slide off his knees. 'What? No. You sorted out New York, and since then I've done nothing—'

'Because I sabotaged it,' he said. 'Anyway, I'm through with these staycations, these holibobs or whatever you want to call them.' He squeezed her hips, his gaze serious. 'I have loved them, Hester. You know that. But I want to take you somewhere real.'

Her heart sped up, and her palms were suddenly clammy. 'What do you mean?'

'I'll need to arrange a few things tomorrow, but would you come away with me on Friday? For the weekend?'

Hester gripped onto his shoulders as if he was a life raft. 'Where?'

Jake laughed. 'Don't look so terrified. Whatever I've told you, whatever Beth may have said, I don't hate this country. There are some parts I love. Let me take you to one of them.'

'Are you sure that's a good idea? Aren't you still supposed to be resting?'

'What I'm planning won't involve any heavy lifting: I'm suggesting a relaxing weekend away. Will you think about it, at least?' he added, when she gave him a sceptical look. 'Let me know by tomorrow night?'

'I'm out with friends,' she said. 'Our usual Thursday catch-up.'

'Let me know by the time you get home, then.'

'I will,' she said. 'And . . . thank you.'

Jake laughed softly. 'You don't know what I'm planning, yet. It could be a tent in a field somewhere.'

'As long as you're there, it'll be perfect.'

She said it without thinking, and when the words echoed in her head and threatened to derail her, she leaned in and kissed him again. He kissed her back, holding her tightly, stealing her breath and her thoughts, until there was nothing left but sensation. He kissed her so thoroughly she felt her limbs lose their strength, all her heat and energy coiling low down in her stomach, her nerve endings alight at the places where their bodies touched: their lips and thighs, his hands on her waist, hers in his soft curls.

'Do you really have to go?' she whispered against his neck.

He groaned and slid forward. 'I should, I—'

'Stay.' She bit his bottom lip.

'Hester.'

He cupped her jaw in both hands and planted a firm kiss on her lips. 'I am going to go back to my hotel, and you . . .'

'Me?'

He shook his head. 'Friday, Hester.' He pushed gently on her thigh and she reluctantly stood up, then held a hand out and pulled him to his feet.

'You did this on purpose, didn't you?'

'Did what?'

'Left me like this.' She gestured to her swollen lips, her entire body humming with desire.

'I'm not exactly immune,' he said softly. And then, 'Come away with me, Hester. I don't want to do this now, when my head's pounding and the whisky's still burning in my stomach and Adam's waiting downstairs. If our first time is make-up sex, then it's not the most auspicious start, is it? Let me do this properly. Let me get this one thing right.'

'You've just proved my point,' she said, grinning at him. 'You made sure I wouldn't be able to say no.'

He pressed his thumb to the side of her mouth, then replaced it with his lips. 'Think about it,' he whispered, then he turned and walked out of her flat, closing the door gently behind him.

She lowered herself onto the sofa, his words replaying in her mind. *If our first time is make-up sex, then it's not the most auspicious start, is it?* She wanted to know, more than anything, what Jake thought it was the start of.

She tried not to think about the one thing she'd promised herself she'd do that evening: tell him the truth about her non-existent travel history, about the fabrications of

217

Australia and Italy, about how she was grounded, hiding behind her ability to weave stories.

She had promised herself that one thing, a silent promise to Jake, too, and he had come all the way over here to apologize, to make things right between them, and she had been a coward. And now he wanted more for them than their faux vacations, with her as tour guide, him as willing tourist. If they were beyond her acting as his travel agent, did that mean she could leave Australia and Italy in the past, wipe the slate clean and be honest with him from now on, without having to go back? But even as she stood and went to the window, watched him climb into the back of a familiar dark car, she knew she couldn't get away with that.

The problem was that now, the choice she had told herself he had to make – to either accept what she'd done and forgive her, or decide to move on and never see her again – was no longer a choice Hester wanted to offer him. Already, the thought of losing Jake was too much for her to bear.

Chapter
Twenty-Four

Thursday

'You have bagged yourself a holiday romance?' Amber said, as they sat at one of their favourite hammered metal tables, the shrieks of people running in and out of the fountain undimmed despite the turn from Indian summer to autumn, the nip in the air that Hester loved so much shimmering through her like a chilled glass of wine. 'Someone who doesn't actually go on holiday, because you refuse to get on a plane?'

'You know it's not about refusal,' Hester said, surprised that she'd picked that part of her friend's assessment to respond to, but finding it easier and more familiar than her blossoming relationship with Jake. 'I would *love* to get on a plane and fly off to wherever it is Cassie wants to send me, but there are certain parts of me, like my legs and my brain and my lungs, that overrule my wanting.'

'It's your head,' Glen said. 'All of it is in your head. That panic attack you had at Stansted? In your head.'

Hester rolled her eyes. 'I know where it comes from, Glen. I know exactly when my phobia of flying started. But knowing doesn't make it any easier to deal with.'

She watched as sympathy softened her friends' expressions, and wished she'd zoned in on the whole holiday romance thing, instead.

'Anyway,' Amber said, rescuing her, 'back to Jake. You were tasked with giving a guy a load of fake holidays, and now you've thrown in a fake holiday romance for free? Was that an add-on, or something?'

Hester returned Amber's smile. 'You're outrageous, you know that? No, of course it's not an add-on. We just . . . we like each other. He is kind, and funny, and genuine. And he's not ugly, either. Why does it matter how it's come about? Loads of people meet at work.'

'So you've told him about the flying issue?' Glen asked. 'He knows you made up all that Australia stuff, because there's no way you could have possibly been there?'

Hester stared at the wine in her glass.

Amber sighed. 'Glen's right, Hester. Obviously it takes a while to get to know someone, but this is a fundamental part of who you are. And especially if you started off pretending. It can't go anywhere, really, if you're not being honest with him.'

'I am not defined by my weaknesses,' she said.

'No, you're not. But you don't want to be defined by your dishonesty, either, do you?' Glen raised his eyebrows, looking at her over the rim of his glass.

'It was a few little fibs, so I could give him the experiences he'd asked for. I didn't tell him I was the world's greatest flyer, or brag about all the places I've been to.'

'You sort of did, though,' Amber said. 'You took Glen's stories from Oz, and mine from Japan.'

'Exactly,' Hester protested, 'because you offered. You encouraged me to do this from the start.'

'Because we didn't realize you liked the guy so much: that you were willing to look after him when he got sick, that he was prepared to track you down to your home address to apologize for being a twat. We love you, Hester.' Glen draped his arm around her shoulder. 'And however this plays out, whether he goes back to New York in a few days and that's the end of it, or you both decide you want to stay in touch, to keep whatever this is alive for a longer haul, you're not going to be able to live with yourself if you don't admit that you've lied to him.'

'We know you,' Amber added. 'With your friends, with people who matter, you don't lie.'

Hester groaned and slumped forward, resting her forehead on her folded arms. 'What if he hates that I did this?'

'Then it's not meant to be, is it?' Glen rubbed the back of her hand.

Hester blinked up at him. 'There's always an air of mystery, of unreality, about holiday romances, though. They're not a deep dive into each other's lives.'

'Not emotionally, anyway,' Amber said.

'No jokes,' Glen replied, his face unusually solemn. 'This is not a holiday romance because you're not on holiday, and who even cares about labels? Just tell the man, Hester. Sooner rather than later. Tell him, or tell him you can't go away with him and that it's over.'

The truth settled, hard and heavy, in Hester's gut. Her friends were right. Whatever this was, however long it was destined to last, she couldn't keep hiding the truth from Jake. She would go with him this weekend, and hope that, in the scheme of things, he would see it as a small anomaly: a blip on the landscape of their short relationship. It was early days, time to change things around.

'Come on,' Glen said, 'enough of being serious. You and Amber have to go and stand in the fountain as penance for making me talk about a guy for so long.'

'What?' Amber said. 'No!'

'Not a chance.' Hester laughed, picking up her drink. Glen took her handbag from the seat beside her and put it on his lap, then did the same with Amber's before she had time to react.

'You're not getting these back until you have tried to dodge the water spouts for at least five minutes. Off you trot.'

Hester exchanged a glance with Amber, then they both got up and walked over to the fountain, where a teenage couple were standing in the middle, kissing, oblivious to the water raining down on them. Hester imagined it was her and Jake, and tried to ignore the giddy rush of desire that went through her. It wasn't the first time that day that it had happened.

'So you're going to tell him then?' Amber said, as they stepped onto the square, facing each other, their shoulders hunched in preparation for the water assault. 'You're going to tell Jake everything about you and planes, about what happened with Betty, and why you've been grounded for so long?'

Hester squealed and jumped forward as a cold jet of water shot up her back, then pelted down on her from above, soaking her in an instant. 'I am,' she said, laughing and shivering as Amber was similarly attacked, a group of people watching them from the sidelines.

She didn't add that, since she'd met Jake, she hadn't really felt grounded at all.

Chapter
Twenty-Five

Friday

The following lunchtime Hester found herself, weekend bag in one hand, wearing a comfortable but – she hoped – attractive outfit of hip-hugging dark jeans and a thin red jumper, her other hand hovering above the doorbell of a large, stone house in Greenwich. She'd clipped her hair back, away from her face, and had on a snug pair of slip-on shoes. She felt relaxed and confident, and she would not, would *not*, be intimidated by the size of Beth's house.

The previous evening, soaked and shivering but still laughing after her trip under the fountain with Amber, a towel from God-knows-where wrapped around her shoulders, she had called Jake and told him she'd love to go away with him for the weekend. She'd already booked the afternoon off with Cassie, her boss more than happy to grant her permission after discovering that things were fine between her and Beth's brother. Hester had stopped short of telling her exactly *how* fine they were.

Jake had been pleased, a burr of excitement in his deep voice as he'd told her he would book everything. She'd almost felt the tension between them, almost believed that, if she looked up and over the Thames, in the direction of the Duval, she might see some kind of shimmering thread linking her to him. It was ridiculous, but she was enjoying feeling this way: the freedom and carelessness of it, giddy with lust and longing, thinking about him when she shouldn't be, despite the issues she still needed to deal with running underneath.

He'd told her to meet him at Beth's house at lunchtime, explaining that it was in Greenwich, an easy train ride from her office, a short taxi ride or longish walk from her flat. When she'd asked why, he'd said that he wanted to borrow Beth's car.

And now, here she was, standing outside the hulking, grey stone magnificence of Beth's house. It wasn't how she'd pictured a foster carer's home, but she had got the sense, from the way Beth had been comfortable in the upmarket London hotel, and Jake's ability to pay for whatever her staycations had required, that they were a family with money. And despite the posh facade, there were obvious signs that this was a family home.

A couple of plant pots along the front of the house had been pulled over, and a small plastic spade was sticking out of another. There was a cluster of bikes, ranging from tiny trike to adult upright with a basket, leaning against the wall, and there were stickers stuck to the inside of one of the downstairs windows: fairies and a unicorn, various dinosaurs and one large rainbow, a pot of gold gleaming at the end. It was clear that, whatever the state of Beth's finances, she was ploughing all her time and resources into looking after these children who hadn't been born into the privilege, or given the opportunities, that she had.

Smiling, Hester pressed the doorbell. There was a moment of silence and then a cacophony of noise from inside, a young voice shouting, 'I'll get it!' before the door was flung open and Hester was greeted with a boy who looked nine or ten, a shock of carroty curls above a freckled, interested face.

'Are you Hester?' he almost shouted.

'I am.'

'Great!' He held out his hand. 'I'm Connor. Jake's in there, with everyone. Did you know that he got hit by a *car*?'

'I did,' Hester said, hiding her smile at the boy's wide-eyed amazement. 'He was pretty brave, by all accounts, saving Mrs Dewey like that.'

'It's fucking wild,' Connor said, then turned and led her down a wide, cream hallway that Hester thought was a bold colour choice, considering most young children's enthusiasm for Sharpies. But it worked, acting as a blank canvas against the colourful toys, discarded at a moment's notice, and the bright paintings framed along the wall, a variety of styles and skill levels: a catalogue of all the children Beth had brought under her roof over the years.

'I heard that, Connor,' said a familiar voice as they emerged into a large family room at the back of the house. It encompassed kitchen, dining room and sitting area, a squashy sofa facing a wall-mounted television, two young children sitting on the rug with a series of coloured blocks between them. The space ended with a glass wall dissected by French windows, a plushly green garden beyond, where Hester could see a trampoline and a tiny football goal, along with a myriad of more bright toys.

'What are you going to say?' Beth folded her arms and gave Connor a straight stare, breaking the serious mask for a second to flash Hester a welcoming grin.

'But Jake said—'

'It doesn't matter what Jake said, and I will be dealing with him later. What do *you* say?'

'Sorry for swearing,' Connor muttered.

'Sorry *who*?'

'Sorry, Hester,' he said, turning to look at her, his shoulders stiff, like a robot under command. 'Sorry for swearing.'

'That's OK, Connor. Thanks for the apology.'

'Can I go outside now?' he asked Beth.

'Sure. Come back in for cake in ten minutes, though, OK?'

'Yay!' He ran outside, the telling-off forgotten in an instant.

'What have you been saying, Jake?' Beth asked, an eyebrow raised.

Jake levelled his sister with a smile, then his eyes met Hester's and lit up as he stood from the dining table, coming round it to greet her. 'Hester.' He pulled her into his arms and kissed her cheek. He was wearing a navy wool jumper with the sleeves rolled up to the elbows, and dark jeans.

Tamsin was sitting further down the table, slumped in her seat, ostensibly tapping away on her phone. Hester recognized her forced nonchalance, as if she just *happened* to be sitting there when Jake was, too. Her heart went out to the teenager. Jake Oakenfield, she was learning, was a heady crush to have.

'Hey,' she said, returning his embrace, indulging in the smell and feel of him, but still self-conscious: she could almost feel Tamsin's eyes burning into her.

'Oh no,' Beth said, 'you don't get away with it that easily. Have you been swearing in front of Connor? Hi, Hester,' she added, 'make yourself at home and I'll bring you a cup of tea.'

Jake kept hold of her hand, leading her back to the table. 'He greeted me with a rugby tackle. Usually I'm up to the challenge, but I may have sworn a bit when he barrelled into me.'

'You didn't tell him it was effing wild, though?' Beth switched on the kettle.

'No, because it wasn't. It was effing painful.' His gaze slid to the two toddlers, who Hester could see were engrossed in their bricks. 'I didn't realize he'd overheard. Besides, he knew exactly what context to say it in; he didn't learn it from me.'

'That's not the point. We shouldn't be encouraging him to swear.'

'I know that,' Jake said. 'But I'm not used to this. Kids. Being here.'

'And why is that, do you think?'

Jake rolled his eyes. 'How are you, Hester? Glad you found us OK. Dried off after the fountain?' Amusement gleamed in his eyes, and Hester could see he wanted to say something else, but that it was probably not for Beth or Tamsin's ears.

'It was freezing, but probably deserved,' she admitted. 'Glen said we were getting too serious.'

'This is Glen and Amber?' Jake asked. 'Bar manager and marketing executive?'

'That's right,' Hester said. They'd spoken a little about her friends during the call last night, and she could see he was trying to show an interest in her life outside their staycations. It didn't seem forced, but it did seem earnest, as if he'd convinced himself about the nature of their relationship and was laying down the building blocks for whatever that was. The thought excited and terrified her.

'What's this about a fountain?' Beth asked, bringing two cups of tea to the table and sitting down, her gaze flitting between Hester and the children playing on the rug.

Hester explained about her night before, leaving out the nature of the serious discussion – namely her need to tell Jake the truth – which had led to Glen coercing her and Amber into the fountain. Beth listened and laughed, the conversation turning to the nights in Jake's suite, as she was eager to hear what a virtual holiday consisted of.

'It forced me to think outside the box,' Hester said, 'but it was also a treat, having Marty and the hotel's resources at my fingertips. I got a taste of what it was like to be a VIP guest.'

'You were. To me, anyway,' Jake said quietly, and the look Tamsin gave her was pure venom.

'I was working,' Hester added with a laugh.

'But not any more,' Beth pointed out. 'You must have done a pretty good job if he's taking you to his favourite place in the world – other than the West Village, of course.'

'Favourite place in the *world*?' Hester turned to Jake.

He averted his gaze, which meant that Hester could examine him. He looked so much better than he had on

New York night; so much better than when he'd turned up at her flat, with his bloodshot eyes and regret. The bruise on his face had run through its gamut of colours and was starting to fade, and it made her wonder about the bruising on his chest that she'd caught a glimpse of.

'It's somewhere I'm pretty fond of,' Jake said eventually, then exchanged a look with his sister, as if to say, *Don't spill my secrets.* 'Somewhere I knew I'd be able to book for a couple of nights.'

'I love Norfolk,' Tamsin said. 'Beth took us there last summer. We played on the slotties in Sheringham, and had fish and chips on the prom. I even went swimming in the sea, in this neon pink bikini I've got.' She smirked at Hester, then gave Jake a bright smile.

'It sounds great,' Jake replied, no hint of annoyance that she'd given away their destination. 'I loved going to the arcades in Great Yarmouth when we were young. And on that rickety old rollercoaster.'

'It's a death trap,' Beth said. 'Look at it with adult eyes and you wouldn't set foot anywhere near it.'

'Are we going to Great Yarmouth?' Hester had also been there when she was little, with her mum and dad. There had been a pony-and-trap ride, she remembered, and what must have been the country's smallest reptile house, with a craggy-looking alligator she wasn't sure was even alive.

'No,' Jake said. 'That's not where we're going. You'll just have to wait and see. I'm nipping to the bathroom before we leave.' He finished his tea and went upstairs, while Hester used the downstairs cloakroom, which was painted bright orange with murals of fish and mermaids and other, dubious-looking sea creatures on the walls. When she stepped back

231

into the hall, Beth was leaning against the wall, arms folded, not even trying to pretend that she was doing anything other than waiting for her.

'You know,' she said, smiling warmly at Hester, 'when I asked Cassie to arrange for someone to book Jake a holiday, I didn't realize it would work out quite the way it has.'

Hester's cheeks burned. She couldn't hold the other woman's gaze. 'I'm sorry if you think—'

'You don't need to be sorry about anything,' Beth cut in. 'I was worried about him, after the accident. I mean, of course, because he was pretty banged up. I will never forget the call I got, the rush to A&E and the sight of him in that hospital bed, looking pale and bruised.' She shuddered. 'But once he was discharged, I was still worried, because it was as if he'd been defeated by what happened. I think it came from losing control – which is the thing he hates most. But then you turned up and, well, I don't need to tell you his turnaround has more to do with you than it does those virtual holidays or the comfort of the hotel.'

'I really like your brother,' Hester whispered.

Beth's eyes gleamed. 'I can tell. You forgave him pretty quickly after an encounter with him and Rich, which is evidence enough. But he's a good man, despite his few shortcomings, and I just hope . . .' She paused, and Hester could see that she was debating whether to say anything else: whether to interfere or step back. 'I hope he doesn't hurt you, that's all.'

Hester opened her mouth to reply, but Jake appeared at the top of the stairs. He walked down them and bent to pick up the battered canvas holdall just inside the door, but Beth tutted and took over. 'I'll put this in the car for you, you sad little invalid.'

'Thanks,' he said quietly.

Beth hefted the bag onto her shoulder and opened the front door, and Jake turned to Hester, his face brightening. She returned his smile, feeling a thrill of excitement at the promise of their secret getaway. It could be the Great Yarmouth seafront or a tent in a field, a Holiday Inn next to Luton Airport or a youth hostel in a car park. As long as Jake was with her, she knew she would enjoy it.

She hoped that Beth's worries were unfounded, though if they weren't Hester was pretty sure it would be the other way around, with Jake's heart the one in danger of being bruised. She pushed the thought away, took his hand and followed Beth out to the car.

Chapter
Twenty-Six

Friday

'I'm supposed to be taking *you* away for the weekend,' Jake said, as Hester settled herself in the driving seat of the old Mercedes and adjusted its position.

'You have broken ribs,' Hester replied. 'I'm not a doctor, but I would have thought driving is pretty uncomfortable.'

Jake sighed, his jaw tensing, and she knew his frustration was with himself and not with her. 'Everything is uncomfortable, so I should drive.'

'Your logic is ridiculous, and I'm here now. My seat.' She tapped the steering wheel. 'And this is such a nice car.'

'Beth fell in love with it on sight, but it doesn't get much use now she's usually ferrying half a dozen kids around. I thought we'd be doing it a favour, as well as us.'

'Doing the car a favour?'

He nodded as she switched the engine on, looked behind her to turn the car around in the large driveway. Beth had said goodbye to them at the door and then closed it, for fear of small legs rushing past her, so there was nobody there to wave them off. Hester didn't know why she'd thought of that.

'We don't want it to rust,' Jake explained, running his hand along the dashboard. There was love in that gesture, perhaps a whole host of memories.

'So which way, then? Do you have directions?'

Jake reached into the door pocket and took out a battered *A to Z*.

Hester glanced at him as he flicked through the pages, and couldn't hold back her laughter. 'Are you taking me to Norfolk, or the nineties?'

The grin he gave her was pure, unadulterated happiness. It was a smile that could blind spaceships. It spoke of camping weekends and endless summer holidays where the sun never faltered; festivals with friends, music and beer in coolers; all responsibility gone, all problems far away, left at home with the door firmly shut. Hester was frozen in place. All his weariness, his cynicism, was gone in that moment, and she was overwhelmed that he felt that way about this: about them. She turned back to the windscreen and gripped the steering wheel.

'We can get there using this, and I'm sure when we're close enough I'll remember the way.' He hadn't realized the effect he'd had on her. 'We don't need a sat nav.'

'Which way from here then, Hot Shot?' she asked, trying to regain her composure. It was one weekend. He was happy, and that was a good thing.

Jake glanced around him, getting his bearings, and then directed Hester onto the A2. She quickly got the hang of

the car, discovering its quirks and personality. The one positive thing her phobia had given her was a determination to drive as soon as she could, and even though she lived in London, and couldn't afford to have her own car when she needed one so infrequently, she made sure she drove as often as possible. She took her mum and dad for pub lunches on the Kent Downs, and always took on the driving whenever she, Amber and Glen managed to get away for a night or weekend. She enjoyed being in control of her destination.

'Beth's such a natural with those kids,' she said, once they were heading towards the Blackwall Tunnel, the traffic heavy but not overwhelming.

'She's wanted a large family for as long as I can remember,' Jake said, turning towards her. 'I was roped into endless dolly tea parties and picnics when I was little. I don't know how she kept track of all her dolls' names, but she did. She was made to do this.'

'She and Duncan didn't want kids of their own?'

Jake sighed. 'She had two miscarriages early on in their relationship, before they were married. They were already talking about foster caring – Beth has always wanted to help, has always had this wide reach, looking out for everyone beyond her immediate circle. But when she lost her babies, she got scared.' He wiped a hand over his face, Hester catching the movement out of the corner of her eye. 'And then she went into fostering, full steam ahead. There's still a chance – she's young enough to have her own children, too – but I don't know if she's prepared to go through it again: losing another one.'

'That's so sad,' Hester said. 'She is a wonderful mum.'

'The best,' Jake confirmed. 'To those children, the younger ones especially, she *is* their mum. And she tells me that's enough for her, but—' He shook his head. 'I don't know what conversations she and Dunc have had, obviously. I'm not around much.'

'It must be nice to see her,' Hester said. 'To have had a chance to catch up with her properly, since you've been back.'

Jake smiled. 'Yeah, it has. As much as I've moaned about being stuck here, there have been some definite plus points.' He slid his hand onto her thigh and squeezed, just as they came to a stop on the tunnel approach. 'Seems we're not the only ones heading out of the city for the weekend,' he murmured.

'Late September's an ideal time for a mini break,' Hester said. 'There's the possibility of perfect, crisp weather, walks in the sunshine *and* crunchy leaves.'

'Pubs with real fires,' Jake added. 'Dogs lying in front of the hearth, decanted bottles of red wine and the smell of woodsmoke. The crackle of the logs burning.'

'Fingers numb with cold; long, hot showers to defrost; warm beds with patchwork blankets on the end; moonlight sneaking through gaps in the curtains.' Hester sighed. 'Waking up and switching on the kettle that's way too small but sounds far too loud; teabag sachets and packets of shortbread biscuits that you put straight in your bag so they get replaced every day.'

Jake laughed. 'Looks like we've got it sorted. You're pretty good at this, you know.'

'Good at what?'

'Conjuring up the perfect holiday. Making it sound desirable, wherever it is. No wonder Cassie values you so much.'

Hester put the car into second as the traffic moved and they drove into the darkness of the tunnel. 'You weren't too bad yourself,' she said lightly. 'I especially liked the dog in front of the hearth. What kind of dog would it be?'

'A German Shepherd or a sheepdog. Something big and strong.'

'Oh of course,' Hester said. 'Nothing small or cute. None of your poodle crosses.'

'Not in Norfolk,' Jake replied. 'You want a runner; something that can drag you across the fields, that forces you outside even when the rain's blowing sideways. All that space, you have to make use of it.'

'Sounds pretty different to your West Village.'

'What can I say? Over the last week or so I've been seeing things a bit differently. I've been reminded that life doesn't have to be small and neat, everything put away in separate boxes. And that, even if you'd like it small and neat, that's not always how it turns out.'

'Beth said you like being in control: that losing it was the hardest part of your accident.'

'She did, did she?' He didn't seem upset, or angry, that they'd been talking about him. 'Yeah, she's right. It's been a bit of a wake-up call. And you – your life isn't small and predictable. It's not like you can settle into a proper routine. How often are you away, going overseas for research trips or to meet hoteliers?'

Hester focused on her speed, on following the signs for the M11. This was a really big roundabout: she needed to concentrate properly. She chewed her lip and tried not to freak out. This was the moment. Time to tell Jake the truth and start again.

'It depends,' she heard herself say. 'There are three of us besides Cassie, so it's usually a case of where the trip is, and who's available. How often do you go away? If you're visiting coffee plantations and making deals, are you gone for long stretches?' And there, just like that, she'd batted it away. She hadn't lied, had she?

'Sometimes a couple of weeks,' Jake said. 'But it's planned out well in advance: everything tightly scheduled so I can meet the producers, work out if we're suited and a deal's going to be beneficial for both of us, then get back to the US and set up the order, arrange the imports, the distribution.'

'And in between,' Hester said, 'people-watching with coffee and newspapers on Sunday mornings.'

'Exactly. My favourite time of the week.'

Was there a woman? Lots of them? Did he see a few on and off, like a young, attractive man in a thriving city might well do? She wanted so much to ask him, but then he'd bat it back to her and she would tell him about Pierre, and how there had been nobody since, not for a good few months, and nobody in her recent history – or even her distant history – who'd come close to making her feel the way Jake did. But every thread of conversation suddenly felt littered with potholes, and she realized she didn't want to tell him the truth while she was driving; when she couldn't even look at his face, his reaction, when she admitted it.

'Have you seen your parents while you've been here?' she asked. It occurred to her that she knew nothing about his and Beth's mum and dad.

Jake shook his head. 'Mum sent flowers. Lilies, of course, because they're her favourite.'

240

Hester thought of the lilies she'd seen in his hotel bathroom. Had he really relegated his mother's gift to the toilet? But she supposed if she'd been in a serious car accident and her mum hadn't even bothered to come and see her, she might not be that pleased with a bunch of flowers either. Was this part of the reason he didn't like coming back to the UK? That fact that had intrigued her when Cassie had first mentioned him, just before she'd left to go to the Duval that afternoon? That seemed like such a long time ago, now.

'She really didn't come and visit you?' Hester asked. 'What if she did while you were in the hospital? If you were on lots of painkillers, then—'

'She didn't, Hester. I would have been shocked if she had done.'

'But you were hurt.'

'Once Beth told her I was going to be fine, that there was no serious damage, she decided it wasn't necessary. And I'm glad, really. It wouldn't have been a particularly warm encounter. She saved both of us more pain by staying away.'

'You're not close, then.' The road was opening up, the sky stretching out above them, a cool blue with thin white clouds streaking through it, the beginnings of the Essex countryside laid out like a quilt on either side.

'No,' Jake said. 'My dad left when Beth was ten and I was eight, and instead of that making our family tighter, Mum gave up on it, almost as if there was no point once we weren't a neat little unit any more. At least it made Beth and I closer. We looked out for each other. But then . . .' His words drifted off and Hester glanced at him, frustrated that he had turned to look out of the window and she couldn't see his face.

'But then?' she prompted gently.

'Then I found out that Mum had lied.'

He said it so simply, giving it the weight it deserved. Hester went hot and cold all at once, sweat prickling her armpits, the steering wheel sticky against her palms. She couldn't reply, but he went on, regardless.

'She'd told us that Dad had left because he'd found someone else, which I guess I didn't fully understand when it happened, because I was young. He didn't seem to want to see us, and I thought I'd accepted it. But then, several years later, I tracked him down, forced him to talk to me. I questioned him about it, and it turned out that it was Mum who'd had the affair, who'd told him he wasn't part of the family any more. I thought he was lying, playing us off against each other, but when I asked her about it, she admitted it.'

'Shit, Jake,' Hester managed.

'She hadn't wanted us, not really, but she hadn't given Dad the chance to try, either: turning me and Beth against him by lying about who had ended the marriage. It—' He coughed, cleared his throat. 'Since then, we've not really been in touch. I haven't spoken to her for months, haven't seen her in a couple of years. I was surprised, actually, to get the flowers.'

Hester could taste bile at the back of her throat. His mum had lied. It was the ultimate betrayal, and he hadn't forgiven her. 'But even so,' she almost whispered. 'She didn't even call you in hospital? Or when you got to the hotel? She's . . . she's never tried to make it up to you? Never asked you to forgive her?' She swallowed, rushing on, as if she could escape the reality of this revelation. 'And then Rosalie,

who you've only known for a few days, paid thousands of pounds so you could recuperate in comfort, came round to check on you, ate pasta with us and told stories about her boyfriend watching Italian porn films.'

Jake laughed, but it sounded forced. 'Rosalie is very different to my mum. Are you close to your parents?'

Hester nodded. 'We see each other most Sundays, and talk in between. They only live in Blackheath. They're very supportive, and I know I'm lucky to have them.'

'And they're proud to have a daughter with a jet-setting lifestyle, I bet.'

Hester looked in the mirror, then behind her, and moved into the fast lane, overtaking a lorry that was overtaking another lorry on the inside lane. She liked the way driving gave her time to think, a natural pause when she wasn't quite sure of her answer – when she wasn't sure how she was supposed to recover from Jake's admission. He had been scarred, probably forever, by the lies his mum had told him.

'I think they'd be supportive of me whatever I chose to do,' she admitted. 'There are some aspects of my job that they don't quite . . . understand. It took them a while to get their heads around our staycations.' She forced a grin.

'You told them about us?'

Us. Not: your work project. She nodded. 'They got out the photo album of our Amalfi holiday, helped me refresh my memories so I could make Italy authentic.'

'It worked,' he said, his voice light.

The silence stretched, the sound of the road beneath their wheels like a barrier between them. When Hester next glanced at Jake, he had his fingers pressed to his lips and was watching her closely, his eyes vividly blue in the sunlight filling the car.

'And now you're sharing *your* memories,' she said, too brightly. 'Tell me what we're doing this weekend. What you've got planned for our Norfolk adventure.'

'We covered it earlier,' Jake said easily. Whatever had caused that pensive expression hadn't made its way into his voice, and she wondered if she'd imagined it. 'Walks, a pub with a fire, long hot showers, big beds.'

Hester shuddered, pleasure and anticipation running through her at the thought, pushing aside worries about parents and lies and the past, so that everything was focused firmly on the road ahead, and on Jake: on the future.

Chapter
Twenty-Seven

Friday

Once they got to Norfolk, Jake directed her away from the main city, Norwich, and up towards the coast. The weather stayed good, the sky blue and clear, the fields they passed carpets of green and brown, the trees turning to red and russet and gold.

After the discussion about Jake's mum, which had sullied the mood and left Hester with an unshakeable sense of dread, she tried everything she could to get back that care-free smile from the beginning of the journey: *Jake's A to Z grin.* She already thought of it as that, and wondered if it could be bottled; used as a treatment in cases of extreme sadness. *The Famous Jake Oakenfield A to Z Grin.* But then she realized she didn't want to share it with anyone, and of all the strange thoughts she was having, that was the most disturbing of all.

'Holkham beach,' she said, because she'd finally squeezed

one of their possible weekend destinations out of him. 'Isn't that in *Shakespeare in Love*? At the end, Gwyneth Paltrow survives the sea wreck and walks across the beach, and it's supposed to be the beginning of *Twelfth Night*? Although I barely noticed it was a beach, because I was crying so hard I couldn't see the screen.'

'Which time?' Jake asked. 'Go straight over this round-about.'

'Ooh look, pigs!' Hester pointed at a field with small, dome-shaped huts and large pink pigs lounging and strolling, their legs encased in mud.

'Pigs!' Jake laughed. 'It's been a while since I've seen a field of pigs.'

'Not many of those in New York, I would imagine.'

'Got it in one, Hester Monday.'

'Anyway, what did you mean, *which time?*'

'I meant which time could you barely see the beach you were crying too hard? Everyone's seen *Shakespeare in Love* at least ten times.'

'Oh, every time. It's impossible to watch it without sobbing. He loves her so much but he can't be with her. He has to set her free, and imagines her living this new, wonderful life on the other side of the world.'

'You old romantic.' He said it in a New York accent, reaching up and chucking her cheek. But then his fingers lingered there, catching the tear that slid down to meet them. 'Wait, you're actually *crying?*'

'Just thinking about it is so sad,' Hester said, sniffing loudly, blinking to clear her vision so she could focus on the road. Why was she so emotional? What was this man doing to her, stirring up all her feelings, letting them rush and rejoice inside her, where before she'd had them firmly under control? Was this what a heady case of lust did to you? Something whispered at the corner of her mind, questioning her choice of 'l' word, and she shoved it violently away.

'Just *thinking* about *Shakespeare in Love* makes you cry?'

'Shut up, Jake,' she said, laughing through the last of her tears. 'It's a very sad film. Bittersweet, which is the worst combination, because it's sad *and* happy. You cry for what the characters have lost, and also what they've found, and it mixes you up inside. Don't laugh at me.'

'I'm not laughing at you,' he said, his voice low and soothing. Throughout the journey he'd been touching her knee, her thigh; resting his hand on hers when it was on the gear stick. Now he reached over and kissed her cheek, his breath hot on her face. 'I would never laugh at you, Hester. Not unless you were purposefully trying to make me.'

Hester exhaled, her desire rising up at that simple touch, at his words, which hinted at a *them*, at a future where they knew each other better, and made each other laugh. She had to resist turning her head to meet his lips: if she did, they would end up in a ditch, and she wouldn't get to do all the other things that she wanted to do with him.

'We're just along here,' he said a few minutes later, and Hester turned into a quaint, bustling high street, with a green-grocer's and an old-fashioned jewellery shop with a low, black awning above it; a pub housed in a Tudor building with a steeply sloping roof. There was a holiday feel to the place, still: adults with takeaway coffee cups shadowing children licking ice creams as they walked down the narrow pavement; a small troop of twenty-somethings on bicycles, their helmets Smarties-bright. Men in tweed jackets and

247

pink trousers strode across the road, and women carried actual wicker baskets. It wasn't like any corner of London Hester could think of.

'Turn left just here,' Jake instructed.

She found herself bumping down a narrow alleyway that opened up into the tiniest car park Hester had ever seen, low buildings crowding in on all four sides.

'Wow. You're really challenging my parking skills.'

'I'd forgotten how small it was.'

'How long is it since you've been here?'

'About eight years,' he admitted.

'Easy to forget.' She eased the car into the one remaining space and turned off the engine. 'So. This is it.'

'It is,' Jake confirmed, 'and I've been waiting to do this all day.' He reached over and kissed her, his touch slow and lazy, as if he was confident that they had all the time in the world. Hester kissed him back, trying to let go of her swirling thoughts, trying to buy into the myth that they had forever, instead of just a couple of days.

'We should get inside,' he said, after several minutes in which he'd managed to drive Hester mad with desire, sitting in the slightly musty Mercedes, in the cramped car park surrounded by buildings with windows.

'We should,' she agreed. He tucked an errant strand of hair behind her ear and climbed out of the car.

Hester lifted both their bags out of the boot, slapping Jake's hand away when he went to carry them inside.

'I can take them in,' he said.

'Nope. You sort out our room. I'll bring these.'

Jake rolled his eyes and led the way, and Hester put the bags down in the cosy reception of what turned out to be a beautiful boutique hotel, its downstairs floor a restaurant, coffee shop and deli. Its decor was decidedly rustic, with exposed brick walls, wooden tables and benches. Small rooms and hidden nooks throughout gave it a warm, secretive atmosphere that Hester loved instantly.

Jake booked them in and collected their room key.

'You're on the second floor,' said their host, his expression cheerful behind black-framed glasses. 'Would you like help with your bags? The stairs are quite narrow.'

'If you wouldn't mind,' Jake said. 'I had an accident a little while ago, and I can't lift too much.'

'He doesn't like me being the pack pony,' Hester added, but she was relieved the man had offered. Carrying both bags, sideways, up a narrow flight of stairs seemed like a recipe for disaster.

'Of course.' He took their holdalls and they followed him up an old staircase, the floorboards creaking under three pairs of feet. He opened the door and left the bags by the window, told them to call down to reception for anything they needed and, after checking Jake's booking for dinner, wished them a happy stay and closed the door behind him.

'I thought we could eat here tonight,' Jake said, 'then make a decision about tomorrow. There are a few other pubs and restaurants in town, and some along the coast, if you'd prefer.'

Hester nodded, but she was distracted by the beautiful room. It was an old building, so the floors and walls were uneven, like a cardboard dolls' house made for a school project, and the wall behind the headboard of the wide bed was exposed brick like downstairs. The bed and chest of drawers were made of polished dark wood, the armchairs by the window worn brown leather. There were paintings of wildflowers adding a wash of bright colour, and a hint of marble bathroom was visible beyond a panelled wooden door.

'Jake, this is so lovely,' she said, sliding her hand over the soft, pale green blanket covering the bottom half of the bed.

'No fairy lights,' he said, stepping towards her. 'But the rest is an authentic Norfolk holiday.'

'I feel like I've been hustled,' she admitted, running her hands up his chest to his shoulders. 'I've been working like a trojan to take you to all these exotic locations, and you've just been biding your time, waiting to pull this out of your arsenal.'

He bent his head and wrapped his arms around her. 'But I never would have thought of this if it hadn't been for you. The moment you opened the door to the suite after I'd been walking up and down those bloody stairs, and you were in that red dress . . .' He let out a low groan that, if Hester had been trying to hold back her desire, would have pulled away the last of her restraint. 'With Australia surrounding you. All those animals, the paddling pool. Actual sand.' He laughed gently. 'You shared all those memories with me. You stopped me wallowing in self-pity, reminded me how fun life could be when you stopped being so fucking serious. It made me want to share my memories, all of myself, with you.'

'Jake,' she whispered, his words throwing water on her desire. 'I need to tell you that—'

'That what?' He kissed her, trailed his lips along her jaw, down her neck.

'That Australia, Amalfi . . . those virtual holidays?'

'Staycations,' he murmured, sliding his hands lower, cupping her bum, kissing the juncture where her neck met her shoulder. 'Holibobs.'

Hester laughed. 'Stop it, I'm being serious.'

He brought his face back up, his gaze communicating so much that she shrank from her responsibilities, unable to say it with those blue eyes, so full of heat and longing, directed at her. 'So am I,' he whispered, and kissed her again.

And then there was nothing else; no room in her head for anything but this man, with his soft jumper and his warm, strong hands, and the skin under his clothes and the thoughts and feelings inside him. She wanted to drag them all out as moans and whispers, as the pressure of his palms and slide of his fingers, until he was as lost, as exposed, as she was.

They fumbled at each other's clothes, their haste making them clumsy, Jake laughing into her neck when his sleeve got caught in the button of her jeans, his shoes hitting the wooden floor with a heavy thud that had them freezing for a second, eyes wide, and then deciding wordlessly that the owners must be used to it.

Hester pulled him to the bed and he pushed her down onto it, the blanket soft and ticklish against her bare skin. Her gaze went to the bruises blossoming across his chest but he didn't hesitate, didn't give her time to pause as he moved down her body.

'Where do you want me?' he murmured. 'How do you want me? Which bit of me do you want?'

She wanted to say all of him, everywhere, but then his head was between her legs, and she could only say, 'Oh God, there. Like that. Don't stop,' and then words deserted her, and she gave herself up to the feel of him; the sensations that had never been so intense, in her body and her blood and her skin, and in her heart. It felt like she was cracking open, letting Jake in, letting out parts of herself that had never seen the light of day.

He came back up the bed, pulling her into his arms, kissing her forehead. His own skin was covered in a sheen of sweat, his body anchoring her to the bed and to him.

Her hands slid down his chest, tracing the scar at the edge of his ribcage, then lower, following the trail of dark hair that ran down his stomach. He was hard, and she held him, stroked him, her body reigniting at the moan she drew from him.

'Give me a second,' he murmured, and pushed himself off the bed. Hester watched him, his movements easy and confident, only a second of hesitation as he bent over, rifling in his bag.

He came back to the bed and settled down beside her. He brushed her hair away from her forehead, then stroked down her body, to her hips, and brought her flush against him. They kissed and kissed, every touch taking Hester closer to somewhere she hadn't known she could go. She took the condom from him, ripped open the foil packet, put it on him.

Jake settled on top of her, his eyes the blue of pure heat. 'I have wanted you, Hester Monday, with me like this, since that first day.'

'I want you too,' she said. 'I have, every day. I do, now and always.' She wasn't in control of the words: they were running away from her. But they didn't make Jake pause, instead his gaze burned brighter.

He moved closer and Hester opened up for him, her eyes fluttering closed as he went deeper, as they moved together, everything lost except the slow, careful rhythm they created. 'Hester Monday,' he murmured. 'Fucking hell.'

'Great review,' she whispered back, their gazes catching, her desire and happiness mirrored in his eyes. He laughed into her neck, gripped her tighter, deepened his movements, until even those words were gone, and she knew that it wasn't just her body she was giving to him, but a whole lot more that, after this moment, she would never be able to take back.

Chapter
Twenty-Eight

Friday

They stayed in bed as the sun slipped lower in the sky. Hester didn't ever want to leave it. She would be happy if she and Jake commandeered the room, like squatters, except with room service on speed dial. As she lay with her head against his chest, tracing the shape of his bruises while he stroked her hair which, even though her body was exhausted from the pleasure he'd given her, made her tingle to her toes, she wondered how many days in this hotel her rent would get them, or a single night's cost of his hotel suite.

'We've got a dinner reservation,' Jake said, sounding as reluctant to move as she felt.

But it was hunger that finally convinced her they should stick to it, and as they made their way downstairs, Jake wearing dark jeans and a grey shirt that he looked so good in Hester immediately wanted to rip it off again, she tried to catalogue her emotions. There were too many, she realized, so she gave up and decided to enjoy herself.

The food was superior pub fare, her cheeseburger coming with Jenga chips built in a tower on her wooden serving board. She wouldn't have forgiven the pretension, except it was the best burger she'd ever eaten, the meat seasoned to perfection. They shared a bottle of red wine and each other's food, Jake cutting her a piece of his steak before she'd even asked him.

'You're wishing you'd chosen this now, aren't you?' he said as he put it on the side of her plate.

'No way. This burger is delicious.' A bit of mayo oozed down her chin and he leaned forward and wiped it off. She tried to slice through the brioche bun, tomato and burger, but it started to collapse. 'Oh look,' she huffed out, and picked the whole thing up and held it towards him. He took a bite, his eyes widening in appreciation.

It was a scene worthy of *Lady and the Tramp*, and Hester wondered if the other guests were quietly asking their servers for sick bags. Candles flickered on the tables, and a string of LED lights – Jake had pointed them out when they'd been led to their table – were nestled in autumn garlands around the room, the rustic leaves and twigs casting their nook of the restaurant in an orange glow, as if they were dining in Cinderella's coach while it was still part-pumpkin.

If Glen and Amber could see her now, she thought happily, they would be utterly disgusted. And then she remembered their conversation the evening before, Hester's promise to them that she would tell Jake the truth. But now he had that look in his eyes, like his A to Z grin wasn't far off, and she could not spoil this moment. Even if it was partly self-preservation, it would also be heartless. She still had time.

He told her about his job, about how tasting coffee was called "cupping", how it was as much about maintaining relationships with the growers and importers, about balancing spreadsheets and managing cost-levels, as it was about travelling to beautiful, often remote locations and sampling coffee variations. As he spoke, she realized that the most innocuous conversations were fraught with danger.

'You must have eaten in some great places over the years,' he said. 'Tried so many different types of food.'

Hester nodded and speared one of her remaining chips, dipping it into the pot of spicy mayonnaise. 'I do think there's something about English pub food, though. It can't be beaten.'

Jake laughed. 'Really? What about Thai? Japanese? Or are you saying you're really a homebody, that you love your job and like going away, but always prefer coming back to England?'

Hester stared at the knots in her wooden board. Could restaurants really be sure the wood was disease-free; that it wasn't harbouring bugs that had been hibernating in it for decades? Even with the wood treated, you could never really be certain, could you?

'Hester?' he prompted.

'I am a homebody,' she said eventually. 'More than you realize. In fact, Jake—' She put her knife and fork down, looked up at him.

'Yes?' A smile dented those perfect, full lips that had kissed every inch of her skin and had her moaning under him. Her body whispered at her not to do this; not to ruin all those future opportunities.

'I need to tell you something.' She swallowed. Those future moments wouldn't last very long if she kept this from him.

'OK.' He was still smiling, unaware of what was coming.

'It's just that—'

'Was everything OK with your meal?' their server asked, reaching down to take their plates.

'Delicious, thank you,' Hester said.

'Really great, thanks.' Jake reached across the table and took Hester's hand, and it was such an unconscious gesture, so natural, that she bit her lip and swallowed the emotion in her throat and decided she would tell him later.

'So where are you taking me?' Hester asked, watching Jake dry himself after his shower the next morning, noticing the way his movements automatically slowed when he got to his torso.

'You'll have to wait and see.'

It was early, and after they'd got back to the room the night before, sleep hadn't been on either of their minds, so she felt heavy with tiredness, but knew that her euphoria would carry her through whatever plans Jake had. She wondered how much their time in bed had hurt him, but he hadn't once drawn attention to his injuries, and she'd found herself thinking that, if he was holding back because of them, then she wasn't sure she'd survive the sheer pleasure of sex with a 100 per cent fit Jake Oakenfield.

'What about breakfast?' she asked.

'I checked with the manager, and they're serving until ten, so we can have it when we get back.'

'Until *ten*?'

'This is the countryside,' he reminded her. 'Not everyone rushes about at a hundred miles an hour. But you do need to get out of bed now.'

'Otherwise we'll be too late for breakfast?'

'Well, there's that. But there's also the fact that I am a heartbeat away from coming back to join you, and I have a feeling we'd miss breakfast, lunch and dinner if I did that, so come on.'

He refused to let her drive this time, promising her it was only a few miles and he had to start behaving normally. She let him, watching as he adjusted the mirror and bent to move the seat back to accommodate his longer legs. Soon they were out of the quaint town and into beautiful English countryside, passing fields and copses of trees, driving through picturesque Norfolk villages with flint cottages and old-fashioned, bright red telephone boxes; one turned into a tiny community library, another nothing more than an elaborate spider palace.

The trees sang with autumn colour and Hester opened her window, the cool air rushing at her like a long-lost friend, leaving the taste of the sea on her lips. She drank it in, gulped it in big waves, and when Jake opened his window as well, the car was a vacuum of sound and wind, a make-shift convertible, tangling her hair and caressing his curls, their thrilled laughter swallowed up immediately.

By the time Jake turned onto a thin track, and Hester could see that they were heading for the sea, the horizon a flat silver line shimmering under the golden pearl of the new sun, she wanted to tell him that nothing could beat that: she didn't think it could get any better.

He parked the car in the beach car park, alongside a couple of other early risers, and together they got out and put their coats on, Hester zipping hers to her neck against the early morning chill.

The beach was a strip of pebbles, stretching as far as the eye could see in both directions. Behind her, beyond acres of flat marshland, the buildings of a small village – perhaps not even that – faced the water. A windmill stood, sails akimbo, as if saying, 'Look at me.'

Jake took her hand and they walked closer to the water, past a cluster of men and women in dark green anoraks and with telescopes on tripods, angled to watch the seabirds that ducked and dove above them; past a pile of clothes which, Hester soon saw, belonged to a lone man swimming, surely freezing slowly to death in the North Sea.

'Sheringham and Cromer are that way,' Jake said, pointing to the rise of cliffs in the distance, the horizon now a streak of gold, a thin layer of mist shrouding the fields. 'And eventually, if you follow the coast round, Great Yarmouth.'

'East, then,' Hester said, 'because of the sun.' She took it all in, the space and the sky, the impossible colours of the sun as it rose, meeting land and water, pebbles and rooftops. How did she ever believe she could organize a worthwhile virtual holiday, when the reality of a place, its beauty, was something that could never be fully captured without being there? She knew she would get out her phone and take photos, and that they would never do justice to the memory of this moment.

'What's the other way?' she asked absent-mindedly, as a large dog, a Labrador, she thought, raced boisterously past them to get to the water, his nose held high in excitement.

'Hunstanton, then further west there's King's Lynn, and then those flat, furtive fens,' Jake said, intoning seriously.

She looked at him and laughed. 'I didn't know you had a talent for alliteration.'

'I don't really,' he said. 'How can the fens be furtive? A place can't have the capacity for creeping.'

'True, but it sounds good.'

'Thanks.' He gave her his small, lopsided smile, and then a second later the grin was back, the full A to Z, and it stole Hester's breath as much as the sunrise. He pressed his cold fingers against her flushed cheeks and kissed her, long and deep, their feet crunching in the pebbles as they shifted their weight, finding the perfect position and angle to make this kiss the best, better than all those hours in bed, better than that first kiss in the New York restaurant, when Hester discovered that he was falling for her, too.

'Beach kiss,' she said, when they broke apart.

'Yup,' he replied. 'A staple of any good holiday.'

'As is a selfie. I don't have any photos of you, I realized.'

'Oh, and when did you realize that?' He raised an eyebrow, and she walked him back towards the waves, wanting to get the sea and the golden haze in the background of her shot. 'When you were lying in bed, thinking about me, and realized you couldn't picture me properly?'

'Don't be so filthy,' she said, laughing, and then widened her eyes in mock horror. 'Oh, that's what *you've* been doing. I see.'

'No need. You were imprinted on my mind from the moment I saw you in the hotel corridor, in your white shirt and navy skirt, your hair tied back and that calm, professional look on your face. Except, once you were in my suite and I told you I didn't want a holiday, then, for just a second, you looked so mad . . .' He shook his head.

'And which expression do I have when you picture me? Calm and professional, or silently furious?'

'I quite like the one I saw in bed yesterday afternoon,' he murmured into her ear. 'And last night. And this morning.'

'Well, I'm not doing *that* face for our selfie,' she said. 'Come on, stand next to me.' She shuffled backwards, closer to the shallows. The waves weren't big, but they would break halfway up their shins if she misjudged.

'Where do you want me?' Jake said, echoing the day before.

He stood behind her and draped his arms around her shoulders, his cheek pressed to hers. Hester opened the camera on her phone, switched the view and, for a moment, could only look at them: this beautiful man, with his curls and his blue eyes and his weekend stubble, and her, looking brighter, sunnier, than she could remember her reflection being. Their cheeks were flushed from the wind, and above all, she realized, they both looked happy.

She pressed the button, turned the phone sideways and pressed it again, wanting to capture the moment even though the moment itself was so much more than the image she was creating of it.

'I want this kind of life when I'm old,' she said.

'Taking endless pictures of your own face?'

'Walking on the beach, being close enough that you can just get out of bed and see the sun rising over the water. Going home for breakfast when you're chilled and wind-swept and your stomach's groaning. Going back to bed with coffee and numb toes.'

262

'And the paper,' he said.

'What?' She turned to look at him.

'You've levelled up my Sunday mornings,' Jake said. 'Made them sound even better. How am I going to be satisfied after this? There's no beach in the West Village. No you, Hester. What am I supposed to do now?'

She couldn't take her eyes off him, and his gaze didn't leave hers. The air between them seemed to disappear, the beach receding, the cries of the seabirds and crash of waves against stones fading to nothing.

But then, out of the corner of her eye, she saw the Labrador, tail wagging and tongue out, barrelling straight towards them. She just had time to notice the dog's owner looking startled and calling out 'Arbuthnot!'; had time to think what a stupid name it was before she realized the dog wasn't planning on changing course.

'Jake, watch out!' She turned to push him out of the way. He sidestepped, holding out his hand for her so he could pull her away too, but it was a second too late and she felt the dog's paws meet the middle of her back, heard him bark delightedly at finding a new playmate, before she lost her footing, let go of Jake's hand so as not to bring him down with her, and then landed, face first, in the water. She blinked, drew in a breath, and then a wave – one of those small ones she hadn't been bothered about – broke over her head.

Chapter
Twenty-Nine

Saturday

Jake's concern matched that of the dog walker's, a couple of the birdwatchers rushed over, and Hester's embarrassment was fully compounded when the Labrador, Arbuthnot, thought she was playing dead and snuffled at her face, licking her cheeks and hand before Jake pulled her upright, checking her over with his eyes, squeezing her shoulders until she met his gaze.

'Are you OK, Hester?'

'Golly I am *so sorry*,' said Arbuthnot's owner.

'All right, love?' asked one of the birdwatchers.

'I'm fine,' Hester said. She went to take her hair out of her mouth but Jake did it for her. He held it up in front of her face to show her it wasn't, in fact, her hair, but a bit of seaweed. 'Oh God. I am *not* fine!'

'What is it?' the dog walker asked urgently. 'Where do you hurt?'

'In my soul,' Hester said, and thought she heard Jake snort. She shot him a look, could see his lips pressed together, saw him fighting it. 'It is *not* funny, Jake Oakenfield.' She took the piece of seaweed from him and hit him with it. 'Not. Funny.'

'Do you need to sit down, dear?' the other birdwatcher asked.

Hester couldn't help it: she burst out laughing. She hid her face in her hands, dropping the seaweed. She heard Arbuthnot bark.

'Oh dear,' the dog walker said. 'She's hysterical.'

'She's fine, I think.' Jake was trying to sound solemn. 'Thank you so much for your concern.' He pulled Hester against him and pressed her head into his shoulder, not caring that she was soaked, and thanked the strangers again until they left them, Arbuthnot's owner hardest to encourage away. Then she could feel his shoulders shaking as the laughter spilled out of him, and it set her off again too, and she wouldn't have been surprised if it brought everyone on the beach back over to them, as they stood in the shallows, the sun rising higher in the sky while they cried with laughter.

'We need to get you dry,' Jake said, once their laughter had subsided and Hester had started shivering.

'I won't argue with that,' she said, her teeth chattering.

He took off her coat and unzipped his leather jacket, but she stepped away from him. 'Your Top Gun jacket,' she protested, but he dragged her back.

'You need to wear it. The car heater's temperamental.'

'It's a ten-minute drive.'

'Hester, don't argue.' He forced her sleeves into the coat,

266

then took her hand and started walking back across the beach. 'Let me look after you for once, OK?'

'OK,' she said quietly. 'Thank you.'

Once they were back in the car and Jake had turned the heating up to max so that it noisily wafted cold, musty-smelling air around the interior, Hester pulled out her phone. 'At least this survived,' she said, shaking it and then unlocking it. 'I think, anyway.' She scrolled through a couple of apps, played a few bars of a Vance Joy song, the speakers loud and clear and not at all crackly. 'Thank God for that.'

'God forbid your phone should die, even if you get hypothermia,' Jake said. 'At least you'll still be able to post on Instagram, once your fingers start working again.'

'Hey! Don't be so fatalist, Jake. And those selfies are prime Instagram fodder. Look.' She held up her phone, and he glanced quickly at the screen, then took another, longer look as he waited to turn right at a junction. She saw his jaw clench, his Adam's apple bob.

'I seem to remember you telling me it was better that you missed your train than that I passed out, cold and alone, on my hotel floor.'

Hester laughed. 'I did not say *cold and alone*. But I *was* worried about you. Not being able to breathe is a bit more serious than being pushed over by a friendly dog on a beach, into salty water and seaweed. Ugh.' She shuddered as she remembered the feel of it in her mouth, the cold sliminess of it. She tried not to linger on the fact that he hadn't commented on the photograph.

'How are you feeling?' he asked. 'Chilly?'

'Not particularly cosy,' she admitted, and he picked up speed.

Back at the hotel, he told her to go up to the room and run a bath, and he'd get some coffee and breakfast brought up. She did as she was told, her legs stiff and heavy in her sodden jeans. Once inside the room, she unpeeled her clothes, her skin pink and shiny, still damp and cold underneath them, and ran a bath, pouring in a liberal amount of rose-scented bubble bath from the tiny bottle on the side of the tub.

The room warmed her up as it filled with scented steam, and Hester climbed into the wide bathtub, the taps in the middle, suspended on the wall and out of the way. She sank into the water, twisted the hot tap on more, closed her eyes and let the salt and the memory of the seaweed drift away, leaving only Jake and his kiss, his unhindered smile and their selfie behind. She would never get tired of the weight of his arms around her shoulders, or the brush of his stubble on her cheek.

Through the fug of her thoughts she heard the door open, heard someone whistling and knew, even though she'd never heard him do it, that it was Jake. She knew his tone, the presence of him, even when she couldn't see him. There was a clink of crockery as, she imagined, he put a tray down, and she wondered what he'd wangled from the kitchen staff. She wouldn't mind scrambled eggs or a croissant, or just buttered toast. As long as it came with coffee – coffee that he, the expert, approved of – and she could warm herself up from the inside as well as the outside, she didn't care.

The whistling got closer, she heard Jake's feet padding to the threshold of the bathroom door, then the footsteps and the tune stopped. Hester kept her eyes closed for a moment more, then felt the water move, sloshing towards her.

She opened her eyes and slid up the bath in surprise. 'Jake! What the hell?'

He was getting into the other side, still in his jeans, his checked shirt and his socks.

'What are you doing?' She almost screeched it, as the water level rose and the damp seeped into his shirt, the bubbles clinging to his sleeves.

'You told me that when people climb into bathtubs with their clothes on, it is the purest expression of feeling or conviction.'

Hester gasped and laughed. 'I did, but I meant on TV. In films!'

'Why can't it happen in real life, too?'

'Because real life doesn't work like that. Jake, you're soaked. Your jeans! They will never, ever dry out.'

'There's a heated towel rail: I noticed it this morning. Why can't real life work this way? Why can't I express the force of my feelings by climbing, fully clothed, into a bathtub with you?' He took her hands and slid his legs forward, outside her hips, caging her.

'What feelings?' she asked, her shock fading as he caught her in his stare and held her there.

'My feelings for you, Hester. For the way my life has changed. For the way *I've* changed, since you knocked on my door all those many hundreds of days ago.'

'It was last week,' she said quietly. 'Not even a fortnight.'

'I know. So how can it be that I feel like I've known you for so much longer, that I know enough to realize you make me happy even though we've barely scratched the surface? That I want to keep getting to know you, long after my accident is a distant memory and the bruises have faded to nothing? *You* are the lasting impact, Hester. The one that's really changed me.'

He'd kept her hands in his while he spoke, and he squeezed them now, as if to underline what he was saying. She'd heard him, of course, but had barely been able to take it in. What it meant and how it was affecting her, churning through her like a tornado, disrupting all her emotions so she could see that they were spinning but couldn't grasp hold of a single one.

'Hester?' he said quietly. 'Please say something.'

'I—' she started. 'I don't . . .'

'Don't know what to say?' He raised his eyebrows, offered a hint of a smile. 'It was a bit much, I know. But I had to say it. I wanted to say it on the beach, before Arbuthnot spoiled the moment.'

'You didn't need to get soaked, too.'

He lifted one shoulder in a shrug, his smile fading. 'If it's too much, then—'

'It's not – not at all.' It was her turn to squeeze his hands. 'It's just that . . .'

'It's OK. I've got breakfast outside, so when you've warmed up we can—'

'No, Jake. Please don't.' He had started to rise, but she held on tighter, refusing to let him go. 'I *do* know what to say, and I feel it – all of it. All those things you said. I felt them and I understood them and I wanted to hug you, to kiss you and fall on you, because that's how it is for me, too. You're *my* car crash: with your blue eyes and your A to Z smile, and all the ways you've made me laugh, and the way you touch me.'

He gave her a bemused smile, brought his hand up to

cup her cheek. 'But?' he whispered. 'That was an unfinished sentence, if ever I heard one.' His eyes were searching hers, and she saw the hint of worry at the way she was responding to him.

'There is something I have to tell you,' she said. 'Something I should have said a while ago: at the very beginning, really. But it might have – I'm sure it would have – changed everything. I don't think we'd be here now, if I'd told you this thing, this . . . this *thing*, right from the start.'

'OK.' He sat back slightly, and Hester knew that this was the moment it all went wrong. He'd climbed into the bath to prove his feelings to her, and now she was dismantling what they'd started, piece by piece. The only thing she needed to decide was how to break it to him: give him the outline, rip off the plaster and hope the sting faded over time, or give the context and the background, lead up to it and ease in gently? 'What is it, Hester?'

She sighed. 'Can we get out of the bath first? The water's starting to go cold, and I—' Her voice hitched. She silently cursed the way her stupid emotions had moved up to just under the surface, ready to make this ten times harder to tell, and deal with.

Jake's reaction was instant. He gathered her to him, wrapped her in his arms, the fabric of his sodden cotton shirt heavy but somehow comforting, bubbles clinging to her hair and his cheek. 'It's OK, Hester. It's fine. Whatever it is, everything will be all right.'

She pressed her head into his neck. She really wanted to believe that was true.

Chapter
Thirty

Saturday

They sat cross-legged on the bed, facing each other and wearing the hotel's oversized towelling robes. Hester couldn't help thinking they were there to taunt her, reminding her of the first time she met Jake, pointing out that she was about to fuck it all up. *Oh, get over yourself,* said a small voice inside her, but another, larger one told her that this really did matter. A lie was a lie, whatever its size.

They both cradled cups of coffee – she couldn't face a croissant or a pain au chocolat, even though they were huge and crispy-looking, all those layers of butter and pastry and chocolate. She would be sick, she thought.

Jake was looking at her calmly, but there was a tightness in his shoulders now, an anticipation after the way she'd led up to this.

'So,' she started, sighing the word out so it rippled the thin layer of foam on her Americano. 'I told you about Betty, the woman I met on the plane? It was a flight to Edinburgh, when I was twelve.'

Jake nodded. 'She died, didn't she?' he said quietly.

'She did,' Hester whispered. 'But . . . I met her almost as soon as we'd sat down. She asked if I wanted her peanuts, because she didn't like them. She was in the seat in front, but she turned around to talk to me: she checked with my mum, who was sitting behind me, first, and then we started talking. She told me about all the places she'd been, and when I said I wanted to travel, that we'd been to Amalfi the year before and now I wanted to go everywhere, she said we were kindred spirits.' She hated that she was having to tell Jake about one of the most defining parts of her life under these circumstances: that she'd allowed it to get to this point.

He reached out, lifted the end of the belt tying her robe together, and held it between his fingers. He noticed her watching, and shrugged.

'I feel like,' she went on, speaking slowly, 'since it happened, I've made more of it – of our conversation, because of what came next. Betty was fun. She talked a lot, and she had this energy – she made me laugh. I was twelve, and I wanted to be like her. She showed me a piece of malachite that she carried with her. She told me it was the guardian stone for travellers.' Hester had taken it out of her bag when they'd put their dressing gowns on. She'd been clutching it, and now she uncurled her fingers, showing it to Jake. It sat, like a portent, between them.

'This is hers?' he asked softly.

Hester nodded. 'We'd been talking for a while, she was telling me about a holiday to Sardinia that she'd been on, and then her smile faded, her eyes sort of lost their focus. She muttered, "Excuse me," and sat back round in her seat. I shrugged – I didn't think anything of it, really – and then, when I turned round to talk to Mum and Dad, there was this startled exclamation, and I saw that she'd slumped against the man sitting next to her.'

Jake discarded her belt and took her hand, placing his palm over the piece of crystal resting in hers, his skin hot from gripping his coffee mug.

'Then it was this . . . this rush of shouting and confusion: of panic. The flight attendants were calm, but their voices were firm. I didn't really understand it, but – Dad moved me back into his seat, next to Mum, so I was further away from what was going on. He asked if he could help, and I saw them move Betty into the aisle. She wasn't moving, and her eyes were closed. The attendants were crowding round her, and one of them addressed the cabin, asking if there was a doctor on the flight. I asked Mum what was happening, but she just showed me the festival programme, trying to get me to tell her which events I wanted to go to.'

'She was protecting you,' Jake said.

'They both were: Mum and Dad. We were close to Edinburgh, so they didn't divert the flight. I remember them moving Betty into another seat, on her own, at the back of the plane, and I thought, for a moment, that she was OK. The rush around her had faded. The whole flight was quiet – I could feel the heavy weight of it, even before they covered her with a blanket.'

There was a pause, and then Jake murmured, 'I can't imagine.'

'It was terrifying,' Hester said. 'It would have been, I

think, even if it hadn't been Betty.' She shook her head. 'We had to walk past her, when we were getting off. Dad said they would need to have a doctor come on board and examine her. He was gentle, when he said it, but he looked so upset. I didn't even know her surname.'

Jake moved closer to her, and Hester winced, because he'd obviously decided that this story was about her and her past, and not about the two of them, or how she'd behaved. She wished now she'd chosen to give him the headline first. But she was nearly there, so she kept going.

'Everyone was getting off the plane, and when I picked up my rucksack, I saw it: the piece of malachite. Betty must have dropped it, and I couldn't bear the thought of it being left there, on the floor. Of her not having it. But I couldn't give it back. Nobody saw me, so I slipped it in my bag and we walked off the plane, leaving her behind.'

'Hester.' Jake wiped his thumbs under her eyes, scooping up the tears that had started to fall without her realizing. 'I am so sorry. I can't imagine how awful that must have been.'

She took a deep breath and tried to smile at him. 'You are beautiful, do you know that?'

He frowned. 'Hester, I—'

'I just had to say it. I have to tell you that you are beautiful and that I have had the most amazing time with you, and that whatever happens now – next – I will never forget you.'

'I don't understand. What are you saying?'

She exhaled. 'We had our break in Edinburgh, but all our happiness was forced. The weekend was tainted by what had happened on the flight. But I didn't realize how much it had got to me, how much I'd been affected, until we went to go home.'

'What do you mean?'

Hester took a sip of coffee. 'I remember this intense feeling of dread as we got closer to airport security. Everything came back to me, the whole thing replaying: the horrified shout from the man sitting next to Betty; the flight attendants' studied calm as they laid her in the aisle; I remember feeling sick and my legs shaking as we neared our gate, and the way Mum and Dad tried to coax me, gently, onto the return flight.'

'But you couldn't do it?' Jake asked.

'No. I couldn't. I had a panic attack, and we ended up getting the train home: a longer journey that was also torturous, because I felt sick and scared and also guilty about the missed flight, which I had wanted so much in the first place, and I couldn't stop crying. But . . .'

'But?'

She took a deep, steadying breath. 'Ever since that day, when I watched Betty die on that aeroplane, I've been scared of flying. I've had a phobia. I've not made it onto a plane since.'

The silence that followed was heavy, a car engine coming to life outside the window the only thing that broke it. She saw Jake's brow rumple, a deep furrow forming between his eyes. 'Well, that's understandable,' he said. 'It sounds like a terrifying flight, and I . . .'

She saw the moment it hit home.

He looked at her, his blue eyes widening. 'Your job,' he said. 'You're a—'

'I've never been anywhere,' she confirmed. 'I haven't been abroad since the holiday in Amalfi, not on a plane since that flight to Edinburgh. And it doesn't matter, not really, because you don't *have* to visit exotic places to be a travel agent. If you can sell the holidays, you can sit at your desk and never move from it. Cassie knows I can do it, although she would like me to go to the resort openings and build relationships with the owners, to participate fully. She's going to make me soon, which means I'm going to have to be honest with her too, or face this fear: see if I can do something about it, finally.' She knew she was rambling, but she was doing it for Jake, to give him a chance to take it in.

'But when I asked you—' He swallowed, tried again. She watched as he shifted backwards on the bed, and wondered if he was conscious of doing it. She was hyper aware all of a sudden, as if her brain was trying to absorb every moment of the time they had left together. 'When I asked you to show me all the places you loved, the places you'd been that mattered to you—'

She shrugged. 'I didn't think you were expecting a virtual tour of a few Devon beaches or the Yorkshire moors.'

'So then, what? Australia – what was that? Those stories you told me, about the lookout point? About the bungee jump?' His voice was harder, but there was also desperation. He took her hand and squeezed it. He wanted this not to be happening as much as she did. 'Those stories were real, Hester.'

'Yes, but they weren't mine. They were Glen's – the lookout story, anyway. I got him to tell me all about his holiday, and send me the photos. The bungee jump never happened: that was about me trying to get on a plane again, to go on holiday with Amber and Glen. All those feelings were real, but the circumstances, the location, was different. I researched and rehearsed everything for our staycations, so I could be convincing.'

Jake dropped her hand, and when his eyes hardened as well as his voice, that was the worst moment. She was cold again, despite the hot bath and the towelling robe. 'And Japan?'

'Japan was going to be Amber's memories,' she whispered. 'But you let me off that one.'

Jake's smile was humourless. 'So you were actually quite pleased when you arrived and Rich was there, and I was drunk? I noticed you made your excuses quickly, but I thought it was because Rich had been rude to you.'

'He *was* rude to me, and I didn't want to stay when it was like that. There was suddenly no point to those cherry blossoms or my fairy lights. I felt mocked.'

Jake shook his head, his fingers pressed to his lips. 'And you didn't think to tell me the truth then, when I came to your flat and apologized for how I'd behaved?'

'I thought it was too late by then: that if I told you, you'd walk away from me. I was already falling for you. I just needed a little more time.'

Jake ran a hand through his curls, his stare fixed on the bed covers. 'So you can't – you can't get on a flight at all?'

Hester closed her eyes. 'I'm so sorry, Jake. I'm sorry I lied to you.'

'Why did you?'

She opened her eyes and forced herself to look at him. 'Because it's what you asked me to do. It was my job, and I knew I could do it: I could take you to those places without you having to leave your hotel suite. I could cheer you up and take your mind off your pain like Beth wanted me to. So I did it because it was just another job, but also . . .' She felt a fresh well of tears spring up as she saw that the pain was back on his face, and knew she was the one

279

who had caused it. 'But also, I did it because I wanted to see you again. I didn't want to tell you I hadn't been anywhere, that someone else would be better off looking after you, because I was desperate to come back to your hotel suite. I wanted to find out about you, and make you feel better.'

He couldn't meet her gaze. He ran his hand over the thick towelling material of his robe. 'So if we . . .'

'If we what?' she whispered.

'You couldn't come and see me, in New York?' He looked up, his eyes latching onto hers.

'I want to get over this, more than anything,' she said. 'I am *desperate* to go to New York. I was even before I met you. Now I want it even more.'

'How could I not know this about you?' It was a murmur, more to himself, she thought, than to her.

'Because I kept it from you,' she said. It was too late to be anything other than completely honest now.

'You could have told me the truth,' he said. 'Told me you could do the virtual holidays, but that they wouldn't be your memories.'

'I thought you'd tell me to go.'

'I wouldn't have,' he said quietly. 'Because I didn't really care where it was: I just wanted to see you again.'

Hester laughed, because if she'd known that then she never would have lied. He could see the irony too, she knew. He sighed and looked at her so tenderly she thought she was fragile enough to deserve it, and that in a moment she would shatter into tiny pieces.

Jake rubbed his cheek. She could see that his brain was working at a million miles; that he was distracted.

'What are you thinking?' she asked quietly.

He shook his head. 'I don't come to London very often, and I – I don't know if . . . I mean, we don't know each other, do we? Not really. This has proved that. And there's a whole ocean between us. It feels as if . . .'

'It's too difficult,' she said, finishing his sentence for him.

Despite all he'd said in the bathtub, climbing in with her to prove just how strongly he felt about her, she could almost feel the panic radiating off him: his realization that the distance between New York and London was big enough to begin with, but would seem much bigger, almost insurmountable, when only one of them could make the journey. And however much Jake liked her, he had made it clear from the beginning that his home, his safe place, wasn't here, but in America.

His sigh was deep, his whole torso shuddering, and she saw his face crease in pain, for just a second. He reached out and took her hand. 'I'm sorry you had to go through that: seeing Betty die. I can't imagine what that journey was like, how horrible it was, especially if it's stopped you from getting on a flight since. You lied to me, and you've had so many chances to put it right, but—'

'I know,' she whispered. 'I was so worried about what you would say: what you might think of me.'

He smiled, and it was so sad and full of regret that she knew what was coming even before he said it. 'I care about you. A lot. But I just . . . I don't know what we're doing here. What sort of future is there for us? And we could stay here, for the rest of the weekend, and I already know how good it would be, but I'm not sure if that's what I want any more. It's just . . . it's suddenly got so complicated.'

She nodded. She felt it too: that now the truth, the reality of her situation was out there, it threw the boundaries of their different lives – their different locations – into stark relief. She should feel encouraged that he didn't want her just for a dirty weekend if that was all it was going to be, that he would rather do the honourable thing and call time on it now, but she was struggling to feel encouraged about anything.

Hester saw Jake swallow, watched him look away from her and blink before turning back, being kind enough to meet her gaze, even as he was breaking her heart. 'You've let me build up this picture of you that isn't true, let me imagine possibilities that can't ever happen, and I understand why you did it – I promise you I do. But I can't do this right now, Hester. I need some time to work out how I feel.'

Chapter
Thirty-One

Saturday

Hester was dreading the drive home. After they'd found dry clothes and packed up their things, she took the bags out to the car and Jake settled up with the hotel. She doubted he'd get a refund for the second night they weren't going to spend in that glorious room together.

She felt exhausted, hollowed out, a victim to the eternal *if only* that kept playing through her head. *If only* she had decided from the beginning not to lie, to do the nights without those personal memories – the ones that belonged to other people. He'd been interested in finding out about her, and he thought the only way he could do that was to link it to all the places she'd been. They'd both done what they could to spend more time with each other, playing this little dance, though neither of them understood it at the time. She was an idiot.

Except, she thought there was more to his reaction than

disappointment in her dishonesty. She remembered Beth telling her that losing control was the hardest thing for Jake, and perhaps that moment of complete exposure: admitting his feelings for her, climbing giddily into the bathtub with her, followed by her revelation that she couldn't follow him out to New York – perhaps would never be able to – made him see how ludicrous it all was: that being with Hester was a further loss of control, one that put the life he had built for himself – far away from London – in jeopardy.

She told him she would drive again, and after a minor protest, he let her. He looked shattered, and after five minutes, once he'd directed Hester back onto the road that would snake its way through Norfolk, round the edge of Norwich and then back onto the A11, he fell asleep.

Hester thought that was probably the easiest way for it to end. She focused on driving, trying to keep her mind blank, but it stubbornly decided to run through everything. Their evenings in his hotel suite: dancing to 'Waltzing Matilda' in that stupid paddling pool; drinking cocktails and eating calamari on the window seat with a view of London rooftops; how he'd kissed his way around Central Park on her stomach, and then brought her into the crook of his arm to sleep after the doctor had seen him, and it had felt like the most natural thing in the world.

There was a queue leading down to the large roundabout at Mildenhall, and they came to a standstill for ten minutes. Hester took the opportunity to look at Jake. He had his arms wrapped protectively around himself, his forehead resting against the window. Stubble was a brown brush along his jaw, making his lips seem pinker, and his dark eyelashes looked impossibly long against his skin. His hair was a tangle of curls, and Hester wanted to run her hands through it, to find that one, perfect ring she'd seen on Amalfi night, when everything had seemed possible: when she'd been intent only on hooking him, and not keeping hold. She wanted to kiss every inch of his face, to crawl inside his battered leather jacket with him and go to sleep in his arms.

Instead, she would be saying goodbye.

He woke up as they reached the M11.

'Sorry,' he said, blinking awake. He sat up straighter and rubbed the back of his neck.

'Don't be,' she replied. 'You must have needed it.'

She could feel him looking at her, could almost hear him trying to work out what to say. But what could he say? He'd told her he needed time, that everything had got too complicated, and she wasn't going to push him. She turned the radio on, the cheerful pop songs sounding frantic in the space between them as the soft green countryside hardened to London suburbs.

Hester drove the Mercedes slowly into Beth's driveway and turned off the engine. She waited a second, unsure, now that they were here, how to do this.

'Hester,' Jake said.

'I should make a move.' She reached into his footwell and took her handbag. He put his hand over hers, and she looked at him. Traitorous tears filled the corners of her eyes, and she could see her pain reflected back at her.

'Hester, I—'

'I'm going to go now.' She opened the car door. 'Bye, Jake.'

She didn't give him time to reply. She got out of the car, took both bags out of the boot and put Jake's on Beth's doorstep. Then she hauled hers over her shoulder and, while he was pulling himself out of the passenger seat, she walked down the driveway and out onto the pavement. She wouldn't wait for a taxi outside Beth's house. She would find a bus, or she would walk, despite the heaviness of her bag and the sky filled with grey clouds, dark with impending rain.

By the time she got back to her flat, her nose was blocked from crying and her neck and shoulder were screaming out that she should have got a taxi after all. It was mid-afternoon and the sun was gone, the thick cloud blanketing it before it had a chance to protest.

Hester dumped her bag in her bedroom, switched on every light in her flat and curled up in her chair with a cup of tea. Her goodbye had been sniffy, she knew, but Jake had made his decision, and she had wanted to get out of there before the tears became a torrent.

Once again, she had been held back by her fears: by that one, defining event sixteen years ago and all its ripples and repercussions. And now, not only was it stopping her from going wherever she wanted, spreading her wings as much as she craved, it had lost her the one man she'd felt like she could love.

She'd moved from tea to wine, had ordered a Chinese that, a text told her, was out for delivery, and the rain was splattering fat, fast drops against the windows when her phone rang.

She reached for it, knowing the selfies she'd taken were still on there. Part of her wished her phone had been ruined when she'd been knocked over on the beach, that those brief moments of perfection could fade in her head, and not be left behind as a reminder. She wouldn't be able to delete them herself.

When she saw who was calling she almost didn't answer, but how could she not?

'Beth?' Her voice was a squeak as she remembered the conversation they'd had in her hallway. *I hope he doesn't hurt you.*

'Hester, are you OK?'

It wasn't what she'd expected. 'Yes,' she said automatically. Then, 'No. No, I'm not. But it's my own fault.'

She heard Beth sigh, long and loud. 'For what it's worth, I don't think it's about the fact that you lied to him.'

'You don't?'

'Not completely. If it is, then it's an extreme case of overreacting.'

'You didn't tell him that, did you?'

'Of course I did. You didn't really expect me to hold back, did you? But I promise I did it in a nice way.'

Hester waited a beat, and then found she couldn't not ask. 'How is he?'

'He's very confused, I think,' Beth said. 'I can't remember the last time he talked about anyone the way he's spoken about you. He *never* talks to me about his love life. We're usually an ocean apart, so he can sidestep the issues and I have no way of finding out. But ever since that first day in his hotel room, I haven't had a conversation with him that hasn't included some mention of you. I was sorry to hear about your phobia. That flight sounds horrendous.'

'He told you?'

Beth sighed. 'When I opened the door and it was just him there, looking so bloody hopeless, I knew things had gone wrong. Once I'd started to coax it out of him there was no holding him back. The stoic, reticent brother I know and love was nowhere to be found. He told me that you'd been lying to him, but I'm sure that's not why he broke off your weekend. He's got this safe, uncomplicated life: his apartment; nights in New York restaurants with his friends; his job where, despite the travel, a lot of it is about managing imports and stock-levels, and everything's OK as long as all the rows on his spreadsheet balance. You coming clean with him like that, I think it made him realize, perhaps, that his priorities are changing. You've blown his quiet, regulated existence out of the water.'

'I should never have lied to him.'

Beth made a noise of disagreement. 'A small lie. He's suddenly realized that this – *you* – what you have together, could shake everything up. He's running scared, I'm sure of it.'

Hester's doorbell rang, and she put the phone under her ear as she opened her door and went down the stairs, past the familiar graffiti, to get her takeaway. 'You think that's it?' She had guessed that might be part of it, and it had made her wonder if he'd been imagining a long-distance, international relationship, where they added detours and stopovers to their existing travel plans, so they could see each other between hotel scouting trips and plantation visits.

'It's this control thing,' Beth said, her voice fuzzing in and out as the signal became patchy in the stairwell. 'He didn't expect to care about you so soon, I suppose. He decided to throw caution to the wind, and now he feels like everything he's built up is at risk, because of his feelings for you. It's much easier for him to stop it in its tracks, use your admission as an excuse to halt proceedings before either of you lose your hearts.'

Hester winced. 'Hang on, Beth.' She accepted her take-away, thanked the delivery driver for coming out in such filthy weather and gave him a tip, then climbed the stairs. 'I totally get all that,' she said. 'I care about him, too. More than seems logical, considering how long I've known him. It's exhilarating, but it's also a bit scary, and I under-stand that if we're hardly ever going to be able to see each other . . .'

Beth sighed. 'He's miserable, you're miserable, and the irony is it's because you make each other so happy that you're both feeling this way.'

Hester stopped on the landing below hers, Beth's simple assessment knocking the air out of her. Jake made her happy. Happier than she'd been in a long time. That was worth fighting for, wasn't it, despite all the complications? The light buzzed above her. *Yes yes yes*, it seemed to say.

'So what are you going to do?' Beth asked.

'Jake said he needed time to think,' Hester said. 'I should give him that.'

Beth laughed humourlessly. 'Now all the kids are in bed, Jake's version of thinking is to hole up in Dunc's study with my husband and some bottles of beer. I don't know how he's expecting that to clarify his mind. What an idiot.' Hester could hear the fondness in her voice, and her heart twisted, because she understood it completely, even if her feelings for Jake were very different to Beth's.

'I love that idiot,' she said, and then sucked in a breath.

Beth, too, was momentarily silenced by Hester's admis-sion. *Was* it an admission? Did she mean it, or was it a throwaway comment?

'So,' Beth repeated. 'What are you going to do?'

Hester put the takeaway on her kitchen counter and stared at the half-empty bottle of wine.

'I don't know yet,' she admitted, screwing the lid back on the bottle and getting out a plate. 'I have to give him time to think about it, to hopefully realize that, even though it's all happened so quickly, and that it's not going to be easy, that it's worth taking a chance on.'

'And if he drags his heels?' Beth prompted, then Hester heard her say, away from the microphone, 'Two secs, Tamsin, and I'll be there.'

Hester sighed. 'If he drags his heels, then I'm going to have to show him myself, aren't I?'

She could almost hear Beth's smile down the phone. 'I think you are,' she agreed. 'Chin up, Hester. Get a good night's sleep, and hopefully I will see you very, *very* soon.'

Hester hung up the phone, and for the first time since she started to tell Jake about Betty and the flight, the kernel of warmth that had been growing inside her for the last ten days started glowing again.

Chapter
Thirty-Two

Monday

By Monday morning, Hester was swinging wildly between a strong sense of resolve, and the certainty that Jake had had time to think, beer or not, and had decided that what they'd had – what they'd started to have – wasn't worth it.

Her phone had stayed painfully quiet throughout Sunday, a day she'd spent vigorously tidying her flat, walking to the local supermarket and buying a selection of healthy foods that, she knew, she would be bored of after a few days, and clearing up the photos on her phone. She had spent far too much time looking at the selfies of her and Jake, and even more time staring at her dark, silent screen and willing it to ring. It hadn't.

When Glen had messaged their friends' group chat on Sunday evening to get all the details of her dirty weekend, Hester had distracted him by asking about his football match and his and Elise's visit to the nearest cat sanctuary, because they wanted to adopt a rescue. When Amber had joined in and tried to turn the conversation back to Hester, she'd simply told them it hadn't gone that well but she was fine, and it would be easier to talk when she saw them.

She'd realized that, since meeting Jake, conversations with her friends had been decidedly one-way. She knew they would argue that it was because she was the one with the news, the life crisis, the problem that needed solving, but Hester felt as if she'd been monopolizing their time. She resolved to be more friend-focused in future. If she was going to take nothing else from her time with Jake, she could see it as a chance to press the reset button.

'Good weekend, Hester?' Seb asked, giving her a longer glare than usual as she walked in.

'Lovely, thanks,' she said breezily, and put a double espresso on his desk.

She might be an emotional, conflicted mess inside, but outwardly, she was going to be on it. She'd dressed in tight, dark jeans and a thin shirt in a rich, deep purple that was loose enough to be comfortable but snug enough to flatter her figure. She wore brown leather ankle boots with a low heel and brass buckles on the sides, and had put her hair in a high ponytail. She'd painted her nails Coca-Cola red and taken longer with her make-up than usual. She was composed, professional, and ready to face the day.

As she took off her coat and sat at her desk, she noticed the pink Post-it note she'd stuck to her computer screen on Friday morning, a note she didn't need because she was already too excited to forget it. *Leave by 12.30* it said in black Sharpie. She chewed the inside of her cheek, then crumpled it up and threw it in the bin.

She was halfway through her emails, jotting down notes for a luxury, month-long family holiday in Mexico she'd been asked to arrange, when Cassie came out of her office. She looked poised as always, wearing a bottle-green jump-suit that was more suited to a red carpet than a travel agency office.

'Good weekend, Hester?' she asked, a neat furrow between her brows.

'Yeah, it was fine thanks. Great, in fact,' she added, when she remembered that of course Cassie knew she'd been going away, because she'd asked for Friday afternoon off. 'Really lovely. Good to get out of London.'

Cassie smiled. 'Excellent. And did Beth get hold of you?'

'Beth?'

'I had a couple of missed calls from her,' Cassie said. 'A voicemail asking if I could get you to call her.'

Hester frowned. 'I spoke to her over the weekend, so . . . maybe she'd forgotten she already had my number?'

'Oh Good. So you've been in touch, then?'

'We have.' Hester had been grateful for Beth's call, had known it was about helping her brother out as much as making Hester feel better. But as good as Beth was at fixing things, she couldn't change Jake's mind. He had to come to a decision by himself, and from the lack of contact since she'd dropped him off, she thought he'd made it.

'Shall we go and get a coffee?' Cassie said. Hester glanced around the room. Danielle and Seb were both working away, the tap tap tap of their keyboards loud in the echoey space.

'Me?'

'Yes.' Cassie smiled warmly. 'I've got an opportunity I want to discuss with you.'

The coffee shop was Monday-morning busy, as if everyone was trying to talk and laugh their way into feeling enthusiastic about the week ahead. The coffee machine squealed, the barista shouted out which drinks he'd made, and Cassie took Hester to a table by the window, where the Thames was visible as a thin, silver line above the river wall.

Hester sat and stared at nothing, her palms clammy, while Cassie got their drinks. She wondered what details Beth had left in her voicemail, whether she was about to get a pep talk or a commiserative pat on the shoulder about her failed weekend away. Hester sighed. A stay at a hotel in *this* country, and she had managed to fuck that up, too.

'Right then.' Cassie put a latte in front of Hester and sat opposite her.

Hester pulled her mug towards her, wondering whether Jake would approve of this particular blend.

'I want you to go to Italy,' Cassie said.

Hester slopped coffee over the rim of her mug. 'Italy?'

'That's right. There's a boutique spa hotel opening in Positano, along the coast between Amalfi and Naples. We've got nothing on our books for that stretch of coastline, and it would give us an advantage. Everyone goes to Amalfi, but this town has got so much charm, and it's closer to Naples, a shorter boat ride to Capri. It's a beautiful hotel, Hester, and I want us to build a relationship with the owners, arrange preferential rates and packages for our customers. I want you to do all that.'

Hester stared at her boss. This was it. The great falling-apart. The crumbling of everything. 'I . . . I don't know what to say.'

'You say yes,' Cassie said, 'because you need to do this. You are such a strong agent, Hester. You can weave magic spells with the customers, make them fall in love with a place just by talking about it. You have that knack, and I keep thinking how much better you could be with first-hand knowledge. You could build a rapport with the hoteliers, too, if you met them instead of talking on the phone. I want you to do this.'

Hester's hands were shaking. She didn't dare try and pick up her coffee cup. 'I do too, but—'

'And the flight is a lot shorter than to Saint Lucia or South Africa.'

Hester stared at her. Cassie raised her eyebrows and sipped her drink.

'You know?'

'I know there has to be something,' Cassie said. 'All those excuses, one after the other, missing out on trips that anyone in their right mind – anyone who had chosen this as a career – would be desperate to go on. This seemed like the most obvious answer.'

Hester nodded. 'I can't fly. I haven't since – not for a long time.'

'Then it's time to make a decision,' Cassie said simply. 'I'm not unsympathetic. I don't know what's behind it, and I would never belittle it, but you're treading water where you are. I want you to step out of your comfort zone, to prove to me – and most of all, yourself – what you're really capable of. You've shown your imagination, and ingenuity, with the project for Jake—' Hester hoped Cassie hadn't noticed the noise that slipped out, some kind of involuntary whimper— 'and you need to keep going. Positano. A week at the beginning of November. I've put your name down for it, and I know you can do it.' She put her hand over Hester's on the table. 'You can do this, Hester.'

Hester nodded, not sure she could speak. Cassie's faith in her was heartening, but her ultimatum – one Hester couldn't blame her for – was forcing her to make a decision. To face her fears or change her life. To get on a plane, or to find a completely different career.

'Can I have a few days?' she asked.

'You can have until the week before,' Cassie said. 'But if I end up sending Seb or Danielle, then you and I will be having a very different conversation, OK?' She squeezed Hester's hand. 'You could be my best agent, Hester. Give yourself the chance to reach those heights.'

The breeze was fresh, the clouds charging through the sky as they walked back to the office. They stepped inside, and were immediately assaulted by Danielle.

'Oh my God, don't either of you check your phones?'

'Danielle,' Cassie said sharply, and the younger woman shrank back.

'Sorry. I'm so sorry, Cassie. I shouldn't have spoken to you like that. It's just that someone called Beth has been trying to get hold of you. You, Hester, mainly. She's tried your number Cassie, and I tried both your mobiles, but—'

A sick feeling churned in Hester's stomach as she took out her phone and saw the missed calls from Danielle. But there were none from Beth. 'Did she say what it was about?'

'No, but she said you had to call her back as soon as you could.'

'Right. Thanks, Danielle.' She took her phone outside and stood against the river wall while people walked past and the wind tugged at her high, confident ponytail.

She called Beth's number, and she picked up after one ring.

'Hester, is that you?'

'It's me,' Hester said, frowning. 'What's wrong?'

'Oh, thank God. I didn't have your number anymore, and neither did Jake.'

'What?' Hester said sharply, and a couple of women walking past turned to look at her.

'It was Tamsin,' Beth hurried. 'Turns out she's got a massive crush on Jake, and when she overheard that you and he had . . . well, that it wasn't going so well, she deleted your number in both our phones: the call lists; Jake's messages – everything. Jake was only here for a few hours on Saturday afternoon, but Tamsin can be so stealthy when she wants to be.

'I am forever leaving my phone around, and she decided she was doing us both a favour. I couldn't find your number, and I didn't know why – until I found out what she'd done. I called Cassie yesterday evening, when I realized what had happened, but I don't think she can have got my messages.'

'So, hang on. Does that mean that Jake wanted to get in touch with me, but couldn't?'

'That's the thing, I don't know,' Beth admitted. 'When I spoke to him yesterday, he was back to being tight-lipped. He told me he was checking out of the Duval today, that he'd lived off Rosalie's generosity for long enough. He tried

297

to do it on Friday because of your weekend away, but she held the suite for him, and he went back on Saturday night so he didn't have to sleep on my camp bed.'

'He's going home?' Hester whispered.

Beth sighed. 'Maybe he's been here long enough to satisfy his doctor's wishes, or maybe he just doesn't care any more. I told him that he had to get in touch with you before he left, even if it was just to say goodbye. He owes you that.'

'What did he say?' Hester could barely speak past the lump in her throat.

'He didn't say anything, just told me he'd call me when he got back to New York. He's such a stubborn sod sometimes! He hasn't turned up at your office?' She sounded hopeful, but Hester knew Danielle would have mentioned it if he'd been there while she'd been having coffee with Cassie. A man like Jake appearing at Paradise Awaits would not go uncommented on.

'He's not been here,' Hester said.

'OK,' Beth said. 'Well, maybe he's got some other things to do first and *then* he's coming to see you? Once we're finished I'm going to give him your number again. He might have wanted to call you yesterday, but had no way of getting hold of you – unless you got in touch with him, which you obviously didn't.'

'I wanted to give him space,' Hester said quietly, thinking that Jake could easily have got her number from Marty if he'd wanted to. 'He might not have any intention of contacting me. Maybe he's made his decision, and he's going to walk away.'

'And what are you going to do about it?' Beth whispered. She didn't sound hopeful any more.

Hester gazed up at the churning clouds, the pigeons being buffeted by the wind. 'I think I've only got one option, haven't I?'

Chapter
Thirty-Three

Monday

Hester walked over Hungerford Bridge and decided that it was too cool for sweat to be running down her back, for her hands to be clammy, but her body wasn't listening. Looming on her horizon she had a trip to Positano that she wouldn't be able to take, forcing her to look elsewhere for work, and she had Jake, hours away from flying out of the country and leaving her life for good.

Perhaps he had wanted to get in touch with her yesterday, but Tamsin, the clever little devil, had taken that option from him? Maybe he hadn't said anything to Beth when she asked because he didn't want her to interfere: he wanted to do things by himself and regain some of the control he'd lost. Or else he didn't want to see her at all, he didn't care that Tamsin had deleted her number – had used it as another way to mentally shut the door on their time together. But that, Hester realized, was not good enough for her.

Yes, she'd lied to him, and she couldn't take that back. She knew it had changed his opinion of her, had made him see the complications of any relationship they embarked on in vivid technicolour, but did that really mean it wasn't worth fighting for? She needed to talk to him again now he'd had time to think. She needed to convince him – in the way that she convinced people, every day, to spend thousands of pounds on a luxury holiday – that he wanted her.

The Duval looked as imposing as it always did, and Hester swallowed before walking up the stone steps, the doorman smiling warmly as he opened the door. She went to the piano room first, wondering if she could find Marty, but the room was empty save for a woman in half-moon spectacles reading a Jane Casey book. Hester tried the concierge's number, huffing in frustration when it rang and rang and then went to voicemail, and, with no options left, took the lift up to the suites.

A few moments later and she was standing in front of the Merryweather door, a slideshow of memories assaulting her: the first time she'd knocked and Jake had answered, not particularly pleased to see her; her second trip, when he was mesmerized by her imaginary escape to the Rockies; Australia and Amalfi and New York; wanky Rich and drunk, puppy-dog Jake. That was the last time she'd been here, their relationship spilling out of this luxurious, unbelievable place and into her real life, her flat and her thoughts, her heart.

She knocked on the door, not wanting to announce herself in case he was inside and reluctant to see her. When she'd left it long enough and there was no answer, she knocked again and called out, 'Jake, it's me! Hester! Please open the door.'

She waited a moment longer, then jumped as she heard a lock turning.

'He's checked out, I think,' said the voice behind her, and she turned to see Sagging Man, the occupant of the Avalon suite, wearing a dark suit and white shirt, looking more polished than the last time they'd met.

'Oh, really?'

'Not actually seen him today, mind. But I think I heard him talking to one of the staff earlier. Asking them to put his case in storage while he saw a couple of people, telling them he'd pick it up later.'

'That's great, thank you. He didn't happen to mention who he was seeing?'

'Not so as I heard, no. Sorry.'

'Not at all – you've been very helpful, thank you.' She waited until he'd walked to the lift, her thoughts racing too fast to want to share it with him and engage in small talk, then she took the stairs to the ground floor.

Sagging Man – which she realized was a cruel nickname for him – thought that Jake had checked out, but it was an overheard conversation. She had to know for certain.

She waited behind a well-groomed couple, then approached the reception desk when it was her turn. Her heart sank a little when she saw it was the dark-haired man from her first visit. He didn't look particularly happy to see her, but that might just have been his resting frown face.

'Can I help you, madam?' he asked.

'Could you tell me if Jake Oakenfield is still checked into the Merryweather suite?'

'Can I ask who you are?'

'My name is Hester Monday. We've been working

together.' That seemed like the easiest summary, without going into detail about virtual holidays, blossoming romances and disastrous weekends away.

His thick eyebrows came together in concentration as he looked at his screen, then back up at her. 'I'm afraid I don't have you on my list, madam.'

That wasn't surprising. 'OK, but could you tell me if Jake is still checked in?'

'I'm afraid I can't give out that information. Not if you're not on my list. I am sorry, madam.' This time, despite the heavy-set eyebrows and impassive face, he did seem genuinely regretful that he couldn't help her. It didn't make Hester feel any better.

'Do you know if Marty is working today?' she tried. 'Sorry, I don't know his surname.'

This time there was a flicker of a smile, of recognition. 'It's his day off, I'm afraid.'

'Oh, OK,' she said. 'Thank you anyway.' She walked away from the desk, pausing in the centre of the large, ornate foyer when she realized she had run out of options.

If she went on the information from Sagging Man – which was all she had to go on – Jake had checked out already, but had asked the hotel to store his case until he could come and get it. Who was he going to see in the meantime? Was he really going back to New York today? The thought made her insides churn unpleasantly. She wandered aimlessly into the lounge and perched on a banquette, the cream and gold striped fabric smooth against her palms.

When she took out her phone, the screen had a single notification.

304

Jake's got your number again now. Everything crossed!
Beth. xxx

Hester put it on the table and rubbed her forehead. He hadn't called her, and the calls she'd made to him since discovering Tamsin had deleted her number had gone unanswered. She was in limbo. The only thing she could think to do was wait here, in sight of reception, until he came back for his case. He could be hours, or Sagging Man could have got it wrong and he could be gone already. She messaged Beth.

Can you ask him to call me? He might say no, but can you ask, at least? Hx

Her reply was instant.

I will ask again. Keep your spirits up, chuck. Beth. xx

'Can I get you anything, madam?' She looked up to find a waiter staring down at her.

'Oh no—' she started, and then hesitated. 'Actually, can I have a pink lemonade, please?'

'Of course,' he said. 'Make yourself at home.'

She frowned at him, and then realized she was perched sideways on the edge of the seat, as if ready to bolt. She turned around and settled onto the bench, her handbag beside her.

She was sitting there, sipping her pink lemonade, with its strawberry decoration and its fresh mint, regretting that first stupid lie about Australia and all the ones that had followed, when Rosalie found her.

Chapter
Thirty-Four

Monday

'Ah, the pink lemonade,' Rosalie said. 'It really is one of the Duval's highlights.' She was wearing a jacket in lemon yellow, the skirt beneath matching. Her leather handbag was chartreuse green, her jewelled earrings the same shade. Just as autumn was about to really kick in, Rosalie Dewey was a vision of spring.

'It's delicious,' Hester agreed, and the thought of having no reason to come back here, to order it and delight in its presentation before she'd even taken a sip, made her feel overwhelmingly sad. 'How are you, Rosalie?' She forced a smile.

'May I?' Rosalie indicated the chair opposite, and Hester nodded, waiting while she sat down.

A waiter was upon them in an instant, and Rosalie ordered the same as Hester, and a bowl of miniature biscuits. 'They're beautiful,' she said to Hester. 'Dainty versions of all the English favourites – custard creams and bourbons, jammy dodgers, but with fresh cream in the centre. One of the chef's creations. But we're not here to talk about the patisserie. What are *you* here for, darling Hester?' She raised a groomed white eyebrow.

'I came to see if I could catch Jake before he left,' she admitted. 'But I think I'm too late, and even if I'm not, he might not want to see me. He might have decided none of this is worth it, and we might end up having an angry, awkward conversation in the foyer, and then the frowning man at reception would be genuinely disapproving of me, rather than just mildly irritated.'

Rosalie stared at her, lips parted. 'I think you'd better tell me what's going on.'

Why? Hester wanted to ask. But then she realized that, because Jake and Rosalie were fond of each other, she might have some insight into how he was feeling, or what he might be planning.

'I'm glad you got those biscuits,' Hester said, smiling.

'This story requires fortification, does it?'

'You did ask. I expect you'll be regretting it pretty soon.'

'If I'm able to help in any way, you *or* Jake, then I don't believe I'll regret it. You take your time, Hester dear. And leave nothing out.'

Hester did leave some details out, namely the intimate ones, because they were for her and Jake alone. Other than that, she let her words spill out, in between sips of pink lemonade and biscuits that were almost magical, tiny but bursting with flavour, custard creams elevated to something magnificent that you wouldn't dare dunk in your tea. If rich children came here for dolly tea parties, they probably went out of their minds with delight at the miniature biscuits.

Hester told Rosalie everything else, not sparing the agony of her conversation with Jake in the Norfolk hotel, and going over, again, the event at the root of it all. The flight that had started out as fun, because this older woman with red hair and green eyes had been paying her attention, taking Hester into her confidence, declaring them the same. Then the panic, the horror of watching the reaction to her collapse – because Hester hadn't seen Betty after that: not until she was laid gently on the floor.

When she described trying to get on the return flight, the way her legs had buckled, and how all her fear and sadness – that had been locked tightly inside her for their whole Edinburgh weekend – had come rushing out, Rosalie placed a wrinkled hand over hers.

'My dear girl,' she said. 'You talk about it as if it was only last week.'

'I can't seem to get rid of it,' Hester explained. 'It was like a horror film, with the aeroplane as the monster. I can't make it past the monster, even though I really, *really* want to.'

'And it was after that, that Jake decided to end your weekend?' Rosalie's eyebrows rose.

'I had to explain to him why I don't fly. Why the things I'd told him – or some of them, during those nights upstairs – weren't true.'

'He didn't fly into a rage when you told him what you'd done?'

'No, he was disappointed. Sad. Confused, I think, because it changed what he knew about me. I think, mostly, it changed how he saw us: the possibility of any future.

It was already complicated, and I'd just added to that. Angry might have been better.'

Rosalie sighed. 'I can see why you would think that, but anger is very rarely better, and rages aren't to be tolerated. A man who keeps control of his emotions is, in my experience, the best kind. Not that he should hide them, as Jake I think has a tendency to do, but it makes him measured. And that gives me hope.'

'Hope?' Hester sat up straighter. That word always sounded so good: it was a shimmering firefly dancing in the air, surprising and desirable. And if Rosalie had hope, then Hester believed she could have it, too.

'He's a considerate man, I'm sure of that. And if he's giving himself time to think about everything you told him, then he wants to see it from your perspective. He could have told you that it was over and closed the door without a second thought. But he hasn't done that.'

'I know,' Hester said. 'But I have no idea where he is. Beth thinks he's getting on a flight home today, and the man in the suite opposite thought he heard Jake asking the staff to look after his case, but reception won't tell me anything and there was a mix-up with my number, so—' she shrugged. When she laid out all the things she didn't know, which were stopping her from seeing Jake again, her firefly of hope guttered and died.

'What do you want to happen?'

It was such a simple question, it emptied all other thoughts from her head. 'I want him to come and find me, to tell me he forgives me and that there's a chance for us, so we can go back to how it was before.'

'Really?' Rosalie asked. 'Back to before? Not forwards?'

Hester picked up a ginger cream and pulled it in half, then nibbled the side without the cream. 'Forwards is so complicated.'

'Because Jake lives in New York. Do you want him to move back to London so you can be together?'

Hester shrugged and sighed, then looked at Rosalie instead of staring at the table like a sulking teenager. Everything that had happened over the last few days, with Jake and with Cassie, had made it clear that she needed to face up to things.

'I love that he lives in New York,' she said. 'It was one of the most exciting things about him, before I'd even met him. I have always wanted to go there, and I – I don't want him to change for me. I fell for the man that he is, with his blue eyes and Top Gun jacket, low voice and stubbornness, and – all of it.'

'So then,' Rosalie said, sitting back and undoing the top button of her jacket, so that Hester could see the matching yellow outfit was a dress, not a skirt. 'If forwards is complicated, what do you want to do about it? What have you done about it, in the past?'

Hester knew instantly what she was talking about. It felt strange, sitting in this lounge with its glitter-ball chandelier, everything fit for a visit from the Queen, talking about the darkest parts of her.

'I've had counselling,' she admitted. 'It helped with a lot, but not with . . . that. And I tried the straightforward way. I booked a holiday to Spain, with Amber and Glen. All-inclusive for a fortnight: cocktails by the pool, endless sunshine, a Kindle full of books to read. I was so excited, and I genuinely thought, having my friends with me, all the promise of that holiday, that I would be able to do it.'

'But?' Rosalie hadn't lowered her voice or hooded her eyes in sympathy.

'But I had a panic attack in the airport. I almost made it to airport security, but then we started moving towards it, with all these other people, and all I could think of was that moment on the plane, when people were crowded around Betty, and all the other passengers were sort of buzzing with alarm. That feeling of not understanding anything, except that something was very wrong: it was a huge wave of emotions and memories, and I felt like I was drowning in it.'

'You didn't get on the plane?'

Hester swallowed, her throat thick as she remembered it. 'I didn't,' she admitted. 'I forced Glen and Amber to, though. They didn't want to leave me, or go without me, but they couldn't lose out because of me. I sat in the Wetherspoons with a free cup of tea and waited for my dad to come and get me.'

'You were brave to try it.'

Hester shook her head. 'The worst part was, I really thought I could do it. I was nervous, but the excitement was so much greater. I felt strong and confident and capable, and then, suddenly, I wasn't any of those things.'

Rosalie called the waiter over and ordered two more lemonades. 'When I was diagnosed with breast cancer,' she said, 'I couldn't read a book or watch any television. Not fiction, anyway. I thought: how dare these people be getting on with their lives, having parties and babies, finding love, while I've got this thing growing inside me, stopping all my plans? And of course it's all drama, so characters died and had cancer too, and suffered horrendous tragedies, but then I thought: they will walk off set and forget about it for the night, or; they don't exist, and the moment I shut the page all their horrors will dissolve into nothing. I was envious of them all.'

Hester nodded. 'I can understand that. It's like life is going on without you, passing by while you're stuck in one place. It's not the same, but I do get it.'

'Of course you do,' Rosalie said. 'And since I've been in remission, which still feels like a dream, I haven't opened a book or watched a drama. I've made a list, I've ordered books from the library by authors I love, and they're waiting to be picked up. But I can't do it.'

'Because it reminds you of having cancer,' Hester finished.

'And it's the same for you. Your problem is nothing to do with the aeroplane, the flight itself. It's the thing you've used to close the lid on your grief, because as much as you only knew Betty for an hour – less – it's still grief. But perhaps not just grief for her, but for you, as well: for the loss of innocence she represented. Seeing someone die in front of you is a horrendous thing at any age, let alone at twelve, when you're absorbing everything, working out who you want to be. No wonder it changed you in such a fundamental way.

'You're using the aeroplane, the horror of that flight, to squash down your fear and grief, and all those other feelings that came along for the ride, and what you need to do is take the lid off and let it all out. You need to face those difficult emotions head on. Numb isn't better, however much it feels like it is.'

Hester stared at Rosalie. She felt like she'd been put in a straitjacket, all her limbs and muscles tensing at the talk of aeroplanes and grief. But there was something else there, a kernel of something shinier and more welcome, almost as if that firefly of hope was waking up again, a tiny flame burning inside her.

'I think Jake will come round,' the older woman went on. 'From what I saw of the two of you, I believe he's already in too deep to get out, dry himself off and walk away. And if that's true, then you're going to have to make a decision about what you want. I'm pretty sure sexting, or mutual masturbation over Zoom, isn't anywhere near as satisfying as the real thing.'

Hester just about managed to not spray Rosalie with pink lemonade. The older woman had a wicked gleam in her eye, and as Hester covered her mouth to stop the laughter filling the Duval's quiet, elegant lounge, she sent a silent thank you to whoever had allowed her to bump into Rosalie right when she needed to.

'Rosalie,' Hester said. 'We're going to make a deal.'

'We are?' She looked intrigued, rather than wary. This, Hester realized, was how she should be living her life. Holding nothing back, saying yes and seeing what happened.

She nodded. 'You're going to help me do something, and then I'm going to come with you to the library, and we're going to take out those books you've put on hold.'

Rosalie didn't say anything, she just held up her glass, and Hester clinked hers against it. It was a toast that, she hoped, she would remember forever, for all the right reasons.

Chapter
Thirty-Five

Monday

Monday afternoon, and the Heathrow Express was busy. Hester sat in the aisle seat, her handbag on her lap. She was clutching it against her, her knuckles white with the force of her grip, as if it contained all her worldly possessions and she couldn't possibly lose it. If she lost her handbag, she thought, she would lose her shit right along with it.

A family sat at the table ahead of her, two small children squealing excitedly about their imminent trip to Disneyland. If they weren't already hopped up on some kind of sugar, then God help those parents when they got to the candyfloss stall. The man in the seat next to her was dozing, and she envied him the ability to do that, knowing the train journey would end in fifteen minutes. Hester felt, right then, as if she might never sleep again.

She and Rosalie had sat in the lounge of the Duval and made the arrangements together, the older woman clasping her hands round Hester's when her fingers were shaking so badly she could barely tap them on her iPhone keyboard. When it was done, they'd walked to Rosalie's local library, which was just around the corner in a building that, Hester decided, was exactly how grand a library should be, with a vaulted ceiling and stone columns either side of the double doors.

Rosalie seemed to have no trouble walking up to the information desk, giving her name and unfolding a fuchsia pink shopping bag – no canvas totes for her – then putting the books into it. Hester noticed a couple of dark-looking crime novels, the latest Hilary Mantel and a hilarious, hot romance that she had read in the Devon holiday cottage the year before.

Every new thing she found out about Rosalie made Hester like her more. And having the older woman behind her, knowing that she had faith in her, was the main reason she was sitting here now, hurtling towards Heathrow, feeling like her stomach was two sharp bends in the track away from coming out of her throat. What would the Disney-bound family think about that? she wondered, and was surprised when her face managed to contort itself into a smile.

'Going to meet someone?' asked a young woman from across the aisle. She had kind eyes and a put-together look about her that made Hester think she was a schoolteacher.

'What makes you say that?' she asked. 'Do I look . . . uhm, excited?'

The woman's smile widened. 'I can't work out if it's excited or terrified. They mean a lot to you, whoever they are.'

Hester nodded, trying to swallow past her dry throat. She forced a laugh. 'Going to meet my destiny on the Heathrow Express from Paddington. I should be in a golden chariot or something.'

The woman laughed along with her. 'As long as it has wings, otherwise you'd come to an ungainly stop on the M25. This is probably the best way to go, even if it's not quite fitting for whoever's waiting for you at the other end.'

'What about you?' Hester asked.

'I'm meeting a friend who's coming back from California, so she'll be impossibly tanned and relaxed. I haven't seen her for a while, so I'm going to put my jealousy aside and take her out to dinner.'

'Shouldn't she be taking you out to dinner, if she's just had an amazing holiday?'

The woman shrugged. 'Maybe. But I know she'll have brought me something wonderful back. It's one of our rituals: whenever we go away without the other, we have to bring back a gift.'

'Do you often go on holiday together, then?'

'Oh yeah, every chance we get. But I've got a big work project on at the moment, so I missed out on California.'

'That must have been gutting,' Hester said, thinking how lovely it would be if holidays with Amber and Glen were easy; where the only two variables they had to worry about were time and funds.

'We'll sort something out in a few months,' the woman went on. 'We always do. Anyway' – she glanced up as people started gathering coats and bags, pulling things off the overhead racks – 'good luck with your destiny. I'm almost tempted to follow you, to find out who it is.'

Hester laughed, but didn't tell her: she didn't want to jinx it. 'Have a great time with your friend. I hope she's got you the best holiday gift.'

They said goodbye and she watched the other woman

walk off the train. Then she stood, gripping the handle of her handbag in sweaty palms, and was relieved to see that the dozing man had woken up and was following her off. It was easier to think about other people and be concerned for them. She didn't want to feel concerned for herself: that would only make this harder.

The walk from the station to the airport was a maze of corridors and escalators, and Hester forced herself to keep her steps steady; not to run, not to falter. The world was a starburst of noise and colour around her, but she felt removed from it all, as if she was watching it through Instagram's most unrealistic filter. She was questioning herself all the way. Had she made the right decision? Was this utter madness? Was she getting her hopes up, setting herself up for a huge fall? She tried not to think about how much it meant, and what she would do if she got there, and it didn't work out.

She followed the overhead signs, passing people standing in groups with their suitcases like dogs at their feet; couples walking hand in hand; children running towards the brightly coloured shops, cafes and restaurants at the fringes of the cavernous space. Hester went to the bank of check-in desks and, finding no available seats, walked over to the wall and slid down it, until she was sitting, cross-legged, on the floor. She still had time. It wouldn't be a mad dash.

She took her phone out of her bag, and wasn't surprised to see that the screen was full of notifications.

Cassie, who she had spoken to after she had left the hotel with Rosalie, sending her a message of encouragement:

Good luck, Hester! I am so proud of you for doing this. xx

Hester chewed her lip. She wished she hadn't had to tell her, but she needed to explain why she wasn't coming back to the office. Cassie had been understanding: she knew Hester had had an unusual couple of weeks. She hadn't told Amber or Glen or her parents, because she didn't want to have to phone them later and tell them she'd failed.

But she *wouldn't* fail, she told herself. She had to be positive. She looked up as a group of men and women walked past, all wearing long dark coats and suits: business people on the way to or from an international conference? One of the men was tall with dark curls, and Hester's pulse thrummed, but then he turned around and she saw the face wasn't Jake's.

He wasn't here. Why would he be?

She went back to her phone, reading the WhatsApp from Beth.

Did he get hold of you??? He said he was going to. Call me, Hester! I am keeping my phone well away from Tamsin. xxxx

Hester inhaled. She could feel one emotion separate itself from the tangle inside, rising up and through her, spreading into her limbs and coiling around her heart. She went back to the chat menu and looked at the message at the top of the list, a tear squeezing out as she opened it.

Please pick up, Hester. Where are you? I have got this so wrong. I need to see you so I can apologize to you and then kiss you. Beth gave me your number again – bloody Tamsin!! Please let me make it up to you? I miss you. Jake. Xx

Hester wiped her face on her sleeve and read the message again. She knew she needed to reply to him, but how? What to say? There was nothing she could say, except the truth. She'd learnt that much over the last few days, at least.

I'm sorry too. I do want to see you again, but there's something else I have to do first. Lying to you wasn't right, and I have to fix that before I do anything else. I miss you already, and I'm sorry I won't get to see you before you go home. Maybe I could visit you in New York? H.

Her fingers hovered over the message, and then she added one final thing, hoping it wasn't too much, wanting to be completely honest with him.

You have made me so happy. x

She pressed send, waited to see it land, delivered, in their conversation, and then switched her phone off. No more messages, no more distractions. She got up, dusted her jeans and jacket down, and walked over to the check-in desk, where people were beginning to queue.

Would the flight attendant be suspicious, she wondered, when she found out Hester only had hand luggage, and it was just her handbag and not even a small case? She felt rusty, out of touch with the protocol, while everyone else seemed at ease, bored or excited, around her.

Every moment that passed felt like an hour, and by the time she reached the front of the queue and showed her phone screen, with the ticket she'd booked online, and her driving licence, her mouth was dry and her fingers fumbled with the zip of her purse.

The woman in the smart navy and red uniform, her dark hair piled high and tied back with a wide, matching hairband, smiled as she asked her questions, and didn't seem to notice that Hester was sweating, or that her words were stilted.

Was this how a terrorist would behave? she wondered, as she collected her boarding pass. Would they take her and lock her in a tiny, bland room and interrogate her for days and days, without food and with only a plastic cone of water to keep her hydrated, while they asked her about terror cells and bomb-making kits, and why she carried a small, cuddly crocodile in her handbag? The thought was almost a relief, although thinking of Stanley Mk 2, nestled between her make-up bag and portable charger, brought on a wave of sadness.

'Miss Monday?' The woman was speaking to her again.

'Yes?' Hester said, then cleared her throat.

'Enjoy your flight to Edinburgh.'

Hester nodded and tried to smile, and then she had to hold onto the desk for a second, hoping she was doing it surreptitiously and didn't look how she felt; as if she was about to come apart at the seams.

'I'm sure I will,' she managed to reply. 'Thank you.'

Chapter
Thirty-Six

Monday

She forced herself to walk around the departure lounge, spending all the allocated time in the shops, sniffing the different bottles of perfume, counting how many types of vodka were on offer, and which countries they came from. She searched for and found Jake's Ocean Haze aftershave, balked at the price even in duty-free, and then saw to her utter delight that there were some free samples: silly little sachets that peeled open to reveal half a drop of scent that you could sniff or smear on your skin. She checked nobody was looking, then took a handful and put them in her bag.

The fear of being sprung with all those freebies, and having to explain to a pair of surly airport police why she had them: because they reminded her of the man that she was pretty sure she loved despite knowing him for only ten days, but she had fucked up their romance because she was terrified of flying; that she was trying to put that right with this very trip, even though it meant he would be going back to New York before she saw him and she was too late, but wasn't it better to fix *herself* first, because how could she fix them without doing that? Well, it kept her thoughts occupied, along with looking at the shelves in WH Smith and wondering if Rosalie had cracked open one of her library books yet. She would message her and ask once she got to Edinburgh. *Once she got to Edinburgh.* She had to lean against the display of Jamie Oliver cookbooks until the wave of dizziness passed.

And then she was with her fellow passengers, hovering at their departure gate, the first few getting their boarding passes checked and heading towards the plane. Hester tried to distract herself from her growing unsteadiness, as if she was slowly losing bone density, by working out who the other people were and why they were flying. That couple were going to look for Edinburgh Festival venues, for their two-person comedy act that involved clown outfits and leather whips, hoping to find a tiny theatre that looked like a dungeon; the large group of female friends were on a low-key hen party, none of them up for bunny ears or penis straws, but when they got to their hotel they would play Trivial Pursuit with a bottle of tequila and go whitewater rafting the next day; that tall man standing in a waxed Barbour jacket, slightly aside from everyone else, was a hired assassin on his way to scope out a hit on the businessman who ran the lion's share of ghost tours in the city, so that a rival ghost tour operator could take over his pitches. Would the assassin's victim become an Edinburgh ghost himself, thus achieving a level of irony it would be impossible to match?

Hester wished Glen and Amber were with her, so she could discuss all these crucial details with them. She wished Jake was there, to hold her hand and tell her she was doing great in his deep, even voice; to distract her with his blue-eyed gaze and his opinions about *Godfather II*, and another phrase he'd learned in Italian for her to puzzle over and then melt at.

She walked, a strange mixture of robotic and loose-limbed, down the tunnel, her body behaving as if she was about to get the worst migraine of her life. Her vision blurred at the edges and her stomach felt too high and present, as if it was about to launch its contents up her throat. She stayed close to the wall, pressing her palm flat against the cool surface, and hoped nobody thought she'd had five gin and tonics in the lounge bar.

But, she told herself, this was much further than she'd got last time, and a second later she was stepping across the threshold onto the tiny plane, where it all came rushing towards her: the claustrophobia and terror, the confusion and panic. She could barely read her boarding pass to see her seat number, and she'd forgotten it, even though she'd been repeating it to herself like a mantra while she'd been haunting duty-free. She was caught up in the shuffling procession of passengers, waiting for people who were putting coats and hand luggage into the overhead compartments. She clenched her damp hands into fists, resisted telling them to hurry up so they could all get this flight over and done with. She wasn't sure, anyway, that she'd actually be able to speak.

She had a window seat. She sat down and hugged her handbag as if it was a parachute that could save her if anything went wrong, but she couldn't resist glancing at the other passengers as they busied themselves around their allocated spaces. Was that man's face too pale? Was he sweating slightly? That woman's hand was trembling: was she afraid of flying, like Hester, or was it something more? An image of Betty, being laid out in the aisle so the flight crew could administer CPR, slid behind her eyes. Hester gripped the back of the chair in front.

Her seat shifted as someone sat next to her, and she turned to discover that her neighbour was the assassin. Of course it was. Did he have his gun in a violin case? Airport security would have had something to say about that. Hester decided his weapon must be waiting for him in Edinburgh, tucked away somewhere nobody would think to look: the gable of the roof he would be shooting from, perhaps, or some corner of an overgrown graveyard, sinister with its elaborate mausoleums.

It should have helped, this speculation, but she felt dizzier with every passing moment. And then, the thing that had her pressing her forehead into the fabric of the seat in front of her, her breath shortening and her eyes watering, was the gentle ping reminding her to fasten her seatbelt. What was it about that? Was it then, as they had begun the descent to Edinburgh, that they'd placed the blanket over Betty, then strapped her in like any other passenger, the two actions distressingly contradictory? That must be it, Hester thought. That was the memory that was turning her muscles to liquid.

'Are you all right?' the assassin asked.

She glanced at him, her vision swimming, and said something in her head that she wasn't sure had come out of her mouth. She was gasping like a goldfish on dry land.

'I'll get help,' he said. 'Hang on.' He raised his arm to get the attention of a flight attendant and Hester grabbed it, surprised at her own strength as she pulled it down.

'No,' she gasped. 'No, please don't! I'm . . . this is my first flight in a while. I'm nervous – but I'll be OK.'

'You will?' he asked. His voice was quietly pitched. He didn't sound like an assassin.

She nodded. Swallowed. She had to be. 'I will,' she said firmly. 'I am going to be fine.'

'OK then, but if you feel extra panicky just let me know, and I'll get some help.'

'Thanks,' Hester said, the kindness of this stranger making her blink furiously against a swell of emotion.

She put her seatbelt on, kept her lips clamped together while the attendants ran through the safety briefing, and accepted that she was going to tremble like Tickle Me Elmo throughout the whole thing. But it wasn't a long flight, she told herself, and Edinburgh was beautiful, despite her associations with it: that strange weekend that should have been full of so much excitement, but had a pall of sadness hanging over it, like early autumn mist; the horror of returning to the airport, the way her body and mind rejected getting on another plane in such a visceral, extreme way.

'It has already happened,' she whispered to herself. 'This is different.'

She closed her eyes when the plane started moving, when it made its interminable route along the runway, taxiing round to take its position in the queue, then waiting, the sound of its engine a low thrum, for a seemingly endless time. Hester licked her dry lips, kept her eyes squeezed shut as the assassin busied himself next to her, listening to the slide of fabric as he removed his coat, his low grunts as he got settled. She focused on his noises, on the way his bulky presence made her chair shift, and pressed herself more firmly into it.

And then the engine roared to life, the vibration filling the plane, the wheels juddering beneath them as it picked up speed, built up momentum. Hester gripped her armrests, felt the press of the hard edges against her palms, as the plane tilted up, up, at an angle too acute to really be believed, and she thought: *It's too late to get off. Anything could happen, and it would be too late.*

She used to enjoy the roller coaster swoop in her stomach, the way her ears popped. She had loved every new sensation on those flights to and from Amalfi. Now she craved nothing, numbness, all her memories and her senses wiped clean, relief from the tumbling thoughts that came crashing down on her as they rose, higher and higher, in the sky. She might have made a sound, a whimper, but she was beyond caring. She closed her eyes and squeezed her armrests and pressed her boots into the carpet, and waited for everything to stop.

And then eventually, *eventually,* the aeroplane evened out, and there was a collective sigh as the seatbelt light went off and people started chatting. Hester arched her back, wiggled her fingers experimentally, and opened her eyes. The plane interior was bright, innocuous, and nobody was staring at her or looking terrified. Nobody was paying her any attention at all.

With slick hands, she reached into her handbag and took out Betty's piece of malachite, and Stanley Mk 2. She held the gemstone in her left hand and the cuddly crocodile in her right, and focused on her breathing.

She was doing this for Betty, who had been kind to her and made her feel special, who had loved travel like Hester was just beginning to, and who had had her time cut unexpectedly short. Hester could have been seeing the world even though Betty couldn't, but she had been stuck. She needed to start moving again.

And she was doing this for Jake, who had made her happy, who had been funny, warm and honest, who had cared about her, and who she hadn't told the truth to. She hadn't given their relationship a chance. From the first time she'd lied, made his opinions of her – his expectations about them and what might be possible in the future – unreliable, she had been dooming it to failure.

And mostly, she was doing this for herself. For all those trips she'd wanted to take but hadn't had the courage for. For holidays with Amber and Glen, for Paradise Awaits hotel openings, for seeing more of New York than the film sets in *On the Town*. She was doing this for Hester Monday, and it felt terrifying, and exhilarating, and like it would never, *ever* end.

'I'm sorry, Betty,' she whispered to the green stone.

'I'm sorry, Jake Oakenfield,' she said to the crocodile. She glanced up, and saw that the assassin was watching her with undisguised curiosity. She knew she had tears streaming down her cheeks, and that she was throwing boulders in glass houses by making judgements about this guy, because honestly, she must look completely nuts.

'Your crocodile is called Jake Oakenfield, hey?' he said, reaching into a bag he'd kept between his feet and handing her a tissue. He was speaking to her as if she was a child, and Hester couldn't blame him.

She rested her crocodile on her knee and accepted the tissue. 'Thanks,' she said. 'No, my crocodile is called Stanley Mk 2. Jake Oakenfield is the man he reminds me of.'

'A man who a crocodile reminds you of?'

Hester smiled. 'It's a long story. I don't think this flight is long enough for it, thank God.'

'You're doing pretty great for someone who's terrified of flying,' he said. 'Apart from the floods of tears and clutching that pebble and the Jake Oakenfield crocodile as if you'll die without them. But I won't tell anyone, I promise.'

'Thanks. I'm surprised I've made it this far.'

'Well, no turning back now,' he said. 'Whatever happens, however hard the next hour is, the next place you'll see will be Edinburgh. You've basically done it. Getting on the plane was the hard part.'

Hester stared at him, her tears drying on her cheeks as his words sunk in. 'I have, haven't I?' she whispered. 'I've really, really done it. Thank you.' The truth was so overwhelming, so startling, that she reached over and hugged him. He was solid and warm and definitely resisting, and she wondered if he would call for help anyway, but for him this time instead of her. He smelled good. Not Ocean Haze good, but pretty nice.

He lightly patted her shoulder, and she realized she wasn't doing anything to dissuade him from thinking she had lost the plot. She sat back and gave him a sheepish smile, then rubbed at the shoulder of his jumper, which she'd left damp with the remnants of her tears.

'Sorry,' she said. 'This is just a big deal for me.'

He nodded, amusement dancing in his eyes. 'I can see that.'

'And you've helped. A lot.'

His eyebrows rose. 'As much as the pebble and Jake Oakenfield?'

She nodded, a fresh wave of tears threatening to spill. 'You've all helped,' she admitted. 'All three of you.'

'But it's mostly been you,' he said. 'I mean, as much as these things must mean something to you, the reality of it is, it's a crystal – a bit of rock – and a small, cuddly crocodile, and a stranger who has only handed you a tissue. You've done this all on your own, really.'

Hester stared down at the objects in her hands. 'A bit of rock, a cuddly toy, and an assassin.'

'I'm sorry?' the man asked.

She looked up at him, horrified. 'No! I mean – sorry. I just . . . you're right. They represent something, of course. But it was me, wasn't it? I did this.'

'Nobody else sitting in that seat,' he said. 'Crying on me.'

She laughed. 'Sorry about that.'

'Don't be. If it helped you get through it, then I'm happy to be of service.'

'What are you doing in Edinburgh, anyway?' It was probably too late to sound like a normal, interested human being after all the weird behaviour he'd had to put up with, but she had *done* it, she had got on a flight and she was nearly, *nearly* in Edinburgh.

'Oh,' he said, with an air of disinterest, 'I've got to meet someone about a ghost hunt. It's not as interesting as it sounds.'

'Well, it sounds like fun.' Hester nodded and smiled and turned to look out of the window so he wouldn't see her trying hard not to laugh, and as she did, the lights of Edinburgh appeared below her. Below *her*, Hester Monday, as she flew, in an aeroplane, towards the airport.

Chapter
Thirty-Seven

Monday

The landing was almost as horrifying as the take-off, but Hester was galvanized by the fact that she had made it so far, and that helped ease her tremors slightly as the plane juddered onto the runway and then, after another lengthy period of taxiing, came to a stop.

She followed the other passengers off the plane, and went through arrivals in a daze, her legs shaking as if she'd been doing squats for the last hour instead of sitting in a cramped window seat.

'OK?' It was the assassin, his large hand on her arm.

'I'm good,' she said. 'Really good. Thank you again.'

'Have a great time here. It's a beautiful city.'

She nodded. 'Good luck with your ghost meeting.'

'Ta.' He doffed her an imaginary cap and then was lost in the crowd.

Hester walked through the airport and out to the taxi

rank. The air was cool, and smelled damp but with no sign of rain, and she was glad that she had her jeans and her boots on, and a short jacket over her purple shirt. She just about remembered putting them on, the outfit an act of defiance against how sad and lost she felt after losing Jake. She couldn't believe it was the same day.

A day when she'd woken up and hoped she'd speak to him; a day when she thought her career might be over, because her boss wanted her to travel abroad. And now she'd been on an aeroplane, the one thing that she had, for the last sixteen years, seen as an impossible feat. It hadn't been easy. It had been one of the hardest things she'd had to do and she felt emotionally and physically wrung out by it, but she'd done it.

'Where to, love?' the cab driver asked.

'Princes Street, please.' She climbed in the back, her handbag on the seat next to her.

As they drove into the centre of Edinburgh, lights warming in the gathering dusk, the buildings becoming bigger, more stately and proud, she realized she had never really given this city a chance: she had dismissed it as keeper of one of her hardest memories, just like she'd sometimes dismissed herself as flawed, incapable, a bit of a Raggy Doll. But she'd been unfair to them both.

The taxi driver dropped her off at the end of Princes Street. She paid him and said goodbye.

Hester stood on the pavement, the buses and trams sliding past, the roads damp from an earlier rainstorm, and breathed in. The glowing, twinkling lights of the Princes Street shops enticed on one side, and Edinburgh Castle, the dark buildings that marked out the Royal Mile, loomed on the other, with Princes Street Gardens, a sunken sanctuary of sweeping lawns and trees in their autumnal coats, between them.

She found a coffee shop with an upper floor, ordered herself a large coffee and a tomato and mozzarella panini, and sat on a stool by the window. She looked out at the city, at the modern and old crammed in together and somehow making it work; at stone walls guarding centuries of memories, at shops with their promise of a brighter future if you would only buy this top, this book, this lipstick.

Hester sipped her coffee and ate her sandwich, finding that she was suddenly ravenous. When it finally sunk in that she had done it, that she had got on an aeroplane, all by herself, and made it through with the help of a friendly assassin, she took out her phone and turned it back on.

She didn't know what she'd been expecting: for her phone to light up with messages from people wondering where she was, asking what on earth she thought she was doing? But the only two people who knew where she was, what she had undertaken that afternoon, were Cassie and Rosalie.

Or at least, that was what she had thought until now.

Because there was a single notification on her screen, waiting for her like a beacon, and she realized it was highly possible that Rosalie had bumped into Jake at the hotel, or that she'd actively sought him out, to tell him what Hester was planning.

It was one message, from Jake. A message that, in some ways, felt like a goodbye.

You are amazing, Hester Monday. x

She walked across the road and down into Princes Street Gardens. There were fairy lights hanging in some of the trees, and as she strolled along the wide, even pathways they came to life, picking out spots of glossy green, red and burnished orange, the rich, heady colours of autumn, the last hurrah before the leaves fell, their job done. It was a beautiful park, busy with people crossing from the old town to the new, or from new to old, heading home from work or out for the evening, to indulge in late-night shopping or find a play, or a film, or an evening tour of the castle.

Hester strolled through the gardens, gazing at the city surrounding her, and chose a bench to sit on. It was just about dry, but cold through her jeans, and she shivered slightly, wrapping her jacket more tightly around her.

She took out Betty's piece of malachite, holding it in her palm, as she'd done hundreds of times over the years. The guardian stone for travellers. Betty's talisman, that hadn't kept her safe after all, but had seemed so important to her in Hester's brief time speaking to her, that she hadn't been able to leave it behind, to be swept into a bin bag along with the rest of the plane's detritus.

It had been her job, she thought, to keep Betty's dreams alive. She had known nothing about her, really: about the family and friends who must have grieved her loss. This was the one thing she should have been able to do.

'I've finally done it, Betty,' she whispered. 'I got on a plane. I don't know if this is the start of something, if I can do it again, but it's a big leap. An achievement. And it's not your fault, you know, all of this. Of course it isn't.' She swallowed. 'I'm sorry for what happened to you, and I hope you don't mind that I took this.' She placed the malachite on the bench next to her, and stroked its smooth surface with her fingertips. She looked up at the bright white lights in the tree above her bench, the leaves shuddering in the gentle breeze.

People walked past, laughing and talking, soaking up the atmosphere of the calm gardens and the vibrant city beyond, and Hester sat on the bench, looked out over the green space, and wondered how being there, how the flight that she'd been dreading – the one she'd been waiting to take for sixteen years – felt so monumental and also, so straightforward. She had done it, and she had discovered that, even though it was still scary, she could get through it. She could override her fear with courage, determination and her will to succeed.

'Goodbye, Betty,' she whispered. 'I'm going to leave you here, now. I just think it's . . . it's time to move on.' She cleared her throat, swallowing down the roughness that had gathered there, wiping her eyes to rub away the sting.

She stood and walked further into the park without looking back, stopping to read the inscriptions on the benches she passed: *To Arthur, 1921 to 2004, a proud father, husband and brother; Ethel Stevens, always in our hearts; William McArthur, 1967 to 2020. Gone too soon, but never forgotten.* She wondered where Betty's tribute was, and who came to look over her and talk about her. She wondered if anyone would pick up her piece of malachite, and what journeys it would take in the future. She hoped it would go on more adventures than she'd taken it on, although when she thought back to those nights at the Duval – Australia and Italy, the walk to the New York restaurant – she realized she hadn't been playing it entirely safe. From the moment she agreed to Jake's plan, she had been opening herself up in a way she knew was risky.

Even now, with things as they were, she thought it had been worth it.

Hester walked to the centre of the park, where a large, lit-up fountain held centre stage. It was beautiful, the iron painted turquoise and gold, with an ornate sculpture at its centre. Mermaids supported the lower part of the tower, water spilling down from above them, into the circular pool surrounding the structure. There were four women seated at the top, and one more female figure highest of all, her gaze cast down on the rest. The water was a glassy blue, the lighting a soft yellow, the dark, imposing hulk of Edinburgh Castle a magnificent backdrop behind.

She stepped closer, looking for a sign to tell her what the sculpture represented, who the women were. The falling water was soothing, the traffic sounds of Princes Street fading into the background. She wasn't the only one here, people taking a last chance to see the sights before the gardens closed for the evening.

She felt a stab of anxiety. She had nowhere booked for the night, just another flight, *another flight,* back to London tomorrow lunchtime. But Rosalie had assured her she would have no problem getting a room, and that if she did, Hester should call her. She was almost tempted to do that anyway, sure that the older woman would sort her out a suite at the Balmoral or somewhere equally fancy. But Rosalie had helped her so much, and she didn't want to take advantage.

She would walk from here to the Royal Mile, find a pub in the old town, then book a room on her phone rather than trail through the streets, knocking on hotel doors until she got lucky. That was the modern way, and Hester was a modern woman now: a woman who could book a flight and be on it three hours later. She smiled, giddy with the realization, and looked up from the plaque she had been staring at but not really reading.

There was a man standing on the other side of the fountain.

He was a silhouette in the twilight, his features masked from her view by the flare from the golden lights, and still Hester felt her body respond, as it always did. Because she recognized the outline, recognized the shape of that leather jacket and his frame and those curls.

It was Jake Oakenfield.

Chapter
Thirty-Eight

Monday

'Hester Monday.' His voice was deep and loud, reaching her across the fountain.

'Jake,' she called. 'I— you're not in New York.'

He walked forward, still on the other side of the pool from her, but close enough to the lights, now, that she could see his features. Those blue eyes and the whisper of a bruise on his temple. He was clean-shaven, and he looked good. *So good.* Wearing jeans and a navy hoody, with his Top Gun jacket on, open, over the top.

'No,' he said. 'There was somewhere else I needed to be.'

'In Edinburgh?' She laughed, incredulous. Happy. Confused.

'Wherever you are, Hester. I have to admit, I didn't imagine it would be here.'

'Did Rosalie tell you?'

He nodded.

'Come round here,' she said. She could see a few people watching them, curious about their half-shouted conversation.

He shook his head. 'How did it go? The flight?'

She exhaled. 'OK. It went OK. I mean . . .' She swallowed, felt the emotion rising up inside her. Damn him and the way he did this to her, every time. 'The guy I was sitting next to thought I was a lunatic, but I thought he was an assassin, so I guess we were even.'

A bemused look passed across his face, and it left behind the ghost of a smile. *Come on*, she thought, *give me that A to Z smile*. 'I'm glad, Hester,' he said. 'I am so bloody happy for you. And – and proud. I have no right to be proud of you, but I am.' He ran a hand over his face. 'I need to apologize.'

She shook her head. 'Come round here, Jake. Or I'm coming to you.'

'No!' He held a hand up in front of him. 'No.'

'No?'

He stepped up onto the low wall surrounding the fountain. 'Jake?'

'Hester.' He smiled, and then stepped down into the pool with a loud splash. Hester gasped, and she wasn't the only one. The water came halfway up his shins, eddying and swaying around him, as if caught off guard by its unexpected occupant.

'Jake, what on earth?'

'I am so, so sorry, Hester,' he said, as he walked towards her. The water sloshed around his legs, and someone muttered, 'He is going to get arrested,' but Jake was undeterred. 'I am sorry I walked away from you. From us. I shouldn't have done that.'

342

'But I . . . you had every right—'

'I had no right,' he said. 'None at all. You told me everything. The hardest part of your life: the event that has shaped and changed you, and instead of understanding, instead of sheltering you from that memory and pain, I was selfish. I was scared of what it meant for the future I already wanted with you, but instead of dealing with it, I ran from it.' He kept walking, the water seeping into his jeans, the fabric darkening over his knees. 'I thought about me, not you.'

'But I'd lied to you,' Hester said. She held her hands out, as if coaxing someone over the last few feet of a perilously high bridge. 'You had every right to be mad with me.'

As he got closer, she could see more details. His dark eyebrows; his full, pink lips; the cord of his hoodie stuck inside his collar, the hood slightly off-centre. She thought she could see the exact spot on the sleeve of his jacket where she had pressed her nose and sniffed, as they stood outside the New York restaurant in Soho.

'I'd done exactly the same thing,' he said.

'What?' She frowned and beckoned him forward. Everyone else around the fountain was openly watching them now, but Hester didn't care.

'You decided to lie so that you could come back to the hotel and see me again,' Jake said, stopping just past the fountain's central structure, the mermaids behind him. 'I asked you to come, to take me to your favourite places, so you thought you had to lie. But I didn't really want a holiday. Not a real one or a virtual one, though I loved them, because you made them so good. But what was really important, what I loved most of all, was being with you. Spending time with you.'

She swallowed. 'Jake, I—'

'You did what you had to, and so did I. It was no different, and I should have been encouraged that you had wanted to see me even then: that it hadn't simply been a job for you, one you were doing under sufferance because I was a grumpy, uncharismatic sod. I should have been flattered, and instead I pushed you away when you had opened your heart to me. When you told me you couldn't fly, that you couldn't come to New York even if you wanted to, it was a shock. I thought of my life over there, and it suddenly wasn't enough, not without you in it. But then the thought of giving it up, of changing everything I've spent years getting just right, just how I like it – I panicked. I thought it would be easier, safer, to stick instead of twist.'

'Oh God, someone's coming,' a voice said, and Hester looked up to see two torch beams in the darkness, wavering and heading towards them.

'Jake,' she said, 'get out of there.'

'No.' He shook his head. 'I'm not finished.'

'But you can do this out of the fountain, can't you?'

'There's no bathtub here. I have to work with what I've got.'

'Jake!' She laughed, her heart soaring, her hope so complete, now, that it was arcing out of her, mingling with the golden glow of the fountain and the twinkling fairy lights in the trees, and the glaring torch beams seeking them out.

'It took me a while to realize,' Jake went on, 'that having you in my life, changing it, changing *me*, was the best thing that could have happened. That I should have accepted and embraced it, not run away from it: that I should have seen how lucky I was. But I ran away and I blamed you, and those were the worst two things I could have done. I don't know if you can forgive me, but I want you to know how sorry I am.'

'Can you get out of the fountain, please, sir!' a voice boomed.

'Shit,' Hester whispered.

'Could you give me two minutes, please?' Jake asked, turning towards the policemen, his voice as steady as if he was asking someone for a cup of coffee.

'I'm afraid you'll have to get out now, sir,' said the voice. It was calm, but with a hint of steeliness that Hester knew shouldn't be ignored.

'One minute,' Jake said. 'Humour me, please?'

Hester could see the policemen's faces now, as they exchanged a glance and then looked back at Jake.

'Thirty seconds,' one of them said. 'Then we're arresting you.'

'Jake!' Hester squealed.

He turned back to her. 'I love you, Hester Monday.' He took another step forward, and another, until he was at the edge of the pool. 'I have loved you since I opened my hotel room door on that first day and saw you standing there, looking at me.' He stepped up onto the low wall. Hester heard a gasp, and realized it had come from her own throat. They were spotlit in the policemen's torch beams, and Jake was dripping on her, but she didn't care. She reached her hands up to him.

He didn't take them. 'Every moment since, my love for you has been getting stronger, and I don't know what I'm supposed to do without you. I don't know how it's going to work, or if you even want it to any more, but I couldn't go back to New York without finding out if there was a chance for us. If there was a possibility that we could, the two of us, make it work somehow.'

'That's your time up, sir,' one of the policemen said.

'Oh, come on, Karl,' said his partner. 'He's declaring his love for the lass.'

Jake took Hester's hands. His touch was like fireworks jolting through her, and it was like the smoothest, softest balm against her skin. She took a step back and he jumped down, then turned to the officers. 'I'm not in the fountain any more,' he said.

'I know,' replied the policeman who wasn't Karl. 'But we have to wait and see what she says, don't we?'

Jake nodded, as if it was perfectly reasonable for them to have an audience. He turned back to Hester, looked down at her with his blue eyes, and she could see his confidence wavering. 'What do you think?' he asked softly. 'Can you forgive me?'

Hester squeezed his fingers and then let go, moving her hands to his waist. 'You came all the way to Edinburgh to ask me that?'

'I would have travelled all the way around the world to ask you that, Hester. I want a life with you. I love you. It wasn't the kind of conversation we could have over the phone, even if you'd been picking up.'

She nodded. 'I'm sorry about that, I just had something I needed to do.'

When he smiled at her, it was impossible for her not to do the same. 'You did. You did it. I realize I am muscling in here, on what is a pretty monumental day for you already, but I didn't want to wait. I thought if I did, I would be too late.'

'I'm quite enjoying my monumental day,' she said, and then realized that wasn't true. She had to be true to herself, and to Jake, always. 'No, scratch that. I am *loving* my monumental day. I'm so happy you're here. It wasn't the same with Stanley Mk 2, though he did help a bit.'

Jake laughed and slid his hands up her arms, her nerve endings tingling to life. 'What are you talking about?'

'I'll tell you later,' she said. 'Right now, I think there's only one thing I need to say.'

'Yes, please,' Karl called over. 'Please do get on with it.'

'Don't rush her,' said his colleague. 'This is important stuff.'

'Thanks.' Hester shot them both a smile, then turned back to Jake. 'Jake Oakenfield. I am completely, head over heels in love with you. I think a part of me has been since before I met you, because when I saw you standing in the doorway of that hotel suite, in your dressing gown, with your irritated expression and that bruise on your face,' she reached up to smooth her thumb over the place where traces of it lingered, watching his eyes widen, then soften to something so tender she almost couldn't continue, 'it was as if I knew you. As if, from the moment I picked the Merryweather door, it was meant to be. Because there was just something about it that felt right. When I knocked on the door, I got this feeling, and then when you opened the door, the feeling went right through me, and settled inside me, and hasn't gone away since. I realized it was love. And it's all for you.'

'Great speech,' he murmured, bending his head towards

347

hers, his eyes brighter than she had ever seen them. 'Do you think it would be OK if I kissed you now?'

'Please God,' said Karl. 'How long can one love declaration take?'

Hester laughed and reached up to lace her fingers through the curls at the nape of Jake's neck. 'I can't believe you walked through the fountain,' she said. 'I hope you have a change of clothes.'

'That would spoil it, surely?' he whispered against her lips. 'I wanted you to know that I meant it, all of it. And now, I think you do. I want everything you have to offer me, Hester Monday.'

'You might regret saying that, you know,' she said, and just before he pressed his lips against hers, he gave her his A to Z smile.

Hester kissed him back with everything that she had; with her newfound confidence and the certainty of being in love. She pressed herself against the body she would never tire of feeling, ran her hands through the curls she wanted to tug forever, tasted his full, plum lips and felt his certainty, too. Against the backdrop of the beautiful park, with its fairy lights and its autumn leaves and the castle gazing down on them, to the gentle shush of the fountain and the whoops and cheers of their accidental audience, Karl and his colleague wolf-whistling with wild abandon, Hester soared higher and higher in Jake Oakenfield's arms.

Chapter
Thirty-Nine

Sunday, some weeks later

'Hester, what can I do you for?' The tall, broad-shouldered man with the denim apron flashed her a blistering smile.

'I would like some lemons, some avocados and courg— zucchini, and some of those plums. What kind of plums are they?' They were small and dark purple, a rich colour that she couldn't stop looking at.

'Merryweather,' the man, Calvin, said. 'You know that, Hester.'

'I *do* know,' she replied. 'I just love hearing you say it. They're my favourite kind of plum.'

'They're actually a damson,' Calvin said, not for the first time. 'And why don't you buy some fruit in season, instead of something that's been forced? What about some nice plump cranberries?' He gestured to the box, the berries inside glistening like rubies.

Hester thought for a second. 'OK,' she said. 'I'll have some of those too.' She waited while he weighed out her groceries and put them in the tote bag she held out to him.

'I'm not gonna have those plums for too much longer,' he added, accepting her money.

'I'll just have to make the most of them while you do, then. Catch you later, Calvin. Have a good Sunday.'

'You too.'

She waved and walked along the pavement, her eyes still, after six weeks, drinking in the tree-lined streets, the quaint boutiques and cosy restaurants of West Village. She was getting to know it so well. All its quirks and hidden corners, the beautiful brownstones that she couldn't believe were single homes, the green, leafy spaces. She had seen so much of it on Google Maps over the years, planning out the visits she hoped she would take. Now, here she was. And it was a visit with no end point; at least not one she had to think about.

The coffee shop on the corner, with its yellow-and-green striped awning, the chairs and tables outside that made the pavement around it almost impassable but which somehow nobody seemed to mind, was one of her favourite places. Especially at this very moment.

She looked through the window and saw him, sitting at their usual table. He looked up, as if he could sense her watching him, and grinned. Her insides danced, unable to get used to the sight of him, the proximity of him: the reality that this was her life, now. With Jake Oakenfield, in New York.

She pushed open the door and it dinged to announce her, and Jake stood up and walked towards her, as he did every time, as if he couldn't quite contain his excitement either. They had been apart for ten minutes. She was surprised there wasn't a Disney soundtrack following them around.

He kissed her full on the lips and pulled her to the leather booth, sitting her beside him so they could both look out of the window. This was where they had sat for the last four Sunday mornings, having breakfast and people-watching, sharing the newspaper. Hester hoped it was a ritual that would continue until they were too old and frail to make it down the street from Jake's apartment.

'What did you get?' He put a hand on her thigh and squeezed gently, reigniting the tingles that had just about settled after that morning. He could see the effect he had on her, the amusement dancing in his eyes, except there was desire there, too. He wasn't immune.

'I got plums,' she said, leaning in to kiss him, moving his hand further up her leg. They were hidden from the view of the other customers in the cafe, but not, she realized, as she glanced to her left, anyone walking past the large picture window. She moved away from him as a woman gave them an incredulous glare and then walked on.

Jake stifled a laugh and took his hand off her leg. 'More plums? Are you going to make jam this time?'

Hester shook her head. 'I don't know how to make jam. I'm just going to eat them. We both are.'

'They're so sharp,' he said. 'There are so many other delicious fruit you could get.'

'But none are called Merryweather.'

'I'm going to veto this, you know. This obsession with plums. It's not healthy.'

Hester smiled at him. She loved his faux seriousness, and his amusement, and the moment his eyes went dark with lust. She loved his A to Z grin, and his curls, which were longer and lusher than they had been in London, and the fact that his bruises were all gone; from his face and his ribs, though the scar would take longer to fade.

She had been right, that very first day, when she'd decided that a fully fit, undamaged Jake Oakenfield would be a man to be reckoned with, and it wasn't just his looks, but his touch and his confidence. There was no longer any wincing or hesitating when he moved, when they were in bed together, when he lifted her up or moved over her, and she loved all of it, all of him, more every day.

'You can't veto my plums,' she said now. 'They're symbolic.'

'What if I replace them with New York cheesecake?'

'Oh. Oh, well. Maybe that would be OK.'

He raised an eyebrow. 'Really? You're giving in to me so easily?'

'Cheesecake tastes better than the plums. They *are* a bit sharp.'

He laughed and stroked her cheek, then he kissed her, pulled her closer, holding her against him. Hester rested her head on his shoulder, breathing in his delicious Ocean Haze scent, and they only broke apart when their food was brought over: Eggs Benedict for Jake, pancakes with bacon and maple syrup for her.

She gazed down at her delicious breakfast, poured the syrup over pancakes already swimming in butter, and thought that, not in a million years would she have been able to give Jake a virtual holiday to West Village and done it any kind of justice. But her brief stint as a staycation organizer was firmly in the past. She would never regret it, because it had led her to this man, and to this place, but it wasn't what she did.

Cassie had been surprisingly fine with Hester's decision to move to New York, ostensibly on an extended holiday but, hopefully, if she had anything to do with it, permanently. Hester had expected a 'good luck' and a pat on the back, but Cassie had suggested she keep working for Paradise Awaits. She could do the customer meetings via video link, and Cassie was trying to grow her contacts in North America anyway: Hester would be perfectly placed to build those relationships. Of course Hester had said yes. It was the best of both worlds, and it meant she had purpose and income while she was here, rather than lolling in Jake's apartment, watching her savings dwindle and being a kept woman.

Leaving Amber and Glen, and her mum and dad behind had been the hardest part. Hester had never been away from any of them for long, and suddenly she was flying – *flying* – away from them, to live halfway around the world. But alongside her parents' sadness, Hester had seen the relief, as if they had known she was lagging behind, not living up to her potential, and was now, at the age of twenty-eight, doing something about it.

The way they had welcomed Jake into their home – for a Sunday roast, of course – her mum refusing to accept his polite kiss on the cheek and handshake, instead pulling him into a tight hug that left him wide-eyed and Hester worrying about his still-bruised ribs, her dad's vigorous pat on the back, had spoken volumes about how they felt about this near stranger. Her dad had warmed to him instantly, drawing him into a long discussion about golf, and Hester had watched, hiding her laughter, as Jake had tried to engage with a topic he knew nothing about. Even Chess had deigned to let Jake stroke him, and that was the moment, she knew, when he had been fully accepted into the family.

Amber and Glen had declared, at first, that they hated him. Even though his presence in Hester's life had, in a roundabout way, led to her 'getting her shit together', as Amber so astutely put it. They were incandescent with rage that he was taking her away from them, so Hester thought the best thing to do would be to bring him along on one of their Thursday nights out.

Of course they hadn't been able to resist his charms for long. Who could? He had agreed that red and white wine were both far superior to rosé, flashing Hester an apologetic look as he did, and then proceeded to wrap Glen and Amber around his little finger. He told them they were welcome to come and stay with him and Hester in New York, that he would love to take them, and Elise too – if she fancied it – on a tour of all the best, lesser-known places: to give them the proper Big Apple experience.

By the end of the evening, Amber and Glen were singing his praises, and when Jake pulled Hester onto the plinth of the Festival Hall fountain, kissing her while they both got completely soaked – it was a theme, it seemed, with him now, and Hester didn't know whether to be worried or not – Amber had shouted that they had better get married, or she would never speak to either of them again.

But even though it had been awful, in some ways, uprooting her life in London to come to New York, it had mostly been exhilarating and thrilling, and filled with possibility. Jake had started to take her to all the places they'd talked about that night in his hotel suite, and more – corners of the city that he knew and loved. They had been to Central Park so many times already, but she thought she might have seen about a thousandth of all it had to offer.

Hester had been stuck in one place for so long, it had felt right that her next move should be an extreme one. And the flight from London to New York hadn't been easy: she hadn't been able to wipe out over a decade of terror with one short return trip to Edinburgh.

But Jake had been at her side, distracting her with stories about the trouble he and Beth had got into when they were younger, how he had followed his confident big sister round with a foolhardy loyalty that had got him into countless scrapes. He had ordered her two large G&Ts from the flight attendant and then talked to her in awful, broken Italian that made no sense but still sounded sexier than anything she'd ever heard, and then, when she was still trembling and tearful, he'd whispered all the things he was going to do to her when he got her back to his apartment, and that had consumed her so completely that for the last half of the flight she was too wound up to be scared.

Luckily, he had made good on all his promises – he had managed to wind himself up thoroughly, too – and Hester had spent her first night in New York, her first night abroad since the age of eleven, having the best sex of her life. It was a great way to start this newest chapter.

'Two things,' Jake said, after they had finished breakfast and were strolling back to his apartment, their fingers entwined. He had a navy scarf wrapped around his neck, above the leather jacket he was still refusing to put away even though the weather was getting colder, autumn struggling to hold off winter. Hester had told him the accessory made him look more Biggles than Maverick, but he just gave her his A to Z grin and said he was keeping it on until he couldn't deal with the cold any more.

'OK,' Hester replied. 'What's the first one?'

'I think we should go to the beach next weekend: get away somewhere. I could take next Friday off work.'

'Really? I'd love that! Where would we go?'

'Cape May, possibly, but there are lots of options. We'll have a look when we get home.'

'Yes please. We can have a levelled-up Sunday morning.'

'That's what I was thinking,' Jake said.

'What's the second thing?' She let go of his hand and wrapped her arm around his waist, bringing him closer. To anyone who saw them they were just a young couple, out for a Sunday stroll. Hester wanted to tell everyone they passed what it meant to her, that she was here, in this city, with this man: how much she had changed in the last few months. She was buzzing with it.

'Jake?' she prompted, when he hadn't said anything. She heard him sigh, and a kernel of unease knotted in her stomach. 'What is it?'

He led them closer to the wall so they weren't in the way of other people, then turned to face her and took both her hands in his. It reminded her of that night in Edinburgh, at the fountain, but his expression was so serious, without any hint of laughter in his blue eyes, that a chill ran through her.

'Jake?' she said again.

'I wondered if . . .' He stopped, chewed his lip, and Hester brushed her hand over his cheek, down to his jaw, feeling his weekend stubble against her palm.

'Wondered if what?'

'If you wanted to start looking at apartments with me?'

She blinked, trying to understand what he was saying, picturing his smart place with its exposed brick walls and masculine furniture, pine and charcoal kitchen, the Yale blue tiles, the sofas a soft grey. Although now, of course, there were the personal touches she'd added too: photos of her with Amber and Glen, and Vanessa and Lyron. The one of her and her Mum and Dad in Amalfi was blown up and framed on the living room mantle, and Stanley and Stanley Mk 2 were cosied up together in the bedroom.

There was also a shot of her, Jake and Rosalie, their glasses filled with champagne rather than pink lemonade, the Duval's beautiful lounge in the background. Rosalie had insisted on taking them for a meal there before they left, and had, during the course of that hilarious and rather hazy evening, invited herself to stay with them in New York. They'd been in touch with her since and she was planning on coming out nearer Christmas, to take them shopping on Fifth Avenue. She had told them that they were stuck with her for life, something which, Jake and Hester had later agreed, they could only feel lucky about. Not only had Hester come to care for Rosalie – and she knew Jake felt the same – but if it wasn't for her, they never would have met.

'An apartment?' she repeated now. 'Why? What's wrong with yours?'

'That's exactly what's wrong with it,' he said. 'It's mine. I want one that's *ours*.'

For a moment, Hester couldn't speak. She felt shaky, as she'd done on the flight over. She pressed her lips together, and Jake squeezed her hands.

'What do you think? Is it – is it too soon? Am I moving too fast?'

Hester shook her head, felt the tears well up and slip out, and let him wipe them away with his thumbs.

He brought his face down to meet hers, and she whispered against his lips. 'No. Not too fast. You really want us to find a place together?'

'Yes,' he said, kissing her gently. 'And that brings me on to the other thing.'

'There's another thing?'

He nodded. 'Where you want to be. If you want New York to be your home, or if you want to go back to London. I know you miss your parents, and Amber and Glen. Now it's easier, now travelling's not out of the question, I just – I didn't want you to think this was it. I wanted us to talk about it.'

Hester blinked. 'But . . . London? You hate London.'

'Not any more,' he said. 'There's Beth and Duncan, and Rosalie. My mum.' He winced. 'I've been wondering if I should . . . anyway. I think it's something we should talk about: where we want to live, longer term.'

'You'd move back to London, if that's what I wanted?'

He took her hand again, squeezing it. 'I'd go anywhere, as long as it was with you. You and me, Hester Monday.' He enunciated her name, taking time over all four syllables, as if he loved saying it, as if he couldn't get enough of it. 'Wherever you want to be, I want to be there, too.'

'You and me,' Hester murmured, in full agreement, and

wondered how she could possibly choose: New York, with all its bright, shiny newness and possibility, places to explore and things to see; or London, with friends and family, a much less restrictive home, now that she knew she could get on a plane and go anywhere. She could go on holiday with Jake, travel to a hotel opening for Paradise Awaits, escape with Amber and Glen on those trips they'd talked about but never taken together.

It was like two doors in front of her, a fifty-fifty choice. Except this time, she thought, the choices – the possibilities – seemed endless.

Still, she realized, she didn't have to decide right now. There were other things to do, on this chilly, sunny Sunday. And, as if reading her mind, Jake bent his head towards hers, and then she couldn't think about anything at all, because Jake Oakenfield was kissing her, on a street corner in New York, his warmth embracing her and his Ocean Haze scent surrounding her; his lips and stubble, and his hands on her back, setting every part of her alight.

It was better than any staycation she could have planned, even with every resource the Duval had to offer, even with her imagination stretched to its limits. It was proof, yet again – and she was finding examples of it every day, almost at every turn – that actually living life, taking chances and risks, not holding back, was so much better than make-believe.

Real life was not worth missing out on, not for anything, and Hester Monday wasn't going to let another minute of it pass her by.

Acknowledgements

This is my eleventh book, and in some ways it's a bit of an unexpected one. I cooked it up over a few strange weeks during the first summer lockdown. The characters and the story, the settings that I loved – and missed so much – came to me almost fully formed.

As always, from the moments of inspiration to the finished book, there are so many stages, and so many people, who have helped to make it what it is.

A huge thank you to Kate Bradley for believing in this book and accepting a slight deviation from my usual stories, for all her enthusiasm and for taking yet another chance on me, and her insightful notes about how to level it up. Thank you, also, to Lynne Drew and the whole HarperFiction team for embracing The Staycation. To Hannah O'Brien, Sarah Munro, Namra Amir, Sarah Shea, Susanna Peden and Chere Tricot for all their support. Thank you to Anne O'Brien for the copy edits that tightened everything up.

I am in love with the stunning, sunny holiday cover, so

a huge thank you to Caroline Young who designed it and made it so standout.

Thank you to my agent, Hannah Ferguson, for being so positive when I sent her an email titled: A lockdown book that's not about lockdown, and for being behind it from the very beginning. Thank you, as always, to the whole Hardman and Swainson team.

MEGA thanks to Kirsty Greenwood, epic friend and cheerleader, who put up with my incessant messages during the frantic fortnight when I was writing the first draft and being overly giddy about it; for being the first person to read it and for telling me I had to send it to Hannah. I'm not sure Hester and Jake would have made it into a published book without her input and encouragement.

Thank you to Sheila Crighton for early reads, endless enthusiasm and sparkly emails; to the whole Book Camp crew for always being at the end of WhatsApp with advice and hilarity (and for that glorious, sunny week in October); and specifically, to Cathy Bramley for picking the perfect title for this book: it seems entirely obvious now, but it really wasn't to me. A big thanks to the authors who read Hester and Jake's story early and were so lovely that it made me feel like my indulgent lockdown novel could find an audience.

Thank you to my husband David, who put up with my lack of communication while I was writing this. I sat in the same room as him the entire time, but he had to deal with a typing ghost rather than a wife. He was unfailingly patient, bringing me coffee and dancing round the living room with me when I needed to clear my head and stretch my limbs.

Thank you to Mum and Dad, who have let me read

author quotes to them over the phone, and who I will have to try very hard not to think about reading this book, though I know they will – Mum on audio, Dad on his iPad – because it has a bit more sizzle than my usual stories. Thanks, always, to Lee.

Thank you to the bloggers, readers and other bookish people on Instagram, Twitter and Facebook who have put up with me going on about it, who have joined in with my excitement, and haven't got bored of me (or at least haven't told me they've got bored of me). Shouting about a book gets it into more people's hands, and I'm so grateful to everyone who has mentioned it.

Finally, thank you to you, if you're reading this. It is nerve-racking sending something slightly different out into the world, but I am very proud of The Staycation, and I'm so glad you've picked it up. I really, really hope you enjoy it; that it gives you a big chunk of escapism, a healthy dose of humour, and a generous sprinkling of romance. If you can't go on a luxury vacation or have a holibob (sorry!) in a hotel room, then I hope Hester and Jake's story is the next best thing.

If you haven't discovered Cressida's delightful Cornish Cream Tea series, read on to enjoy the first chapter of *The Cornish Cream Tea Bus*.

Chapter
One

My Dearest Charlie,

Gertie is yours, to do with what you will. I know that you cherish her, but you do not need to keep her. She is a gift, not a millstone around your neck. If the best thing for you is to sell her and go travelling, then that is what you should do.

I have so much to say to you, but my time is running out. I hope that these few words will be enough to show you how much I love you; it's more than I ever thought possible.

Look after yourself, think of all the happy times we spent together, and know that you can do anything if you believe in yourself enough.

Remember, my darling niece, live life to the full – you only get one chance. Make the most of your opportunities and do what is right for you.

All my love, always,
Your Uncle Hal x

Charlie Quilter folded the letter and pushed it into the back pocket of her jeans. She blinked, her eyes adjusting to the gloom, and tried to stop her heart from sinking as her dad stopped beside her in the garage doorway. His sigh was heavy, and not unexpected: he had been sighing a lot lately. She could barely remember a time when his narrow shoulders hadn't been slumped, and she had forgotten what his laughter sounded like. But on this occasion, she felt the same as he did; the sight before them was not inspiring.

The 1960s Routemaster bus, painted cream with green accents, looked more scrapheap than vintage, and Charlie could see that its months left in the garage without Uncle Hal's care and attention had had a serious impact.

'God, Charlie,' Vince Quilter said, stepping inside the garage and finding the light switch, 'what are you – we – I mean . . .' He shrugged, his arms wide, expression forlorn.

Charlie took a deep breath and, despite the February chill at her back, unzipped her coat and unwound her thick maroon scarf. The wind assailed her neck, newly exposed to the elements after the pre-Christmas, post-break-up, chop-it-all-off graduated bob that – she now realized – had been an ill-advised choice for this time of year.

'We're going to fix her,' she said purposefully, putting her bag against the wall and laying her palm flat against the bus's cold paintwork. 'We're going to restore Gertie, aren't we, Dad?' He was staring at the workbench where all Hal's tools were laid out, rubbing his unshaven jaw. Hal's death had hit him harder than anyone else, and while Charlie felt her uncle's loss keenly, she knew it was nothing compared to what Vince was going through. 'Dad?' she prompted.

'Sorry, love. That we are.' He started rolling up the sleeves of his jacket, thought better of it and took it off instead. He switched on the heater and rubbed his hands together.

Charlie felt a surge of hope. She hurried over to her bag and pulled out a flask of coffee and a Tupperware box. 'Here, have a brownie to keep you going. I thought we could do with some sustenance.' She took off the lid, and a glimmer of a smile lit up Vince's face.

'Always thinking ahead, huh?'

'This was never going to be the easiest task in the world, practically or emotionally. Brownies baked with love – and hazelnuts and chocolate chip, because that's your favourite kind.'

'Your food is the best, because it's baked with love and extra calories,' her dad said, taking one of the neatly arranged squares. 'That's what he always said.'

'Yup.' A lump formed unhelpfully at the back of Charlie's throat, as it had been doing at inopportune moments ever since her uncle Hal had been diagnosed with an aggressive cancer at the end of last summer. So many things reminded her of him, and while dealing with practicalities – assessing the state of his beloved Routemaster bus, for example – were easier to focus on without the emotion overwhelming her, his sayings, his nuggets of wisdom, always knocked her off kilter. They were so ingrained in her family now, but it was as if she could hear Hal's voice, his unwavering cheerfulness, whoever was saying the words.

'Love and extra calories,' she repeated, wincing when she noticed a deep gouge in Gertie's side. 'How did he get away with being so sentimental?'

'Because he was straightforward,' her dad said through a mouthful of chocolate and nuts. 'He said everything without embarrassment or affectation. He was a sixty-eight-year-old man who called his bus Gertie. He meant it all, and was never ashamed of who he was.'

Uncle Hal had given scenic tours on Gertie, the vintage double-decker Routemaster, that were legendary throughout the Cotswolds. He was an expert bus driver and a world-class talker. Everyone who took one of his tours left feeling as if they'd made a friend for life, and the testimonials on TripAdvisor were gushing. His untimely death had left a huge hole in the Cotswold tourist trade, as well as his family's life.

And now Gertie belonged to Charlie; left to her in Hal's will, for her to do with whatever she wanted. At that moment, all she could see in the bus's future was being dismantled and sold for spares, but she was not going to let that happen. She couldn't imagine herself taking over her uncle's tours, even though she had spent many hours on them and had been taught to drive the bus as soon as she was old enough. Her expertise was in baking, not talking.

Her dad finished his brownie and started examining Gertie's engine. As a car dealer he knew his way around vehicles, but had admitted to Charlie that he wasn't that knowledgeable about buses. Charlie had argued that it was just a bigger version, and nothing could be that different.

She cleaned the chocolate off her fingers with a paper napkin and climbed on board the bus. It had taken on a musty, unloved smell, and was bone-achingly cold. Charlie walked up the aisle of the lower deck, her fingers trailing along the backs of the forest-green seats, and opened the cab.

Her dad appeared behind her, wiping his hands on a rag. 'The engine seems in good enough shape, but I only know the basics. And in here?' He gave another melancholy sigh.

'It's going to be fine,' she said. 'She needs a bit of sprucing up, that's all. A few things need fixing, there's some cosmetic work, knocking a couple of panels back into shape, and then Gertie will be as good as new.'

'I could give Clive a call,' Vince said, worrying at his scruffy hair, 'get him to come and give her a once-over, see what condition her vital organs are in.'

'And in the meantime, I'll tackle in here. We've got the Hoover, cleaning sprays, and I can make a list of what needs repairing. The toilet probably needs a good flushing out.' Charlie made a face and her dad laughed.

'You sure you want to start that now?' he asked. 'Shouldn't we find out if she's salvageable first? You don't want to waste your time cleaning her if the engine's buggered.'

'Dad, the engine is *not* buggered. She's fine. Hal was driving her right up until . . . he wasn't any more. He never mentioned anything being wrong with her.'

'Yes, but you have to agree she looks—'

'Neglected,' Charlie finished. 'Which is why we're here. I guarantee that once we've given her a bit of love and attention, things will look a hundred times better. Gertie is going back on the road, that's all there is to it.' She grinned, and it wasn't even forced. She had almost convinced herself.

Her dad looked at her fondly. 'You're a wonder, Charlie. Anyone else faced with these circumstances – with this,' he gestured around him, 'and Hal, and everything you've been through with Stuart – would start a lengthy hibernation, and nobody would blame them. Instead you've baked brownies and dragged me here, and you're not going to leave until Gertie's gleaming. You don't even know what you're going to do with her when she's restored!'

Charlie's smile almost slipped at this last point, because that was worrying her far more than the state of Gertie's engine or how many panels needed replacing. What on earth was she going to do with a vintage, double-decker bus, when she worked in a café in Ross-on-Wye and her main skills were baking and eating? 'I'll think of something,' she said brightly. 'One step at a time, Dad. Fix Gertie, and *then* decide what to do with her.'

She put the key in the ignition and a satisfying thrum reverberated, like a heartbeat, through the bus. The engine was working, at least. She cranked the heating up to max – she didn't want her fingers to fall off before she'd polished the metalwork – then turned on the radio.

'Gold' by Spandau Ballet filled the space, and Charlie took her dad's hands and pulled them up in the air with hers. She forced them into an awkward dance down the aisle, bumping into seats as they sashayed from the front of the bus to the back, and sang along at the top of her voice. Soon they were both laughing, and her dad let go of her hands so he could clutch his stomach. She dinged the bell and tried to get her breathing under control. When Vince looked up, Charlie could see the familiar warmth in his eyes that she had been worried was gone for good.

It was impossible not to feel cheered in Gertie's company. Hal had been convinced there was something a little bit magical about her, and while Charlie had always argued that it was Hal who inspired the laughter on his tours, at this moment she wondered if he was right.

They could do this. No question. Despite all that had happened to her over the past few months, she knew she could restore Gertie to her former glory. What came next wasn't so certain but, as she'd said to her dad, they could only take one step at a time. Right now, they needed to focus on bringing the bus back to life.

They worked all morning, and even though Charlie knew the bits they were fixing were only cosmetic, and a small part of her worried that when Clive came round he would tell them that the engine was too old, or there was too much rust in the chassis, or any one of a number of things that meant Gertie would not outlive Hal, she felt so much better for doing it. The radio kept them buoyed, and at one point her dad even whistled along to a Sixties tune, something that, only a day before, Charlie and her mum would both have thought impossible.

The simple act of working on Uncle Hal's bus was taking the edge off their grief. It reminded Charlie how much she had loved spending time with him, a lot of it on board this very bus, and how big an influence he'd been on her. That didn't have to stop just because he was no longer physically with her. Hal would be part of her life for ever.

It was after one o'clock when Vince announced he was going to get sandwiches. Charlie ordered an egg mayo and bacon baguette and, once her dad had strolled out of the garage with his jacket done up to his neck, she climbed to the top deck of the bus. She sat above the cab – her favourite position as a child because she could pretend she was driving – even though, inside the garage, the view was less than inspiring. As she did so, she felt the letter in her back pocket. Hal had left it for her in his will, and it had been folded and reopened so many times the paper had begun to wear thin along the creases.

It no longer made her cry, but the words still affected her deeply. He had never married, had never had a family of his own, so she had been like a daughter to him. Losing him had been a huge blow – his cancer diagnosis a mind-numbing shock followed quickly by practicalities as his condition worsened and he needed more care – but at least she had been able to spend time with him, to let him know how much she loved him and how much he had shaped her life. And she would always have his letter. It was bittersweet, but so much better than the irreversible cut-off of losing someone suddenly.

She was still lost in thought when she heard a woman calling her name, followed by a high-pitched yelp. Charlie ran down Gertie's narrow staircase and out of the open doorway.

'How are you doing?' Juliette asked. Before Charlie had time to reply, Marmite raced up to her, his extendable lead whirring noisily, and put his tiny front paws on Charlie's shins. Charlie scooped the Yorkipoo puppy into her arms and closed her eyes while he licked her chin. However miserable some aspects of life had been recently, Marmite never failed to bring a smile to her face. He was six months old, and more of a terror with every passing day.

'OK, I think,' Charlie said. 'But don't look at the outside, come and see what we've done inside. Dad's getting someone to take a proper look at her, and in the meantime we've been giving her a polish. He's just gone to get lunch.'

'I know,' Juliette said, unclipping Marmite's lead and following Charlie onto the bus. 'I saw him on my way here. He's getting me a sandwich, too.'

'So you can stay for a bit, before you go back to Cornwall this afternoon?'

Juliette nodded. 'It's been so good seeing everyone. But I'm still not sure, Char, how you're really doing. What's going on up here?' She tapped Charlie's forehead. 'You're putting on this amazing front, but I need to know before I go home that you're OK.'

'I'm fine,' Charlie said. 'This morning has helped a lot. Dad was concerned that Gertie wouldn't be salvageable, but just look at her! She might need a bit of work under the bonnet, some patching up, but it's given me hope.'

Juliette surveyed their morning's work, the metal uprights gleaming, the walls clean, the seats vacuumed to within an inch of their lives. 'She looks great, Char, almost as good as new. But I'm not as convinced about you. Since I've been back you've been so busy, working at The Café on the Hill, helping with the catering for the funeral. You haven't stopped, even for a day. You should be taking some time out.'

Charlie groaned. 'Why does everyone think that's best for me? Keeping busy is what helps in this kind of situation.' She led Juliette to a seat halfway down the bus. Some of the chairs were sagging dangerously, but this one, she had discovered earlier, was still fairly firm.

'Are you *sure* you're OK?' Juliette said after a minute. Her voice was low, her slight French accent always adding a seriousness to her words, though in this case it was probably intentional.

Charlie remembered the first time she had heard Juliette speak, on a packed train from London to Cheltenham; she'd been chatting with someone on the other end of her mobile, and had occasionally slipped into French. Charlie had been sitting next to her, and after Juliette had finished her call and offered some expletives in both languages, Charlie had asked her those same words: *Are you OK?* Juliette had been reserved, embarrassed that she'd been entertaining the whole carriage, and so Charlie had told her how *she'd* had a no-holds-barred telephone row with her then-boyfriend in a hotel doorway, not realizing that a wedding party were waiting to get past her into the ballroom, and how some of the guests had looked quite shocked when she'd finally noticed that they were watching her.

She'd made Juliette laugh, and by the time the train had pulled up in Cheltenham, they had swapped numbers and agreed to meet up. That had been almost seven years ago, and their friendship was still strong despite Juliette's move to Cornwall two years before, with her boyfriend Lawrence. Charlie was still touched that Juliette had come back for Hal's funeral, staying for a couple of weeks to catch up with friends in the area. She had been on Gertie countless times when she'd lived in Cheltenham, and Charlie hadn't asked her if *she* was OK.

'I'm not doing too badly,' she said now. 'I've been getting on with stuff, which is better than wallowing in the empty flat, or at Mum and Dad's. Dad's so cut up about losing Hal. Today is the first time I've seen him smile in what feels like for ever.'

'I know you're worried about Vince, but you have to think about yourself, too.' Juliette put a hand on her shoulder. 'Because it isn't just Hal, is it? It's only been a couple of months since you and Stuart . . . finished. And you're in the flat, hosting viewings, unsure where you're going to go once it's sold. I know you don't want to go back to living with your parents, and you can't live on Gertie, as tempting as it is.' She laughed softly.

'That's looking like one of the better options, actually,' Charlie said, chuckling. 'What *am* I going to do with her, Jules? I can't be a tour guide. I'm a baker, a caterer. I don't have the gift of the gab like Hal did. But, despite what he said in his letter, I can't sell her.' She rubbed her hands over her eyes, realizing too late that they were covered in cleaning spray.

'This is why you need time,' Juliette pressed. 'You need to stop thinking for a bit, give yourself some space before you make any big decisions. The place in Newquay wasn't brilliant, but our new house in Porthgolow, it's perfect, Char. It's so close to the sea. It's beautiful and quiet, and the people in the village are friendly. Come and stay for a couple of weeks. Bea would give you the time off, wouldn't she? The hours you've put into that café, you're probably owed months back in overtime.'

'Working is good for me,' Charlie insisted but, even as she said it, the thought of returning to the café in Ross-on-Wye, even with its spring-themed window display and the ideas she had for seasonal cakes and sandwiches, didn't fill her with as much joy as it should. There were too many other thoughts crowding her mind.

'Take a break,' Juliette continued. 'Come and stay with Lawrence and me. I'm sure Marmite would get on fine with Ray and Benton. They're easy-going cats, and Marmite's still so small. And the most adorable dog in the world, by the way. I'm so glad you've got him to look after you.'

Marmite was sitting on the seat in front of them, scrabbling at the back of the cushion as if there might be a treat hidden somewhere in the fabric. Charlie picked him up and settled him on her lap, rubbing his black-and-tan coat. She pictured the two of them walking along a sandy beach with crystal blue water beyond, to a soundtrack of seagulls and crashing waves. It was certainly a better image than this bland, functional garage or the flat she had shared with Stuart, now empty and soulless. She didn't want to run away from the hard things in life, but she knew her friend was right.

'Let me talk to Bea,' she said decisively. 'I'll see if I can get a couple of weeks off.'

Discover more delightful fiction
from Cressida McLaughlin.
All available now.